OUR FRAIL
BLOOD

Also by Peter Nathaniel Malae

Teach the Free Man
What We Are

PETER NATHANIEL MALAE

OUR FRAIL BLOOD

Black Cat
New York
A paperback original imprint of Grove/Atlantic, Inc.

"Mother" from ANNE STEVENSON: POEMS 1955-2005
by Anne Stevenson. Copyright © 2005.
Reprinted by permission of Bloodaxe Books.

Excerpt from "Oysters" from OPENED GROUND: SELECTED
POEMS 1966-1996 by Seamus Heaney. Copyright © 1998
by Seamus Heaney. Reprinted by permission of Faber and Faber Ltd
and Farrar, Straus and Giroux, LLC.

Printed in the United States of America
Published simultaneously in Canada

ISBN-13: 978-0-8021-2078-6

Black Cat
a paperback original imprint of Grove/Atlantic, Inc.
841 Broadway
New York, NY 10003

Distributed by Publishers Group West

www.groveatlantic.com

13 14 15 16   10 9 8 7 6 5 4 3 2 1

As all else,
this book
is for Christina

Of course I love them, they are my children.
That is my daughter and this my son.
And this is my life I give them to please them.
It has never been used. Keep it safe, pass it on.

—Anne Stevenson, "The Mother"

Contents

The Felices   1
Upland Examiner in the Kitchen of Big Victor
September 2, 1967

Part I: Anthony

1. Murron Leonora Teinetoa   7
   E-Mail in East Palo Alto
   October 25, 2007

2. Anthony Constantine Felice II   17
   Iraq War Protest at the Mount Shasta Amphitheater
   November 12, 2003

3. Murron Leonora Teinetoa   33
   The Flowers of Elysium Fields
   October 31, 2007

4. Anthony Constantine Felice II   56
   Dream of the Camp America Cabin
   May 3, 1996

5. Murron Leonora Teinetoa   73
   Critical Review of Shakespeare
   November 13, 2007

6. Anthony Constantine Felice II   90
   Soup Kitchen of St. Joseph's Cathedral
   June 3, 1993

The Felices   103
Christmas Lights of Big Victor
December 12, 1963

Part II: Richmond

7. Murron Leonora Teinetoa   109
   Land of Endless Possibility
   November 29, 2007

8. Richmond Lincoln Felice   126
   Walk Across Manhattan
   June 20, 1999

9. Murron Leonora Teinetoa   140
   Discussion After the Long Day
   November 30, 2007

10. Richmond Lincoln Felice   151
    Drive Through the Tenderloin
    March 10, 1996

11. Murron Leonora Teinetoa   168
    No Country for Old Men in Starbucks
    December 9, 2007

12. Richmond Lincoln Felice   181
    Flight to Montparnesse
    April 13, 1993

    The Felices   195
    Summer Vacation at the Grand Canyon
    August 8, 1956

Part III: Johnny

13. Murron Leonora Teinetoa   201
    Scrapbook of Anthony Constantine Felice Sr.
    January 4, 2008

14. Johnny Benedetto Capone   218
    Afternoon Drink at Blinky's Can't Say Lounge
    April 28, 2004

15. Murron Leonora Teinetoa   237
    Calling Forth of Lazarus
    January 10, 2008

16. Johnny Benedetto Capone   257
    Share of the Rosy-Flush Clip-On
    January 8, 1981

17. Murron Leonora Teinetoa   271
    Blackjack at the Ohlone Indian Casino
    January 15, 2008

18. Johnny Benedetto Capone   283
    Last Shot at Peter Entry Films
    March 22, 1979

    The Felices   297
    Vision at the Upland Independence Day Parade
    July 4, 1955

                    Part IV: Lazarus

19. Murron Leonora Teinetoa   303
    House Hunt with Anthony
    March 2, 2008

20. Lazarus Corsa Felice   326
    Recall of the Hell Hospital
    October 6, 1997

21. Murron Leonora Teinetoa   339
    Boiling Water in the Room
    March 12, 2008

22. Lazarus Corsa Felice   351
    Enrollment at Università degli Studi di Palermo, Sicilia
    March 19, 1987

23. Murron Leonora Teinetoa   366
    Terms of the Correspondence
    March 13, 2008

24. Lazarus Corsa Felice   386
    Arrival of the Package
    July 23, 1982

The Felices   402
Jimmy Baldwin of the Upland Little League
July 29, 1954

Part V: Mary Anna

25. Murron Leonora Teinetoa   407
    Motherhood on the Terrace
    March 25, 2008

26. Mary Anna Felice   424
    Abstinence at the Estate
    July 4, 1998

27. Murron Leonora Teinetoa   438
    Nakedness on the Big Date
    April 1, 2008

28. Mary Anna Felice   449
    Spring Sports Banquet at Hayward State University
    May 16, 1993

29. Murron Leonora Teinetoa   461
    First Day with Mary Capone Felice
    February 9, 2010

30. Mary Anna Felice   472
    Seventieth Birthday Party for Anthony Constantine Felice Sr.
    September 6, 1983

    The Felices   482
    Prayer at the Upland Carmelite Mission
    July 8, 1953

The Felices
Upland Examiner in the Kitchen of Big Victor
September 2, 1967

When little Limus Baldwin, younger brother to Jimmy, whipped the paper like a Frisbee over his shoulder, weaving heavily down Third Street on his silver Schwinn ten-speed, the frame's center saddled with sixteen more deliveries in town before the clock struck noon, they came out to the porch of their house, Big Victor, and picked it up. He had his father's meerschaum pipe in his mouth, unlit as of yet, about to be smoked at the oaken kitchen table while plucking through the vitals of this very paper. She had on her Big Mama apron, clean as of yet, about to be messed with the day's early baking at her stove. She was excited about the news, maybe delirious in some dormant chamber of her heart, having no understanding of the flak her family would soon enough face from certain elements in the town of Upland, thinking from her fairly uninformed historical perspective that the Victory Parade she'd witnessed in the autumn of 1945, their first year in California, was something of the standard when it came to the reception of her country to its veterans, but this would change in time, as certainly as the seasons, an awakening of sorts to a darker dream not to be pondered as of yet.

Now, in front of her husband, head down as if she were prepared to push through a crowd to save her own child, she stomped into Big

Victor. Their daughter, the last of the brood, was an hour into practice for the Upland Junior High School softball team. This first Saturday in September, ten minutes before twelve, the sun as bright as it would ever be, the oranges on the counter fatter than grapefruits, the sheen on the rinds glowing with the fertile nutrients of Southern California soil. The grove behind Big Victor still put out the best citrus in America, the entire state of Florida be damned. She stood next to his spot at the head of the table, gripping the bridge of his chair, and waited. He came in casually, rolling the rubber band off the paper as he walked, as if this were just another day in their life, perhaps to balance her predictable southern Italian response of pure emotion, this due to the contents of today's issue of the Upland Examiner, *purportedly on the first page. And then, also, he didn't expect good news when good news was supposed to happen, especially to loved ones, the survivor's trait sometimes proven beneficial and called guardedness, sometimes not and called cynicism. However defined, residual drip-down of the Great Depression. Now he was really dragging the moment out, stretching the dramatic undercurrent as if it were a piece of taffy in his hands, now lighting his pipe, looking over at his wife with mischief in his eyes. Maybe he believed in the good news this time, maybe the man from the paper had kept his word. Maybe he was just bathing in hope.*

"Anthony!" she shouted.

"Okay, okay."

He unrolled the paper and laid it across the table.

"Dear God!" she shouted. "How wonderful!"

A cloud of applewood smoke drifted over his long face, goose bumps running the lengths of his arms, still muscular from his early years in the coal mines. They'd gotten the front page all right, the whole of it. Article on the left, photos on the right. Four black-and-white portraits of his boys in their dress formals, each, except one, on his way to Vietnam.

"Anthony!"

"It looks good," he said. "Really good."

"Are you happy, honey?"

"I am," he said. "I really am."

The phone rang. He walked over to the living room, the floorboards of Big Victor creaking like a saloon in an Old West ghost town, and picked it up.

"Anthony Felice Sr."

She went to stand at her husband's side, the creaking less severe but still there, always there for the twenty-two years of the family's residency in these elegant yet warm, colossal yet intimate Victorian halls, there as the children ran across, ran through, ran up the house in the wild middle of a hide-and-seek game, there during the prayer before dinner, there during the debate over Kennedy and Johnson and Nixon and a hot plate of pasta fazool, there watching Cronkite in utter silence, palms at the sides of their bottoms, rocking back and forth as if at sea, there serving tea to neighbors, beer to coaches, wine to priests, most of the guests ignoring the strange sounds, strange emissions, strange utterances that came of a familiar and beneficent source, the creaking erupting during the fistfights, the creaking steady in the ad hominem attacks, there during the epithets and false accusations, there during the making up, the apologies, this sole and trusted witness to all lovemaking, there while they slept in their own hidden corners, as a son, a brother, someone no one deep down really knew and maybe couldn't love or like anyway, the tragedy of the species, crept through the dark corridors in the midnight hour, on the spy's toes, in the crook's covetous trance, and there after the joy and beauty, the horror and ignorance, the familial flame which in harsh and soft winds both was the ever-flittering story of the Felices, and then there for two more families, six years in Spanish with the Aragons, three in Vietnamese with the Nguyens until over four smoggy summer days in the early nineties the creaking floors gone forever, Big Victor torn to the ground, turned to a lot more or less, or a site, its resurrection considered in strictly fiscal terms by out-of-state contractors from back east, then declared a week later unlikely via fax, finally deemed impossible in a single phone call from a man in New Jersey, confirmed by all involved by running memo, the Fourth Street Grove sold like a black-market good to a foreign entrepreneur whose name no one but a few parties in the old neighborhood knew, the whole of Third Street blasted for the erection of a super-sized porn theater baptized as Mr. Peeps and a convenience store christened as Larry's Liquor.

For now, Anthony Felice Sr. said, "Thank you, Ron. I will give them your best." Then: "Yes, I will. Definitely will." And: "You, too, Ron. Absolute best to the missus."

The calls came in fast, thirteen before lunch. Congratulatory, kind, grateful. It was a day to celebrate, and nothing else. Some of the callers were on their way over. She would be ready, she was born to cook for many. She would host her guests with tuna salad sandwiches and assorted fruit, black licorice for desert and hand-squeezed orange juice from the grove. Aniseed biscotti in little brown bags to be taken home for the kids. She would not say much except for the soulful greeting and gentle salutation inherent to her person, she would watch the Flecks and Mr. Bierce and Principal O'Connor speak to her husband on the paper's front-page topic, dropping plaudits like flower petals on a trail, and she'd return to the kitchen beaming from their praise of her boys, knowing that no one but God could take away the greatness of this day from her family. She would wash the dishes looking out the window, she would take in none of the specifics of the conversations, content with the kind tone of them. No thought at all about the certainties of this life, that benumbing minute when the loss of all things innocent even dreams even love would return to the same doorstep where this joyous day had begun.

PART I
Anthony

I

Murron Leonora Teinetoa
E-mail in East Palo Alto
October 25, 2007

I DON'T KNOW WHY SOMETIMES, but I try.

Once I get home, my mother says, "Is it one of those come-hell-or-high-water days, baby?" and while I'd like to be honest about it and say, "Yes, those bastards are talking about cutting my column," I realize that in the grand sum of things my concern about the job is rather small, not because it means less to me or to the world but because I really have no say in the long run who stays or goes at the *Chronicle,* even when the who is me. Which, obviously, means everything.

Focus on the stuff in your life you have control over, I say.

"How was *your* day, Mom?"

"Very interesting," she says, the cryptic avoidance of my eyes meaning something that, I'm sure, will eventually reveal itself.

I go straight to the underwater-blue glow by the telephone, the one with the virtual rainbow of tropical fishes happily blowing bubbles into the darkness, make them vanish with one tap on the keyboard, check my e-mails. If Lokapi is going to take Prince for the weekend, I want to know how long he's keeping him and when and where the pickups and drop-offs are going to happen.

A couple coworkers, especially the divorced ones, think it's weird that I don't feel any animosity toward Lokapi. Being a single mom is tough enough without having haters on your contact list. The haters always want you, too, to hate. "It's not natural to be so nonjudgmental, Murron." "Are you even human, girl?" "Should you hand Prince over so nonchalantly?"

Forget weird. I consider their suggestions to be somewhat *stupid* because when it comes down to it, from top to bottom, inside and out, my kid is one-half Lokapi. No matter how much I or anyone propagandize Prince, some genome on the spiral ladder will be summoning blood to revolt, and I know this. And even if I did feel the way they say I'm supposed to, I still wouldn't exhibit those feelings in front of Prince, who's savvy and sensitive enough to know when someone's being devious.

So I let Lokapi have Prince as much as he wants. From the start, we've never involved the courts, and it's my deepest truest hope that we never do. I don't really see how anyone else should have say over our son's life and, luckily, so far, Lokapi feels the same way.

I flick through the standard e-mails—weekend playdates at the Watergarden, doting Richard and his downie.dick (@aol.com), enough spam to either save or kill a third-world nation—and then drag to one I've never seen before: iker4u@gmail.com.

When I open it, every so-called relative I have is on the CC, even my mother: Richmond.Felice@ubs.com; LazFelice@aol.com; 17GodBlessAmerica76@gmail.com; Paxetbonum@yahoo.com.

Hello everyone. As you know, I have been the primary contact over the past few years when it comes to Mother's health. This is due, of course, to my decades of work and leadership in the health care industry. Mother's systems are now shutting down. If you wish to get your good-byes in before she goes, I'd strongly encourage you doing it soon. She will be at the Elysium Fields Hospice in East San José. I have spoken with Janice Ashton, the hospice administrator,

and she informed me that all visits are terminated by 7:00 p.m.
Please respect her wishes.

Mary Anna

I put my hand on my chest, the palpitations of my heart increasing. Weird that I feel no sadness about the news, just a vague, lingering dread, the kind I get before a triathlon. I want to know how these people found me. Prince runs into the room with my mother who doesn't want to look me in the eyes.

"Who's that, Mama?" Prince asks.

He's bouncing on his toes, shadowboxing like the UFC fighters he watches at Lokapi's, shirtless, barefoot, his hands wrapping and rewrapping his lavalava around his tiny waist. The yellow and blue flowers on the fabric stand out so beautifully against his copper skin. With my encouragement, he's been learning Samoan customs and phrases at his father's place, but it sometimes feels like our apartment is not completely our apartment. That Kapi still lives here, and that I don't have anything comparable to offer my son when it comes to culture, and lineage, and language, and name.

Which takes me, circularly, and by default, back to the original position: Yes, I want you to embrace your father's heritage, honey. Because it's his, it's also yours, okay?

I look up at my mother. She's carrying the load of inheritance for Prince. And my big brother, Gabe, to a much much smaller degree. By that I mean we love having him, but we rarely have him. We're not yet sure who's got Gabe's heart, but we have our hopes, and our theories, and definitely our doubts.

Mom's moving into the kitchen to wash the dishes, still ignoring me, which says all I need to know about how the Felices have found me. I respect, though, her desire to avoid a verbal shouting match. She's crossed a line by passing on my contact information, but it's for a good reason. Which is a horrible thing to say, of course. I don't know my mother's would-be mother-in-law, but I'm sorry that she, or anyone, has to have their "systems shut down."

"I guess they're relatives," I say.

"What'd they want! What'd they want!"

"Not those relatives, Prince."

"Oh. Not *mine* then."

Quick, always has been.

If they've never been relatives to me, they've obviously never been relatives to him. Because you're either there for family or you're not. Which means you're either family or you're not. Sounds harsh, but it's no less true for its harshness. And a kid knows. I did. A kid can tell all those things that we adults have forgotten in our bloated self-reliance. The seemingly easy stuff like: Does that person right there care about me, Mama? You can put up a fight for a while—"Oh yes, she does care about you, baby. And one day you'll see how much"—but a child knows. After a while, you have to take off the training wheels and let the kid ride around the neighborhood to see for himself. And all you can hope for when he returns is that the emptiness he's just witnessed will make him closer to you, make him love you all the more for having always been there.

Or else that he's wiser.

"Can you make sure to cook him something healthy?" I ask my mother.

"Of course, baby."

She feels guilty for her betrayal. While I won't make it worse, she should feel guilty for a minute or two. Maybe. But from what I know of them, I can't stand the family she wanted to marry into to make me.

"Thanks, Ma."

"*Fia ai hamukepa!*"

"Hamburger, honey?" My mother, too, has picked up on some of the Samoan.

"Yeah!"

"Yes, Grandma," I say. "Thank you, Grandma."

"Sorry," Prince says. "Thanks, Grandmama."

"You're welcome, honey. You listen to Mother."

"I know. I do. I will."

"Quiet, Prince."

"Got it, Grandmama!" He's shadowboxing again—*pop, pop, pop!*—his hands and arms an untraceable blur. I follow his head, and watch his dark eyes. I can't believe how fast and angular his punches are, the way he steps in and cuts out, his body lithe and pliable. How daring the expression on his face is, almost reckless. "Okay, Mom! Don't worry! I'll protect my two favorite ladies in the world!"

"Ladies?"

"Right, G-mama!" He jumps up onto the couch, reaches out for a Wiffle ball bat, cuts at the air, and sings, "I'm Samurai Jack, Samurai Jack, Samurai Jack!"

"Sit, please," I say.

He jumps down, lands with both legs folded beneath him, hands already locked across his lap in mock subservience, eyes crossed. An old game we've been playing for so long I can't remember how it started. The joke is that he'll straighten his eyes, slowly rising as he achieves visual reacclimation, once I release him from custody.

"Okay, hon. You've paid your dues. You're free."

He's coming up now, back to normal again. "*Fa'afetai lava.*"

"You're welcome."

"That means thank you very much," my mother translates.

"Mom," I say.

"I'm sorry. I know you know that stuff. Just excited to learn."

"It's fine. I get it, Ma."

"I'm so proud of Prince for picking it up!"

"As am I," I say. "*Kama lea loa kaukala Samoa.*"

"*Ioi!*" Prince shouts.

"That's really good, too, baby. You talk like a native."

"Well, I did live with a Samoan for four years, Ma. I know a few words."

My mother smiles at me. I force a smile back, pouring a glass of chocolate Silk, then head into the rear of the apartment. Sip by sip. Some guy I dated once told me that: *Life is a matter, sexy, of sip by sip.* Bravo. Probably worked like a charm on one of his bubble-blowing nymphets. I let the soy milk circle around for a minute inside me. Hoping. But knowing better. Knowing better about the worse to come. I open the window to our patio, which is so small Prince can barely fit on it, and try to breathe a bit. But there's no breeze, the polluted stagnant Bay Area air unable to expand, as if it's held in by the walls of a dirty laundry closet. I can feel it coming up in my stomach now like the water in one of those famous French fountains.

Damnit, it's been almost a good month.

I walk over to the toilet and look into the mirror before I squat to face the blindingly clean porcelain. Mom scrubs it for me daily, thinking I don't know. I do know, and I appreciate it, but I have no clue what to say about it.

The resignation on my face reminds me of the football games Lokapi and I used to watch together when Prince was an infant. Afterward, every coach of the losing team had the same look while shaking hands with the other team's coach. The tight, closed lips pulled back into the mouth. An admittance of some sort, a series of contradictory statements finalized by the spying public, something like: Okay. I know. You've proven me wrong. Thank you. Fuck you. See you next year.

Finally something good I've borrowed from the competitive male world. Don't have a clue who I'm competing with, but it feels completely right to try to conquer this thing. On my own. For my son. To not concede to emotion.

Mom pokes her head in, and I slowly stand. Used to pop up when I'd kept it under wraps. Now that everyone knows, or everyone I care about anyway, there's no point in keeping up appearances. I just have to watch for my mother's overflowing font of compassion, which could ruin my progress. When I was a spiker on the high school volleyball team years ago, she used to scream every time I came down from a block at the net. The apocalypse fifty times a match, right when the rubber of my shoes kissed hardwood. My ears would bead on the high-pitched siren each time, almost as if there were no other parents or coaches or friends gathered there in the gym to make noise. Even today, it's embarrassing to think about. I didn't understand it then. I think I do now, which basically means I'm a mother, too. Still, you have to fight the instinct, at least in public. Not the instinct to be worried about your child. You have to fight the instinct to lose your balance in drink, or whatever be your vice.

"Baby?"

"Mother. Please."

"I'm sorry. I just thought you'd want to know about it. That's all. That's the only reason I did it."

But my mother knows the importance of balance. She's proven it. Been sober, perfectly, ten years and nineteen days. We celebrate that birthday, rather than the one that happened fifty-eight years ago. She calls it "attaining inner harmony." I admire my mother for conquering alcohol, but I don't admire her any more now than I ever did. Just didn't know it then. I was only a kid, after all, a loud and worried girl confounded by her sex and her inheritance, Lazarus's daily absence from our lives. Or else I was a six-foot oddity who secretly loved books and late-night skinny-dipping alone, stupid with her own terror of inadequacy. "It's okay, Mom."

"Okay."

"We'll deal with it. Just like anything."

"Okay, Mur."

"Anything else?"

"Well, yeah."

"What?"

"Do you want to see her?"

This surprises me. I guess I have a right. Even if it's never happened before. I don't know if she'd want to see me, or see us, but maybe. But then. Seeing her means seeing them, the Felices.

The last time this problem came up, I twice rejected my mother's advice. When Lokapi and I got married, she told me to invite the Felice family, every one of them but Lazarus. I did the opposite. I didn't think anyone I'd never met before should come to my wedding, regardless of whether or not they were my progenitor's blood. And then I wanted, I remember, Lazarus to sit on the precipice of my public rejection, force him to just one time look down at his feet and think of what he'd done in absentia. Because I knew that when the moment of his comeuppance came, I would forgive him in the very next second, no words, no more tears, just my naked arm to be escorted down the aisle.

Instead, I got exactly what my mother predicted. Despite the invitation, Lazarus never showed up. Lokapi had 452 guests, 90 percent of whom I'd never met, including a 51-person *malaga* visiting from Western Samoa. I had 36 friends from college and work and two relatives, my mother and my big brother, Gabe.

And also dearest Prince, of course, who was in my belly.

"Well. Yes," I hear myself say. Maybe it's time I got to know them by first name, help them in their time of need. "I think I do. I do want to see her."

"I'm so glad, baby," she says, letting out her breath. "We'll all go. Prince, too."

"Yeah. But no. I'm not sure about Prince, actually."

She says nothing, which means she doesn't agree. That's okay.

"I don't know if it's right."

"Well, you just tell me if you want to talk about it, Mur, okay?"

"Okay. Anything else?"

"No."

"'Kay then."

"But."

"Should get out there with Prince."

"Still."

"I know, Mother."

"Know what? I didn't say anything."

"You don't like me doing this."

"Makes me sad, that's all."

"Well, I don't like doing this, either. And it makes me angry, not sad."

"Don't be mad, baby, because—"

"Makes me pissed."

"—that always makes things worse."

"Okay, okay. Not—"

"It does!"

"—the AA lesson right now, Ma. Please. I never agree with them, you know that, but at the same time, it doesn't bother me that they helped you. I'm happy, in fact. Grateful. I don't care about method. I've said it before. It's the results that matter—"

"Baby?"

"—and you know why? Because there's a whole lot of stuff out there to be mad at. There is literally a huge trash bag of shit being air-dropped on someone's head *right now*. But forget I said it, okay? Just forget it. What? What now?"

"Do you want water?"

"No, thank you."

"Milk?"

"Noooo. I mean, yes. Yes, I do. Half a glass. You can put it outside the door. Sorry. Don't worry. But I've really gotta take care of this now, okay?"

She ducks back out with a firm nod which loyally but melodramatically translates into *Be strong, my only daughter,* and I turn on the fan to drown out the noise. I don't know why, but I start to undress. My blouse unbuttons so readily I remember the time a few months ago when it opened to my sternum in a brusque San Francisco wind on the Marina. I was on a lunch date with a "novelist" who lied, I later found out, about having a novel on the shelves. When I called him on it, and asked how he thought he'd successfully push the fib past a literary critic, he'd said, "But I *am* a novelist. In my heart, I *am!*"

And yet I was lying then, too, or I was concealing, anyway, which is officially somewhat different. I was so skinny that I worried he would see my secret in an exposed rib, and so I turned and ducked down, spastically coughing as cover, nimbly buttoning up in the feminine panic of exposure. I held my right hand to my heart for the rest of the date, a pledge of allegiance to my fears and insecurities.

I fold the blouse and lay it across the sink, step out of the pants and fold them, too. I don't look at myself yet, I can't. I know that I'm better today than I was yesterday, and far better today than last week. This is a test. I roll my panties off and then, the last contortionist step, reach behind my back and unhook my bra. My breasts spill out of the containers in a roller-coaster drop and then, almost in an instant, stop moving in their relative weightlessness. I stand upright and press my chin to the middle of my protruding clavicle and look at them from above. There is no outward slope to the nipple, the udders dry of milk, empty of fat. I hate my breasts. I have no breasts. They're more like flaps, like the drape at the automatic car wash. My pubic bone still presses against my skin as if it's an alien interred in my stomach, which sticks out a bit and always reminds me of that stupid movie line where some French girl praises the contours of a potbelly.

I take one more look into the mirror and say, "Last time, Mur," drop down to my knees, finger the trigger at the back of my throat, shamelessly ready even as it rushes out of me—nose, mouth—to start the next streak of promise to self, and beat this demon without a name inside me.

2

Anthony Constantine Felice II
Iraq War Protest at the Mount Shasta Amphitheater
November 12, 2003

HE WAITED UNTIL THE WIFE LEFT on her day's errands, whatever they were, and then crawled into the attic. He brought down a dusty box with half a dozen faded, peeling German stamps lined neatly across one corner. He sliced the masking tape with a razor and carefully unfolded the top flaps, reached inside, and came up with a pair of tiger-striped fatigues. Looking them over, he bet, to his physically fit credit, that he could still slide into these army issues without sucking in his fifty-nine year old stomach, pinching the cheeks of his fifty-nine year old backside. Suddenly he felt strong, and left the box where it was, evidence of his recurrent crime of dabbling with yesterday.

In their room, he opened their lucky drawer and took out a T-shirt, shriveled from use, fading. He'd bought it from a street vendor at a Blue Angels performance on Veterans Day, Moffett Field, 1993. He absolutely loved the shirt, a masterful misdirection, playful trick of a T-shirt twist. From afar, his brothers and sisters in peace would take in the peace sign symbol with affection. But as they'd near, the visual mirage would change and the real image, to Anthony's delight, would take shape. The vertical stem of the sign was actually the body of an airplane, the arms of the sign actually wings. And not just any airplane. It was a fortress of destruction, the B-52 bomber caught in an aerial shot, blessed by the heavens above, as if, Anthony thought now, only God's eye, infinitely higher than man's, could truly appreciate the splendor. In print over the photograph was the word PEACE, and beneath it the punch line: THROUGH SUPERIOR FIREPOWER.

"A T-shirt TKO," Anthony whispered to himself.

Once he'd heard that Richmond had said the shirt was something only a noncombat veteran could wear, that a B-52 pilot would find it despicable. Shameful. The first point of admittance to a soldiers' club, Richmond had said, was the understanding that one killed despite, not because, and never for pleasure. In any nation, any era.

"Piss on him," he whispered again, holding the signage at eye level. "The golden boy switched teams."

Over the years, he'd worn the shirt to family functions, anyway. Sometimes they'd make a quick joke, acknowledge that they had been, most gratefully, entertained. So well entertained, in fact, that could they move on to something else now? The shirt rarely created what Anthony desired: conversation, intimacy, brotherhood.

Now he was alone with his shirt and put his head and arms through it. The cloth dropped down his muscular torso, waving, for a few seconds, like an antique flag of a forgotten war. For the first time in forty years, he slipped into his fatigues, still a perfect fit, just like he'd known. Then he fastened on his mountain boots, thought twice about the fashion alliance that would arise with some nature-loving hippie, took them off, dropped them in the kitchen trash bin, returned to the attic.

The box was right where he'd left it. He went in deeper than before and came out with a pair of olive-green, knee-high paratrooper boots. He double-timed back to the kitchen and spit-shone the toe, the heel, the tongue, and any other square of black leather he could find. He got a wet rag and dabbed at the dust on the olive-green canvas and then laced them up tight, as if he were about to engage in precisely that activity the boots were designed for, a full-speed collision with the earth.

At various times in the late sixties, Anthony and his younger brothers had leapt from planes during Airborne School at Fort Benning, Georgia, all except Johnny voluntarily joined up. After boot camp, each of his younger brothers—Richmond, Johnny, and Lazarus—got their orders to land in Vietnam. Tony's spearheading jump landed in Berlin. The greatest irony and tragedy of his life. No one, not even his soon-to-be-veteran brothers, ever asked how he let it happen, getting stationed in West Germany with the rampage and death going on in his name on the other side of the globe. He'd been assigned to eyeball the Soviets across the wall.

The folks back in Upland viewed his orders as just that. The military told you what to do, and if protocol saved one of their sons from the glory of war, they were grateful. His mother had once confided this to the wife, how nice it was not to have to worry about Anthony on the Berlin Wall, "although he was doing his duty, after all, and that's what counts." But his brothers knew the truth. Not even Johnny had ever levied the accusation that anyone cleared for combat, regardless of their orders, could *opt* for combat, both patriot and parrot.

In Berlin, he built a reputation for being a brawler. His nationalistic fervor had finally found its home, and he was free in West Germany to take his old arguments to the next level. The belligerence of ideologues most welcome at the bars. Any slight against the flag he took personally, the tiniest insult against his country enraged him. He was popular, considered courageous by his peers, even a tad crazy, a mind-set that they not only admired but were defined by. They'd been taught, even while not in war, that survival was contingent upon the auspices of war, and as war was inherently crazy, it thus required courage to endure it. Spaten Oktoberfest was his beer of preference, chased by a shot of Jägermeister.

His girl asked him to marry her on her twenty-first birthday. He hadn't thought of it before, but why not? She had saved a thousand bucks for a ring, she would be a good mother, she was conservative, frugal, loyal, cunning. He'd need the cunning as protection against anyone tossing out the one ad hominem hand grenade from which he couldn't protect himself: You of all people didn't go to Vietnam? You, the zealot with the American flag wallet? Not even as a truck driver, not even as an MP? Well, how can you say anything about it, bud?

So they married. Tried to have kids right from the start. Before they'd decided on a list of names, three years had passed. She failed test after test. He took it upon himself. He slurped raw oysters at sunrise, mixed dried African tree bark into his afternoon protein shakes, ran three miles in the fertile evenings. He felt strong, virile. He was not yet twenty-five, he was at the peak of his physiological potential. They went to the bookstore and bought a copy of *Kama Sutra*. That same night, they sampled strange positions, finished in weird angles. He made it fun, naked Twister, dress-up Thursday, once or twice a month in a West Upland peach orchard. On a drunken night when he was feeling especially rambunctious, he lifted her up by her feet and held her there like a deer carcass being drained of blood, letting gravity assist, as he joked, "the lazy freestyle stroke of those little fishies." He stayed positive, he insisted postcoitally that he could feel her belly growing already, he practically felt that he could will the little being *into* being.

Finally they visited a doctor. He took Anthony to the side and said it wouldn't happen, not with her, anyway, nearly winking. He'd married a barren woman, empty of an heir.

Now he came out of his house in his B-52 for peace T-shirt and dusty tiger-striped fatigues tucked into the paratrooper boots, the laces wrapped tight up the length of his calves like the laurel wreath on the noble shins of a Roman emperor. He climbed into his four-door, six-wheel, V-8 American-made Ram truck, the gunner mounting his turret, the Air Force Academy sticker across the front and back windows both, the Air Force Academy license frame outlining the custom AFAGDAD plate. He hadn't seen his error in acronym until it was too late, and he tried to drive about, as much as possible, at night, until the new one came from whatever California prison made license plates. It still hadn't come. A few weeks back, disaster had struck when a trucker at a red light in Redding had snickered.

He'd fired back, "Stands for Air Force Academy godfather, you liberal son of a bitch!"

"Who's liberal, you stupid fuck?"

"You can't be a dad if you're a fag!" Tony shouted. "It's Adam and Eve, not Adam and Steve! Where the hell did you come from?"

"Came back from Iraq, tough guy, First Marine Regiment, how 'bout you?"

Tony nodded with respect and said, still nodding, "Well, thank you for your service to this—"

"That's what I thought, you goddamned wannabe."

"—country. Hey!"

When the light turned green, the trucker swerved his eighteen wheels in front of Tony and drove fifteen miles under the speed limit, which was twenty-five miles per hour. Tony couldn't see anything but the WASH ME message fingered into the dirt of the sliding door and two naked-lady mud flaps that seemed, although faceless, to laugh at him all the way home.

He was crossing that same intersection, now making the descent down a small hill, trying like hell not to think about his nonexistent war record, his botched domestic life with the wife, his delinquent, missing, artistic namesake, a.k.a. the "other party." He hadn't talked to the "other party" in almost two years. He hadn't said his name— Anthony Constantine Felice III—in the same time. He'd heard that the "other party" had applied for a name change—Duk Soo Kim. He thought about his goddaughter instead, Leila Nakamitsu, and her postcards with the official academy insignia on the back corner. It probably was like a dollar bill, he thought, had some mysterious Masonic code to counter any counterfeit. In each three-sentence note, she always wrote about the latest coed dance and the beautiful skies in Colorado and how much she appreciated the trust fund he'd set up in her name for once she became a second lieutenant. He liked to pull from his mind the image of five F-16s in sleek formation, zipping like birds through the clouds, at her graduation at Falcon Stadium. The president would pin the bars to her lapel himself, having visited West Point and Annapolis the two years prior. This stroke of luck so thrilled him that he vowed to visit Colorado Springs before she finished her plebeian year, with or without the wife.

Hundreds of California black oaks were crowding his side of the road, but he looked the other way. He then saw thousands of western junipers and incense cedars and ponderosa pines climbing so sky-high that the outline of the trees blurred like a dense blanket of green, as if they were warming the mountainside. But this image he'd seen every day for the last decade never impressed Anthony, even when they'd fled the liberal Silicon Valley for, unbeknownst to them, the liberal town of Mount Shasta. It wasn't that he'd seen better, it was that he doubted anyone could destroy it. Would take a million years to cut down all those trees, he thought. "So why not!" he shouted now. "Why not get the bums some jobs, huh? These tree huggers are nothing but sewer rats who found free rent on a pine branch! Not enough rat traps in the world, I'll tell ya!"

He'd argued with neighbors at barbecues, principals at teachers' night, bus riders and tweakers at the Greyhound depot, septuagenarians at town-hall bingo games. He'd made certain that everyone in the municipality of three thousand understood that he was the only resident who wasn't, as he referred to them, "a mental environ-mentalist." He was so proud of coining the term that he made a baseball cap with the words pressed to the face of the crown and placed it square on the cardboard cutout of Abbie Hoffman in drag in his garage. He'd nearly been arrested at his son's graduation party for threatening the drunken valedictorian who'd said, "Well, Mr. Felice, if you think your truck's so good for the air, why don't you go outside and wrap your lips around the muffler, and I'll fire up the engine?"

Now he accelerated across the crevasse and into the heart of downtown Mount Shasta, where the cars were already door-to-door tight along the walk. Everything he hated right there in the square, at least a thousand protesters. This was the enemy, his leftist neighbors, the dirtball hordes. It was like the sixties all over again, unshorn hair, flaring jeans, and turquoise love beads, a drug-induced time warp to Hippieville, California. Stupid kids who could barely start a car spouting about a world they hadn't even seen yet, smart-ass college grads with their grandiose arguments and snotty rationalizations, the affluent sellouts of his own generation. Even the pink grandmas were here pumping their arthritic fists in the cool Shasta air. The polar-bear apologists, the degenerate poets, the freeloading transients.

They weren't just taking over downtown Mount Shasta—they were taking over America. He couldn't sip on his coffee without being lectured about the virtue of recycling your paper cup to save a bitternut hickory tree in Minnesota. He couldn't turn on the television without his masculinity getting assaulted by gay men obsessed with interior decoration, Oscar-winning pimps barking gangsta threats into the camera, Larry King lobbing softballs to Jimmy Carter, the anti-American BBC, the tragedy of Comedy Central, the mental environmentals of the Discovery Channel. He couldn't step outside his house without slipping on the solicitation leaflets for every imaginable humanitarian cause, sub-Saharan AIDS, middle-aged breast cancer, washed-up shellfish, inner-city immigrants, one-legged triathletes.

"Like a herd of cows on a football field," Anthony said, running a hand over his crew cut in the cab of his V-8.

He recalled his favorite flick—before he'd discovered Paul Newman's radical politics—*Hud,* the scene where the steers infected with foot-and-mouth are shot down, one by one, by the government men.

That's what these people are, thought Anthony, shaking his head. Rotting from the inside out.

"The masses are in need of their executioner."

He parked behind the compost dumpsters at Orgy of Organics, the sustainable-farms food store where he wouldn't otherwise be caught dead, and grabbed the laminated sign he'd had made the day before

at Kinko's for $82.27. At tax time, he'd try to write it off as a donation
to the Republican Party. He lifted the sign high over his head and
marched toward the rally.

He didn't get far before fearing that the "other party" might be
present, had maybe even organized this shameful gathering, and
then just as he remembered that the wife had said the "other party"
was at an artists' retreat in New Hampshire, he realized that nothing would change if his namesake were here. That the whole point
of this mission was holding fast for the next generation, which still
included, Anthony supposed, the "other party," Korean ingrate of
his American adoption.

If he were here, the "other party" would probably laugh at Anthony,
mock the front side of the sign with its red backdrop, the Soviet
hammer and sickle under the words IF YOU DON'T LIKE IT, YOU KNOW
WHERE YOU CAN GO . . . The "other party," despite his smarts, would
completely miss the clever irony behind the history of the statement,
how unless you were partial to China, North Korea, Cuba, or a few
Scandinavian countries, there was, in fact, nowhere for a commie to
go, not on this earth, anyway, which led to the other side of the sign,
more redness over a bed of flames, one word . . . HELL!

He walked by the Shasta Pizza Parlor where he used to take the
family on Friday nights. Seeing his own stout figure in the combat
fatigues made him *suck in the gut! puff out the chest! tuck in the chin!*
even more, the erect militaristic posture that the wife, as far as he
knew, no longer enjoyed. If she was here today, it could be the end of
their marriage. Very possible that she wouldn't take this latest embarrassment, might even slap him right there in public.

After Child Protective Services had stepped in six years ago and
taken the "other party" from their home, the marriage had actually
seemed to strengthen. The circumstance of having lost a third of their
family to a commie government institution had so infuriated Anthony
that he'd pondered selling his best stocks to hire a solid attorney to
get the "other party" back. The wife had spared him this pain and

found them pro bono representation from a first-year private lawyer at the Heritage Foundation. Anthony was instructed to think about that first day at the airport seeing the "other party," the first time he heard the word "Da-da," the first wobbly steps in infantdom, the best report card brought home by the "other party," all the promise of an American life anytime he thought the anger would consume him.

His poor performance with the committee astonished the attorney. "I told you what to say," he repeated over and over. "Then you go and say the opposite. And rail on the kid, no less. Right there in front of all of them. Why the hell did you need me there, anyway?"

"Hey! We want what we paid for!"

"You don't mean the kid?"

"That, too!"

"That's why you won't get the kid, right there. Get it? And, anyway, you didn't pay me a dime, buddy."

"Hey! Ever heard of tax dollars? Ever heard of half my paycheck?"

"Ever heard of nonprofit?" And then: "Do you even work?"

"Hey! Stay on the topic! What are we talking about here?"

"You're an idiot. You don't deserve to have a child."

"Fuck you!"

"You *are* a child."

Child Protective Services refused to return the "other party" because of "insistent and alarming self-righteousness on the part of the probated father, as well as indoctrination bordering on abuse." It was worse inside their home. Having the words spelled out so explicitly had put Anthony's marriage in serious jeopardy. The "other party" was sent to a foster home in Yreka, and the wife swore to get him back. She kept the lines of communication open, all without his cooperation. When the "other party" called home, he answered, "Is this the other party to whom I am speaking? . . . Would the other party like to speak to my wife?"

By the end of the year, the "other party" was old enough to speak for himself, two years from eligibility for the selective service. Everyone but Anthony listened to what the "other party" had to say. But why should he listen, after all? Had he not provided a roof, a thousand meals, political education? What had he done wrong? Whose throat had he put a knife to?

When the committee finalized the recommendation to permanently remove the "other party" from their home, Anthony had never seen the wife so mad. Not at the committee, or even the "other party," but at him. This had caught Anthony off guard, and even now as he hurried toward the rally, he was hurt in his heart by her fury. He didn't believe in unconditional love. When he'd told her this, as softly as he could, she'd said, "You don't make any sense. You're the only extremist on the planet who doesn't believe in unconditional love."

Thinking on the wife's anger and what he was about to do today made him feel panicky, and so he focused, without thought, on the onward march through downtown Mount Shasta, still keeping the soldierly gait he'd learned in West Germany, hoisting the sign high above his head.

He was right there at the fringe of the masses and he cut directly through the crowd, thinking on the beach charge at Normandy, the enemy encampments up ahead. He thought of trouncing cockroaches in the garage. For so many years he'd called these people pinkos, and reds, and it was no coincidence that everything was hued now in a shade of blood. It was like that Rolling Stones song "Paint It Black," except it was "Paint It Red," and except fuck them, fuck the Rolling Stones, too.

"There aren't enough shotguns in the world," he said.

So far his sign and its politics had not been detected. There were dozens of other signs here, each homogeneous in message. He would change that, or die trying. He made it to the stage front. Listened for a minute, let the venom build.

A pink grandma shouted into the microphone about the alleged inside job at Tower 7 and now they were chanting: "We want the truth! We want the truth!"

What the hell did these people know about life? About loyalty, sacrifice, honor? His own goddaughter knew more about these universal concepts than all of these jerks combined and, at twenty, she couldn't even legally drink a beer.

Anthony's eyes were glazed over but not tearing, certainly not that, and by the time he came back around to where he was, and why he was there, no fewer than twelve angry hippies had formed a half circle around him. Surrounded by the enemy. His back to the podium. He didn't know what the hell they were saying, but it didn't matter. He was exactly where he was needed, right in the front line, middle of the war.

"Fuck you!" he fired back. *"Fuck you! Fuck you!"*

"Get outta here, you clown!"

"Find some love in your heart, man!"

"You're a Nazi! A fucking Nazi!"

"Heil Hitler! Where's your swastika?"

"Hey!" he shouted, confused by the accusation. "I fought those people!"

He didn't think it untrue. Because he'd been willing back then on the wall to fight Nazis if they'd sprung back out from their holes, he'd been willing to keep them from returning to the world, and that was what counted, just like his mother had said, in the end. And this felt like the end to Anthony, a small death, each stinking hippie breath blown into his face.

"Fuck you!" he shouted with all the air in his lungs, all the righteous fire in his gut, the sign about commies and hell brought down like a knight's lance, a torch lighting the darkness. Someone grabbed him from behind and he twisted at once, thrusting the lance outward but missing. Some laughed and others came forward and suddenly an urgent voice in his ear resonated with trust in his system: "Anthony! Anthony!"

It was no angel. Ned Loeffler, the neighbor, the pacifist, a devil. He held Anthony from behind in a bear hug, patting him soothingly on the chest.

"Come on, buddy, come on. We gotta get you home."

"Hey!" grunted Anthony, trying to plant his feet. A plastic cup collided with his shoulder, the liquid splattering across his B-52 for Peace T-shirt.

"Come on, old friend. We got it. We can do it."

They made their way out of the rally, which was growing into a miniature riot, urged on by a new chant: "Clip your Bush! Clip your Bush!"

The organizers had the slogan in print on their black tees. On the back of the shirt was the image of a .45 whose clip was being loaded by a black-gloved hand, a clear suggestion at presidential assassination. My God, thought Anthony, these people are *crazy*!

Anthony shouted over the shoulder of his neighbor, "You fucking pinheads will die in your own shit!" The beer rained down. He was crying now, couldn't keep it back. "Will rot in it!"

They got to the neighbor's car, a late-eighties Volkswagen bus of all things, and he wiped away the tears and said, "Oh, great. Gotta sit in this German piece of shit. Why don't you just send me home in a hearse? Ever heard of driving American?"

"You all right, brother?"

"I'm not your brother," he said, still erect in the front seat, as if the upholstery were toxic.

The first year of his life in Mount Shasta, Anthony had talked politics through the fence with this neighbor, and then one day Loeffler had offered to pay to make the barrier taller, an eight-foot high property divide where no conversations between the oaken blanks could occur. "Probably to grow marijuana," Anthony had told the wife.

"You smell like hemp," he said now.

Loeffler smiled, shook his head. "Well, you smell like beer."

"Hey! What do you expect from those drunks?"

"Don't worry." A change in tone. "I won't say anything to Darlene about this."

"Hey! Mind your own business! You leftists are always butting into my family affairs!"

They made their way back to the neighborhood in real silence, the kind where there is nothing to say, and when he was dropped off at the house, Anthony didn't thank his neighbor for the good save or the kind words or the free ride. He merely nodded, said, "Okay," and walked up the red, white, and blue brick driveway he'd victoriously laid in Bush's honor after the '00 election.

He kept the code of silence, not saying a word to the wife. She was in the backyard planting bulbs. Why did she need to know what had just happened at the protest rally? He went on to his office. At his desk, he fingered the stationery with the bald eagle perched on the tidal wave of an American flag, hoping she would come no closer than the kitchen.

She'd once suggested divorce, and he'd immediately said, "What about my money?"

In order to survive their marriage, he sometimes forced himself to remember the orange grove behind Big Victor. They'd fallen in love there. He'd told her the romantic tales about Anthony Constantine Felice, the good man he was named after. She'd loved hearing the Great Depression stories about hawking bruised apricots on congested, smoky, unpaved street corners, the gritty tales of burrowing through the earth in the lightless coal mines of southern Pennsylvania. He'd shared the black-and-white pictures of his parents' wedding at St. Dominic's, the church packed tenuously with the northern and southern Italian communities, an empty pew in between. How it took only the laying of his father's hand upon his trembling shoulder to feel loved, that he'd needed nothing more from the man, that he'd never forget those tender hands as long as he lived.

"You'da never thought it," he'd said raking a hand over his flat-top hair in his James Dean T-shirt and blue jeans, brown eyes wide with amazement, her head in his lap, the spaghetti-strap dress spread across the fertile ground like a giant fan of woven cotton, cool in the shade of the orange trees, warm Southern California summer, prewar, 1961. "Who'da guessed, huh? That a coal miner's callused hands could make you feel so good. Well, they did. As God is my witness, it's true."

Now he stood out of boredom and a kind of general malaise that seemed to override, or outlast, his dreams during these long, drawn-out days by himself. He looked at the hundred-dollar bill taped to his desk, the head shot of his goddaughter from the AFA 2003 yearbook, and walked over to his shelf of books. He romantically traced the ends of his fingers along the skinny scarlet letters of Ann Coulter's hardbacks, he chummily patted the fat memoirs-as-self-betterment of Bill O'Reilly, he nodded at the character attacks on the Hollywood crowd by Bernie Goldberg, he squinted at the academic free-market books he'd never opened but liked looking at nonetheless, and then the unassuming small print of a book half the size of the others caught his eye for the first time in years. He pulled out the treatise on suicide, Camus's *Myth of Sisyphus,* irritated already by the black-and-white triangles on the tattered cover, its badly yellowing pages. He opened to the first page and read the inscription.

To Tony, the extremist who might like, even need, this book. Love, Rich.

"Traitor."

Anthony had always been the guy who fingered the line between what was right and what wasn't. During fights he'd organize the two sides of the issue because he knew exactly where he stood. Sometimes his extremism would offend even allies, and they'd roll over to the other side to put distance between their skin and the fire of his passion. These betrayers, siblings or not, would only intensify his zealotry. They, his former allies, were now worse than apostates. They were Benedict Arnolds, not worth any benefit of the doubt. Weak, repulsive people, wrong wrong so goddamned wrong, in need of a high-noon hanging in the dusty square, worse than the enemy for the very reason that they'd once been right.

"There is only black and white," he said aloud.

The lethargy snuck up on the bed of his anger once again, and he sat down and fell asleep, his head in the fold of his forearms, dreaming about lions, which he'd never seen, on the coast of Africa. Before discovering why he'd never been there, he awakened under the wife, trespassing. He tossed her off and put his fists up. She reclutched his hand violently, saying something he couldn't make out. He'd caught three words: ". . . that goddamned sign."

So then she knew about the rally. He sat up slowly, not exactly contrite in his politically charged heart, a thread of spittle spinning off his chin. He would let her ramble on for a while, get her just due of didactics, let off some steam. He deserved, he supposed, some flak from the wife. Not because he'd gone to the rally for the wrong reason, but that she was still here after all these decades.

At least, he thought, matrimonial comeuppance hasn't come in the form of a court order to sell any stocks.

"Did you hear me? I said, get up!"

"What?" he whispered, slightly whining, but standing nonetheless.

"The goddamned peace sign!" She rarely cussed. "Follow me!"

Anthony shrugged, eyebrows raised. He stayed a few steps behind her. He figured she'd incinerate his B-52 for Peace T-shirt tonight. Or commit it to the rag drawer for Windex and Pine-Sol like other worn-out war apparel, the RUSH shammy and No Spin Zone sweater. He knew what she was thinking. It was one thing to be on the side of what's right, but to flout common sense and venture into the heart of the storm? What kind of idiot had she married?

She walked past the kitchen and into the garage, just as he'd predicted. She hit the button and this surprised him. He watched the light rise against the darkness, the wife walking straight under the groaning mechanics of the garage door into the late day. He stood there in dramatic suspension, wondering what was about to happen.

In the driveway, she was pointing down at the pavement, her back to the house.

"Anthony! Anthony!"

He was short of breath. The rat-dogs were barking next door where, he imagined, Loeffler already knew what he didn't know, and yet would soon learn. This was one of those times when he'd be left with nothing but his unflappable principles, the old code of self-reliance confirmed by our betters of yesteryear.

"Get over here, Anthony!"

Finally he came out, trying not to look around, not to look at her or the ground she was pointing at. He looked at his feet.

"You will clean this up at once!"

There it was, the rainbow-colored peace sign, big as a hula hoop, the spray paint remarkably exact on the tributary bricks he'd laid himself.

Anthony turned and marched back up the driveway. The wife, without shame, was dressing him down from behind, Loeffler's rat-dogs barked their mocking applause. He thought about the box he'd opened that morning. The only thing missing was the soldier's specialty, the paratrooper's lifeline. Apparently a necessity in this day and age, even in a hippie outfit like Shasta. Somehow he'd find his hermetic brother now, Lazarus the gun nut, give him a call before night fell on America.

He needed a weapon to defend himself.

3

Murron Leonora Teinetoa
The Flowers of Elysium Fields
October 31, 2007

FROM THE DOOR, I peek my head into Room 129 of the Elysium Fields Hospice and find a lady who looks nothing at all like me, a powder-blue surgeon's curtain pulled up the right side of the bed. I don't know how anyone, even the elderly infirm with damaged passages and congested sensories, could sleep through the smell of this place. The Elysium Fields Hospice, from door to door, stinks. Like putrid meat. She's got mustard smeared across her cheek like some finger-painting project for toddlers, the neck stick-thin. Sad. She must be less than eighty pounds. Above her head on the bulletin board, a single piece of red paper has a picture of a cup of water with a thick cartoonish X through its center.

I take a few quiet steps toward her bed, not just to look at her face closer but to clean the mess she's made, apparently falling asleep during lunch. A hamburger is spilled open across the floor, the trail of pickles and tomatoes starting in the deep hollow of her collarbone. I reach down to pick up the hamburger and realize, almost at once, that the ominous stillness of this poor woman means only one thing.

Jesus.

I reach out for her wrist to confirm by touch what the eyes already know, and there's nothing there beneath the cool skin, even the blood has gone dead cold. I don't want to think how long she's been lying here like this, pulseless in a swamp of dried condiments, but it is five long hours after midday, and the dribble of saliva obviously reached the sheet some time ago, a dark egg-shaped stain on the bed. On the other side of the gown, I see another image of evidence of what happened here, a dollop of relish and catsup tangled into the frays of her dusty gray hair.

The anger I feel at this ugly discovery is generalized and somewhat common, I suppose, with no projected target or blameworthy source, but it doesn't feel right that the first time I get to see the mother of Lazarus, my progenitor, she doesn't even know it, and never will know it. As usual with this side of my bloodline, no memory to claim, no shared story, no forward step to take.

I pull out a sanitary wipe from my purse, start to clean her chin. The dried condiments have crusted over and I have to pick at the mess with my nail to get them off completely, an indignity for neither Mary Capone Felice, who's not aware of the intrusion, nor me, who hasn't cared what people think for a long time. At least not people I don't know. Next I dial my mother's number, look at the clock to remember, always, the discovery time of her body.

"Hello!" I hear, and then through the phone, "Hello?"

I walk around the curtain and see, in a weird flash that feels like time travel, my own dark southern Italian eyes on the pillow. *This* is the mother of Lazarus, Mary Capone Felice, assessing me from head to toe, the hard desirous way men do at the beach, though without possession. Her hair is matted and twisted with sweat, and her lips are dried and blistered.

"I used to look like you, honey! But a lot shorter! You're tall as a model!"

I don't feel happy about the discovery on this side of the room, but I do feel partially relieved, and grateful, and then because my mind has never been able to stay put for very long, I'm overwhelmed with sadness for the other woman, deceased on the other side of this curtain.

"Hello?"

I press my lips to the speaker, turn away from Mary. "Oh. Hi, Mom. Sorry."

"You all right?"

"Yes, yes. I'm fine. I'm . . . here."

"Did she recognize you?"

I turn back and she's smiling from the bed, kindly waiting for the return of my attention. "Definitely. I'll tell you about it later, okay?"

"Sure you're fine, baby?"

"Yeah. I have to take care of something right now, okay?"

"'Kay. Bye, baby. Good luck!"

"Okay."

I smile at Mary, and this makes her own smile widen. She has lovely auburn skin, I can see even from here, the soft shade of brown that Gabe used to have after a few days of skating with his buddies in midsummer. I step forward and take her hand. The skin is soft and moist, like a baby's. I guess I'm blessed, genetically, in the epidermis department.

"I'll be back in a couple minutes, okay?"

She keeps smiling as if in a trance, and I lower my head just enough to verify that, yes, she's messed herself. The dark, wide, perfectly oval Mediterranean eyes suspect something shameful, but I try to throw her suspicions off by saying, "You look beautiful, you know that?"

Sounds silly, I know, but I pat her hand the way my mother taught me in Sonoma, except back then the recipient of the affection was our neighbor's gelding, Starfire. "With real human care and concern," she used to say, "because the horse knows." I don't feel meddlesome, and I don't know why this is exactly, but when I begin to lightly stroke the skin from her wrist to the ends of her fingertips, the crusty eyelids close down on each other and the mouth widens just as I'd hoped. In half a minute, she appears to be in a deep sleep.

I cross the powder-blue divide between the patients in this room, each a world unto itself. The woman's name, it says on an unpeeled name tag I find under her bedside lamp, is Amélia Fatima Assuncão Duarte, was, was Amélia Fatima Assuncão Duarte, and I find on the tabletop something that verifies that she was more, to me, than a happened-upon corpse and a beautiful name. She has a letter from a son or a brother or a cousin in Portugal, Sr. Arturo Cardoso Saramago Duarte, and when I pull out the card, there is a black-and-white picture inside of a young girl no taller than this passed-on woman whose beauty in youth perfectly matches her name, holding a fish above her head by the gills, AZORES '33 artisan-etched into the upper right corner of the photo.

"Lovely," I whisper. "I think my brother, Gabe, once caught a marlin this big. He sent me a picture, too. I can see how strong you were, Amélia. Good-bye. And thank you."

I squeeze past an Asian woman pushing her son down the center of the hallway, his elephantine head propped back against the chair as if he's just taken, to the brain, an electric jolt, and his eyes are locked on the faded wallpaper stars of the ceiling. I pass an abandoned cafeteria cart, the meals on the trays in various stages of disappearance.

At the nurses' desk, none of the three nurses look up, each one filling out her own daunting stack of paperwork, a legitimate reason, I suppose, not to pay me any attention. Still, someone has passed away. They're obviously unaware. Or is it that they're already on top of this latest development, their indifferent institutional discovery made far before my terrified civilian own, and they've merely pushed back the pickup and cleanup to deal with other problems in real time?

Maybe the papers they're presently sifting through are the last bureaucratic detail of Mrs. Amélia Fatima Assuncão Duarte. Just like that, it seems not only likely but certain. I don't know this place well enough to appreciate how common an occurrence death is, but

I suspect, by the look of things, by the smell, that they've happened upon more than one neglected corpse in their day.

I'm tempted to ring the bell. Instead, I wait. For one reason only. Maybe someday when I come up here, they'll be busy with paperwork on Mary's behalf, immersed, for instance, in her prescriptive caretaking, or signing off some dietary recommendation about reducing, say, her high levels of salt intake.

"Yes," the nurse in the center says, still filling out forms. She is the tallest and the whitest. The other two are Filipinas. No one has yet to look up. "How can I help you?"

"Um, you probably know this already, but there is a woman who died in Room 129."

I don't feel right about using her name, and suddenly, preposterously, I'm even wondering about my own personal ability to determine if someone has died. I read books for a living, which, at times, puts me at something of a disadvantage in real life. The line between the hope-based possibilities drawn of a book and the hopeless impossibilities lived through in real life has always made for a balancing act. Seeing death like this is a first for me, hopefully my last in a while. I have no idea if it's better to be ready for death or to be ambushed by it. Perhaps it sounds small and American-spoiled to say so, but I don't want to think about Mrs. Amélia Fatima Assuncão Duarte too much once I leave here today.

The nurse is still writing, ten seconds later—unimpressed, I guess, with the facts of my reportage. It's necessary, of course, to be standing here in the flames of her silence, but I don't like being powerless. She knows I need her, and not the other way around.

"Okay," she says, still not looking up. "Let's go have a look."

I turn without any further prompt, and again make my way down the hallway. I don't hear footsteps behind me, but I continue on nonetheless, fairly certain that if she doesn't reach the room herself for whatever reason, she will at least send someone else. I'm nearing the Asian woman with her physically and mentally incapacitated son, the head collapsed on the sarcopenic neck like a ripe watermelon. She's practically motionless with her back to the wall, these two unmemorialized statues of an obviously ended lineage, his mouth blowing a dying bubble of air every few seconds, and I can't afford to slow down, and I won't dare make eye contact, and I'll shut off my sappy maternal heart, heavy with pity and admiration for her stoic commitment, because I want to stay focused. Faster than a heart attack, I can lose my center.

All that I'll allow myself to think, just this once, is that every day, without question, *pro infinito,* I'd do the same thing for my son.

Mary's still sleeping. I guess it's just as well. I look around her half of the room. There's nowhere to sit but in a wheelchair pinned against the door, so I lower myself into the vinyl seat, its bucket-like dimensions forcing my knees together as if I were embarking on a roller-coaster ride. I lean back and roll forward a few feet. The brake is too loose to brace the rubber tire and so I slowly stand, the brown shadows from the weak yellow light rearranging themselves in mock mimicry. As if to balance against the darkness, the second light above the empty soap dispenser is blindingly bright, like the kind in 24 Hour Fitness locker rooms. I wait. To keep my mind from drifting too far from what I'm here, for this moment, anyway, to do, I open the closet door and find a few hangers and a few items of clothes tossed across the base. I hang the clothes, one by one, wondering nothing. This is obviously the outfit she wore to the hospice. No need to use it again.

The wallpaper in the closet is the same design as the wallpaper in the room, which is the same design as the wallpaper in the halls. Simple, uncomplicated, mostly faded stars, the pattern of the constellations indiscernible. The paper is peeling in the corners, and this reminds me of our trailer growing up where the roofline and floor line seemed, by the imaginative misperceptions of a child, to be curling in on the room, like funhouse mirrors at a carnival. There are no mirrors here, though, nothing in which you can see your own reflection. Probably for good reason. There are no photographs, there are no cards, but there is a potted plant of flowers which, until you investigate the dust on the plastic leaves, do a pretty good job of fooling you into thinking they're real tulips. Overhead, the unplugged Zenith television is suspended from a bolted frame, perfectly bisecting the room.

"Well!" I hear. "You must be my missing brother's missing daughter!"

I don't like the roundabout way Lazarus has been attacked, despite the accuracy of it and the irony of his absence yet again, and I don't care for the insensitive summarization of my life in one sentence, especially by a "relative" who, as near as I can remember, I've never met, and so I say to the woman, who, I'm guessing, is Mary Anna, "You must be Lazarus's other brother."

"Huh. Real funny. Huh. Huh."

I say nothing, but, weirdly, she's already sneering.

"So where is she, huh? Your mom got my e-mail, huh? Make sure you don't stay beyond visiting hours."

I move closer to the only sister of Lazarus, and then decide, because her eyes are hostile and her voice is loud, to walk past her. I've been condescended to enough today by women I don't know and then, more importantly, I wouldn't want Mary to wake up over what I hope is not the beginnings of a catfight. I have thousands of questions I could ask Mary Anna, but I get the sense that she doesn't have one for me.

I stand to the side of the door, the unremitting silence and eerie vastness of the hallway making me feel as if one step out of the room would be the first spiral of vertigo down the canyon's descent.

"You should whisper," I whisper.

"You don't know Ma," she says. "She sleeps like a board. Don't worry about it."

"Well," I say. "You don't want her to wake up before they come—"

"Well! I said it doesn't matter—"

"—and—"

"—didn't I?"

"Well, yes. You did. But look—"

"Well, then?"

"—there's—Would you be quiet? God."

She's infuriated by this statement, and why not, I guess, her narrowing eyes pining for the legitimacy of, as Mom used to say to me, "your wrongly presumed big britches," and it's almost as if the duration of her "taking me in" has provided her with facial information confirming what she's suspected all along: that during the years I was missing from her life it was obviously for the very best of reasons. So she's a phrenologist. What can I do but evaluate back? She has a horrible jawline, to start, the crooked disproportionate kind of overbite where the jaw would have to be broken to reset the hinges, and has the habit of chewing on her thin, almost nonexistent lower lip with what appears to be no self-awareness at all.

I don't think she's too happy with herself.

"Sorry," I whisper. "It's just that she just died." Somehow this sounds better, by the thinnest of hairs, than saying, "She's dead."

Mary Anna walks by me, drags the drapes wide open, the light claiming her face immediately. "Mom?"

"No," I whisper, not without urgency. "No."

"Oh, you mean the roommate? The roommate died?" She looks from me to the bed one time, and that's it. She's back on me. "All right. Well. They'll clean it up. That's what they're paid to do. Now, look, we don't want to be in here with a dead body, do we?"

Only because it would be borderline criminal for Mary to wake up and hear our conversation, if she hasn't heard or dreamed it already, I start into the hallway and stand by the door to await the nurse. A young Filipina is coming toward the room now.

"Hi," I say. "How are you?"

"Good good."

"So you know—"

"Yes yes."

"—about—"

"No worry."

"Come on, Murron. Let's—"

"We take care, okay?"

"—go to the snack bar. There's someone there you should meet."

I shrug in concession to this strange confluence of two people who neither know nor greet each other but who evidently desire the same result in this room and say, "All right. Oh, Nurse?"

"Yes yes?"

"Mary's soiled herself."

"What dat?"

"She pooped her pants," says Mary Anna.

"Yeah yeah. I clean her no worry."

"Let's go then."

"And just so I know who I'm walking with. You're Mary Anna, right?"

"Yep."

"Okay. I'm Murron."

"I know that."

"Okay." I smile, and she looks at me.

"Is something funny?"

"Of course," I say, capping the deep chuckle inside by biting my lower lip. "It's not just funny. It's hilarious."

She says nothing but picks up her pace considerably, as if my suggestion of the humorous nature of our exchange is some offensive notion to flee from, rounding a corner without, it seems, an awareness of the possibility of collision with a patient, a nurse, a guest.

"I didn't know," I say, "that they had a snack bar here."

"Well, it's more like a coffee room. Jeez! You are an exacting person, aren't you?"

I shake my head and wonder what I'm getting into, intent, however, on staying even with this woman, who'd very much like me to follow her lead.

"Rich!" she shouts. "Richmond!"

He's the only one in the "cafeteria," which is basically a storage room for therapeutic equipment like massage balls and heating pads, along with a Quik Cook coffeemaker, an Alhambra water outlet without water, and a small foldout table. There are no chairs besides the one Richmond is sitting on, and he's smiling so widely at me that I step right into his hug, which feels not only warm and familial but even, if possible, apologetic. It does feels good, at first, but after a few seconds and his repetition, with simple presumptive irritating melancholy, of my name three times, I begin to think that the hug's now definitely over the top, the forced intimacy and drawn-out length of it, and maybe even inappropriate. I don't want to pull away, though, and so I wait for his release.

He says, "Are you all right, Murron?"

"Oh, I'm always all right."

He evaluates me in a way similar to how Mary Anna had earlier, except he doesn't squint as she did, or exhibit any nervousness. He just looks at me directly, he doesn't even blink, his eyes on my waist.

"Taking good care of yourself?"

Code language for the Bulimia Watch. I don't know how he knows, and the biggest problem is that I'm not even sure if I'm right. Either their suspicion or your paranoia. I swallow at the instinct to be punitive and repeat, "I'm always all right."

"Rich, hon," Mary Anna says, the intonation of her voice so dramatically altered in those two words that I have to double take to make sure she's serious. She is. She slithers her arm around her brother's neck, one hardly subtle Marilyn Monroe stroke of her hand across his upper chest. I'd heard from my mother that she was a lesbian, and she does have the butch look with the butch cut, the butch attitude of get out of my way. And yet she seems to have entered that strange playground of sibling flirtation where the underlying impulses are heterosexual.

He's now smiling at his sister, and has temporarily forgotten about me. It's almost like she's placating him by playing the helpless girl, unassertive female in figurative distress. This is a reductive mind-set I haven't felt for so long that it seems not only foreign but almost immoral. Still, I don't know anything at all about the dynamics between these people and so, basically, I just watch and wait and wonder.

"And how is your son?"

"He's fine." I don't know how they know, so I ask, "Who told you?"

"We'd like to meet him sometime."

"Oh, I'm—"

"It'll be fine, Murron."

"—not sure if—well, look. I've just met you *myself*. Maybe you've seen me as a baby, but that doesn't count. I have no memory of you guys and, well, let me think about it, okay?"

I don't miss Mary Anna rolling her eyes at this last request.

"Absolutely," says Richmond. "Just think about it. It's always nice to have a little help."

"That's true," I say, "sometimes. Depends on the kind of help."

"Well, we—"

"Anyway, I have very reliable help with Prince." Not sure if I should share everything just yet. "My roommate just loves him."

"Well, as long as the roommate—"

"She does," I say, nodding firmly at them both. "She is. Would never hurt Prince."

"Prince?"

Richmond looks at his sister, as if the tone of the question offends him more than me. "You think we can have a minute alone, *fratella mia*?"

"I love when you use the Italian, Rich," she purrs. "Of course you can. I'll take a walk around the place. You listen to him now, Murron. He's got a lot of wisdom he can pass on to you."

I listen to everyone. In fact, I listen, through reading, for a living.

Going out, she slams into a doctor coming in. "Watch where you're going!"

"Excuse me," he says. "I am sorry."

Richmond stands and the doctor says, "We spoke on the phone, Mr. Felice. I am Dr. Patel."

"Yes, how are you, Doctor? This is my sister, Mary Anna."

"Hello. I am sorry again."

"My brother wants to ask you something."

"That is fine. I wanted to talk—"

"So how much longer does she have?"

"—about—Excuse me?"

"Does she have a few months? A year? How long will she live?"

"Well, as I said before, Mr. Felice, the blood transfusion was successful."

"Yes, but what does that *mean*. In practical terms now. Not in doctorly terms."

"Well, Mr. Felice, it means her body took on the blood without complicat—"

"No. What I want—"

"Excuse me?"

"—are figures. Put a date to her—"

"I cannot do that."

"—health level."

"No one can."

"Well, can she die tomorrow?"

"Of course she can."

"All right. Well, thank you, Doctor."

"Anybody can."

"Was good of you to come out and meet with us so promptly."

Dr. Patel looks at me, but I'm not sure what just occurred. "I see," he mumbles, and turns on his heel.

"We don't want anyone suffering any longer than they have to," Richmond says, nodding at me. Mary Anna shakes her head in assent, kisses her brother on the cheek. "These things can go on forever. They tried to do the same thing to my son. Kept pumping him with artificial life. Finally we said, 'You're not going to do this anymore.'"

I don't think that's what the poor doctor just said.

"Sucked the life right out of him."

"I miss Richie," says Mary Anna.

"You know, Murron, he said some very nice things about you."

"Well, I really enjoyed the small bit of time I got to spend with him in Europe."

"Yes," he says. "Some very nice things."

"I got to watch him play once in Paris."

"Yes," Richmond says, patting my hand. "He sure loved his art."

I still recall with much affection catching the train from Palermo to watch Richie do a cello solo of Bach's majestic Suites on the shore of the Seine, dusk descending on the City of Lights, how randomly we dropped down in mid-conversation about our wretched childhoods on a bench where squirrels and pigeons had obviously been feeding on human food for decades, how his timing of a personal concerto made no sense to me whatsoever. The darkened bank across the river was dotting with lights. He refused to set up a money hat for the small but apparently loyal crowd because it was not just the art that mattered, he said, though that was enough, he added, but also the red-and-white triangles drifting with the wind behind him, three of some fifty-odd sailboats that leashed their lines to the dock just before the sun set. This most genuine of human gestures was more payment than he, as a former talentless acolyte of Madame Dalia Sirkin, could have ever imagined in American bucks, or French francs, for that matter. I didn't know Richie well, but I remember thinking, Here is an artist.

I hate to do this, but I don't want to get lost in yesterday. There is another, more pressing matter today. "And what about your mother? Do you think that you should—"

"Hey, Mary Anna."

"Yes, Rich?"

"Why don't you give Murron and me some alone time together?"

"Sure, sure, Rich," she says, hugging him again, and then leaving.

"So Murron," he says. "How's work going?"

"What do you mean?"

"Tough times for you at the paper."

I don't know where he got his information, but it irritates me that he's broached the topic. And then to not say anything about the strange exchange with Dr. Patel. "How do you know about that?"

"Hey now. I read."

Of course. The intellectual of the family. Which could mean a whole range of things. "Okay."

"Not all us Felices are like your uncle Anthony and uncle John."

Lazarus's other brothers, like Richmond, are no uncles to me, but I don't say this aloud because I want to keep open, for Prince's sake, and maybe even my own, whatever possible relations I can. I don't believe in family by blood. I believe in family by *being* there.

"You were asking about work."

"Yep. So?"

"Well, you know," I say. "It goes."

"Goes?"

"Gotta try to focus on the good side of things these days."

"Why bother? That seems like it could be some form of denial."

"Well," I say, "maybe it is."

I did find one thing to make me happy this past week. Within the next few days, I'll write my first positive review of the year, the headline something simple like, "The Principle of Deprivation Made Me Love Nam Le's *The Boat* Even More, More, More."

"So what's the bad stuff?"

"Where do I start? The era. America. Its culture. Tech."

"Tech?"

"Of course."

"How so? I would think your work gets done more efficiently now than it ever has."

"That doesn't matter," I say. "Because the survivability of something, of anything, is an interactive concept. I'm not the only one who's benefited from a laptop."

"You mean online stuff then? Right?"

"Of course. Blogs. Blog reviews."

"I've never read one."

"You will," I say.

"It sounds like you've got some problems, but I wouldn't worry too much about it. Newspapers are the dodo bird of information. A gone way of Americana."

Casually, as if it doesn't affect me or anyone else, he's just stating facts. I don't nod at his annoyingly defensible prognostication, which would be like kissing the hangman before the execution. Instead, I lift one eyebrow, the right, and hold it in suspension, one of a number of signature gestures that used to turn Lokapi off so much that he left.

"Well. The reason I mention this is not to insult you. No, not at all. I respect your passion for the newspaper." Dying but honorable. "I used to feel the way you do about books. Just couldn't do without them. Well, now I live without them more or less, and I seem to be okay." Honorable but useless. "Just thought that it would be a shame if someone with your smarts finds herself out of work someday. You went to Stanford, didn't you?"

I nod, half-smile, lips sealed tight.

"Listen. You have everything it takes to be a part of the business." The business he means, I'm assuming, is stocks. His business. "I could get you into a good, you know, apprenticeship at UBS. I'm sure, if you buckled down in the breach, you'd start climbing the ranks in no time."

So the danger of silence is that sometimes you're misunderstood. Even by a managerial guru, according to my mother's removed rumor-based account, of national repute. I've been on the other end of conversations like this before, the most notable a recent lecture from my brother, after he pointed out that without a Stanford education, he makes more money than I by doing real estate part-time.

All I could say to Gabe was that he's right. It is pretty amazing that he makes $9,000 on a single sale without any advanced education, be it at Stanford or the local junior college, for that matter. I apologized later for saying this kind of pretentious crap, but it sank in, I think, because after the argument Gabe started referring to himself as "the dropout hustler brother," a typically cynical ploy of heaping another load of self-deprecation on himself.

I paid my own way through the Farm, every penny of my childhood savings to tuition, waitressing on weekends year-round and delivering Domino's pizzas between semesters. Unlike most of my classmates, I never traveled to a spring break destination the second the last final was turned in. Four different scholarships have left me with payments on two loans which'll finally die out, at a rate of $118 a month, during my late sixties. Anyone can disagree with my somewhat medieval view of money, but I think I've arrived at the outlook for a reason.

I've lived in East Palo Alto for the past few years because this is what I can afford at the moment. I know how to live frugally, I grew up in a trailer in East Sonoma. Lokapi's "homies" were always talking about "the hood" where they came from, and how only G's and homies survive Fruitvale, California, but I know they never ate peanut butter and jelly sandwiches for a month straight, as I did. As I can. I don't allow Prince to call our neighborhood "the hood." I disabused him of that nonsense when he started sagging his pants in second grade.

"You have good clothes. A nice room. A good family. You eat three meals a day. Yes? Yes? Then pull your damned drawers up."

The single mothers in our apartment complex who brag that they live in poverty are the same women who'd brag about their wealth if they could. If the "East" on their home address were removed from "Palo Alto." But I haven't seen any empirical evidence that money, at its core, shepherds in happiness. I guess money is opportunity, as Camus said in one of his earlier novels, and it can open doors and you don't have to ask the questions everyone else asks like, "Should I maybe not have that, maybe not try that?" And yet money can bring with it all kinds of ancillary issues that even the best opportunity cannot overcome. Like, for one, always thinking you've got an absolute right to have this, you've got an absolute right to try that.

"Thanks for the offer, Richmond, but I'm fine."

"For now, you're fine. You might want to think this over."

"I'm okay. Thank you."

"Think of it as a business proposition."

"I can take care of myself. Been doing that since the age of fifteen."

"I know, I know."

"No. Listen. If I were to hold you to what you think you know, it would mean you have something to say about how I grew up, and that's just not the case."

He's surprised at this, he's quiet, waiting. His self-assuredness is so strong that he doesn't believe the insinuations of what I've just said. He just doesn't see that, as it is, he has no say about my life.

"It's no problem," he says, firmly nodding. "No problem if you change your mind about things."

I've always had trouble with the arbitrary generosity of relations. What's more, I *became* me because of this trouble.

"We're doing great, Richmond. Okaaay?"

"Okay," he says. "Just give me a call if you change your mind."

I start to chuckle. He looks perplexed. I can't help it this time. I'd bite right through my lip if I tried to stop it. The chuckle grows into unabashed laughter.

I hold his stare as I laugh, and he's careful not to join in, and then, as if the moment can't hold on to itself without a pair of hands stroking his wounded ego, we're saved by his sister. Mary Anna smiles at us both, she wants in on the joke. But I'm still laughing and now she seems nervous, curling her lip and baring the upper row of her unaligned teeth, like she suspects she's the subject of ridicule.

"Well! What are you two laughing at, huh? Let's take a walk to that Starbucks on the corner. This coffee is horrible."

We make our way to the busy street, the dizzying pollen-laced sunlight brighter than a desert between the shadows of the trees, the heat twirling off the pavement like a thousand wisps of cigarette smoke polluting the air. I remain silent during the walk, as does Mary Anna, the both of us listening, I think, very attentively to Richmond's impressive

case for the recent progress on the African continent in combating
AIDS, how the key, as he sees it, is no different than the challenges
facing your standard American corporation, how it's neat that all things,
as he understands it, can be plugged into the deceivingly flexible business model, the only difference being that we deal with dollars, they
deal with lives. I want to say to him that every dollar has always affected
every life on the entire planet because there's no such thing as a distinction between money and lives. And since the application of Western
capitalism created the problem on that continent in the first place, it's
just and perhaps a simple matter of circuitous moral obligation that
Western capitalism *fix* it. But I submit instead to the curious goodness
in his voice, the most essential, and underrated, component of any said
or written word to be valued, and it's nice that someone in the obtuse
business world actually cares enough to keep track, however myopically,
of these crazy-because-they're-preventable-and-often-curable afflictions
of the battered third world, and then, also, firstly, what can I really say
to someone who lost a son to the disease?

This lesson is like an antidote to any negative feelings I may have
toward these people. I don't think I like Richmond any more than I
like Mary Anna, at least not so far, but where he's a bit mysterious,
she's easily pitied. I feel sorry for anyone with the kind of naked
emotional belligerence she's shown me. Still, I don't know her, I don't
know him, and it hasn't even been half an hour.

"I have to use the bathroom."

They say nothing and we separate. I nod at the baristas congregated
in the hallway to the facilities and they also pay me no attention,
which is just fine. I can hear them disperse as I turn on the light and
the fan, lock the door, and take two steps to the toilet, where I don't
squat down. Won't. I'm all rattled today, and I don't know if it's seeing death, Mary, or her children firsthand, each, in their own right, a
kind of baptismal affair, but I won't succumb to these dumb visceral
impulses, I simply won't.

Just as the thought forms on my tongue, "I won't," it happens, painfully, since I haven't eaten anything in a while, and am basically dry heaving in violent spasms, my hands clutched to my quivering knees like the umpire behind the plate at Prince's Little League games. It's a short half-minute bout where nothing but saliva comes up, and I'm thankful that there wasn't any blood this time, that it wasn't too long, and that it hasn't come back. I wipe my mouth with the top of my hand, walk to the door, and put my ear to the crack. No one there. I rinse out with my mouthwash. It seems to fizz like Pop Rocks candy after these things, which always makes me think that it's doing its job, cleaning out the battery acid that's meant to be in your stomach disintegrating food. Now I have to risk returning to the Felices, if only because my staying here could prompt another round of spewing bile.

It looks like they're already in a discussion about something very serious. Mary Anna's moving her head up and down dutifully, and he's talking with the composure and elegance of an authority. I come up behind them, unsure if I should cut in.

Neither see me.

"And look, Rich, we can't let Tony and Laz know about this, don't you think?" Her whisper is rushed, fast, like a harsh wind. "They'll take the whole thing the wrong way."

He's still nodding. I'm unsure if I should sit. My own indecision has always irritated me, even though it's a deeply rooted aspect of my personality, and so I decide to take the table behind them and just wait. "Listen. Don't make a lot of noise about this," he says. "Just handle the details and—"

"The last thing we need is Tony getting stupid over Mom's situation."

"That's going to happen anyway, all right? That's *Tony.*"

"He's an idiot. You know how long it's been since he's talked with his son?"

"At least a few years," says Richmond.

"Six."

"Six?"

"Yes. Little Tony changed his name back to the Korean."

"He did?"

"Duck So Kim, or something like that."

"Well, okay. Anyway, back to Mom. Just do as much as you can and don't wait a—"

"Should I let you guys finish?"

"Oh, hey," Richmond says, already leaning back amicably, the automatic way he includes me in their personal space piquing the worst cynical version of my inner critic. He nods at Mary Anna with meaning, secret sibling stuff that likely goes back to the ancient annals of their shared childhood, and if it means what it means between Gabe and me, they'll be resurrecting the topic later in my absence.

"Pull your chair up."

She's looking at me very intensely, terrified, I'm guessing, that I've heard something not intended for my ears. I don't care if they've been talking about Lazarus. Yes, he's their pure blood brother, birthed in the same town and raised in the same household, but to me, he's nothing more than my mother's sperm bank twice withdrawn.

"How long were you back there?" she says.

"Come on, Murron. Sit right here by me, 'kay?"

"You shouldn't sneak up on people like that."

What can I do but begin to question the sincerity of this woman? He's smiling at me, as if he's trying to cover for the brusque interrogations of his sister.

"I don't sneak up on people," I say. "Me get napkin. Me sit down at table."

This makes Richmond smile and he says, patting my hand, "How's it going, huh? You have your father's sense of humor."

"You look," says Mary Anna, reaching out for my face, "like maybe you had some work done, Murron."

I push her hand away, my brows and cheeks scrunched up the way they do when I smell bad cheese.

"Oh, it's all right!" she shouts. "I have lots of friends in Blackhawk who've done it! I've done it!"

"Costs a lot of money," he says.

"Not if you don't pay for it," I say.

"Well, that's certainly true! Date your plastic surgeon!" She loves the scam, it seems, and he's smiling at the notion of free money. My mother says they all love it, in their own loud and strained Felice way, and that it's the Achilles' heel of an otherwise epic family. And the only one who doesn't care about it can't be found. Not since he loaned his last seed, me, to my mother. "Ha-ha-ha! Good, Murron! Good!"

"Listen." I can't believe how up-front she is, how little she thinks of the range of possibility before speaking. "Jesus. Slow down."

"We're listening," he says. "Just take it easy, Murron. Just having some fun with you, that's all. No need to be defensive now."

"That's right!" She leans over the table, her aggression equidistant between Richmond and me. "Hey! I've done it, too. Look." She turns her head back and forth like a toy-store mannequin. I'm sorry to think this, especially with what I'm about to tell her about my nose job, but I want to slap her. "Crow's-feet. Had 'em lasered away. Can't see 'em anymore. A few thousand greenbacks and—voilà!—they're gone."

I'm not sure if Richmond sees what I see—voilà! they're back! or still there!—but I somewhat don't care. The conversation has gotten to the point where my own closed mouth no longer protects me. So much for my theories on the punitive power of silence.

"Listen. My ex-husband paid for the operation."

"Well, you shouldn't do it for him, Murron, don't ever let a man's sexual fantasies dictate what you—"

"Would you be *quiet*, please?"

She's mad yet again but she's skidded to a stop. Not because of my words. Richmond is holding his hand up, like some sovereign from a forgotten age, giving me his approval to explain. For just that reason, I pay him no eye contact at all.

I look at her and say, "He broke my nose." She squints her eyes—she's so mammalian with her responses—but I don't think it's because she wants more of the story.

"You should've called the cops!" she shouts. "You should've never let him see the light of—"

"Would you shut up?"

This time it's Richmond. He's scowling at her.

If I walk out on them now forever, can I really be blamed?

"Why don't *both* of you shut up?" I say.

Her mouth drops, he's lifted an eyebrow. I bet that no one from this clan has told him to shut up, not in this circle of a minuscule pond, and I have to beat them to speaking on this miracle, which basically means *let's stay on topic.* "You guys crack me up. You butt into my business, have no broader sense of what that means, and then when I try to answer your questions, you cut me off."

"Hey! We're just trying to get to know you, we're trying—"

"You're the patient ones in your family, right?"

Richmond puts his hand on my own. "It's your family, too."

I reach over and lift his hand off. "That's where you're wrong. It's not your place to say whether I'm family or not. You've had a long time to figure that out, you know? Just like I did."

"You shouldn't protect him!" she shouts. "He's manipulating you!" I'm not sure if she means protect Lokapi from the police or protect Prince from Lokapi. "You've gotta prosecute him with the full power of the law!"

"Okay. Were you under the impression I'm a DA? I'm a critic, Mary Anna. I work for the *Chronicle,* not the city of Palo Alto."

I'm worried about sharing the truth about Lokapi with these people. That he was not only prosecuted for felony assault but convicted of it, too, that he did a year in the Santa Clara County Jail, which meant nine months on "good time." That there was another year of anger-management classes ordered by the state, and paid for by me, or he'd be back behind bars. That I attended a group session once, for exactly ten minutes, and then got up and left when the therapist had the nerve to label me a victim.

"The victim doesn't hit back," I'd said. "And the victim shuts up."

That what I'd said to Lokapi that day, before and after he'd hit me, the blood running into my mouth like tears, probably should have been prosecutable. Low and illegal, evil verbal blows that he'd never heard before or since, and I know this.

That I didn't leave him, that he left me.

If these people got to meet my son, I'd have to monitor their tactlessness. How fast she'd shove Prince along to easy paternal indictment with those spittle bullets she sprays into the air like a terrorist with his AK-47. She talks as if the bullets couldn't come down on someone's—maybe even her own—head. How smooth his soft invitations would sound in Prince's ear, how he'd seduce my son into a trip to, say, the summer cabin on the north shore of Lake Tahoe, provide Prince with the green-and-blue grandeur that only money can buy in California. Give him a glimpse of the life that neither I nor Lokapi can give him.

"Don't worry," he says, nodding. "We get it. That's fine. She doesn't want to talk about it, okay?"

"Oh, I'll talk," I say, "to the right people."

4

Anthony Constantine Felice II
Dream of the Camp America Cabin
May 3, 1996

HE COULDN'T BRING HIMSELF to do it.

Half a dozen times he'd stood under the oaken doorframe, unable to take two or three steps into his son's room. As if paralysis claimed his muscles the closer he got to the source of whatever it was he wanted to find. For some time now, he'd watched his son ask to be dismissed after dinner, slide with utter sloth out of his seat, laze his way across the living room of the Camp America Cabin, stomach sucked in, head down, eyes down, shoulders slumped, and disappear down the hallway. Once Anthony followed Little Ton, tiptoeing behind him, feeling like a fool, peeking around the corner of the hall with the real fear of being caught. His son cracked the door just barely, one long step in, and was gone.

In Big Victor everyone had a space of their own, a kind of domestic right to privacy, celebration of the First Amendment for which no intervening ACLU was needed. He suggested something of the kind to his wife when asked about his investigative intentions with their son.

"First Amendment?" He couldn't look at her when she expressed astonishment. "What the hell are you talking about?"

"This is the Camp America Cabin and I—"

"Oh, God."

"—think—"

"Will you shut up with that, Anthony? This is our *house*. Stop making it more than what it is. Okay? This isn't Big Victor. That's half of your problem right there."

"Well. I just mean that he has a right to be himself, that's all."

"You don't mean that. I'll prove it."

She started toward their son's room. He reached out and pulled her back. They were chest to chest for a second, and then she pushed off and stood there. He was terrified of the parental realm they were nearing. "Wait. Please wait."

"You don't know what you're talking about," she said. "This is 1996. Kids are screwing in junior high school, Anthony! Like goddamned rabbits! Camp America Cabin? Big Victor?"

"Please. I don't think it's right. Maybe he should have his privacy, huh?"

"Was it right what happened to Mary Anna? Was that right? There's your Big Victor. That's what happens when parents turn a blind eye, Anthony Constantine. That's reality."

He felt like slapping her, not because she was wrong in what she'd said but because she had no right to say it. He didn't raise his hand. She'd probably laugh in his face. She'd slapped him before, several times, but that didn't matter.

The next day he finally decided to invade. While his son was at school, he trooped down the hall, past the aluminum-framed copies of Iwo Jima and the Grand Canyon on the wall, absolutely not thinking. He'd once heard that cowardice was thought and courage was action. He was already somewhat afraid of his son's sense of "otherness," and since the little he understood was strange enough, a larger dosage of the "otherness" would be too much to bear, and he'd stop on what must be done. By the time he'd started down this track of reason, he was already at the room, opening the door with his eyes open, knowing that the melodrama of closing his eyes provided another kind of darkness, something like cowardice, which was thought, he knew, and not action.

The black electrical tape crisscrossed over the door set the tone for the room. There were posters and concert T-shirts of Marilyn Manson hanging crookedly across the walls, Disney characters with nylon nooses around their necks, steak knives through their ears, pirate and vampire paraphernalia randomly claiming every corner of the room. The terrarium with that silly snake sat at the foot of the bed. There was mold everywhere. Thumbtacks held the blinds in place across the window. The only light the room had seen in months was artificial.

He couldn't make sense of this kind of darkness. Couldn't relate to the idea of doom inherent to its proposition, its worldview. He very simply did not know what to do with his son. Unable to invade any farther, he went to his wife and told her the details of what he'd seen. She listened, nodding at intervals, and then said, "I know all of this," and then nothing.

"You already invaded?"

"Investigated, Anthony. Probed."

He had an idea. It felt desperate, but then that's exactly what the situation was. "I don't want to do this," he said, "but I'll do it for the sake of our son. Our family."

"Don't call him, Anthony."

"But maybe he can help."

"Are you *crazy*? He'll just downtalk you again. Jesus. When are you going to realize what he does? An opportunity to grandstand. That's what it is to Richmond, nothing else. He loves that you, his oldest brother, come to him for wisdom."

"Okay, okay, shut up."

She waited a bit and then said, "Just try letting him speak his mind some."

"Who, Little Ton?"

"Who *else* are we talking about, Anthony? Do you think I care about what your brother thinks?"

"What does that mush-head know about anything? He's sixteen years old!"

"He's your son. Start there."

"What does my mush-head son know about anything?"

"Can't we have just one quiet meal?"

"You're giving me the red light at lunch?"

"Red light? What the hell are you talking about, Anthony? Red light? No, I'm giving you a caveat: he's got a lot of thoughts stuffed up in there, Anthony. And he gets his stubbornness from someone."

"Oh, I see! So now that's my fault, too!"

"You're impossible. I can't st—"

"Hey! Whose side are you on here?"

"Whose side? Whose *side*? What a stupid—"

"Hey! I need some support here."

"I can't stand when you talk like this. It's so stupid."

"Well, thank you very much. Gotta set my son straight—"

"Our son."

"—myself. A matter of domestic security."

"Yeah, right. Alert, alert."

"A lotta help you are."

"Why do you come to me, Anthony, if you don't like the answer I give?"

She waited. He saw this and tried to cooperate by not saying anything. He worried that the only time things went forward in his household was when he didn't say a word.

"Okay."

"Which takes us back to my original suggestion. Start with Tony being your son."

"Okay, okay."

"Start with love."

"Okay! Just shut up, please!"

"You're the one talking, Anthony. In fact, that's the whole problem. Always starts there."

"I get your point, I get your point."

"Let the boy talk for once. He's smarter than you think."

"I know he's smart," he said. "I know."

"He won the regionals in Speech and Debate for a reason."

"I know!"

So he tried to ease off on the banter during evening meals, staying quiet when he wanted to talk politics. Just dying to cut up right there on their place mats the latest act of besmirchment by the Arkansan philanderer occupying the White House. Anthony refused to name him or call him his president. Still, he stayed the prescribed course, keeping the subjects of their dinner conversations light, the high school football team, the San Francisco 49ers, and the weather. He didn't think that his son's goth style of dress promulgated a certain political reality in which one didn't care about high school football, one certainly didn't support corporate athletic outfits like the San Francisco 49ers, and, finally, one didn't think that the weather was a worthy topic unless it was illuminating the latest fact about global warming.

But sure enough, his son started to open up. Anthony was so quiet his knees shook under the table. Keeping the words to himself gave him pangs of indigestion. But his own imposed discipline, he knew, would pay off. It had to.

What he discovered after a few days was that he was not only living with but providing quarters to the political enemy. Little Ton talked openly about his admiration for President Clinton (Anthony winced), how he wished he were eighteen so that he could vote him in to a second term (wince again). How he'd get it hands down, anyway, that Dole was a good, likable, bipartisan man (A war hero, Anthony thought, versus a draft dodger) but not a contender by any means, so you might as well be ready. Because the world's view of us improved big-time by the easily overlooked detail that President Clinton (wince) knew how to properly shake someone's hand. (Especially when that someone has tits.) How a man like Richard Nixon probably shouldn't have been allowed near the White House in the first place as either president or visitor, how trickle-down economics meant exactly that: drip, drop, little trickle of piss on the bone-dry tongues of the masses. (Hey! You starve by choice!) How the environment had been eaten up by the villains of corporate America. (Oh, you mean the people who made this country?) That the whole thing was a scam (Like the polar bears!), and it fed like greed itself upon our greed for status and immediacy (Hey! Greed is good, you mush-head!), our belief that a superficial order had to be imposed on the world. It didn't have to be told to us. We bought it. The deal was sold before we really thought about the price.

"Sold? Sold?" Anthony couldn't hold back any longer. He was salivating in this self-imposed muzzle of silence. He didn't think about the implications that, even if it was erroneous or one-sided, his sixteen-year-old son had presented a nicely articulated case. This wasn't about smarts, no, this was about what was right. He'd had enough of this nonsense. "What do you mean by sold? You mean like at market price?"

"Well, I suppose that fits into the slot of my argument. So in a way, yes."

"In a way. In a *way*? Well, why didn't you *say* that? *Hey!* This is a free country! That's what I keep *telling* you! Even mush-heads can say what they want without being hung to die in the town square!"

"Hung to die?"

"That's *right*! That's what *happens*! Open your *eyes*! It's not all live and love and let's be happy out there! People get shot for jaywalking in China! The second kid gets apprehended by the state! It's a—"

"I don't think that's true. I remember reading that families are fined for having an extra kid. But they got a billion people. It's as much a matter of resources as anything else."

"*Hey! Billion! Trillion!* Who the hell are they to take away my *right* to have a kid?"

"Anthony."

"What? How long do we have to listen to this crap without responding?"

"You're not in China," the boy said.

"That's *right*! That's the *point*! Put the bullet through my head before you send me there! I'll load the chamber for you and say thank you!"

"He's trying to express himself."

"Express express express away for all I care!"

"Just calm down, Anthony."

He looked at his son. There was a string bean on his plate that had been halved at least twelve times. Thirteen. Anthony shook his head. Well, didn't he have the right to speak in his own house? Did the First Amendment die on his doorstep, or did it wither like a flower in the blackness and nothingness of his son's goth philosophy?

There was a time when he'd had no doubt about his power to reign in any stray opinion of his son's, especially any political opinion. Now that day was obviously gone. Yet he still had hope. His son was young, he would come around. If he wasn't a good enough teacher to learn his son, then the blessing of living in the greatest country in the history of mankind would rightly open his eyes. Soon. Eventually.

"I believe you're gonna love America someday, son," he said, standing with both hands under his untouched plate. "I'm gonna go outside. I can't sup around mush-head leftists."

He went into their backyard. The cold Shasta air bit down on the edge of his nose and he sat Indian-style under a tree. His life was like this now. Always revisiting the past, knocking on an old friend's door.

He remembered that wonderful day in the spring of 1982—he could see it better than his own wedding. Before they'd entered the dealership, his wife had reminded Anthony three times to keep the real reason for buying the van out of the conversation because "salesmen are looking for any reason to rip you off. They smell desire like coyotes smell blood." He'd agreed, but he couldn't help himself. Inspecting the considerable legroom in the backseat, he let it slip: "Yes, yes, we're gonna need a lot of space, Derick. That's for sure. Because, well, you know, we've got a son coming. A little blessing on the way."

His wife shook her head, the salesman looked at her flat stomach, and Anthony Constantine Felice II beamed as if he were Lindbergh post-flight across the Atlantic.

The vehicle was not fast by any means, it wasn't particularly attractive at first glance, but it was reliable, spacious, and, most pressingly, American-made. By the end of morning, they'd bought the van, good old American blue, American steel, American fiberglass, American rubber. Before the product was out of the showcase window, he'd stuck the MANUFACTURED 100% AMERICAN sticker across the monstrous rear windshield, all to ensure that any traitorous purchaser of a Japanese product would be alerted to their folly while pulling up at a stoplight. When he'd driven off the lot, he'd honked a couple times at the bewildered staff of Billings Ford, his own small gesture of gratitude for selling American. He was proud of these patriots, they were good people, they were friends.

"A dire error letting the Japs get their hands in the honey pot," he said now, shaking his head with disgust, repositioning his weight under the tree.

Victory meant a vanquished enemy, a crushed economy and a crippled spirit. It didn't mean rejuvenated into a world power with the victor's tax dollars to the point of competitor number one. ("Nuts! They won the war in the end! They won!")

First thing home he'd unscrewed the Billings Ford frame around the license plate and attached a red, white, and blue striped frame that read, GOD BLESS AMERICA. His wife was cooking dinner, and though he couldn't hear the lyrics from the garage, he knew "Simple Gifts" was being hummed in tune, a song he'd loved dearly, especially emitted out the voice box of his loyal wife. He'd serenaded her with this same song on their honeymoon night in Berlin, Germany, stuffed with bratwurst and Spaten Oktoberfest.

"We busted up a lot of those Nazi bars," he said to himself, smiling, standing, breathing in deeply so that his chest expanded.

As he paced slowly around the tree, counting his steps like a pirate on a treasure hunt, he let himself be lured back into the dream. They were on their way to destiny, side by side in the brand-new three-door, one sliding, American blue '82 e250 Ford van, not a mile over the speed limit, almost cruising to the rendezvous point at San José International Airport to pick up their son, whom they'd already named, against the staunch advice of the agency, Anthony Constantine Felice III.

"Names are very important to a child's self-esteem," they'd been told.

"Well, that's quite right," he'd said. "Exactly the point of naming him Little Ton."

"Mr. Felice, you might reconsider this. Removing any trace of his birth country is not advised. This is a big change."

"He's two."

"Maybe look into incorporating the last name into a middle name, something like that."

"Kim?" he'd asked. "Kim?"

"It won't be anything anyone sees or reads, Mr. Felice. Only the boy will know."

"Ma'am. The boy knowing is enough, wouldn't you say? Ever heard of a Johnny Cash song called 'A Boy Named Sue'?"

"Great song."

"Great song my backside. The kid hunts down the father for giving him a girl's name. Shoots him in the mud outside a saloon."

"No one's going to get shot here, Mr. Felice. And it was stabbed, by the way."

"What?"

"The father cut the kid's ear off."

"Hey! Stabbed, shot, what the hell are we talking about here?"

"We're just trying to look out for the best interests of the boy."

"Ditto."

Maybe their son's native country was nice, but that was not the point. This was about erasing an old story in order to embrace a new and better one. The whole point was not going back in time. They'd both agreed that neither of them could remember anything before five, and just to be safe they'd insisted on a child under three years of age. No memory, no blockade. Anthony III would be given a chance to be a part of the most pursued story in the world.

When they got to the airport, his wife went to the bathroom "to pretty up," and he sat down in the waiting area of Gate 12, his knees shaking nervously as if he were four and not two years shy of forty. As if the roles were reversed, the child awaiting the arrival of the father.

He rested the airport coffee on a thigh. Scanned the crowd and nearly spilled the contents.

A young couple making out in the corner of the waiting area caught his attention. Their matching short, greased hair, twin porcelain brooches pinning the top collar button, identical ankle-length coats with THE SMITHS on the chest pocket made Anthony wonder how you distinguished between the boy and the girl. You made the guess, he guessed, by seeing which of the two was taller, but he couldn't manage even this distinction when they were sitting.

Americans were the best in the world, yes, but this crowd hardly fit the mold. Not a single Teddy Roos Rough Rider among them, no trail-burning Lewis and Clark, the future looked bleak. He closed his eyes and rubbed them, almost is if doing so would erase what he'd just seen. When he finally opened them again, he saw his mother and father. He stood and walked over.

"Mom. Dad. My God. What are you doing here? I mean, I know what you're doing here but—"

"Oh, honey," his mother said.

"You didn't have to drive up here."

"We didn't drive." She was already in his arms. "This is so *won*derful."

"So you flew then. You flew?" He looked at his father, his chin on his mother's shoulder.

"Son. Very happy for you and Darlene."

"Thanks, Dad. But you flew? Uh, how did you pay for the tick—"

"Rich set it up for us."

"It's *won*derful, honey."

"Where is Rich?"

"Honduras."

"Honduras?"

"He set it up through his secretary."

His mother shouted, *"Wonderful!"*

He didn't know what to feel. Appreciation or irritation. He and Darlene had wanted to do this on their own, have the event exclusively to themselves. This delivery of their son felt like something private between them, like pillow talk.

Childlessness was the defining tragedy of their marriage. It had kept them sad, it had kept them together, it had made them keep the hope up when they otherwise would have walked right through the day, blind to their own need. How did Rich know what was needed today? They hadn't talked in months. They were on bad terms. Rich was a political sellout for his socially moderate positions, Rich thought he was a zealot for being right. Either way, he would have afforded his brother the courtesy of a heads-up.

This kind of shot-calling attitude, Anthony thought, is what brought the rift in the first place.

Suddenly he turned. The teenagers were singing a duet of some sort. Its crass lyrics about sex and drugs were awful, the song awfully rendered, almost forcibly without rhythm.

Like a vaudeville, Anthony thought, performed by retarded children.

Only these two weren't looking for laughs, they wanted to be taken seriously. These sensitive souls wanted everyone around them, especially Anthony, to know how badly they'd been damaged. And when that fact of damage was acknowledged, and only then, there was the need to address the very important matter of who had *done* the damage. Negotiations about the damage would proceed at their discretion, their pace.

Anthony snorted, stepped closer to his parents, almost is if to shield them from the hideous sight and sound of these two ingrates, society's New Deal scourge, and said, "Is it all right if we wait by the gate?"

"Of course, son."

"This is your day."

Darlene emerged from the bathroom and shouted, "Mom! Dad!" He heard them talk through the hugging, but he didn't listen to their conversation. Because this was it. His son was coming through the gate. He saw the boy before everyone else. He skipped up the ramp and someone stopped him.

"You cannot pass this point."

"Anthony!" He stood at the divide between the native and the new American, leaning dangerously over the rope. "Anthony!"

His wife, mother, and father joined him in the chant. "Anthony! Anthony!"

Now he heard the dream out loud. "Anthony!"

His wife's upper body filled their kitchen window, face pressed to the screen. The frost from Mount Shasta had gathered across his forearms and hands and she called him, sharply, again. "Anthony! Come inside now. Your son is gone."

He stood slowly and walked over to the side door of their house, cleaning his feet on the THIS IS A NO SPIN ZONE doormat, and whispered, "Where'd he go?"

"Library to study."

"Good," he said. "Good."

"He's a smart kid, Anthony. He just doesn't know how to say what he feels."

"I don't think that's his problem."

He didn't want to brood over the fight, and so he said nothing more. Still, he didn't know what to do with himself. He stood there in the kitchen for a few moments, focusing, for some reason, on his feet.

This made him think of shoelaces, Little Ton's, which he'd taught his son to tie every day before school. Tony's first clumsy steps across the deck of their pool. His counting up to ten. The alphabet. The kid did it forward and backward at three years of age.

He went into their room and lay down on the bed. He worried that he wouldn't be able to sleep, but he closed his eyes anyway, hoping for an answer in the nostalgic world where he seemed to thrive. He could still see Little Anthony's flushed cheeks, heavy with baby fat. He could see the chubby shoulders beneath the cloth wrapping. The forehead hard and wide and flat like a wooden board.

He'd said, "Look how big his head is! Look at that thing! It's bigger than a cement block! You know what that means?"

One of the workers lifted her eyebrows, the other shook his head, as in, No, I don't know. You tell me what that means before we hand over this baby.

"Means we got a scholar on our hands! Skulls like that are built for one reason and one reason only! You got a big old brain in there, don'tcha Little Ton?" He looked at his wife in disbelief. "Jesus, that's a melon, ain't it?"

"It is, Anthony. It is."

"How *wonderful!*" his mother cried.

Anthony looked up at the workers. "And what's wrong with his eyes?"

Everyone even his own parents went quiet, waiting for the relief of interpretation, something to reverse his course of losing this deal. His wife had told him on the drive over that his ruining of things was okay when it was just the two of them, that she'd always stay, that her heart was his, but now, if they were lucky, it would be the three of them. Another body to consider, a boy in real need. These thoughts, he knew, he could see, were ripping through her mind with the speed and irreversibility of bullets through a paper target, but she kept herself under remarkable control because she, too, was being evaluated.

By the time they'd figured out what his statement meant, Anthony was already stroking the baby's head, cooing, "Have you been crying on the flight, Little Tony? Huh? Look at those swollen eyes. Don't worry, baby boy. You're home now, you're home, Little Ton. It's all right. Oh, don't cry. You're here with Mommy and Daddy in the good old red, white, and blue."

"He's been eating only rice gruel so you're gonna want to be careful with what you give him."

"Nonsense, nonsense," said Anthony, reaching down and tickling the baby with his finger. "He's got a date with a bowl of applesauce, don't you, Little Tony? Our own American baby! You beautiful, beautiful boy! We're gonna take you home."

Now he sat up and flipped his legs over the edge of their marriage bed, the light rapidly fading in the room, the argument with his son hard on his heart. These days the darkness stirred him awake, rarely luring him to sleep anymore. He'd never liked how fast night overtook day. Not since childhood, late summer, picking oranges in the grove at sunset for a dollar a barrel. He was nine, ten, his imagination making too much of the shadows cutting through the trees, long-armed phantoms sticking their hands into his money pot. By the time the light was gone, so, too, would be his hard-earned money, the empty bucket lighter than a copper penny. Vision of terror in the next minute, life of fear up ahead.

He lay down and took in the redwood beams of their cabin ceiling for what felt like hours. When he looked over at the clock, three minutes had passed. He rested there half-awake, his son's toxic politics going down like acid into his system, a clove of raw garlic in his gut. He closed his eyes again, stomach churning, and mentally forced himself out of his life in the Camp America Cabin. Right into another dream, all the way back to his red, white, and blue room in Big Victor, his mother's rattling pots and pans in the kitchen below like the echo, for all he knew, of gunfire on the battlefield.

He loved to ponder Davy Crockett. The Alamo hadn't died in his head like the other idiotic fantasies of adolescence: the World Series homer in the bottom of the ninth inning donning Dodger blue, the arm-in-arm escort of Marilyn Monroe down the Academy Award red carpet. Crockett's feisty survival in his psyche meant something. He'd never told anyone about it, not even his wife, how its consistent reappearance always came in times of personal trouble.

Once again he was there at the Alamo with Crockett, beaver skin crowning his head, moccasins shrouding his feet. The buckshot rifle shook, as usual, uncontrollably. Crockett wore the same outfit, except his beaver was bigger, and he wasn't nervous. After all, this was Davy Crockett, calm, cool, the legend of American boyhood. Everyone else was dead. The adobe walls were wet with the moisture of bodies and blood. Anthony could not say the few words he needed to say before the end. If he could just put the sentiment into a sentence, the feeling to voice, he would face with dignity what he knew was coming. He wanted to share with Crockett, very simply: "I respect you."

He could hear the rushed, angry voices in Spanish, and this made him wipe his eyes with the sleeve of his leather frontier shirt, and lay prostrate next to Crockett, rifle in front of him, the polished butt in his shoulder, trigger finger trembling.

The clapping report of the Mexican guns made him fade into a breathlessness that resonated gray and amorphous, smoke and gunpowder, and though he was still alive, and knew it, he felt truly dead in the depths of his heart. He lay in this dead time for too long, he thought, and at just that point where he felt victimized for the very first time in his life, the dream broke into another world, bright sun, giant creature—*a spider!*—with chiseled claws digging into his neck. He reached up to scratch it away. The spider bit into his hand and bored deeper into the skin of his neck.

He awoke in shock, shouting, "Hey!"

His son's face was looming above him, eyes wide as they'd ever be, clutching a knife to Anthony's throat. He couldn't think. Just like at the Alamo, he was voiceless. Couldn't speak when it counted, couldn't even move. The dream of silence a reality. Couldn't utter a pleading word, couldn't call for his wife in the kitchen. Blood slid down his neck to the sheets, eyes starting to water.

"Now you know what it's like!" The boy was hysterical. "Only *now* do you know!"

He was alone in his own haven of rightness, the vicious shards of leftover light slicing through the shades, his eyes burning with tears.

"Mother!" the boy shouted. "Mother!"

This wasn't his son. And if this wasn't his son, then he wasn't a father. The legacy gone, lost for good. The thought made him bold. He'd never known this person—*had he?*—this demon on the other end of the bowie knife. And how could you love what you didn't know? Namesake? Inheritor? Legend? If he died in his own blood on his own bed, let the bastard fry strapped to a 2,400-volt chair.

This is me against the enemy, he thought.

"Tony!" His wife's voice from the door. "What in God's name are you doing?"

"You're gonna watch your husband die, Mother!"

"Tony! For God's sake! Put it down right now! Put that down, goddamnit!"

"The *Republican* Party! God *bless* America! You're not Korean, you're *American*! Those leftist shitheels are like rats in the sewer! Blah! Blah! Blah!"

"Tony!"

"I *hate* him, Mother! I'm gonna kill him for the good of anyone who'd cross his path! He can't talk his bullshit with a knife in his windbox."

"Tony, Jesus, Jesus, listen to us, son, listen to me."

She was whispering now. Seducing him into tears in that massaging tone of motherhood. Boys always responded to it. But the words were already said. He heard each one. Can't go back on this, can't erase conviction. He'd given this other party free living quarters for fourteen years. The best clothes, best education, weekday barbecues. He'd changed diapers, bragged to family, hoped in the most private regions of his heart for success, happiness, love. This other party had leeched the very blood from Anthony's veins.

"We love you, son," she whispered. "We love you we love you."

Anthony Constantine Felice III dropped his head at the soothing words and began to whimper like the sixteen-year-old boy he was. He dropped the knife on the floor. Was bigger than his feet. Then he dropped to his knees, hairless chin on his collarbone. His chest heaved. He had no time to look up.

"Anthony! No!"

The ex-father jumped off the bed and kicked his heel into the beige hairless jaw, and then beat the boy as he'd beaten no enemy in his life before.

5

Murron Leonora Teinetoa
Critical Review of Shakespeare
November 13, 2007

THE NINETY-POUND WOMAN who's been laid prostrate and unmoving onto the just sterilized hospice mattress is drowning in her own sound. It comes, it seems, from deep down in her muscleless chest cavity, the auditory price, I guess, for the reflexive lungs expelling carbon dioxide at this stage of life, if life this is, the monotonous humming like a cross between the sheep's dumb bleat and the angry growl of Frankenstein's monster. Her gray-as-gravel eyes are rolled halfway back into the skin ceiling of her eyelids, and it's almost as if she has no clue that I, or anyone, really, am standing just a foot and a half from her bed, awestruck with pity and wonder and the very real concept of futility, our deadweight feet stuck to the ground in the storm.

Just yesterday, Mrs. Edward McFadden, as she'd introduced herself to me two days before, died in that same bed with an uneaten sloppy joe resting perfectly on her abdomen. She looked almost regal in her stillness, the veiny hands folded into supplication, her nails, amazingly, manicured. I hadn't gotten over my first visit to this room when the woman I'd mistaken for Mary had spilled her hamburger across her upper chest. She was the first of the dead I discovered here. I don't know which of the two is worse: starting and not finishing your final meal or never starting it at all.

I have always been prone to allowing the abuses of a tragic imagination to carry on unchecked, such that I'd lay still in the ominous Sonoma mornings of my childhood holding in my pee for hours, praying for Gabe to wake up and take one yawning step into the unknown of our family trailer. In the first grade, I was diagnosed with an ulcer. I have fought against this paranoia, consciously, all my life, I have slept, regrettably, with boys and men I shouldn't have slept with just to hear someone's heart beating under the covers through the long night. I used to let Prince cut school when I knew he wasn't sick just to spend an afternoon with him watching cartoons on the living room floor. The orderly image of the sloppy joe riled up the worst kind of senseless terror in me, such that I reached out before the nurses came and took it off her stomach.

When we'd met, I had no clue what I should do with Mrs. McFadden. She told Mary that Mary didn't belong in this room. That she was coasting on someone's dime. Maybe her own family's, which was shameful, maybe the taxpayers', which was a crime. Either way, it was morally wrong to occupy a bed that someone else out there really needed. She said all these things in five minutes' time and with such vigor that it was as if her whole life had been, step by step, a long climb to this last moment where at last she would make one small thing right in the world before falling from the pyramid for good. I don't know how she came to these conclusions or even, really, how she summoned the energy to put the words together, as she was clearly dying—full-blown thyroid cancer, I'd later learned from her son. Her righteousness and piety scared me. I turned the volume up on the television so that Mary couldn't hear the indictments from this stranger, and then I turned the channel, for constant noise, to a random cable news show.

She'd been in the bed for less than an hour and she hadn't stopped talking. She said her own dear son, Ed Jr., would be visiting soon because noontime was the only time he could leave his job. Eddie, she said, was an aeronautical engineer for the air force, the only officer in the history of the military to fluently speak Czech and Mandarin both, and he would never, she said, allow his mother to freeload off the state of California.

When her son came into the room, his stature was so male and erect and official that he seemed, despite the surroundings, unaffected. He wore a short-sleeved collared shirt pressed, you could see, professionally, and the sight of his Middle America flat-top had me bringing a hand to my head to brush the rebellious bangs out of my eyes. She'd gone silent. He hadn't yet looked at her. He didn't say hello to me. Instead, he probed around the half of the room claimed by his mother for, I assumed, something to straighten, or to clean, or to complain about later to a nurse, and his childish resolve to fix and make better for his mother felt wretchedly familiar. As if here was a chance to vicariously witness a microcosmic replica of my own fatherless life, the one where making right by Lazarus was no less than pathetic, no impetus, at long last, to get anything done.

He made me sad. I wanted to run my hand along the healthy blue veins coursing down his forearms like the map of so many country roads, the edges of my fingers barely touching the skin, our senses alerted by a predisposition of metaphysical reverence, the way Gabe and I used to play with the Ouija board as kids. I wanted him to know, without knowing him, that he could mourn.

He went to her side and dropped to his knees. He looked like one of the knights of the comitatus code Gabe had grown up worshipping as a kid, Lancelot and King Arthur, until he'd come upon the samurai of Shiroyama, and now Ed Jr. pressed his nose against the jutting bone of her jaw. Her jaw so displaced and useless it looked like the mandible of some prehistoric fish. Her bulbous hairless skull the shape of a turnip. She closed her eyes and took in her son's smell. I watched in the mouth-open hopelessness of the caged creature at the Humane Society, I watched in the involuntary trance of the hypnotist's patient, and then I woke up and looked away, aware of my fiending eyes, ashamed of my presence. I was on the other side of death with Mary who, like a blessing, was sleeping deeper than Prince does after a day at the beach.

No more than a minute passed before he got up to leave. I followed him into the hall and asked if we could talk. He didn't say yes, but he did stop, and so I said, "You know, I'm sorry to bother you like this—I really don't want to ask you or stop you here like this."

"What is it?"

"Well, it's your mother. I just wonder if—"

"How did you know that was my mother?"

"—you could maybe talk to her? Oh, well, that's exactly what I wanted to talk to you about. Maybe ask her to—"

"Is she bothering that other patient in the room?"

The accuracy of his prediction, in what might have been, on stage or screen, the deadpan delivery of a dark-hearted comic, was so wretched to witness that I wondered, not for the first time on the premises of this foul hospice, what I really truly wanted out of a given action I'd just taken.

"Well, yes. I think it's safe to say she's been saying some very biting—"

"I will handle this," he said, already marching back toward the room, the make-believe comic book hero whom I knew, right then, to be a false prophet with his ironed slacks and flawless flat-top.

I would never repeat to anyone what he said to his mother, the cold militaristic tone, the matter-of-fact delivery of a duty. It was as if he'd missed, entirely, the whole point of my complaint—that I'd tried to render it as tenderly as possible, that it wasn't us, for right now, anyway, who mattered. Instead he took it as an appeal to his sense of fair play, as if there were such a thing in this life. He wouldn't let anyone say he didn't understand the constitutional issues at hand, he wouldn't let anyone point out a wrinkle in his outfit. I was so angry, standing there in the hallway listening to the absolutism of his directives, but there seemed to be no way to make the situation right. I had reached over the fence and unlatched the gate, and now the dog was loose.

I went home later that night and made a batch of sloppy joes, which his mother had kept calling for in her sleep after he'd left, and which she refused to eat because I'd brought them, and which she died under.

Now my upper thigh buzzes with an electric signal matching the sheeplike calls of Mary's new roommate, and I pull out the phone and read a text from my mother.

Oh my God. Did yo read their eMails?

On the patio, I open up my account through my BlackBerry and find that I have eight e-mails waiting like time bombs in my box. I open up the eighth in the queue and read the latest entry, its thread running all the way out to the earliest, everyone in the Felice clan, again, CC'd to each entry, a virtual bulletin board of family dirt.

Hey Mary Anna! Better Hell than the Elysium Fields Hospice!

* *

Rot in Hell, you son of a bitch!

Mary Anna Felice
President of the Walnut Creek Holistic Center for Existential
*   Wellness*
President of the Blackhawk School District Committee on Gender,
*   Racial, and Lifestyle Equality (GiRLiE)*
Chairwoman of the Hayward Theater of the Arts

* *

Hey Mary Anna! You need one more title for your resume: Your P.O.A. is D.O.A. Anthony C.

∗∗

Tony,
You do not have my knowledge of culture. You are blind to matters of the heart. While your view is your view, it is overly erroneous and childlike. Please cease and desist from contacting me again. Your ranting and raving are childlike. Your position is childlike. You are not a part of my life and you do not occupy my spirit or soul, so please do not think that you know why I act the way I do. I feel and love in matters of the heart like a real human being. These are the matters of the heart. You are mad over something you have created, and working with a shrink would help. It is no wonder that your son has not spoken with you this century. I do not see that changing. Please get the help you need.

Mary Anna
President of the Walnut Creek Holistic Center for Existential Wellness
President of the Blackhawk School Disctrict Committee on Gender, Racial, and Lifestyle Equality (GiRLiE)
Chairwoman of the Hayward Theater of the Arts

∗∗

Mary Anna and the other Criminal,
Mom and Dad are not here? That was a Freudian slip of the worst kind, little sister. Last I checked, both still have heartbeats and an appetite, though that might change with you at the helm. I pray every night you haven't seen One Flew over the Cuckoo's Nest.

Or that you haven't seen the ending, anyway, with that pillow-smothering scene.

I never realized that attempting to suggest a better place for Mom would ever be considered nonsense and that you would not want to be bothered with that concept. Where, do I dare ask, would you put your better half, Keri, in such a situation? I bet the Consumer Digest rankings would matter to you then.

Put your pity in the trash can. Why would you mention my wife's name when she hasn't said one word to you? Why would you treat someone who supports your mother so badly? You lefties got it all backwards: you need an hour with Rush. He'll set you straight.

Do you even know what the word "proverbial" means? Here, let me help: You leftist scum POAs "dropped the proverbial ball" right on my mother's head.

Incidentally, as Power of Attorney, you should try to learn the definition of the terminology you're using. It might help.

Tony

* *

Tony:
It is apparent from your note that you feel the proverbial "we" are criminals, and you and perhaps your wife are the saviors for our mother. You cannot be further from the serious heart of the matter. Poor Tony. I feel sorry for you. At what point will you realize that I have heard your rhetoric before? At what point will you realize that I have been studying the heart of the matter of these issues of human health care in this country much longer than you? How dare you question my motives to do right at all times? At what point will you realize that I have been gathering facts about the right thing for much longer than you? The fact is there are no correct answers, as Mom and Dad are not here.

*As power of attorney, I am doing only what I have been directed
to do. That is all.*

*Please DO NOT bother me with any more of your nonsense. My
life is exhausting enough without people like you trying to take over.*

Mary Anna Felice
*President of the Walnut Creek Holistic Center for Existential
    Wellness*
*President of the Blackhawk School Disctrict Committee on Gender,
    Racial, and Lifestyle Equality (GiRLiE)*
Chairwoman of the Hayward Theater of the Arts

* *

Tony and Anyone Else Who Cares,
*I'm glad to see that Tony has found his voice again, although it's
sad that he still can't do anything but pout about being skipped
over as Power of Attorney. Well, I'd have thought that all of the
siblings were wiser and better than that when it came to showing respect to the folks in their twilight years. It's really too bad
because in the end, I'm afraid, all of us have only one funeral,
and you can only hope that the people putting it together are
okay guys and gals.*

*Just so everyone knows, I do not agree at all with the suggestion
to move Mom. Personal politics and familial dynamics aside, I have
to go along with Mary Anna's twenty-five years in the medical world
(the reason I recommended she share, with me, P of A) and that
of the hospice nurse, who both believe it could be disastrous to
move Mom. When I recently saw Mom at the hospice just before
vacationing in Hawaii, she was friendly, in good spirits and just
fine. It was obvious, however, that she had mentally deteriorated
since the last time I'd seen her. So as the other criminal half of*

*this insidious Power of Attorney monopoly, I intend to here drop
the matter, and will.*

Richmond

****

Hello All:
*Just visited that shithole somebody threw mother in and while
I'd like to suspend judgment about the whole deal so I can swat
the cockroach off my knee, I gotta ask: Hey! What the hell are
you people doing? The Elysium Fields Hospice is the misnomer
of the year! Why is it necessary to provide this to you guys: http://
www.consumerreports.org/cro/health-fitness/nursing-home-guide/
deficient-dozen-8-06/overview/0608-deficient dozen ov.thtm.*

*The Gasoline Fields Hospice is in the Deficient Dozen of the
Consumer Report for six years running! That's Mr. Nader's outfit,
Mary Anna, so it should jibe with your political sensibilities. It would
be a good thing to consider moving Mom. Duh. If she's got a day or
a decade—Hey! Do the RIGHT thing!*

Ton

I'm clutching the BlackBerry so tight my knuckles are white with
bloodlessness. What kind of solution could any of these people get to
with their method of communication, if *method* it be called? It's like
they spent all their civility today on everyone outside their blood, the
coworkers at the office, the clerk at the grocery store, and nothing's
left for family but the sour acerbic indigestible lees at the bottom of
the wine barrel.

I'm worried for Mary.

I slide the screen door of her room open and she's awake now,
beckoning me inside, her palm mechanically motioning me over like
a storefront mannequin. It's old habit for her, I think, but no less

sincere an act. Maybe that's what we should strive for. Goodness so ingrained in habit that it's done without thought, in whatever form, however slight, whomever for.

"Come in, honey. Come on. Close that door, honey. And push that wheelchair back against the closet."

"Hi," I say, doing each request with a last superfluous thrust, the clapping report an auditory reminder that the room, this half of it anyway, is purely hers to rule. God knows, it's not much, but it's all she's got for the moment. It seems these days that this issue brings people together or pushes people apart. To give her less, to give her nothing, to give her more.

"What's that noise, honey?"

Somehow I'd tuned out from the barnyard baying of her new roommate. "Oh, it's nothing," I say, nodding at the other side of the curtain. "I think it's the television over there."

"They need to fix it!"

"Here," I say. "Let me turn up our own TV, 'kay?"

We watch the show in silence, a dry yet masterful run of wordplay on the British Theatre Hour. The camera's antiquated motionlessness makes me, conversely, dizzy with the expectation of chaotic movement, trained as I am to Prince's New Age cartoons where our eyes do things they weren't designed to do. I guess the mass social blindness has not yet set in to be recordable.

"This is real nice, honey," says Mary. "I like this."

"Me, too."

"So wonderful of you to come and see me, honey, but I don't want you cutting off your life for me."

"Oh, no," I say.

"You live your life!"

"I want to be here, Mary."

"Well, this is real nice."

"Yes."

"You're smart, honey. What is it?"

"Oh, the show, you mean? Well, I'm positive it's Shakespeare. I just don't know which play. Maybe *Much Ado About Nothing*, maybe *Taming the Shrew*."

The channel listing tells me I'm wrong on both fronts. It was actually one of my favorites as a high school drama club dreamer back in the day.

"It's *Twelfth Night*."

We performed it a dozen times. My best friend, Hazel, was Sebastian, I played Viola. This momentary loss of recall doesn't really bother me, not just because I still remember most of my lines but because I know I've either forgotten or backshelved a lot of stuff over the years. As a mom, your whole being seems to gauge all activity by the single question of whether or not it's good for the child. Who knows? I probably started the process of removing this scene from my brain years ago when, say, I had to pick up Prince from soccer practice on the same night that I bought scratch at Zanotto's for a homemade lasagna.

Now my brain, despite the brilliant dueling of Viola and Antonio on the screen, has wrapped itself around the one present all-consuming sound, Mrs. Dora Calderon's bed-trapped moan which, though steady and unaltered, seems of a lower pitch now. I try to focus on the play, repeating the verse under my breath, "Will you deny me now?" remembering, "Do not tempt my misery," thinking back to our performance at the Sonoma City Opera. It was the only time an amateur troupe had been allowed to take their stage, and this honor seemed international to us, sixteen wily Sonoma high schoolers, most of whom would never leave that town. I guess, when prorated by the last fact, it remains a big event for some of my old thespian friends.

"Or any taint of vice," I recite, pressing my eyelids tightly together to draw it out to the word, "whose strong corruption inhabits our frail blood."

The nurse comes in with heavy feet and loud hands, miserably sorting the medication on her pharmacy on wheels, lavender trimmed in pink. This is a tough job, anyone can see, and probably does horrible irreparable damage to your romantic understanding of the last earthly moment, the crystalline ascension swept away forever by the stench of mass incontinence, the ethereal trumpets of every theology on the planet silenced by the barn animal calls of the near dead. I feel bad for her but, then, I feel worse for Mrs. Calderon.

"Hi," I say. "Will it be easier if I leave the room?"

"Why?" she says.

The answer seems obvious. There's nothing for me to do but provide it. "Oh, you know, for space. Privacy."

"Do you think I'm going to feed cyanide to Mrs. Calderon?"

Her hands haven't stopped moving, her eyes haven't relayed one kind thought. I find the dark humor inappropriate and even offensive, considering the proximity of this place to the cemetery. Assuming the patients, though bedridden and weary, can still hear. And then I suppose you're not supposed to think it, which is exactly the point, but stranger things have happened on this demented planet than her taunt of yet another *Hamlet* ending, and now I'm regretting, weirdly, that I'm even here, that my mere interaction with this woman will make her more miserable than she already is. Which could be bad for Mary, for her roommate, and for any other interred patient in need of meds. I cannot imagine anyone at the Elysium Fields Hospice, patient or staff, not in need of some kind of mind-altering inducement.

"My name is Murron. Really nice to meet you."

She flicks the switch of a pill counter, saying nothing, eyes down, the treelike rows of upright bottles and the windy trails of colorful pills like a Candy Land game board.

"I've been coming here for a couple weeks. Mary seems to be doing pretty well."

She administers Mrs. Calderon's medication, her lungs and stomach issuing an atmospheric disturbance now, the horror of her reality blaring into the hallway and beyond. The nurse is unfazed. She straightens her lower back, turning to her cart to mark a checklist, then pivots on her toes and, in one swift motion, reaches out to mute Mary's television.

I quietly read the ancient verse in closed captioning. "In nature, there's no blemish but the mind; none can be called deformed but the unkind. Virtue is beauty; but the beauteous evil are empty trunks, o'er-flourished by the devil."

She spies me doing this. "You know that when I distribute medication, the television should be off?"

Well, I want to ask, why did you just mute it then? "No, I didn't. Honestly, no one's told me anything about this place."

"But I'm sure you knew that, didn't you?"

I honestly don't know the right thing to say, I don't know the right thing to do but stay in this room. I turn to the nurse with exaggerated politeness. "Thanks for letting us watch the play in silence."

She says nothing, and although I can't stand her, I know that she wields real power here at the Elysium Fields Hospice. As if I need illustration of this point, she counts pills with what I daresay is a sinister punctiliousness, the methodical pace so slow I can tally the hairs on three fingers of her right hand.

Six. Five. Eight.

Now she reaches up and turns the television off.

These games are so unnecessary, but when you're called upon, you have to play. Too much is at stake. It's taken me a long time to get my dream job of dealing with virtually no living person save the egotistical ghosts behind the novels I choose to review. Never mind that each week my position is assessed as an extravagant enterprise by higher-ups at the paper. Too many people have thought, before testing me, that my solitudinous, anti-passive-aggressive personality is a verification of weakness. I hate to play the games people play because I don't like who I am when I play them. But I have never met anyone who can be as quick to the verbal kill as I.

And that's a blessing and a curse both.

I've got to remember that it's not just about me. Perhaps if I were in the bed. Today I have to think of Mary. "Should I be speaking with the head nurse about this?"

"I *am* the head nurse."

"Well. I'll be speaking with your director then."

"Feel free," she says, but she's looking at me now, and that's all I need.

"I would have thought that you were skilled enough to do your job in any circumstance."

"We have our rules."

"Yes. And that's the nice thing about bureaucracies, isn't it? Always someone higher up to complain to."

She says nothing.

"You work for us, remember?"

"Well, I do," she says, "yes, I do remember," and I suspect she's about to back down. Now the trick is somehow getting her on your side enough so that she doesn't take vengeance on the patient you're visiting. It's horrible to have to think like this, the hit-and-miss game of the speculative psychologist, but it's worse to have to be here, to be *in* here.

For a second, I think on what could be the right response to this fickle nurse. "You do look very busy."

Our eyes meet again, and I narrow my own tired pair to a serious but respectful squint, one that indicates I'll listen to her talk about her troubles because, well, I also have troubles. I won't share them, but she can spout all the venom she wants. As long as she does right by me. By *us*. It looks like she accepts the offer in three vicious facial ticks, the involuntary acquiescence evoking unstated sympathy in me, and then in one gesture, she proves me right, at least for the moment, at least while I'm *here*, reaching up over her head without looking and turning the television back on. A reverse dunk with fast, almost frightening, expertise. She's a control freak, but the head nurse has her limits, I can see. Of the two traits, the first probably got her the job, the second has helped her keep it.

"I started here in 1986. I've served thousands of patients. Of every creed and breed, I always say. Of every need."

I nod so that she can see it, so she can appreciate my willingness to listen. She's counting Mary's pills now. I want her to think she's instructing me, whether she is or not. Either about herself, or her job, or this place, any of it.

"All are the same to me, I have no prejudice or personal favorites. If I did, I wouldn't be—what was it you called me again?"

I look up and she's smiling.

"Ah, yes," she says. "The head nurse."

I laugh and it feels better than good. It feels beautiful. I look up at the screen so as not to test the moment's lastingness and silently read the words: "A very dishonest paltry boy, and more a coward than a hare."

She spies me doing this. "Do you like Shakespeare?"

"Yes," I say. "Yes, I do."

"He's so good," she says, "that no one even knows he wrote poems."

"You're right."

"That's how good he is."

I don't miss that she speaks about Shakespeare in the present tense. It's an old manipulation of time used by scholars and professors and other lovers of books, inside code for the club. Suddenly I feel like such a shit. Were it not for the surroundings and my East Palo Alto suspiciousness of intent, I'd say that I'm tickled by her extension of our conversation. Shakespeare in the Elysium Fields Hospice: Why not?

"I think you're right."

"No one compares to him," she says.

"It's a question, perhaps, of numbers. Of output."

"No, it isn't. It's that he *gets* it. And that he writes so wonderfully."

This scolding surprises me, genuinely and gratefully. Who knows? Maybe, unlike me, she's properly identified the play. Maybe, despite my so-called vocational command, I could learn something from her.

Probably a lot. Varied interpretation of text is one of the reasons I took my job in the first place because it demonstrates, before anything else, a sincere interest in a given story. Which means life is important to you.

"You know, I want to thank you. I didn't think about his sonnets that way until now. I guess they're kind of like hors d'oeuvres with Shakespeare. Forgotten by the English-speaking world until February fourteenth."

"Valentine's Day."

I smile, nod. "Yeah."

"The hundred and sixteenth is my favorite."

I don't know them by number. "Which is that?"

" 'Let me not to the marriage of true minds admit impediments.' "

"Yessss," I say, "it's lovely. Something to aim for."

" 'An ever-fixed mark that looks on tempests—' "

" '—and is never shaken.' "

She smiles, the tick gone now.

"A friend of mine," I say, "serenaded his wife at their wedding with that poem."

"I'd keep him forever."

"That's what I keep telling my bosses." She frowns. "Oh, he's a poetry critic," I add.

Here she looks at me with meaning. She's figuring me out, too, I guess. "I hope he's good."

"He is. He's excellent. But that he really loves poetry is more important, I think. And maybe why he's excellent. Too many critics out there are doing the work for themselves and not for poetry."

"That seems counterintuitive."

"I guess it is."

"I can't remember one critic from Shakespeare's time," she says.

"Well." It's good to be humbled now and then, too, you know? She's right. A critic is necessary, but always secondary. That's the nature of the job. We're like the Secret Service or something: our purpose is service without notice, and yet we're absolutely vital. "I think that's how it should be."

And you know what else? I like when I'm wrong about people. I honest to God do. When I surprise myself. And then to actually come out on the positive end. Your own personal prejudices and shortcomings are revealed for what they are, not in the alone time, but in the tête-à-tête with another person. The trick is to pay attention and catch it on the fly, the way—Prince would be proud of me—a UFC fighter hears the trainer's instructions in the middle of the round. I don't know why, or if it's right, really, but I trust this nurse. As if her initial attitude was a kind of test for sincerity, a way to say this place is not for the meek of heart, that she's got enough to take care of without wasting time on a stranger, someone who may be back but who likely, based on precedence, won't. Deep down there in her angry depths, I can see that she cares, that her cynicism is birthed in real concern.

Our silence kills the conversation. But it's not silent. Poor Mrs. Calderon has been moaning the whole time. We didn't talk over her, we talked *through* her. The nurse walks over to Mary at the bed, a return to her own duty, and I turn my head with her, slowly remembering that I, too, have a necessary reason for being here, that I exposed myself, dangerously, to an absolute stranger, and that I did it, at least initially, for someone else.

"I'm so sorry, Mary. I got caught up talking to the nurse."

"I'm Maggie," the nurse says.

"Oh, honey!" Mary shouts, beaming at me the way my mother does when she knows she's right about something. "You talk all you want to your friend here, okay?"

And I think she *is* right. Wherever you're at, whoever you are, it's good to have someone on your side who can recite a Shakespearean love sonnet.

"Don't you dare worry about me! I won't have that! You go right ahead and talk, you two honeys!"

6

Anthony Constantine Felice II
Soup Kitchen of St. Joseph's Cathedral
June 3, 1993

THE CONCEPT OF GOODNESS, he thought, started before all else with the conservation of tradition.

For several days he'd been combing the South Bay for a church to his liking, something that could rekindle the sense of awe he'd had as a child. He wanted his thirteen-year-old son to see that his own story had started here, and that institutions like the church survived for a reason, and that it was their job as a family to keep the tradition alive. He would admit this failure as a father to his son, a gesture of reunion, a reminder of the beauty of the church. The doors were always open, and it was never too late to return until, in fact, it was too late.

He went to his brother Rich. Not just because he'd been a seminarian as a child—"A *failed* seminarian," his wife had corrected, protesting the call he was about to make—but because with the death of an only son one must arrive upon certain truths that others just can't understand.

In fact, he'd thought, as he'd dialed his brother's number for the first time in over a year, that's my God's very story.

Richmond said, "What are you interested in a dead revolution for?"

He tried to let the statement pass through his system. Admittedly, it was hard. He was less than a minute into the call. He didn't think that assessments of history, even Richmond's supposedly profound kind, would help Anthony III or his family. When it came down to it, he didn't trust heady people, the intellectual types who sat apart from the crowd in a kind of indifference that, it seemed, amounted to judgment. And yet despite this attitude of superiority, you were somehow held within their force field of a worldview.

Maybe it was just the power of personality. He'd seen it many times in college. Once the poets and protesters emerged from the cafés and art galleries to actually acknowledge your presence, they acted like their knowledge was so rare that even their defecatory act was a gift. They shat on their brothers and sisters with unabashed flair. Despite his war record, Richmond might have fallen into this category. Or maybe he had always been this way and had since fallen back into it after returning from the war. Rich's wife had once let slip certain unclean stories of guitar strumming in Jack London Square. "An acoustic Fender in his hands, Dylan's lyrics in his head, and Humboldt green in his lungs," she'd said, laughing out loud. The image didn't fit Anthony's vision of a veteran, let alone a veteran who was his own brother. But in truth, he wasn't sure about his brother's political reality, and didn't want to crucify him without the evidence.

After more than four decades with this familial story and having been burned repeatedly by loved ones, Anthony felt that certain truths were finally revealing themselves to him. He didn't know if this was a statement of the power of family to cast blindness on its members or one of his own personal stupidity. He was the first to admit that his sentimental regard for the people in his world made him less than savvy when it came to things like motive, or duplicity, or cuckoldry.

Maybe, he thought for the first time in his life, Richmond's real strength was an uppity version of passive-aggression.

His younger brother was going on now about Nietzsche, how no major Western philosopher since before the insane German had been Christian. He tried tuning it out. He couldn't do it.

"I disagree with your thesis, Rich."

"Oh, no, no, Ton. Can't emphasize this enough: it's not a thesis. We're just talking facts here, real facts. Anyone with any understanding of the thing knows this. It's a place to start the conversation."

"Well, anyway, to hell with these philosophers. They haven't done a damned thing worth remembering, Rich. Not from Socrates all the way to that French prick."

"Sartre?"

"Whatever."

"You know what Sartre said, Ton?"

"No, but I have a real good hunch you're gonna tell me."

"He said, 'Other people are hell.'"

"Listen, Rich. It's questions upon questions with assholes like Sartre. Like a big pile of horse shit. Philosophers have nothing to do with what I'm after."

There was a pause. He knew it meant his brother was about to disagree with him, virulently. He was already readying for this, though, as usual, he didn't know how to prepare for it. He felt ill-equipped when his brother started dropping the big names of history.

"Don't take this personally, Ton, but I've never heard anything so stupid in my life. The Catholic Church is more responsible for Western philosophy than any institution around."

"It's about tradition, Rich. It's about good and evil. It's about something real, see?"

"No, I don't see."

"You offer nothing. Think about it."

"Okay, okay. That's fine. I won't say a word further. In exchange for this, just keep me out of these insufferable conversations, will you?"

"Hey, you ain't doing me any favors either." He tried to lighten up the tenor between them. He still wanted ideas, even if he had to sacrifice his pride. "Especially using words like 'insufferable.'"

"I don't have time for this stuff, Ton."

"Boy, you sure have changed."

"Bullshit. I've always been this busy. You know that."

"Jesus, Rich. I'm talking about your belief in God."

"Ton, my son contracted AIDS at twenty-three. I prayed hard about it. I am not satisfied with the results."

He almost said, "Hey! When you fuck fifty men over the course of a year, that's exactly what happens!" He might have said it before Rich Jr. had contracted the virus. He might have said it preventatively, to save the kid's life. But not when the kid had it, not while dying. Not now, certainly, not dead.

"I'm sorry about your loss, Rich."

"You don't know a thing about pain, Ton."

"Hey! Fuck you, Rich! Who the hell do you think you are? You don't got a monopoly here, man!"

"If you can't be civil about it, don't even pick up the phone."

His wife came out of their room, reached across Anthony's lap, and depressed the receiver button for the length of a full second. By the time he shouted, "Hey!" it was too late. She was gone. She'd been listening on the other line. He was only angry with her for a second. She'd saved him. He owed her.

He went out of the house and took a drive up the 280, not knowing where he was going, fervently nodding as he drove. His "good friend Rush" was talking about why all American transients were Democrats, and how Democrats with homes were, of their own making, one step away from homelessness. How he, Rush, was an instrument of reconciliation between the Left and their street-beggar roots. Anthony was a self-proclaimed Ditto, which meant that he agreed so thoroughly with Rush Limbaugh's words that he bypassed—along with others of the clique—the need to articulate his assent beyond the highly efficient, truly faithful, rightly right "Ditto."

"Ditto!" he shouted. "Ditto!"

He decided to have lunch at César Chávez park. He'd yet to acknowledge the proper name change honoring the Mexican farmer. He ordered the same good old American lunch of a 100 percent beef hot dog and a bag of potato chips—Lays, barbecued, packaged in a tiny town in upper Michigan—to be washed down, as his mother had always called it, by a "pop"—Coca-Cola, glass bottle, imported, without his knowledge, from Mexico. If he'd have known this, he'd have drunk water. The vendor's name was Max, and Anthony liked him. He was a proud American. He worked hard. He positioned himself where he knew the business crowd would either gather for lunch or at least pass. Anthony admired this strategy, though he wished Max would diversify his menu a bit, offer a sub sandwich or something.

He gave Max the money and Max gave him the dog, smiling, and despite having repeated the same phrase every day for several months, this afternoon Anthony felt it incumbent upon him to say yet again, "A tip for a fine job," dropping a shiny quarter in the mayonnaise jar. The coin made no noise, the bottom of the glass layered with dollar bills and business cards. He was fiercely loyal to Max and his wieners and his little yellow cart, the Hot Dog Taxi, as it was called, an unlicensed business entity that the police on this park beat overlooked for an occasional free wiener between calls, and a chance to rest in the shade of the checkered umbrellas.

He took the same route back to work every day, past the porters at the Fairmont, around the black brick of the San José Museum of Art, and then down a block to Park Avenue. He made a point each day to avoid the corner of San Fernando and Market because there was always a cluster of homeless people on the sidewalk, "bums" as Anthony preferred calling them, spilling out of a soup kitchen somewhere behind an iron fence.

Today they reached the street. He went around them as best he could, holding in his breath. He looked up at the building which he'd never looked up at before, and saw, to his surprise, that it was a church. St. Joseph's. He'd never known. He'd always walked past this point with his eyes averted from the failure of the American dream that these people clearly represented, and yet here they were congregating on the steps of a church, defiling the Lord's house. A man asked him for change. He stopped in his tracks and exhaled. He wondered why no one from the church ever called the police. His nostrils flared, his eyes burned with meaning.

"Why don't you bums go somewhere else?"

"Eh, man, I just asked you for a fucking quarter, bro."

"I give my quarters to Americans who work for a living."

"Oh, it's work all right listening to mu'fuckers like you."

"First you beg, then you borrow. First it's a quarter, then it's my house."

"Oh, I done skip borrowing, bro. If I want something that bad, I just straight steal it. I mean, when it come down to it, if I really wantchyo money, I just knock you down and take the wallet outcha pocket."

Anthony walked up the steps of the church, feeling both unclean and wronged. He shook his head and said, "The Seventh Commandment?"

"Survive, mu'fucker. Ask my boy Moses. That's the First Commandment, the Second, the Third, Fourth Commandment. That's the Fifth, Sixth—"

"Take this crap out of here!" he shouted, pointing at the ten-speeds and grocery baskets weighed down with bags and blankets. "How dare you turn my Father's house into a flea market!"

The bum started up the steps, forcing Anthony to walk up backward to the church. He wasn't scared to fight them. He was scared to *touch* them. Pick up in one right hook every unseen disease these walking petri dishes carried, every germ known to a warm body. Suddenly he thought about his nephew who'd died of AIDS a few months ago, and ordered, "Stay back!"

"Tyrone!"

Tyrone stopped at the top step. Anthony had his ass against the door. The church was locked. He couldn't believe it. When he was a kid in Upland, the Carmelite chapel was open year-round for anyone in need. Tyrone turned and walked back down. A priest came up.

"Father. Jesus. Should we call the police?"

The priest smiled. He took Anthony's hand and said, "You are a child of God, my son. But you are not the only child."

"I didn't know they locked churches now."

"Well." The priest nodded. "We had to. Lost some beautiful relics recently, had the confessional defiled. But we're still open for business. The faithful can always get in through the door by the sacristy."

"If only these bums didn't loot and loiter, huh, Father?"

"My son, we are fifteen minutes from our afternoon Mass. Would you care to join us?"

Anthony looked down at the transients.

"The answer to the question you didn't ask would be yes. We welcome *all*."

"Don't take this personally, Father, but I can't believe you let those bums in here after what they did. I mean, how can you make the same mistake twice?"

"Would you come with me?"

They walked down the steps, the priest nodding at the transients who made up nearly a third of his congregation during afternoon Mass. They respectfully parted as he passed through, closing the gap fast on Anthony. They threw out playground glares worthy of the worst film on late-night Kung Fu Theater.

"It wasn't twice. A half dozen times it happened. We lost a beautiful portrait of the Holy Mother last year. It was the only fresco here. Was sent, I think, as a gift from an Italian baron who'd visited San José in the fifties. Bought an apricot orchard, I believe, but I forget what else."

They went inside the church through the prescribed side door the priest had mentioned, and he dipped his finger in the holy water and crossed himself, then nodded at Anthony, who did the same.

The church was beautiful. The pews were laid out in four perpendicular angles so that from the ethereal vantage they made the shape of the cross. The highest point of the domed ceiling was held together by God, his beard flowing down his chest and abdomen like seaweed whitened by a beneficent angle of sunlight, his arms and hands spread out across the dome, his robe patrolled by pink-cheeked angels in midflight, saints shoulder to shoulder along the perimeter above the Latin. The fourteen stations of the cross were actually paintings of Christ's ascent up Golgotha, the backdrop in each portrait darker than the inside of the mouth, the Roman numerals seeming to simultaneously increase in value and horror.

As he followed the priest, he remembered the church of his childhood. The view from his supplicant knees in the carven pews during Sunday Mass, feeling safe in what he couldn't see, knowing that he was surrounded by brother and sister congregants in the same posture of devotion, all present even Johnny awaiting the lulling scent of incense preceding the holy procession toward the sacred altar, the floor of the church cut perfectly in half by the wiry cross his brother Richmond held up over his head, now passing the family with such serenity and purpose that he had to have been led, Anthony believed, by the holy apparition, this blood brother, second blood son to his parents, dwarfed in a clean flowing gown so white it seemed almost transparent. Well, he was proud, too. Back then. Of this ceremony of his family's faith begun in part by one of their own. Of a church that sent knights on crusades to reclaim the holy land, missionaries on missions to convert the heathen, armies overseas to shatter the blasphemous illusions of heretics. Proud of the strength he felt from the ground, eyes closed. Not blind to, but affirmed by, the reality he couldn't see around him.

He used to bike down to watch the weddings on the bright, fertile, vintage summer weekends at the Carmelites, sit on the steps at the abbey hidden by the olive trees, dream about his own wedding in the future, an event way too far off to touch but which he'd indulge in

nonetheless, how he'd carry his bride out of the church in the bed
of his arms, as if he were rescuing her from a burning fire. Once his
father had told the family to pack up for a picnic, and en route to
downtown Upland he'd stopped the car and said, "Let's help them
consecrate their love," parking along the street and walking through
the cool shadows to join the celebration of a marriage to which they
were not invited, and how they'd melded right into the rice throwing
and the cheering, how the bride's father kept biting his lower lip in a
successful effort not to cry. Somehow Anthony's own father had found
out his secret ritual, and this was his indirect way of saying that it
was not only perfectly normal but fully supported by his family, and
society, and God.

That's my father, Anthony thought. A good, thoughtful man.

"Do you have weddings here, Father?"

"We do."

They went to the far end of the church where donation envelopes
and colorful pamphlets were stacked. The priest unlocked a door, nodded at Anthony, and entered the room. It looked like an empty storage
closet at the office. The white paint glistened in the electric light,
nothing adorning the walls but a digital clock, a calendar highlight-
ing holy days, and an aluminum crucifix the size of two intersecting
fountain pens over the door. He looked at the priest with a question.
There was a small table between them, like a desk.

The priest said, "Confession room."

"This?"

"Yes."

He felt as if he was in a barren structure, an architectural purgatory.

"Not exactly what I was raised on, Father."

"Please relax. Now is not the time to embrace passion."

So this was what the modern world thought of the confession
of sin. Splash some man-made light on it in a sterilized closet. The
confessional he'd known in Upland ensured that a significant part of
his childhood was spent in mortal fear, and that was good, Anthony

knew, because a life of pure fearlessness was not just foolish, it was bad for the country. Was unpatriotic. It made for bad kids, bred to be ingrates and cowards and little gods-on-earth. Children needed restriction from on high, and no one was better than the Catholic Church at putting a muzzle over the ego.

As a boy he'd felt his own sins weigh on his heart like heavy stones through the long week. In the school cafeteria during lunch, tossing the ball around in the grove, walking home from Little League practice, lying in bed in Big Victor, his hands behind his head on the pillow, his legs crossed at the feet, the punitive deity of the book of Job looming not just overhead but outside, and in all the places where he set foot, frowning down upon him in judgment. He'd duck into the confessional breathless. He'd sinned many times outside the booth, but Anthony never lied in it. He thus never left the booth feeling worse than he'd felt going in it. It always felt clean and liberating to bound down the steps of the church with a prescription of prayers for salvation, and how comforting it was to know that the wise old fathers of the church had passed down your own personalized map to heaven, and that it was up to you to pick up your cross and follow it.

The priest was talking. He hadn't been listening. "Father?"

"So that's what it comes down to. If the price for one saved soul is this church being burned to the ground, we'll gladly have our shovels and hammers ready before the smoke clears to give it a go again. That's what Christ teaches us. And whatever it is we can get up, we're that much more blessed for the sake of that single soul."

"Father, how can you accept—"

"And for the sake of accuracy, it wasn't transients who looted the church."

"How do you know?"

"The culprits were caught. Three teenagers."

"Kids?"

"And they confessed."

"Catholic kids?"

"Not to *me*. Confessed to the police. Each dressed in all black, black makeup, black hair."

Rats, Anthony thought.

"And it was actually the transients who caught the kids."

Well, it was a good thing to help your local church, Anthony thought, but a transient was a transient. "What were the names of those kids, Father?"

"What's important is that we can help them by example. Be the verifiable proof that a good life is not a bad life."

The priest smiled at his play on words.

"Put 'em away for life," Anthony said.

The priest frowned.

"Well," Anthony said, nodding. "Maybe ten, fifteen."

Either incarcerated in a draconian cell at juvie or locked in the parents' walk-in closet. Both measures were sufficient to Anthony, as long as the period of punishment fit the crime, which meant a good chunk of time out of the kid's life. It wasn't a matter of correction. This was a matter of justice. The kid had to learn that a certain kind of behavior resulted in a certain kind of reality.

"Let's try and find you some peace, my son."

"Those rats should be shot for doing that, Father."

"The church does not believe this. Capital punishment is not Christ-like."

"Knee shot then. Those dark-hearted fucks need to have their kneecaps obliterated. Excuse the cussing, Father."

"Do you have children, my son?"

"Wait a second." Anthony's mind was invaded and occupied by simplistic visions of the Spanish Inquisition, a trading card rosary whose face side was a gaudy, preincineration portrait of Joan of Arc on the stake. "Since when does the Catholic Church not believe in capital punishment?"

"My son. You have too much hatred in your heart. You risk the love dying. This is not something you want."

"Father, I have a son, okay? He's just entering his teens. I want him raised right, thinking right. Now. How in the hell—sorry—do you expect me to support an institution that welcomes those bums down below? That won't defend itself if needed? What should I tell my son, huh? It's not the American way, Father. It's not even—"

"Well, you can tell him—"

"—practical."

"—our loyalty is to God, not the state. That's a good place to start."

"Do you see the Muslims tiptoeing through the world like this? I mean, that damned religion should be outlawed."

The priest pulled a pair of spectacles from his chest pocket. He had to push them up on his face repeatedly, finally holding them at the bridge of his nose with an index finger. So damaged, crooked, and chewed upon that one imagined the manufacturer reclaiming the frames on principle, if ever it crossed paths with this priest. It seemed to Anthony that someone called to guide God's children should take better care of his personal paraphernalia, that his coveted religious vision shouldn't rely upon a cylinder of masking tape.

"Italian?"

"My mother and father are Italian," said Anthony.

"You've been to Italy?"

"No."

Now that he thought it over, only his brother Richmond had gone. Early sixties. He and the other siblings had to hear about it for the next five years. Once or twice in a moment of adolescent weakness, he'd felt deprived. Only looking on and mediating his brother Johnny's selfish shenanigans had thoroughly put an end to the sentiment. By now, he didn't care. His brother probably had dual citizenship, had surely been given a key to some forgotten fishing village on the boot.

"Should go back and see the homeland. Even if it doesn't deepen your faith, it will broaden your horizons a bit."

"*This* is my homeland, Father. I'm an *American*."

"I see."

"With all due respect, Father, I don't think you do. Look around, Father! Sea to shining sea!"

"I'm familiar with the song. I like the song."

"Everything I need to see is within these borders."

"Well, I hope you'll stay for Mass, my son. Or maybe come back with your family. We love having Americans in our church."

The priest patted Anthony's arm and then walked off, his head slightly tipped forward, as if only the steps he was taking were holding him up.

Anthony watched him go, and then with the determination of deep purpose, he rushed down the steps so that he wouldn't have to cross paths with the transients. He could smell them but he couldn't see them, and that, anyway, was a good sign. He hustled back to work, closed the door to his office, made a call to his wife. The promise of delivery of the glory of yesteryear was dead in this valley. His mind was made up about the liberal pocket of America he'd called his home for the last two decades.

When the grand old Catholic Church was lost, all was lost.

"We're leaving," he said. "Starting today, say your good-byes. Not raising my son in this filthy valley of progressive fucks."

By the end of the month they were packed and gone, the house sold for a small loss, their immediate future of a five-hour drive up I-5 in twin sixteen-foot U-hauls the next long and tiresome step to rightness.

The Felices
Christmas Lights of Big Victor
December 12, 1963

They lived in the oldest Victorian in West Upland. The house was at the direct midpoint of Third Street, an experimental project of an early 1930s construction site of solely southern Italians and eastern Poles, and its architectural grandiosity imposed a kind of secondary nature upon the surrounding Victorians, as if they were scaled-down versions of the original blueprint built merely to contribute to its seniority. The personality of the family perfectly fit this dream of the neighborhood meeting point. Of provincial centrality. The family had an obtuse, innocent, and ultimately charming energy evoking at once the idea that the house, which they'd christened Big Victor, was actually the direct midpoint of Upland itself, all of West Upland, all of downtown Upland, even, somehow, the off-limits barrio of East Upland.

Big Victor was shrouded by a field of green lawn extending to the gutters of the street itself. There were no fences between Big Victor and the houses on either side. A line of concrete gently bisected the always neatly trimmed grass, disappeared behind the house, wound under an always sagging laundry line, snaked past a built-in barbecue pit of hand-made, hand-laid, shiny red brick, around a white, four-seat arbor with opposing trellises, to end at a one-car garage, fifteen yards from the back porch of Big Victor.

The windows of Big Victor were as wide, as mysterious, as individually embodied as cave entrances. Octagonal, rectangular, enigmatic, they looked like ornate portholes to a toy submarine, they looked almost Russian in one instance, Chinese in another. Highly stylized. Framed in dark colors that were never the same colors, the hand-carved, hand-whittled ledges were like ancient symbols whose original meaning was long forgotten.

Big Victor was vast in size, intricate in design, completely asymmetrical. A railed porch encircled Big Victor, wide enough on the north and west sides to accommodate several southern porch swings, so narrow on the south and east sides that one couldn't walk between the rails and the walls of the house. Rows of potted plants lined the space instead. At the western end of the house there was a solarium filled with rhododendrons and lilies, the morning sunlight divinely magnified by the vacuum of glass. Each of the seven bedrooms was so unique in its spaciousness that it was impossible to determine which was the master bedroom. Detailed scrollwork put a stamp of authenticity on each room. Every few years there were trades among the children, a room for a room, to "try out" life in a different part of the house. If you counted the attic, there were three floors of the house, if you counted the loft, four floors.

Everywhere was the evidence of family life, which meant mainly the evidence of children. Dirty athletic sneakers at the door, sometimes neatly lined up, sometimes not, depending on the season and the number of siblings participating, depending on the sternness of the last lecture from their father, depending on their love lives, depending on what they could smell brewing in the kitchen, depending on their individual moods. Oiled mitts with baseballs rounding the webbed pockets on kitchen counters, V-neck T-shirts tucked between the cushions of the couch, stacks of school books—algebra, biology, American history—left claimingly in the best corners of Big Victor, flyers and leaflets of every size and color tacked to what was once a visible bulletin board, calendars of cafeteria menus, highlighted holy days, announcements of town-hall meetings addressing civic issues like the color scheme, chaperone schedule, and locale of the high school ball. Upon the tabletops, in the middle of drawers, between the glass and the wood of hallway mirrors were dozens of various rosaries for various relatives, some long dead. On a monthly whim to establish order in the house, Anthony Sr. would attempt to clean up the clutter and Mary would slap his hand at the blasphemy: "Never forgotten! Not ever!"

During the second week of Advent, the boys would climb the ladder and run lights along the roofline, down the four steep corners of Big Victor. The brother on the ground would feed the line like rope to a rock climber, and the brother up top would say, "Got it, got it, keep goin'."

Every few years someone would fall, break a bone, twist an ankle, shout "Shit!," blame it on the brother on the ground and then have that same brother, caught in a laugh attack for hours, sign the cast first. He'd sign it, "I'll catch you next year."

That night the family would gather on the front lawn beneath the dark map of bright, untouchable stars, hugging and shoving each other, betting on which lights had died during the layover of eleven months, an assembly of celebration for more than the Christmas season. The buzz would grow so magnetically that neighbors would come out in curiosity and join the Felices on the lawn, the Miltons, the Flecks, the Bierces, the Wallaces, the more families the better. They got to talking about how nice this was, how absolutely necessary after the horrible tragedy in Dallas just weeks before, and how they'd follow the lead of the Felices if the Upland Hardware Store still carried the product this late into the month of December. Then someone would start up the first verse of "Silent Night," and soon everyone on the lawn was singing, feeling warm in the cold evening.

After the song one of the carolers under ten would remind them: "What about the lights already!"

A shout from inside Big Victor came: "Are you ready?"

"The lights!"

"Are you ready?"

"The lights!"

"Is that a yes?"

"Anthony Sr.!"

"Okay, if you say so," and then in a flash Big Victor was outlined in electrical snow, the gleam off the roof casting sheets of beneficent light on the adjacent homes, and the chirping started up again, the nods of admiration, the children setting chase to each other across the lawn and into that capricious world of shadows, the citrus grove, and another carol was started by the adolescents and affirmed by the joining in of the adults, the hum this time softer in the scintillating glow of Big Victor, and after the last refrain of "White Christmas" was sung, one by one the neighbors drifted home hand in hand, the Miltons, the Flecks, the Bierces, the Wallaces, and then the Felices assembled under the electric lights and tittering stars of winter one last time and, heads bowed, silent, went inside their house.

PART II
Richmond

7

Murron Leonora Teinetoa
Land of Endless Possibility
November 29, 2007

I watch Prince shrink to dot size in the rearview mirror of my Prius, accelerating now to stay with the madness of five o'clock El Camino Real traffic, the endless string of strip malls just behind the walk so unremarkable and repetitive you forget what's there until the car just ahead of you is awash in red light and you're forced to slow, too, and in the three-second interim that nonetheless feels like a minute, Billions and Billions Served enters your already paranoid field of vision, followed by Kentucky Fried Chicken, Taco Bell, Carl's Jr., Subway, the parental panic setting in of not just chronic obesity visiting your nine-year-old only child but of asthma, but of gout, but of type-2 diabetes, and then, in the next second of acceleration, is gone again.

But I'm with them today, I drive faster than I normally would. Probably to avoid thinking about the daily rituals of departure from my son, at the door of our apartment, at the bus stop, just now at one of Stanford's two dozen soccer fields. It's as if the constant act of leaving is no more than a preparation for that one final irreversible exit, either his or mine, in the always-here-too-fast future.

Prince has developed a serious contemplative side in front of other boys, one that precludes him from saying good-bye too loudly to his mother. That's what I know about him. It's not just typical boyish embarrassment in front of his soccer team. It's also that he feels, naturally, the kind of seriousness he thinks I'm driven by, and which he carries in his system through circumstance and DNA both. The proof, I suppose, that he's right about me. And yet I can see him, still, waving maniacally from the uncut yellowing grass only a year ago, half the Under-10 Palo Alto Select soccer team evaluating him with suspicion until, as it was, he scored three goals in their first game for a 4–2 win against Willow Glen United.

Sometimes as a parent, you can't help but detest the way the world works, the speed with which it exacts consciousness on your child, the hope that his conscience keeps up with the horridly naked influx of data, and the way you can watch, as if it's your own personal cinema, the universal issues of being alive take form in his chemical makeup, courage, fear, morality, change, endurance, flexibility. How you know he's dangerously low on one, and nearly high on another. And there are those times when you think, usually falsely, you have arrived, just the two of you, upon an understanding (that will keep forever) of a problem (which will never return). I shouldn't complain. I just mean that it's tough to watch the world, which means watch other people, take your son, day by day, away from you.

The 280 is relatively traffic-free this early evening, and I can drive without too much of the stress that comes of nothing else, really, but an overwrought populace in an impacted valley. The people here, it seems, are always impatiently elbow to elbow, be it in their cars, their cubicles, or their beds. I miss Sonoma at times like this, where you can jog solo along a country road in good faith, the heat rising like coffee steam off the sun-drenched pavement, rolling hill of green clover on one side, symmetrical field of Isabella grapes on the other. No excuse but to run hard in an oxygenated atmosphere like that. Everyone more or less has to be kind or, anyway, tries to be kind because, despite the uninhabited landspace in between, you're bound to see the same person today as tomorrow. Very little changes there but the seasons. Until meth came along in the late nineties, very few vices but the native vice of wine.

I haven't taken the uglier but faster 101 South in years, always opt for the secondary southbound passage hailed by its architects (who've obviously never visited Europe) as "the most beautiful freeway in the world." Sounds like the misnomer oxymoron of the (American) World Series. Still, if one can keep her expectations of beauty confined to "the world" of the Silicon Valley, I suppose the 280 could be exactly that.

I leave behind the towns of Los Altos, Mountain View, Cupertino as I enter Northern California's biggest city, just under a million residents occupying the inland suburban plains of San José, no San Francisco Bay or Pacific Ocean to push the city's pollutants into, the smog hovering this hour like a massive smokescreen for the Santa Cruz and Mount Diablo Mountains. At the exit for Highway 17, the cars slow and cluster for the epicenters of Valley Fair and Santana Row and I check my mirrors in one glance and immediately move into the mess with caution and assertion both.

I open the buzzing cell phone without looking at the number. "Hello."

"Hi, baby."

"Hi, Ma."

"Where are you?"

"I'm on my way to see Mary, why? How are you?"

"I just came from there. I'm fine."

"Okay. Well, how did it go?"

"I'd say good and bad."

"That's how it always is, I guess."

"No. Actually, Mary was great . . ."

During our last visit, the skin around the stress map of crow's-feet seemed old and tired, but the eyes were young in the center, her pupils dancing with life. As if she'd reached some kind of treasure that we, the walking uninterred, had a long way to go to discover.

". . . she was kind and even warm, I'd say. I brought her a card and some rosaries from St. Francis of Assisi. She loved them. She talked about her dog, Rex, the one she had as a kid in Pittsburgh. I was amazed by her memory. She just went on and on with the neatest little details you wouldn't believe. She said Rex was a tan-face, not a black-face, shepherd. That his line could be traced all the way back to Germany. She even named the policeman they'd bought Rex from, the only Italian, she kept saying, on the force back then. No one liked him in the Italian community, but Mary said her family pitied him and was always kind. You know, I wished when I was listening to her that I could've gone back to Upland and listened to her then. Oh, God, what I'd do for that! Nobody cared what she said, Mur. Not her husband, not her children. They'd only pay attention to her once she went crazy. It was like a big game to them. They didn't value her brain, Mur. It's something you couldn't imagine, I think, as bright and ambitious as you are. And then she talked about—"

"Ma."

"Yes?"

"Don't mean to cut you off, but I'm here. Those are great stories. I'm glad it went well. I know how nervous you were to see her. But what was the bad side? Did she mention Lazarus or something?"

"No. She didn't say one word about him."

"Oh. With me, too. So far, anyway. I can tell she wants to—so what was it then?"

"Anthony's there. I can't stand him."

"I know, Ma."

"He's the one—"

"—you borrowed money from?"

"Yes, that would be him."

The oldest brother is the tallest, the most pronounced in his Latinate features, the darkest-eyed, the longest-nosed. I haven't seen a photo of him in twenty years. Back then, I'd believed that my mother's feelings about Anthony were very important to note, and support, both as a daughter and an observer of people, since my mother likes just about everyone she's ever crossed paths with. "Mur. You can find something to love in anyone." She used to say that paraphrase of Saroyan to me more often than hello or good-bye. I think it's still true in Adultland. Hope.

"All he cares about is money."

"You told me this."

"He got that from his father."

"Ma, I—"

"The father's okay," my mother says. "But that's where the son got his obsession with money."

"You told me this—"

"Anthony Jr. is a jerk."

"Well, that seems to be the consensus opinion."

"Mary Anna and Richmond, you mean?"

"Yes."

"All he talked about was how the mainstream news gets made by left-wing traitors. Right there in the hospice, all these people dying around him. He called Katie Couric leftist scum. I couldn't *believe* that. She's so tiny and cute. Like Dorothy Hamill. You remember her? So I turned the TV off and he kept on going. Like a freight train off the track. He's like—"

"Mom."

"—one of those cable news celebrity—oh. Okay, hon. You go inside. I don't like talking like that. It's not right for me to pollute your experience before you even meet that jerk."

"I'll find out for myself."

"You won't—"

"Maybe I'll discover—"

"—like him."

"—some good things, who knows?"

I'm walking somewhat hurriedly through the lot where the valet parking booth is empty again, and, at the end, near the facility entrance, I approach a truck occupying two spaces, its tailgate covered with white cardboard, a *National Geographic*–like photo of a rat chewing its own tail on the left side and the words DEMOC-RATS ARE SQUEAKING BEHIND THE WALL. TIME TO FUMIGATE!"

"Murron? Are you there?"

"I'm here. Sorry. I just saw something sort of disturbing in the parking lot."

My mother's silence means two things. She will not, number one, be able to meet her promise of not badmouthing Lazarus's brother because, number two, the truck belongs to this brother. "Mur."

I take a picture with my digital camera for my coworkers at the *Chronicle* to lose their lunch over. The wall, I see now, is of brick, a Soviet hammer and sickle stamped across its middle. "Yeah?"

"Is it that insane truck of his?"

"Yep."

"That's him. That's Anthony."

"Yeah, I figured. All right. I got a sense of what I'm in for, I guess. The picture and the thousand words and all that."

"Oh, I'd say a thousand words is a conservative figure with a Felice."

"I won't use words like 'conservative' in the next hour, Mom. Try not to talk politics, right?"

"Impossible. Everything is political to him."

"Who knows? Maybe he won't say a word to me."

"Well," she says. "Maybe."

"That's when I'll convert him."

"Hah! That would provide you with a reason to attend Mass with me—"

"Oh God, Mom."

"—because it would be nothing short of a miracle."

"Well," I say, standing outside the tinted doors and windows, one long careful step away from the concrete ash can, the cigarettes and snipes and all kinds of random debris spilled onto the walk, "that was funny. A good note to end on."

"I love you, Murron Leonora."

"Love you, too, Leticia. See you at home."

I pocket the phone with the satisfaction of a warm conversation with my former enemy, the woman I was so angry at during my childhood. I enter the lobby of the Elysium Fields Hospice where the same inpatients from my last visit are waiting in an astonishingly straight row angled sharply to the door, each one, as if their wheelchairs were unbought cars at a dealership. I smile and nod at as many as I can, held by the childlike stares of their pure need, ancient owl eyes in the darkness of infirmity. The two men nearest the lobby bathroom are in rollicking stages of stupor, their eyelashes fluttering like my own weirdly guilt-ridden heart, a kind of survivor's guilt where no one, as of yet, has died. I feel prone to reach out and hold their heads in place.

At the greetings desk, the lobby nurse turns her back to keep talking on a cell phone, and it's okay with me. I don't need to be pampered with a greeting. I sign my name (MLT) and the time (After work) and the reason for visiting the Elysium Fields Hospice (Someone I know is here). I head directly past her desk and into the hallway, the feces-laced air accosting my relatively sensitive nostrils, and I remember my brother, long ago, telling me that if someone doesn't want to talk with you, Murron, then it's okay not to talk with them.

I'm not sure, now, that it's always the right strategy to employ, especially, say, with hesitant foreigners or the chronically shy, but back then I needed something to protect myself, and before I'd really questioned the merit of his advice, the trait had ingrained itself in me as not just habit but a fire suit of sorts. I think, deep down, I've always been afraid of the capacity we humans possess to hurt each other, which, I suppose, means in the final calculation how we can hurt ourselves. When I was a young girl, I'd come home bawling to our mother because someone had shunned me in the playground once again, or laughed at my height as I awkwardly circled the roller-rink floor in Santa Rosa, a result, more often than not, of me having put myself in the invariably vulnerable position of appealing, with hope and need both, to someone I didn't know. "Hi, my name is Murron," I must have said a thousand times. "What's your name?"

Gabe used to tell me, "You can't fix the world in a hug, kiddo," and then, behind my back, go find the poor child who'd mocked me. I hate to say it, but I learned that the meanest people on the planet can be children, who seem, if I remember it with accuracy, to bead on weakness like carnivorous beasts.

Prince has never been that way. I don't know who to thank for this, probably his father, but I feel gratitude about that noble aspect of his personality. He'll protect another child from pain, rather than inflict it on him. His second week of first grade he'd defended a boy at school. I'd called my mother from work to ask what she'd do, and she'd said do nothing. Not yet. Go into the meeting with a clear head, but don't forget who your son is. Wait until you get there to assess the situation.

Prince had been crying, I could see, and the principal was angry. My son held his head down in dejection I've seen before, and it made my initial sadness linger in my heart like a party guest who'll never leave. The other boy was holding a wet rag to his nose, glaring at me as if I, and not my son, had been the one to strike him. I vaguely understood what kind of clash of ego had occurred just by the brash singularity of that entitled look on a seven-year-old, and when he said, "You're the mother, aren't you?" the vagaries vanished. The principal muttered, "Be quiet, Todd," as if the boy had turned a card over for me to see, and then she made her case about zero tolerance of violence on her playgrounds. I nodded accordingly because, to a large degree, I agreed. But not entirely. When she was done, I let the heavy silence sit uncomfortably between us, a prelude to what I was about to say.

"There is another boy involved, yes?"

"Hmmm?"

"You didn't say anything about the first boy."

"Well, I—"

"I want to see the boy my son was protecting. These are children we're dealing with, not robots. I want to see the other boy."

"Mrs. Teeny-toe. I don't think you understand what I'm trying to get at here."

"Where is the boy my son was keeping from harm?"

"I'll be speaking with him later."

"We, Mrs. Bludecker."

"He's at the nurse's office, Mrs. Teeny-toe. I'm afraid—"

"Thank you."

"—you can't—"

"Come on, Prince. We'll be back."

Todd, I learned from the boy, had dragged him face-first through a mud pile in a hidden part of the playground. Several girls had sprinted to the teacher on yard duty, pigtails flailing, fingers pointing wildly behind them. By the time she'd gotten there, Prince was atop Todd, walloping him. Now the dirt had dried along the boy's upper forehead, the wet dirt creased in his neck. He was several inches shorter than Prince and a whole foot shorter than Todd and he had the look of a battered stray cat, traumatized by the injustice of what just happened, terrified of what could happen next. The boy's name was Darrell, I'll never forget, because his barely white T shirt said this in Old English type, right there across one corner of his muscleless chest, in cheap fuzzy black suede.

We went back to the principal's office and accepted Mrs. Bludecker's punishment. She had to maintain order, she said, and I said that's true, and thank you for doing that. I made sure that she publicly declared, to me, what Todd's punishment would be once we left. I was ready to argue forever if it was less than Prince's. It will be the same as your son's, she said, violence is violence. I asked Prince to go sit outside, and after he shut the door, I said, "Violence is not violence. Otherwise a nuclear bomb is the same as a slap. Otherwise neither the cowboys nor the Indians were wrong. I don't think your problem could have gone any better, Mrs. Bludecker. I'm sure Todd here won't drag another kid half his size through the mud again, will you, Todd?"

We got in the car and I leaned across the gearshift and kissed Prince on the forehead. He held me there by my cheeks and whimpered in the same way I used to whimper when the release of tension was too great to bear. I didn't want my son to feel good, no, but I didn't want him to feel bad either. I've never been prouder of Prince. I drove him straight out to his favorite place in San Mateo, two healthy servings of rainbow gelato at Romolo's Cannoli and Spumoni Factory on Thirty-seventh Avenue.

Now I enter Mary's room and the immediate revolt in my stomach happens with such profound force that my knees buckle slightly. I catch myself on the rail of the first bed in this room, glaringly empty of a body, empty of Mrs. Calderon, and reeking of both factory cleanser and human decomposition, Clorox and shit both. Philip Roth once wrote, "Old age isn't a battle, it's a massacre," and he appears to have been right. I cover my nose with a palm and walk by Mary's bed, the curtain pulled halfway to catch the light and let her sleep, Anthony standing outside on the porch talking on his cell phone and staring into the room in unequivocal horror, his dark eyes making the nausea infinitely worse. He looks with his long-nosed Latinate face like an older male version of me. This is not in any way comforting.

Inside the bathroom, I assume the position, hunching over and gripping my knees in automatic mode, and then I reach out and lock the door to the conjoining suite, the click, I fear, too loud, one that a nurse or a guest might investigate. I turn on the fan and vomit into the toilet. The first blast ricochets and splatters across my chin and neck. Crap. There's a urine catch strapped across the toilet that I'd missed in my haste, not only because it's so low it's practically floating on the toilet water but because I never entertained the possibility that anyone would leave behind a 31 Flavors banana-split platter with rim hooks, this because of shame, this because of courtesy, and as the acidic stench of puke penetrates my nostrils and spreads across my throat and tonsils, I puke far more than I have in some time, thinking,

Alzheimer's. Lazy nurse. All kinds of possibilities, you fool, to cross a piss basin in this place.

When I'm done, I reach out, still hunched, and yank the lever, pull my face away fast enough to avoid the "up-splash" of a flushing institutional toilet.

Next I pull the miniature mouthwash out of my purse and swish the magical green liquid through the cavern of my mouth, cheek to cheek, under the tongue and over it, across the tonsils and as deep into the esophagus as I can manage, one gagging cough catching the top of my throat, just one small splash removing any trace of the taste of regurgitation, and also the bile that eats the enamel off the backs of your teeth.

I emerge from the bathroom and he's standing there just outside the door, erect and stationary, but the consistency of his concern means it's genuine, and so I try to walk by him politely to get to the porch and its relatively uncompromised air.

"You all right?"

I smile and nod, open the screen behind the sliding glass, and take a deep breath on the porch. I'd sit but there's no chair, I'd put my purse down but there's no table, I'd walk in a circle but there's no room. I stand in place and he peeks out like a child who's just gotten caught spying on his parents and says, "Is it okay if I join you out there?"

"Yes," I say. "Sure."

I'm still smiling, and I think it's fine to still smile, especially as everyone, even someone your sentimental mother fully loathes, deserves a tabula rasa when you first meet them. If I could rid myself of the last image on my camera, his political cardboard billboard on the truck in the Elysium Fields parking lot, I could give him a brand-new blank slate. If I didn't have to read his shirt (I WANT YOU! TO GO HOME!), or figure out the historical joke of the picture (Michael Savage as Uncle Sam, World War II recruiter in white beard and pin-striped top hat, index finger chasing out illegal immigrants). I close my eyes and decide almost immediately to open them, not happy at all about this bad joke of a facial doppelganger, but ready to force myself to be neutrally kind, just as I would with anyone.

"I'm Murron."

"I know, I know. Jesus."

"Is there something wrong?"

"Oh, no. No. Not at all. It's just. Well, the last time I saw you, you were a little baby. Yeah. This big. I remember seeing you in the Santa Rosa hospital. They took you out of the main room with all the other babies because you wouldn't sleep. The doctor said you had colic. You wouldn't stop crying. I felt so horrible for you I went and prayed in the chapel. Yeah. Huh. That was a good time. We were a close family then."

I don't know what to say. I'm touched by his sharing of this memory. But it's anticlimactic to hear out of the mouth of a stranger the words you wished you'd heard from another stranger, Lazarus the Absentee, who, indirectly, made this encounter happen by being born a brother to this man fifty-eight years ago and also, the important part, making me on a reckless Sonoma evening in 1969.

"That's what I heard," I say. "My mom always used to talk about how you guys were inseparable, how she almost loved the family more than she loved Lazarus."

I can see that he's bothered by my use of his younger brother's name, and though I won't change this personal policy for him, or for anyone, I'll try not to mention Lazarus gratuitously.

"Well, yeah. Your mother's right there. About the family, I mean. We were close. Did everything together. You'da loved it. Used to have barbecues that started on a Friday evening and finished Sunday morning. Then it was off to Mass with a hangover and a belly full of meat. Boy, those were the days, I'll tell ya. Good times. We used to go fish the Presidio pier at midnight. Smoke Cuban stogies and pass a bottle of Jack around. Sing camp songs over the rail. You'da thought nothing else in the world mattered at that moment. Oh, yeah. We used to catch these blue-ridged mutton crabs and cook 'em right there under the stars. It was like having a big American flag over your head, I swear to God. Just beautiful. We had to get there before the Chinese did at sunrise. But we always beat 'em. Yep. Sure did."

"Sounds like a lot of fun."

"Was, you know? It really was. I don't know what happened to the family. I don't know what happened to the country."

"Well."

"Hey! Did you ever get a chance to see Big Vic?"

"Uh, don't think so. Who's he?"

Anthony laughs at a joke I don't get and then digs into the back pocket of his pants, pulls out a blue wallet with a white falcon upon it, the mascot of the U.S. Air Force Academy. He flips through the plastic and then pushes the wallet out at me, the contents spread open to a picture of the Felice family standing before their home, circa 1960, I'd say. It's a lovely picture, the five children of Mr. and Mrs. Anthony Felice, of varied height, in slightly varied dress, but with the same wily carpe diem look on their faces. It doesn't seem consistent with the stoic portraits of this era, the ones where it always looks like someone has died. The group jubilation is astonishing. All except one kid. He's sneering at his father behind his back, very clearly sneering, and no one but the photographer, if he's aware of it, could know. A sneer that vanishes in the air in real time, but memorialized forever. The girl, who must be Mary Anna, is about four or five and has a jump rope hanging from either end of her neck like a lei of tuberoses.

"That's Big Vic right there," he says.

"There are seven people. Which one is he?"

"Big Vic is the *house*," he says, not without a little boy-like pride. "I named it. Big Victor for the big Victorian, get it?"

"Yeah," I say. "I do. It's a beautiful house."

"You can't see it because the photo is black and white, but Big Vic is yellow."

"Okay."

"With white trim. Although, to be honest, there were a few other colors in there. Artisan surprises everywhere in Big Vic. Was like the Winchester Mystery House. You ever been there?"

"I went once with—"

"They don't make 'em like that anymore, huh?"

"No. They don't. They never do."

"Yeah, the photo's perfect except for that moron John."

"Hmm."

"He did that kind of stuff every time. You could count on it. Like sunrise, sunset. John was going to make an ass of himself wherever we went. I used to call him Derry."

He's smiling again, waiting for me to laugh.

"Short for 'derriere.' Get it, huh? Get it?"

"Yeah, I do. When is this?"

"Guess."

"I'll say 1960."

"Hey! That's close! You're smart, huh? December 12, 1963. We just put the Christmas lights up. See the grove back there, the orange trees?"

"Yes."

"That was the grove. We used to play back there. We didn't have video games or this goddamned Internet. I had my first job there. Winter detail that ran all the way from Thanksgiving to Washington's Birthday. Used to keep the smokers going at night."

"Smokers?"

"They were like barbecue pits. The heat kept the trees from getting frostbite."

"Either ice or toxins, I guess."

"No. Either dead or alive."

"Couldn't have been good for the fruit, though."

"Oh, huh, you're one of those greenies, huh?"

I know what he means, but ask anyway, "Greenies?"

"I live in Shasta. The air is clean despite all the hot air from the mentals."

I don't know what this one means. "Mentals?"

"*Mental* environmentalists. They like to sleep up there in the trees. Anytime someone wants some firewood to keep the cabin warm, you gotta wait four weeks for the mentals to come down from the treehouse. *Hey!* They wanna live like squirrels, shoot 'em down like squirrels. Rats."

"Well, I think extremism makes one lose focus, you know, whatever side you're on."

"Hey! Those rats—"

"I think the nurse—"

"—ain't worth a rusty Lincoln copper—"

"—is here."

"—penny, I'll tell ya."

I make my way past him with a gentle but firm nudge and slide the tattered screen door open as quietly as I can, nod at the Filipino nurse, who not only doesn't nod back but doesn't seem to know I'm in here at all. It's okay. I've seen this before.

"I'm Anthony Felice Jr.!"

She looks past me at Anthony, but it's friendly and not condescending.

"Hey! I want to thank you for taking care of ol' Ma here. How's she doing, by the way? Should whisper, huh? Oh, but I guess you're gonna wake her up, anyway, huh, doesn't matter. Can I open the curtain then? Is that all right to say hi?"

"Op course it is. But I hab to administer pirst the medication. Porty-pibe milligrams of moor-peen, all right?"

"Wait. What did you say again? Can you repeat that? I didn't understand what you said."

"Forty-five," I say.

Anthony shakes his head with such obvious elitist insinuations that I want to hook my hand into his arm and escort him out of the room. She didn't talk at first, I suspect, because she's embarrassed about her accent. I feel compassionate and grateful, he feels slighted and angry. I imagine that our respective political positions on the issue, whatever they are, have no more to do with anything but our respective feelings at this exact moment. Any clever puns, any word-play labels, any fire-brand speeches, any manipulated intellectual maxims, any referenced historical figures evoked in the predictably identical future are, I'd bet, sprung directly of this sentiment, right here, right now. And yet it seems to me that any real modern Californian who once or twice sets foot outside the house these days must know that it's fairly easy to follow a first-generation Filipina tackling English as a second language.

"Of what again? Was that medication you said? What kind? Can you repeat that?"

"Morphine," I say. "Don't you speak English, Anthony?"

"Morphine! Forty-five milligrams? What the hell?"

She drags the curtain halfway up the length of the bed and it's clear Mary has been awake the whole time, her eyes wide open and terrified, though glazed, the inflated tongue pushing her jaws open like a giant slug trying to escape a hole in the lawn. I suddenly realize that, cutting out the belligerence of his statement, Anthony has made a valid probe of policy.

"She's all right," I ask, "right?"

"She pine."

"I was just wondering, though, why she's on so much morphine?"

"Moor-peen help with pain."

"Hmmm," I say. "She didn't seem to be in any pain a couple days ago."

"You *here*?"

Why would anyone return to the Elysium Fields Hospice so *soon*?

"Yes. I was."

"Yesterday say her hips hurt."

"Did she fall?"

The nurse shakes her head, holding my stare in a pleading, almost desperate way that breaks my heart. I think I understand what it is. She wants me to know that she's only carrying out orders. Despite

Anthony's right to be here with his mother, I wish I were alone with this woman for a minute and we could speak freely, accent and all.

"You know, she's been in the bed," I say softly, "the whole time."

The nurse shrugs and says, "Maybe sore. I don know."

"You don't know?" asks Anthony.

"Can we somehow give her water?" Tacked to the wall above her pillow, a mere inches from Mary's head but clearly out of her line of vision, there's a red printout of an encircled water jug with a line crossed through its center. She'll probably vomit water, I imagine, or any fluid at this point of inundation. Morphine, I'd read somewhere, is a derivative of heroin. Or maybe it's the other way around. Either way, you vomit up what you most desire, water. "She seems thirsty."

The nurse looks up at me, fully ignoring Anthony. "Thee pamily don't want her take moor-peen?"

"Nooo!" Anthony shouts, and it startles me, but I recover fast. "Do you think we want to kill her? Hey! I'm her oldest son and I never signed onto this institutional assassi—"

"Anthony!" I shout.

"—nation— What?"

I lift my eyebrows, my heart in my throat, unable to look down at Mary on the bed. I hope he gets it, I hope he shuts up just once. Jesus.

"Oh. Yeah. Okay. Wanna talk *outside*? Will you join us *outside*?" he asks the nurse, but she's already on her way out the door, presumably to pass off the responsibility to a higher bureaucratic source.

"Should we talk outside, Murron?"

"No," I say, pushing by him and going to Mary's side. "Let's just be quiet, okay?"

She looks up at me the way a wounded dog does at the scene of the accident. I pet her head with as much tenderness as I can given what she's just heard, and tell her it will be all right, Mary, it will be all right, though I'm not exactly sure what that means.

It's not always good to live in a land where anything is possible.

8

Richmond Lincoln Felice
Walk Across Manhattan
June 20, 1999

IN THE CUSTOM-MADE SUIT he'd bought at a little villa on the western
Italian coast, its sheen of stark black fabric like the clean transmission
on a brand-new analog television, he walked at a good stride through
the heart of Manhattan's famed Wall Street, knowing when he saw the
peak of the Twin Towers that his destination was near. The main office
of the company he'd done so well by, and they him, Paine Webber.
He'd always felt alive walking these streets, no different now at 53,
and though he had no friends here, meaning he knew no one in New
York who wasn't in the business, and though he sometimes wondered
how you could really get to know another person on an island whose
concentration of stories was greater, now or ever, than any other place
in the world, he somehow felt very much a part of this city. He could
breathe on these streets, the unpredictable, uncontrollable flow of
people a constant reminder that life life life was everywhere, and was
exciting, and was real. He never felt queasy with the smallness of his
person in New York. To the contrary, he could exist without thinking
about himself, he was "verb, pure verb."

   Last night in the anticipation of another sleepless early morning,
he'd put on his coat and cap and walked over to the Strand before it

closed. He'd found a poem in a book of poems by an Irishman named Heaney that he enjoyed and respected on the first read, loved and purchased on the second. It was the last line that got him:

> I ate the day
> Deliberately, that its tang
> Might quicken me all into verb, pure verb.

The line perfectly captured how he felt as an exec at Paine Webber, doing communion with the moneymakers in the business. He'd aimed from the very beginning to be a figment of action, a producer of results, more than a mere subject of the whirling and incessant power seizure that went on with every interaction, big or small, between two or more humans. Business, in this sense, was truer than any academic exercise, theory, dissertation, lecture, symposium, or otherwise that, by definition, stayed safe in the cool vacuum of the classroom. Untried in the trials of the real world. They'd bend and break in the test of the furnace, melt in the relentless heat, and no one was held accountable in tangible terms. They were already on to the next big idea when the meltdown was starting. But he was a force within the universe of business, he was "verb, pure verb," he could not afford to stop and ponder his, or anyone's, pain. Not from nine-thirty to four o'clock East Coast time, not from the opening to the closing bell of Wall Street, those tinny chimes of achievement.

Everyone around him stopped at a red light. He also stopped, elbow to elbow, watching the taxis accelerate by. He loved the way the pedestrians of Manhattan fell into flow with the vehicles of Manhattan. Where else in the U.S. did this happen? The green and red lights were more like suggestions than mandates. The first pedestrian set foot into the perilous street, trusted by the next pedestrian down, who was trusted by the next, and by the next, and so forth, and so on. All the way down the line. An unwritten, fully abided civilian contract toward progression. Head-down on a cell phone, munching an energy bar, fiddling with a briefcase, a true New Yorker commenced to the next destination with the committed drive of hard rain. From above, he thought, it must look like a line of human dominoes. Or corpuscles of blood in the vein. One fearless hustling en masse organism.

The crowd moved into the street and he went with it, looking straight ahead with soldierly faith, ready for whatever would happen between now and the soon-to-be now.

Lately he'd been going to the poets again. Guys and gals like this new Irish discovery of his. Reading them whenever he could. Couldn't read them enough. He wished he'd never lapsed way back when. But that couldn't have been helped. Poetry was a form of daydreaming. Ironically, poetry was the opposite of what the Heaney poem promoted in the first place. He had to be verb, pure verb. Only a select few could daydream for a living.

Brokers were experts at the fluctuations of the market, he reasoned, poets the experts of the fluctuations of the heart. Simple, sensible compartmentalization. Businessmen had no place speaking to the condition of the species, and poets had no place speaking to the business. He thus never went anywhere near the business books. Read instead through the *Journal* at breakfast and the *Economist* at lunch.

He couldn't explain why the poems brought peace to his heart.

Was it merely ritual? he thought. Nostalgia? The mind's way of battling the past-tense eraser all around us?

It had started forty years ago on Saturday trips to the Upland Public Library with his mother and siblings. He'd get home to Big Victor with books stacked to his chin and disappear. Lock the basement door to pull through the last chapter of Faulkner, who could have been a poet, without interruption.

Faulkner.

He loved the man. Wasn't sure he understood the man, then or now. Maybe that's why he'd continued to go back, lured by the sensation of discovery in increments, tiny spoonfuls of truth serum.

"*As I Lay Dying,*" he whispered to himself, publicly hidden in the layered noise of New York, "was my favorite book."

Sometimes he'd use the rhythms of Faulkner's prose to soothe himself, not fully processing the meaning, leaving the story line to his subconscious. Because whatever stayed in the labyrinth of memory was meant to stay.

This was what impressed Richmond most. Making a map dot like Yoknapatawpha County alive in some Parisian's mind seemed almost miraculous. He used it as a kind of benchmark for the commitment one should have to one's own story. Since the world was filled with stories, it could remember only so many. It was your job to keep your story alive. This happened through the telling of it. In real life, away from the page, you told it by achievement, by seeking, always, quality of the highest order. When it came down to it, you had to have the impulsive nerve to impose your story on the consciousness of others. That was the truth no one wanted to admit. You couldn't falter in the bright light of social pressure, tiptoe in the echoing accusations of elitism. You couldn't double take for response. You had a story to tell. What's more, they *had* to hear it. Maybe he loved men like Faulkner because they'd taken the risk to make themselves known ad infinitum. And whether time would deem the risk a success would matter only to the living. And the failure wouldn't matter to the living. Because the story would have justly died if it wasn't good enough to live.

He stopped at a shawarma stand, breathless not so much from walking as from pondering the writers who sustained him. He pointed at the browning chunk of lamb spinning in the burning light. Then he looked down at his watch. Three-thirteen. He would be there with the other brokers, even if this vendor lagged, with a few minutes to spare.

He handed the young man the money, uninterested in the change. He turned and looked up at the sliver of sky knifing between the skyscrapers and raised to his toes to see more, the silver luster infinitely brighter than the three dimes in his palm. Usually he waited less than a minute at a street vendor's stand. He liked that. The shaving of the lamb was fast and efficient. And while he had problems with the way Middle Easterners viewed world affairs, he respected at minimum their work ethic, and believed that a few more decades in the prosperity of his country would reverse their anti-American sentiment. The vendor was young, maybe still in his teens. He squirted garlic sauce across the meat and said, "Yo, hea you go, man."

Then he summoned a passing woman: "Yo, Rita! Rita!"

"Fuhget about it, Pablito."

"Me esperas, mami! Tengo un gran kebab para ti, mami! Y gratis seguro!"

"Go fuck yourself, Pablito."

"Hahaha!" He looked at Richmond and stopped laughing. "Ju want something else, man?"

Richmond shook his head no, then walked to a bench to sit and eat.

This is New York, he thought, where shawarma sold by a Puerto Rican is no surprise.

You can't make conclusions so fast. Maybe never could, not now at fifty, nor back then when he was the Puerto Rican kid's age. Richmond turned nineteen his third week in Vietnam. Almost a month in, he was still looking for anything he could relate to. He tried to buddy up to a vet from the Gulf Coast, asking if it bothered him that a Mexican was running point. A stupid question. He was trying to make conversation. Stupid reason. The man looked at Richmond like he'd just been insulted. As in who in this godforsaken hell is your cherry ass to question who's running point in this outfit? Or to assume that I'm stupid enough to put my life in the hands of an incompetent? Or to assume the racial issues back in the world upon me? Or to mistake a New York Puerto Rican for a Mexican?

His was a five-man team running covert recon missions on the Laos-Vietnam-Cambodia border. Unlike his brother Lazarus who actually killed people, Richmond was a medic. He'd never fired his .45, though he'd unholstered it countless times. He didn't want to kill people, he wanted to heal people, even at risk to his own life.

He'd once been a promising seminary student back in his late teens. And then, also, in a forward-thinking way, one that assumed his own charmed survival through a tour in Vietnam, he chose to be a medic since the knowledge could be directly transcribed, upon his return to the world, to a career in medicine. It might even impress a few civilians, while, by contrast, the skill set of cleaning an M16 clip would mean nothing except to a lunatic serial killer.

Once in a hooch on a safe LZ over the course of a bath-warm, sponge-wet Vietnamese night, he read the entirety of a package from his mother. She'd sent the paperback he'd asked about during a phone call months earlier, Styron's novel *The Confessions of Nat Turner*. Reading the passages, he couldn't keep the story free of his own team's diverse racial composition, which was either proof of the betterment, however leaden, of American society or of the absolute need, however loaded, of the camaraderie birthed of war. The intimate dance with death called all to the floor of slaughter. He defied anyone to claim that their time together was defined in any way other than brotherly, truly brotherly, and yet he hadn't spoken with one since he'd flown out of the Southeast Asian peninsula thirty-one years ago. Not one. They each could be dead, or alive but without home. One of them, Richmond thought, may be in Vietnam right now. Vietnam forever. Coconut could have bought his ticket, having gone back for another tour, and already on his crap-shoot third with Richmond in '68.

"Coconut," he said aloud now. "Coconut."

The heavy gunner from Hawaii. The army didn't make helmets big enough for his gargantuan Polynesian head and so he wore nothing but a bandanna, which was nothing but a black T-shirt ripped right down the middle and cut into two strips with a bowie knife. Richmond had watched him do this, had oddly never considered the improvisation. Coconut could make a radio out of tinfoil and a fork, could haul his twenty-five-pound 60 as if it were a five-pound 16, could construct the best hooch, which meant the driest, in two minutes, could find inner peace in the deadliest bush in Vietnam. Richmond imagined

Coconut's village on Molokai as a smaller version, in strictly topo-
graphical terms, of Vietnam. The opposite of where he came from.

"It don't mean nothing," he said.

The statement surprised him. That's how they used to talk in the
bush. Dropping bombs of nihilism into the conversations. "Don't mean
nothing." "Fuck it." But Richmond didn't talk like that. Back then
he'd feared that the use of the vernacular would dumb him down,
would unlearn him of proper grammar. The brownness of the language
terrified him. His dream of a life in verse was more poignant than
ever in the jungle, maybe had kept him alive. His team called him
Poet, first with denigration, then with affection. He worried that if he
talked like they talked he'd never compose anything of permanence,
his pockets empty at the toll bridge between the base continent of
commonspeak and the deserted island of poetry.

Coconut never spoke more than a sentence at a time. Naturally
happy to communicate in grunts. And he called everyone "bruddah,"
even the enemy. Whom he called "dose little slant-eyed bruddahs."
He talked about them as if they were merely children given grown-
up guns that just happened to be instruments of destruction and
that just happened to be aimed at you. Coconut's equanimity about
the greater political reality necessitating their life-or-death situation
simply amazed Richmond. It was almost transcendent.

Coconut seemed to understand the Vietnamese in a subtext of
language inaccessible to others on the team. Anytime they had to
deal with the natives, Coconut was the first to squat down in the
middle of the circle, drawing diagrams in the dirt for the benefit of
a gawking crowd of Montagnards. They'd happily peck at a popped
can of beanie weenies like a brood of human chickens. So naked
and soil-encrusted they looked like they'd been born of the earth
itself, bastardized sons sprung of the mother planet. Not a trace of
the just-passed moment, fire built, fire put out, literally less than five
minutes of planning, cooking, and eating, nearly unfathomable to
Richmond in the awake time of his basically safe and perfectly clean

Upland, California, rearing. He'd been incorrigibly lost in translation too often in Vietnam.

He and Coconut could sit for countless hours without the need to speak. This was almost more foreign to Richmond than the red Southeast Asian soil itself. He could practically hear the echoes of the Felice family conversations from across the ocean. But this was silence of the purest sort with Coconut, no need to accommodate the other person with a word, even as the jungle around them pumped out its untraceable sounds, avian symphonies with no curtain time.

He realized now that Coconut had taken him under his wing those first few weeks in-country. He'd kept Richmond alive, had kept him on the radar.

What we know about life, he thought, is that time moves, always, too fast. We can't ever get ahold of it, just can't get our hands around the truth. Not even the truth of our memories. We're like monkeys trying to make amateur shapes out of a palmful of water. The memories, Richmond reasoned, mean something only if we're wiser for their remembrance, or if we get a chance to relive them with the very people in the memory. Those people, he thought, are by now so far gone in your life, or so much different now that they're just as good as gone, or so far under the ground, or so far whatever, that the excursion down memory lane, in strictly business terms, strictly useful terms, is too often a futile operation.

Now he took one last bite of the shawarma, tossed the considerable remains of it into the garbage can, and walked toward the building in which he was to give the first-quarter report on the overall status of his eighteen West Coast offices.

Inside the Paine Webber building, he handed over his ID badge to the security guard, saying nothing, giving the guard no eye contact at all. He took the badge back without acknowledgment. He got into the elevator and hit the button for the fifty-eighth floor, and stood there looking at himself in the golden shine of the doors. When they opened, he walked through the office, nodding curtly and respectfully at employees he'd met before but couldn't say a word about. He tried recalling his brothers at war. His arms ran with goose bumps at the realization that it wasn't just Coconut. He couldn't remember *any* of their real names. Five men. Not one. And not just that. He'd never inquired if they'd even made it back stateside.

On his twenty-second birthday, he'd brooded over the possibility that he actually hadn't made it back. That something of his very essence had died in Vietnam. Something like his soul, his inner being, the stuff that mattered. He really didn't know why, but he went to a few rallies to hear speeches. He stood far outside the crowd, balancing on the balls of his toes, his hands filling the bottomless pockets of the dark green army jacket all the way up to the forearms. He was waiting for something of which he knew nothing. Not in the occasion, and neither out of it. Not a supporter of, not a rejecter of. He didn't know what to do about it. He felt neutral. A little more than a year after the Summer of Love, September 1968, Richmond Lincoln Felice was back stateside ready once again to figure himself out for good, meaning for betterment.

He grew a handlebar mustache and did Dylan songs at the local café, no microphone, no sheet music, just a busted desk chair with painted-on rainbow stripes. He sat ankle over knee, a used Fender occupying the triangle of his lap, face dropped in deep sorrow like a saint in a Renaissance fresco. He was a mediocre musician but had a mysterious stage presence that kept a few regulars from leaving. He never said a public word. Never touted a position. He watched on the TV a poet named Robert Lowell walk the streets of D.C. with a crowd of long-haireds on his heels. He read Mailer's book. He smoked grass in the local park at midnight. He wondered.

After several months of this downtime, no one but his wife knew that, day by day, this disposition of wonderment had become increasingly forced. That he was being, as he was always prone to be, an American romantic.

Had he missed something when he'd quit Uncle Sam's army, a handbook with a prescribed list of approved behavior for vets?

In a weird way, he couldn't believe that that's what he was now, a bona fide veteran with a CMB, the latest edition of the fine men he and his brothers on their banana bikes and wooden foot scooters had searched out for stories at the VFW Hall in downtown Upland. Though he never dared say it, he might have even been a hero. Maybe. Probably not. Okay, definitely not. But there was a major problem. No one of his generation gave him the respect a veteran inherently earned in returning from the theater of war. He hadn't been spit on, but he also didn't feel like a veteran in the public eye. Which was maybe the most important thing back then, especially during the alone hours. If you knew yourself to be x but no one treated you like x, were you in fact x?

When his wife told him, "Get a job, we need money," he didn't ask a question, didn't half-step. By the time she started to show in the belly, he was two months into trimming pine trees at the park near their house. He had been accepted into the business school at the University of California, Los Angeles. Within a year, Richmond was on the dean's list, the first of seven straight semesters. By the time he'd graduated magna cum laude, his son was almost three years old, and he was off to Princeton for a master's in business administration.

Who had time to look back? he thought now, making his way into the Paine Room, saying hello to colleagues, firmly shaking hands. Big Vietnams, little Vietnams. The next flying bullet could have your name on it. You had to earn your life, you couldn't take a break. Who had time for a mental respite?

I don't, thought Richmond. No one with any success does.

Verb, pure verb.

Someone handed him the papers. He had no idea what they were about. Didn't care. These people would get precisely what they wanted. And what's more, he was the chosen one to give it to them. Was all about articulation. All about holding down the boardroom.

His reputation at Paine Webber was spotless. Still, he took the papers because a big part of the business, he'd learned long ago, was taking the papers graciously even if you had no intention of taking in the *contents* of the papers. A cursory glance, a nod of conviction. This wasn't dishonesty. Was another handshake. Respecting the process. People were involved. He did the same at art galleries. Even the best of them, MoMA, the Louvre. One of ten times he came upon a gem. Would practically set up a cot right there under the soft lights in the showroom. Who knew how it happened? If the report was meant to be reviewed, ingested, studied, it would present itself like a Rodin replica in the middle of an American strip mall.

He took his seat, smiling absently, unaware that he'd lost eye contact with everyone in the room, and that a few had even registered this breach of etiquette. He read the lead sentence of the promotional pamphlet: "Here at Paine Webber we keep our eye on the prize." This obviously was right. A girl had once laughed in his face. He'd just recited Rilke to her in the German. A freshman in high school chasing the senior cheerleader. Shooting for the stars. Afterward he swore he'd succeed just to spite her. The last he'd heard, she was waitressing in a karaoke bar in Pomona, and he hadn't asked about her since. That was just after Vietnam. That was justice after Vietnam. He'd forgotten her name. The spinster at his favorite Italian villa had embroidered his handkerchief, RLF. He'd forgotten her name, too. May have never known it. Money talked. Got him what he wanted. He'd forgotten the name of the villa. Pleasantries were good to give but weren't exactly important. Not a single nicety made a bit of difference in the imperial annals of history. Faulkner once told his own daughter that no one remembers Shakespeare's little girl, my dear. He could remember the villa if only some warm Mediterranean scents could be airblown through the sterile vents of this office. Where no evil virus had ever lived. He could recommend Italian cuisine at least for the Christmas party.

Well, maybe he did have too much on his mind today. Could use a memory drain, a neurotransmitter toilet. But he recoiled from the thought. At the very hour the scientists would invent one, our story would be done, we'd be finished as a species. Your memories made you. You had to love your story. Because you had a place in your story. And yet memory, it seemed, was very simply an impediment to good business. You had to keep your eyes up and away from the ground. Appearance. Composure. The collective singularity of purpose. Clarity of vision, execution without the fetters of outside influence. Clairvoyance, clairvoyance. It was do, it was go, it was ignoring any consequences that didn't contribute to enterprise.

In order to do good business, thought Richmond Lincoln Felice, you have to deny the reflexive devices to search out, reflect upon, and then eliminate the contradictions of life. Which means in translation the ways in which you've outright failed.

"Since yesterday was Father's Day . . ."

He looked up, blinking. He'd completely forgotten. Not forgotten this year. But forgotten for good, as in forever. He'd stopped recognizing it after Richie had died, six years without the holiday, and somehow without even a said word between them, his wife had known exactly what he'd wanted, and gave it without a glance of dispute. She said nothing, signed no card, bought no present. No mention of this gesturelessness except, in a kind of parental balance, the understanding that Mother's Day had also died.

". . . and so in honor of that, because you know none of us could have gotten here without a loving shove from behind, it's the truth that however great we all think we are, we've gotta remember those who put the food on the plate, right, who—"

"Okay, Todd," someone said, not without a hint of affection. "We get it."

"Yeah. Well. Anyway, I thought we'd go around the room and ask you to share what you love about your father. Can keep it short but sweet. Don't be afraid to spill it, though. There's always something each of us can learn from old Dad, whoever's dad it was."

"Hear, hear."

"Rich? You wanna start?"

A bad day. He was sweating. Didn't dare look around. He dried his forehead with the RLF handkerchief. Back in the San José office, he had a baseball cap with the word WAR emblazoned across the front. He'd don it sometimes when things were going badly, and he had to remind himself to fight through it. In 1993, he might have worn it every day. He'd bought the hat in the fall of '81, his first year in the business, looking for Bach albums at Tower Records. The three capital letters were burned into the black backdrop, redder than a ripe pomegranate, the brim curled militaristically, no measurable resemblance to how the Hispanic fans of the group for whom the cap had been manufactured wore it. He'd redefined it for himself, a simultaneous act of business brilliance and cultural ignorance. The genius and the fool. He was a Nietzschean, a fine businessman.

At home there was no hat to hold in all the pain in his cranium. The untouchable demeanor he maintained at the office softened, and often he'd stand in the early morn before the fourteen-by-eight oil on canvas for hours on end, each minute a reminder of his own private sin of piety. He punished himself, he never sat. But the subject of this piece sat, a dead-eyed teenage boy with full-blown AIDS sagging on the edge of the bed, stabbed by the cutting shards of intricate shadows, as if the moon itself were cornered in Richmond's living room casting its own dead eyes on "The Virus." He'd bought it for $6,000 from an art dealer named Junker in the Mission. Sometimes it seemed that he could take on the pain of the painting if he really tried, the fresh scabs of the deep abscesses on the side of the body, the bones of the ribs spurred against the skin as if the rib cage itself were screaming to escape its host, the ghost-white, bloodless face exhausted in the flood of torment that came with each eternal moment of a heartbeat, remaining until the heart was shocked enough with the horror of what it kept alive to finally quit the only function it had ever known.

"Rich?"

He said, fast on his verbal feet, "That its tang might quicken me all into verb, pure verb."

"What's that?"

He didn't dare look around, dabbing at his head again. "I'm sorry," he finally said. "Was thinking about something else. Please excuse me. But it can't wait."

He rushed past the group and out into the main area of the office. He went directly to the bathroom, a steady stride even when his shoulder collided with the door harder than intended, right by the folded towels and flattened newspapers cornered on the motion-detecting sinks. Mirrors outlined in shiny golden trim. He couldn't look at them. Instead, he twisted into the handicapped toilet. No one had a handicap up here. Not in the most expensive real estate in the world they didn't. He whipped around and locked the latch anyway. So that no living person could see this pathetic display of anti-business.

He stood in a puddle of piss, trembling. He pressed one hand against the wall to support his body, fingertips softly stroking the grout between the tiles. Then, without the offense of sound, he wept, his face dropping into his free hand as if he were blocking from vision the very site where this hideous violation was occurring. The code broken on unclean ground. Where the damaged came to hide. He could stay in the stall until the end of the day for all it mattered. Until the pores of this story were dry as a desert. He feared that these tears probably didn't count in the end. He was held to the same standard as he held everyone else.

Life, because of death, went on.

"My son," he nonetheless whispered, over and over, as far into the hour as he could stand of himself.

9

Murron Leonora Teinetoa
Discussion After the Long Day
November 30, 2007

I WALK THROUGH THE DOOR of our apartment, saddled with the dying story of newspaper, feeling so low inside I take in a deep breath before entering. A friend just fired, or "let go" is how they'd put it. The journalistic euphemism always at the ready, an especially valuable skill when cutting the cord on one of your own. Let us find the beauty in betrayal. Trick the about-to-be-executed into one final smile for the camera.

Can't come up with a euphemism, though, for Giorgio Grant's thirty-one years of relatively devout service to those good people of San Francisco interested in the adopted son poetics of the brilliant Thom Gunn ("His traditional style carrying this untraditional theme," he'd written, "is so startling, contradictory and yet sensible—he's cleaning his underbelly by lashing his back with iambic meter; he's the trainer and the lion taming himself; he's his own dominatrix and supplicant—that I took a walk across a few of our fourteen hills before picking up the book again"), the sagacious masterpieces of Kay Ryan ("No one can touch this woman. Pound for pound, she's the wisest scribe on the planet. I would never attend a Kay Ryan reading so as to hide the small shred of self I have left from her knowing eye.

I am absolutely terrified of her"), or even a recommended literary meandering through, say, the watercolor aesthetics of Derek Walcott ("Walcott is in love with himself and thank God for that. I can't wait for him to wonder about classical music or sculpture. He's our last Renaissance man, mon, the Caribbean Da Vinci").

And so now the survival of the last legitimate lit crit venue on the West Coast pends entirely on me. No more poetry, just fiction. Godspeed, good luck. My paycheck neck on the fiscal chopping block of the *San Francisco Chronicle,* the figures "wholly [my] responsibility since [I'm] the last of the Mohicans. No one's left. Jeez. Look around, would ya?"

Well, I've looked around. I know who I see. What's most ironic is the ease with which these supposed progressives get caught in the old capitalist trap, that nothing is worth keeping that doesn't earn money. Not even the existential story, which buttresses the "hard story," imposes quality on all story, at a place where story matters *most*. Plenty of things that go into making this life work can't be quantified on a short-term spreadsheet, but who'd ever know?

I didn't see it coming, even in this dumb and happy, shortsighted state without culture. California. The state of mind without culture. I guess I'm at fault for failing to prognosticate the possibility of apocalypse. The first obligation of anyone trying to love anything is that you have to preserve what you love. Preservation, in its truest definitional form, means the daily warding off of death.

In college I was so much into the notion of fairness that I was afraid to say something could be bad. I tried hard not to say that one opinion was better than another. I stayed away from the easy elitism of academia, principally the presumption that a scholar's word trumps all others. Their interminable claim on credentials. This was easier for me than for most others at Stanford because I wasn't intimidated by the life experiences of our professors. The exchange for a brain, it sometimes seemed, was that you didn't live, that you observed life from the safety bubble of the classroom, through the vicarious existence in a book. Their authority was mitigated, or at least asterisked, by the absence of real experience. The liquid lens of the safety bubble distorting what's real.

But then came the Internet. Abuser of equal opportunity, the egalitarian's wet dream. Where any street-corner quack can rile up a thousand hits, private public playground for nuts of every sort. It's as if none of these people understand the idea of earning one's keep, of making your bones. The pendulum has swung too far to the other side when any kook can blog about books, and no one will say that his opinion is worse than another's, even when the other opinion comes with the sacred stamp of the *San Francisco Chronicle*, a tradition going back to the middle of the nineteenth century.

The editor of the tech page once said to me, "I thought your kind is into equal access for everyone."

"I am," I'd said.

"So what's the deal?"

"I'm into quality more."

The deep contemplative trawl has always ruled the book. However little they'd lived, my professors were right. Sensationalism perishes on the page, as it should, because men and women are willing to die over one divine word. I'm not being romantic. How is that possible? I'm not one of those people, after all, who does what I admire, and thus I recognize my water-girl status. I don't have the talent to write a lasting narrative, and my heartbreaking realization of this years ago was nothing short of a chain-breaking moment, where I was finally free of the unattainable story of my own great expectations.

"Hi, Mom," Prince says.

"Give me a big hug."

Maybe it's tough to take my mind off the place I just left because it felt like I lost the argument. But what about my son? Doesn't he have a right to critically acclaimed books? Why should he read some vanity-press crap from a Facebook friend when I, or someone like me, could have done the siphoning for him?

"Why are you still watching television? Where's Grandma?"

"In the back room."

He pulls his head away, arching his spine and tightening his stomach, and I pull back just to test his strength. He doesn't have to try too hard to break away, taking my bag without shame and hefting it over a shoulder like a junior postal worker on his route. Prince loves to show me how tough he is because, he thinks, one day he may have to shield me from the meannesses of the untamed world outside our apartment.

Preserve, ward off death.

This life makes me sad sometimes, which maybe is just another way of saying it wears me down. I've tried to protect him from the dysfunction that can occur inside our little apartment, the domestic trials that can ruin your insides. All with the hope that if I fortify his internal spirit, he'll be safer in every endeavor, he'll be more prone to survive. I don't care about success as much. If he has it, in whatever way, I'll be happy for him. If he doesn't, I'll be here to remind him how fast things can change in this life.

I pour a glass of moscato, sip so slowly that I can feel it wet my lips, tingle across my tongue, and trickle into my system, warm as coffee down the throat. It feels so good, almost like the wine plays a trick on the mind's processing system, such that the digestion goes directly to the heart, not the intestines. My chest is heavy with nourishment, and I feel the *thumpa thumpa thumpa* of my heartbeat so pristinely I can almost hear it.

"Hi, baby."

She kisses me, I kiss back. "Hey, Ma."

"How was work, baby?"

"I guess if I were to critically assess it, work really sucked."

"I'm sorry, baby."

"A very bad book entitled *Tuesday*. By Moneymaking Moron. You wanna laugh, Mom?"

"Yes, I do."

"Today they complained about the novels I chose to review this past year."

"Really?"

"Yeah. Can you believe that? Two of them are finalists for the National Book Award, and another gal was called 'a Marilynne Robinson in the making' by the *Times*. For what it's worth, I said she 'perfectly understands that goodness comes from looking up at, and not looking down on, the reader.'"

"That's a very nice sentence, honey, but I don't understand."

"They want Moneymaking Morons like Nicholas Sparks."

"I like him."

"I know."

"Don't get mad, baby."

"I'm not, Mom. I just want to—"

"He writes a clean story."

"—finish my anecdote. Yes, I'm sure he does. Look at his photo on the jacket, for God's sake. He looks like a Romney son or something. His whole family in the shot. Dog, too."

"Don't be mean."

"Joking, Ma. Somewhat. But back to my day. So they asked me to review some novel about bulimia because—"

"Oh my God."

"—because, here I'll quote, 'It's a real hot thing out there, Mur, and, well, your firsthand knowledge on the topic could enlighten a whole generation of girls.'"

"It's none of their business!"

"Amen."

My mother is considering the therapeutic benefits of me delving into me. Or what ails me. "That is horrible, but, honey."

"No, Mom. No Sparks in my column, no barf book on bulimia. They're *wrong*, okay? My job is to review books that matter, not save the world."

"But—"

"Or save myself."

"How could you—"

"No!"

"Okay."

"Don't want to argue, Ma. Actually wanted to make you laugh."

"I know, baby."

Suddenly I remember two lines of an unpublished poem I'd written entitled "Anger": *Anger is the elixir for internal surrender. Anger has a lot to lose, including itself.* "We can move on, can't we?"

"Of course, baby! We can do *anything.*"

"You're funny. Okay. So how was your day today?"

"Well, something important happened."

"Good?"

"No. Well, maybe it *can* be. But I don't think so. Oh, I can't say."

I wait, knowing I'll have to ask. My mother's always belaboringly building up to drama, partly out of her indecisiveness, partly out of her desire to lure you in. I think she thinks that prompt delivery would somehow mitigate the compositional power of a story.

"So?"

"Prince watched a documentary today on cable news."

"Here or at school?"

"Here."

"And?"

"It was about that shooting at that southern college."

"Virginia Tech?"

She nods, says, "I'm sorry. I didn't know."

"About what? The shooting or the—"

"No, no. That he watched it."

"But you were here the whole time, right?"

"He watched it at Jaeshong's house."

"Okay." This surprises me. Jaeshong's parents are famously strict. It's one of the reasons I've felt relatively comfortable having Prince visit so regularly. There's only one way this happened. "So Mr. and Mrs. Han weren't there."

"No."

"Did you talk to him about it?"

Prince has returned. The somber tone of our conversation, I suspect, keeps him from asking me about my day.

Anger finishes the child was a middle line.

"A little bit, but I don't like talking about that stuff, baby."

"I understand, Mom. Who would?"

"Are you mad, Mom?"

"No, hon," I say, ruffling Prince's hair and pulling him in again. Life is crazy. Here I've been worried about the books my son will read one day, and he's been taking in the most selfish massacre of the young century on TV. These types of ironies occur more often than someone like me is willing to admit. "Just kind of worried. Did you watch the whole thing, hon?"

He nods. "That guy was crazy."

Another line: *Anger is the mother of every murder and the spurned son of every sage.*

"Maybe worse than that," I say. "Now, you listen to me, Prince, okay?"

He looks up at me, unblinking. I remember now. Senior year at Stanford, a poetry class with Eavan Boland. She said I had the poet's fury to "keep the word alive," and was disappointed when I'd called her eleven years ago about the job offer at the *Chronicle*.

Anger always ends in peace, I'd written, *one way or the other.*

"Some people will try to say there was a reason he did those things. I don't want you to listen to those people. What he did was absolutely wrong—"

"Evil!" my mother shouts.

"A lot of people," I continue, "will feel pain and emptiness for the rest of their lives because—"

"Him."

"—of what. Yes, honey. You're absolutely right. Because of *him*. And of what he did, honey. Even his own parents and family have—"

"I know, Mom. I saw it. They said they're ashamed for three hundred years. They read a letter."

"Those poor people," my mother says.

"He was a coward, Prince. You know why? He didn't try to find love, you see? It's out there, honey. All over the place. Sounds silly, baby, I know, but you remember you can always talk to me about *anything*."

"Okay."

"And your grandma, too."

"And Dad, right?"

"Of course."

"How about Uncle Fatu?"

I nod. "Um-huh."

"How about Auntie Peka?"

"Yes. The Teinetoas are a good family, honey. You have a good name. You can talk to any—"

The phone rings.

"—one of. Hold on. Give Grandma a hug. And you promise to talk to me if you feel like it, okay?"

"Um-huh."

I pick up, not relaxed exactly, but somewhat relieved. "Hell—"

"Murron."

"Yes? Who's this?"

"You are not to interfere with Mother's care, do you understand? You are allowed to visit with—"

"Mary Anna."

"—her, but that is all. You will not be allowed to speak to her care nurses disrespectfully."

"What are you talking about?"

"Murron. Murron. You will not speak to me the way you spoke to them, are we clear?"

"They weren't changing her diapers!"

"You will cease and desist from this at once, and that is not a request."

Suddenly the moscato does another system switch, the *thumpa thumpa thumpa* relocating in the middle of my head. *Cease and desist?* I close my eyes, the swirling tidepool starting in my stomach, then open them and find my mother standing next to me.

What is it? she silently mouths.

Nothing, I mouth back.

"Mary Anna, I'll go where I want to go. Do what I wanna do. Are we *clear?* That's what happens when you turn eighteen, if I remember correctly. That was two decades ago for me. Clear-minded people do what they want. You don't have any say over what I do."

"Oh, yeah, right. Smart-ass. Ms. Independent. That's exactly like you, isn't it?"

"Are you kidding me?"

"You're just one angry little girl, aren't you?"

"Hey! You don't even *know* me! Don't call here and bring your *shit* to my house! You don't know a thing about where I come from! And what kind of *idiot* uses the words 'cease and desist,' anyway? Why don't—"

"Yeah, sure, uh-huh."

Click.

My mother looks up at me, horrified. Both of her index fingers are plugging my son's ears from the anger. "What is it?"

"She hung up on me!"

My mother's almost crying. I take another deep breath, keep my eyes away from Prince's accusation of hypocrisy.

"Who, honey, who?"

I breathe out. "That would-be sister-in-law of yours."

"*That* Mary Anna?"

I pour a full glass of moscato, my hand trembling, a buzzing sound coming from somewhere down below. "Mother?"

"My phone," she says.

I hope, I pray, I want so badly for this to be an old friend from her AA society in Sonoma, or one of her church cronies at St. Luke's, even, by God, the late and delinquent Lazarus of yesteryear.

Please be Lazarus.

"Hello?"

Right from the start I can hear the yelling through the phone and I think less of myself than for my mother, who wouldn't be involved without this call, who couldn't defend herself from a pillow attack by kindergarteners, and then the old guilt creeps into my heart of all those times in childhood when I'd bathed in my own wounds at my mother's expense, the woman who single-handedly raised my brother and me on $400 a month, the instinct to defend a parent rising in me, as it does in my own son, so profoundly.

"Prince," I say. "Go to your room for a minute."

Right when his lavalava disappears down the hallway, I grab the phone from my mother.

"—and she is not to visit her any longer and if you would *please* cooperate with us on this, Leticia, it will be the best thing for everyone involved. She called me names and she had the nerve to tell me I had no business—"

"Mary Anna."

"—telling her—"

"Mary. Anna."

Beneath the anger, a pause. She didn't remember the important detail from our coffeehouse conversations that I have a roommate. She thought she'd get my mother's damaged, unprotected ear.

"Don't you ever contact my mother and bother her with your guilt-ridden bullshit. *Ever!* You bully hater bitch."

"What? Is that a reference to my—"

"You heard me. Bully. Hater. Bitch."

I hang the phone up this time. I'm embarrassed by how good it feels. I don't care for the moment. Despite myself, I want to patch things up with my mother.

"I'm sorry, Mom. I feel so much venom around people like her."

"It's okay, baby." She pats the top of my hand, absolution for my predictably belligerent response to what I view as injustice. The irony is a bit much. Being on the other end of pity from a family member you're financially supporting and, a decade ago, had saved from the insane asylum.

"Think so?"

Her hand encircles my own and she pulls it into her chest, bends down, and brings it to her lips. "I know what you're doing, baby. And you're right to fight."

"But I'm not fighting. Just trying to do the right thing, you know?"

"I know."

"Wish it would pay off now and then."

"I know you're trying. Why would *I* of all people think otherwise? You're so brave, baby. I couldn't say all that to her. But I am saying this to you. I love you for taking this on, dear, I really do."

For what it's worth, the words are like flower petals tickling my inner ear, the goose bumps now running down my neck and across my arm like tiny heaven-kissed raindrops that will never evaporate, that will help me rise one day from the pillar of self-hatred.

Up off my knees and into the waiting world.

"I'm gonna go talk to Prince," I say. "Try it again."

10

Richmond Lincoln Felice
Drive Through the Tenderloin
March 10, 1996

IN THE QUIETEST HOUR of the early morning, his wife would finally fall asleep. There was no longer any bed talking between them. He considered her silence during the day to be evidence of her decency, of why he'd married her so long ago. Commitment like this was a lesson of a sort for anyone on the planet. She hadn't added a single dramatic note to the opera of their lives. All of it had come from the outside. And he wasn't being romantic, no. Or, rather, he *was* being romantic, but it was without a choice, really. Or so it seemed. There was nothing else for him to feel these days but the real pain of true love, which he knew to exist now, and could never doubt again.

So when the normalized breathing came, he knew she was down for the night. If he didn't think about things too much, the quiet in their spacious room was very peaceful, and Richmond would rise with no urgency, all to prolong the peace. He'd head down the stairs, holding his breath.

In his office, he'd leave the lights off at first. This was his ritual. Always sit there in blackness for a few minutes, looking down at the void of the hardwood floor under his feet, wondering what he could have said, could have written, could have done to have reversed this course, eradicated this moment, kept his son alive. An extra year even, a single day. And not the kind of day they'd shared in the hospital, his son exhausted on the soiled bed, bones on the bridge of collapse, wrapping of scab-infested skin burning with infection. But a day where the dead weren't calling from the graves, and a twenty-three year-old young man might ponder the world around him, inside him, might think of those who loved him.

There are books of our lives, he thought now, kept closed by the weight of our silences.

He heard the crackle of floorboards overhead, and he knew she was awake. She was coming down the stairs. He sat upright, flicked on the light switch, and waited. She went past the office into the kitchen, and he heard himself breathe out through his nose.

A late-night snack, he thought. Well, that is good. A gesture of nurture to the body. Bottom-line signing of life's petition. Good.

She came back and knocked lightly.

He wasn't sure how to intone his answer, surprised by her rising at this hour, and so he hurriedly stood and rushed to the door, slowing for a split second as he gripped the knob, opening it cautiously, as if there were a stranger on the other side and not his wife.

"I feel like taking a walk." She was dressed for it, energetic, tossing an unpeeled orange from one hand to the other.

He almost asked, At this hour? but instead said, "Can I come along?"

She nodded. He threw on a pair of sweats, slipped into the cow-skin moccasins, a gift from one of the three Christmases after his death, and followed her into the night.

She went fast, as if someone were behind her, and he kept up, exhilarated by the present tense of this action. A few minutes into the walk and he couldn't stay with the now of the moment, sabotaged again by memory. He thought about the early days in this city when they were so ambitious with plans. Younger than the other couples in the apartment complex, Las Casitas, but they felt older than they were, more mature. Whether it was true or not, their plans were bigger, and this secret they held onto together, like a rescue line dropped from a helicopter. Their discussions back then always began with the goal of children, lots of children, "so many," he'd say, "we'll need separate rooms to stop making children."

The thought of children helped him shelve Vietnam and go forward with his life. The song of experience was powerful and permanent, but it wasn't the only song out there.

That was Blake, he thought, discovered at the Upland Public Library.

He missed those years he'd spent hidden in the dusty stacks. Anthony was the first to walk him up the aisles, pushing the frontier heroes and revolutionary fathers on Richmond like a lonely tour guide in some dusty museum. Richmond was sure, daydreaming in a monsoon-drenched hooch, that his big brother was telling the same tall tales in the trenches of a bratwurst smorgasbord in Germany. With Anthony, you had to ignore the repetition and focus on what sat behind the passion of each anecdote, a vague truth waiting to be specified. Yes, it was exhausting, and, no, not much intelligence came out of Anthony's mouth, but Richmond believed that manhood was indeed forged in death, just like his big brother said.

By that qualification, he thought now, stretching out into the street, crossing in three long strides, my own son was more a soldier than Anthony ever was. Died at seventy-nine pounds. Bruised skin and old lady bones, but a man. Died in manhood.

His son never asked him about the war, not one question in the seventeen years he'd lived at home, what the death of another man really meant up close, what it looked like, not shocking or impossible but just sad very sad, how you lucked your way into and out of a firefight, how keeping the self calm was the only real skill left in modern battle, a self-prodded pseudomiracle that sometimes, with luck, saved you. Never wondered aloud why he'd even gone in the first place, ordered under duress or volunteered with pride, the politics or patriotism of it, why each of his brothers save one had also gone, what it meant, even generically, to their parents back in Upland. Once he'd shared at a weekday dinner a scaled-down story about his mother calling the White House every night for two weeks, how the runner had snidely delivered the note—an order for Richmond to write his mother—from some bureaucrat in D.C., and Richie had excused himself in the middle of it.

A soldier's survival of Vietnam was no guarantor of strength to his son. Richie had viewed his year of service as the just price of social cowardice, proof that his father had philosophically buckled to that old bullshit code of manhood, forged by the flames of war. His son's outlook burned up his blood, threatening to unravel the stuff that made Richmond who he was.

And then the outlook, he thought, became a lifestyle. And the lifestyle became a life.

"It's who he was," he said out loud, coughing into his hand to cover the confession, his wife picking up speed as if not only had she heard nothing but that no words were allowed during the sacred hour.

This is San José, this midnight in the first quarter of 1996, this is here, now.

The effeminate mannerisms bothered him early on.

He loathed the way his son stretched out his syllables to hold the conversation. Richmond would go days, weeks at a time without noticing it, and then suddenly he'd catch Richie leaning into the kitchen island, hips pushed out, head thrown slightly back, breaking eggs into a mixing bowl for breakfast. He'd whip the whites and yolks with too much wrist, looking up and talking shop with his mother, beading on the perfect recipe for quiche. The image would stay with Richmond through the bulk of the day, and he would combat its claim on his mind almost consciously, tell himself that his observations, for once, were wrong.

He'd prod his wife with his worries and suspicions, indirectly try-ing to figure Richie out. "Is ice-skating a sport? I mean, it's more like a performance, don't you think? The spinning and the pirouettes are nice, I admit, physically difficult to pull off, but I don't get the appeal there for a young boy." "What is it with the style now, huh? The black turtlenecks with tight sleeves. The designer sweaters from Paris. It's not the money necessarily. But Laz and I used to sport a T-shirt and blue jeans, you know?"

Even an encouraging aspect of his son's life developed, under better focus, into another concern. Yes, he had a lot of friends who were girls, beautiful tempestuous creatures who took care of themselves the way wealthy girls do, but their interactions with his son seemed sterile. They were always whispering into his ear and slapping his knee. Richie seemed incapable of eventuating into the last interaction, the good pairing where Richmond's experience as man might be sought out by his son.

Sometimes if work at the office lulled, his brain would drift without discipline, and he'd throw out a line of reasoning to see what he'd bring in. Let's not forget, he'd start, that Richie's eccentric. An artist. Deeply involved with his music. His ambition drives him but also blinds him. He doesn't yet see them as they are. But he will. Boy, will he. Soon enough, the only thing he'll be interested in. Will drive me crazy talking about it. Will never shut up. He's a late bloomer. A good-looking kid. He's got no zits, but his smarts make him odd. He doesn't know his own potential.

"Richmond?"

They were standing in front of an Afghan liquor store on Second and San Salvador. On the window were colorful, even lovely posters promoting a film in a language that looked like scribble.

"Do you want something?"

"Well," he said. "It's closed."

"Seven-Eleven a few blocks up."

He didn't know this. He looked around and said, "No."

"The park then."

She walked on, and he followed.

Once in the late eighties his wife had said, "Richie's going to the prom with Molly." He reached for his best bottle of port in their wine pantry and said, "Good, very good." He could still see himself pinning the hundred-dollar bill to Richie's lavender boutonniere, saying, "Take your time, son. Don't rush back, okay?"

Later that summer she told him about Richie's first time with a girl. His son must have been a sophomore, just barely sixteen. His immediate thought wasn't about the risk of pregnancy, the curse of a lifelong STD. "Yeah?" he said, and when she asked if he wanted to know the details, he said, "Oh no no no. Let him keep something for himself."

Now they crossed the intersection of San Salvador and Third and the city opened up to Richmond like a clam. He blinked a few times in the twilight. A 522 bus stop popped out like a prominent skyscraper, the hooded dealers deciphering undercover cops in the shadows. Above this, a downtown art studio lit up like a scene from the stage, the clutter of cardboard, acrylic paint, and used easels governed by some limp-wristed charlatan who couldn't make it in San Francisco. He saw all of these features of the city as if he knew them himself, recalling the images like a memory. He could almost feel along the skin over his spine the damp bed of grass under the Calabazas Bridge, that covert quarter where he imagined his son to have taken his johns, the trickle of polluted creek water cooling their naked bodies in the midnight hour.

They were passing the Vietnamese restaurants he hadn't once tried in two decades, and for some reason the CLOSED signs made him sad for their existence, as if the condition were permanent and there weren't an OPEN sign on the other side. A few homeless people were crouched around the dumpster digging into styrofoam bowls of cold pho, their broth-drenched beards glistening like seaweed in a bed of moonlight. The image made Richmond nauseous. There was something uncivilized about them, the frenzy in their eyes almost like war itself, predatory, and he grabbed his wife's elbow and pushed her along, the light at the intersection cycling from red to green without a pedestrian or car anywhere in sight.

She reclaimed her arm almost immediately, and he knew from the fierce pride of her movement that she'd walked these streets before, maybe at this hour, certainly alone. She wasn't afraid, she didn't need him.

Rebecca had told Richmond that their son had gone into these restaurants, and it had surprised him then, but not now. He'd never known enough about his son's life to keep him alive. He'd stayed safe in what he knew about Richie. By the time the boy reached his teens, he didn't dare ask the tough questions. He left that to his wife, the mother as friend, confidante. She knew things about their son that he didn't want to know.

Funny. Tragic. He'd never put any of his money, after all, in a B of A savings account. He'd always scoffed at those cowards who earned 2 percent on their fortune. He loved to research the trends, do the work behind the scenes that no one else would do, and then take the educated risk, get the bone he'd earned. He'd been confident in his ability to rebound, to learn learn always learn. If he'd made the wrong choice, he'd be back, he could recover. But with his son, the money just sat there waiting to be picked up, handled, wagered. The paternal fortune squandered.

In the empty hour of this city, he was learning more about his dead son than when he'd been alive, close enough to touch, real enough to listen to, present enough to love.

He was right there, Richmond thought, looking over his shoulder at Mi Canh House of Pho. My son was right there.

Sometimes he felt like a historical scholar of Richie's life, discovering revealing artifacts about his son in hindsight. Chipping away at the dirt of his grave, sifting rock from bone, separating weed from tendon. There were a thousand known tragedies when it came to his confused species, but this phenomenon of learning more about the dead than the living was especially troublesome. Like some kind of key to a question everyone had. It was as if the condition of living, with all its mad autonomous unforeseen trajectories, was too hard on one's system. That you couldn't take in another human being's story judiciously, not even someone you loved. That is, with the kind of all-consuming study requisite of respecting the experience.

It seemed to Richmond that connection between people was actually the truest kind of denial. Which didn't speak well to the notion of a family. That maybe death was no more than a corridor where the formerly living gathered to be understood by the presently living.

Now they were moving stride for stride down the hidden streets, long stretched-out strides, emerging out of an alley in the darkest hour like two thieves on the make. At Market and San Fernando, they cut across César Chávez park. New territory for Richmond. He heard the deep groan of the city sweeper, felt its middle-of-the-earth grumble, turned his head and it was nearly upon him, awash in red and white lights like a traveling carnival gone astray. He moved closer to his wife, who hadn't slowed or acknowledged the noise, right through the ankle-high amalgamation of detritus, the needles, the bottles, the clothes, in the same forward unconscious push of this gutter machine spinning the wet leaves and broken branches into itself.

They were gaining momentum on he knew not what, sidestepping the half-eaten, graying remains of fast food, avoiding the blacked-out transients sprawled on beds of flattened newspaper, crumpled newspaper pillows, tented newspaper blankets, faster now, almost speed-walking, they passed a brood of pigeons roosting on an unused vendor stand. Lined along the Hot Dog Taxi like planes on an aircraft carrier. Not one pigeon awakened, no bird feared their presence. The words were lost between them, their combined silence loud as a hushed breath in the ear.

The stoplight at the end of the park rotated in the vacancy of this hour, another happening with no discernible cause, civic inefficiency, energy spent on nothing, loss loss loss, and though he would someday remember, he knew, this cold night as one of the important moments of his marriage, Richmond felt further from his wife than ever before. This despite their thoughtless synchronicity, the matching breathing. No habit, no ritual could diminish the chasm between them.

The death of a loved one, he thought, sweeps you up into the highest reaches of connectedness, nearly heavenly, seemingly permanent, and then drops you back down, when it happens, to the sober ground of your life.

His scabbed-over body so magnified on the bed that you forget about your point of contact, not here in this hospital, astride the unbathed, the tortured, the lifeless, but there—*in fact, right there!*—in the warmest hour of the town you grew up in, a few weeks back from the war, arm-in-arm amnesia of the savage jungles of Vietnam, Third Street, Upland, and its beautiful little civilized heart again—*you made it back! were spared!*—the dream of learning the world's mysteries no dream at all.

Maybe, he thought, the vision of their son enshrined in the dying hour had replaced the marital bond. Had become the embodiment of their connection, more so even than in birth. Maybe that's why he'd died. Was all his body could hold. Maybe they, he thought, had taken a toll on *him,* and not the other way around. The pressure of their desire too much, the load of their story too heavy. Impending death, identical tale for the eschatologists to bicker over, read aloud in both directions.

Dear God, Richmond thought, arms looping high in front, behind him, almost violently. I killed my own son.

"What's wrong?" she said.

"Nothing."

"Keep walking," she said. "It helps."

"I know."

"Okay."

Maybe you also knew of his death, he thought, all the way back to his birth, when you'd seen the claws of life choking him not eventually but at once, baptism in stagnant oxygen, his clean uncontemplative nine-month free float through the womb now polluted for good, meaning from here on out, pollution going forward. And from this knowledge of your son filtering the world's backstory for the first time, a kind of blindness occurred, like an anemic queasy from seeing blood.

This the wrong night, the wrong city, to soak the soul in regret. They walked deeper into its dark guts, and just like that, despite himself, he came upon the memory of discovery. Triggered by the far-off tinkling of a storefront sign. The reminder of failure, like the sweeper they'd passed, always back to the gutter of life.

The brothers, even Johnny, wandering through North Beach, right down Columbus Avenue, dropping into their favorite haunts for a drink—Tosca, Vesuvio, the Stinking Rose—slapping hands with the old Italian men summoning women half their age at the velvet-lined entrance of the restaurants. The feeling of freedom increasing with each step, something magnetic pulling them along on this cool San Franciscan night, no mention of money, no talk of business, this two-year-old tradition of tackling the city once a month the best thing they'd done together since joining up.

Now they jumped into Anthony's brand-new '86 Cadillac, piling into the car as if it were their father's Mercury station wagon, their shared blood boiling now, this last night of being united, thoughtlessly, in brotherhood.

They drove through the city, the lights dancing into the car and then streaming out, determined to take the night to task, ride this mad horse of a Caddy the distance. Johnny shouted epithets at pedestrians, one hand gripping the dash, the other clutching a bottle of wine, and here Richmond pressed his face to the window, having no clue where they were, a mere three minutes into the ride.

So much of the city seemed repetitive to him, the same story with different characters, but now he thought that he, too, could live here someday, bring his family to San Francisco and try something new, why not, he'd just cut the biggest deal of his career, securing the account of the premier oil mogul in Bolivia, and what else was money for than to open the world's gate, afford opportunity, get you into the show? He'd done the dirt labor of the young broker, taking mental notes of work ethic during walk-throughs at start-up companies, reading the *Economist* after hours for leads, keeping to the mission of finding the money trees of the fertile Silicon Valley. They'd renamed it, after all, for a reason. The cash was out there, and this thought propelled him to try to relax, taking the bottle of port offered from the front seat, downing the contents in two deep swigs.

"Hey!" Anthony shouted, spinning the wheel with a forearm, chin over shoulder. "Save some for the oldest son!"

"Already gone," said Lazarus.

"Just drive the damned car, woman!"

"Fuck you, Johnny!"

"Afraid he's right this time," said Richmond, smiling. "The lights are nice until they're police lights."

"Why don't you listen to goody-goody back there, Anto-nia?"

"Hey! Keep it down, you civilians! I'm driving!"

Anthony commenced to sing, "The Battle Hymn of the Republic," a few decibels louder than Culture Club's "Karma Chameleon," which was plenty loud on the radio, and just as ridiculous.

They were winding down Lombard Street, trampling rows of bushes and flowers, and he could feel himself succumbing to the fraternal momentum, the easy victory, the release of any aspiration to be better, do right, to be good. Not get bogged down by the herculean concept of purpose. It was as if two or more men gathered in anyone's name was just trouble, but there had to be at least two, and they had to be men. That's how the planet's every tug-of-war began.

Anthony angry at the wheel, Johnny riding shotgun, checked-out Lazarus to Richmond's left. We all go back, he thought, to the same warm womb of Mary Capone Felice. And this was how they'd grown up in Upland, the blind energetic social assumption of his brothers perfectly familiar to Richmond. One had to cooperate, or try to be communal, to pull it off not *for* others so much but *with* others.

That's what he loved about the business. You relied on everyone out there, producers, sellers, consumers, *and* brokers. Being in business was the purest statement of belief in people coming together, in the story of the country earning its keep, that we could get it done better than anyone. His job was to gather under the flashing stream of the market and bark out interpretations of the digits. To sway. And influence. He brokered stocks, this was his life now, and his very first law was to convince at all pure, isolationist costs.

"Hey, Laz." Lazarus nodded, kept nodding. "I think you might wanna look into HP sometime this week. They're putting out some good stuff these days."

"Good stuff," said Lazarus, nodding.

"Yeah. This'll be a strong quarter for them."

"Shut the hell up back there, ladies."

"You shut the hell up, Johnny, and let 'em talk business if they want!"

"Business? Richmond don't know a dollar from a dime. He's gotta get—"

"Shut up, Johnny!"

"I know, never wrong, blah, blah, blah."

But he had made mistakes in real life. He didn't know a thing about his son that mattered, afraid of what he'd find in his boy's uncontained mind. The ultimate teenage contrarian, that's what he'd become, less than a year from the right to vote. The thought of conversation with his only son terrified Richmond, an old failure that was coming, he knew, to constant fruition these days, encouraging him to go back—*fast!*—to the work, to breaking down the easy intricacies of stocks. Inanimate, egoless, always present-tense money. He wanted to like his son. He was tired of loving despite. That's what he'd grown up with, loving people you couldn't stand.

They were speeding down California now, Anthony gripping the wheel in soldierly focus, the green lights luring them deeper into the city. Richmond watched the nightclubs going backward outside and he caught the names—the Roxy, Easy Andy, 24 Hour Diner—the same way he used to catch baseballs, squinting, head slightly turned.

They passed Hyde, Larkin, the car's interior now flooded in fluorescent lights, and as he saw the green roll to yellow on the corner of Polk, three dozen men walked out of a theater, in twos, threes. The light turned red. They slowed to a stop and Lazarus asked, "Where are we?"

"Don't try to act like you don't know," said Johnny. He pushed out a can of beer, and Lazarus took it. "Drink this, boy."

"Nothing shocks you, does it, Johnny?"

Johnny put his head out the window and shouted, "Hey, bitches! I got a golden rod you fags can fight over!"

"Roll the window up!"

Now Richmond's smile spilled into laughter as the window sealed the brothers unto themselves, the unfettered stupidity of Johnny issuing Richmond into condescension-based joy, the regal demands of his elite heart put on hold with the present company, three men who knew, each one, that he was *better*, despite his errors, than they were, he was amazed, almost enthralled, by what he saw outside, couldn't believe that so many men, who weren't men in his mind, would put themselves on public display and risk everything, especially, he thought, when there was so much to lose, he was wondering why a light turned red when it did, the mechanics behind it, the mass coordination of an underground street grid, he watched them spread like a virus across the walk and recognized the waif's swagger down the curb, three fast steps to his black pimp's two, skin of the protruding bone-thin hip bright against the darkness of the guiding hand, limp wrist hooked into the front pocket of this block of a man, the words RELAX ballooning out across his billboard chest.

He slid down fast in the backseat, at least half a foot, ass over the edge, back curled, his eyes even with the horizon line of the hood, which he could see like a dark hollow between his two brothers. Anthony muttered, "Holy shit," which meant that it was too late, he'd seen it and understood, and then, toward the passenger seat, "Shut up, Johnny!"

Johnny was howling with his head cocked back, whipping his head around in search of Richmond, as if he were taking the baton of laughter passed on from a teammate, who was watching him sprint to the finish line of hilarity.

"I said, shut the fuck up, Johnny!"

The car went quiet in a breathless hush that made Richmond's arms run with the kind of goose bumps he'd felt before battle in Vietnam, the mad-rush drug of adrenaline, and as they watched Richie hang to the monstrous arm like a human purse, the tight polyester turtleneck choking his eyes up into the perversely raw face of this man, desperate save-me trust at the kennel, he thought, weirdly, angrily, For fuck's sake! Basic law of physics! Look for cars crossing traffic! Look for cars!

He slid farther down the backseat of the Beemer, Richie luckily not recognizing Anthony's new purchase, the shine of his son's lacquered-with-pomade head claiming his vision for a second, and then gone. The world wide open with the unknown, the absurd, stupidly coincidental life.

Thousands of intersections in this fucking city, thousands!

Now he walked with his wife of twenty-nine years, knowing it was she who was better than him, so loaded down by the weight of yesterday's cowardice, the kind that never outdated itself, that he started to slow, to lose his breath. He couldn't keep up with her fierce clarity on this night. She would have gotten out of the car right there on the corner of Polk and California to claim their son, he knew this, pimp or no pimp, laws or no laws, damn the social shame.

"You know what," she said now, her words startling him. They'd reached the outskirts of the city, entering Guadalupe River Park at the same wild speed. "We used to come here together."

He'd assumed his wife's thoughts were far from his own, but how far away could they really be? "I know."

"Must have been a hundred times. And yet all I can remember is a winter evening in the eighties. The seventies? For the love of God, I just can't get it."

"It's all right. I've forgotten a lot, too."

"You know why I remember it?"

He knew that she was about to indict herself.

"Because I didn't want to be out here. It was freezing. You couldn't see a star in the sky. I just looked up. Felt like I was caught in a box of steel and concrete. And wires. Telephone wires everywhere. Like a goddamned fishnet. And he was moping like he does, you know, when things aren't right, and I just kept thinking over and over, 'I hate my life. I want another life. I don't want to be here.'"

He took her hand and held it to his chest. He didn't want to lose this, too. A transient passed them on the path, but they did not look up. Maybe, if he hadn't ducked down in the backseat, hiding from the truth in a tree house of fake privacy, they wouldn't be here now drowning in memory's wake, she wouldn't walk after midnight ever again, their union unthreatened by yesterday.

"I meant, Rich, that I didn't want to be a mother. That I wanted another life, that something was slipping away—I don't know what. I thought I'd be better in a role that wasn't so . . . giving. I was never meant to be a mother."

"Nobody is meant to be anything," he said, thinking, Nobody should outlive his own son.

"That's not what I'm trying to say."

"I'm sorry. I'm listening."

"Do you believe in God?" she asked.

The question surprised Richmond. He looked over at the sandbox where kids played during the day, their happy heads popping in and out of the red plastic holes like gophers'. But his image spoiled in less than a second. He imagined a drug dealer atop the slide looking

down, squirrels scuttling through the trees, the gray sky almost white
in spots, like cowhide.

"No." He didn't like that he whispered it, which made him sound
unsure. "Not anymore."

"Well, I do," she said. "We've switched, Richmond. I do believe
in God now."

This surprised him again. He'd always relied on her silent atheism,
a safety net he'd jumped into when he'd quit the bridge of theology.
He returned to the old question: How much have I missed of my life
being gone sixty hours a week for twenty years?

"Because if I never wanted to be a mother, I shouldn't be a mother.
That's what's right. You can only be what you want to be. I know this."

"When I was studying for the seminary, I—"

"Oh God, Richmond! Please."

"I'm sorry." He felt on the verge of an inner collapse, something
he'd never felt before.

"I don't want the boardroom speech right now."

"Forgive me."

"To hell with the experts, okay? I don't care what they say. I'm telling
you one thing, and I want you to listen." He nodded, but she talked
right through it. "Don't think you're the only one who can crucify
himself. I pray for sleep. I sit in our closet for hours when you're off
on your business trips. I should've laid down on that shit-stained bed
and died with him. God, I hate this confessional bullshit."

He was hurt but he did his best not to show it. He'd always thought
that the strength between them was confession, that this kind of sharing was uniquely theirs, something others didn't engage in. Something
that, precariously, had survived their son's death. And yet here he was,
questioning it like he questioned everything now.

In Vietnam, he'd known that death made other things in life more
certain. Now he wasn't so sure. Because the deeper you thought on
something, the fewer pillars you found to lean on. It was like every
idea, every belief, everything you'd die for was built, deep down, on

air. Like life was a dream, some poorly delivered gag gift where you got to float on ideas, beliefs, and then nothing.

"Well," he said. "That's all right. We don't have to talk about it."

She took her hand away and walked ahead of him. The hurt was so strong that when he inhaled, his lips trembled. "Should I leave you alone?" he asked.

"You fool!" she shouted. "You goddamned fool!"

She hadn't bothered to turn toward him. She sat down on a bench and wept into her sleeve. He honestly didn't know if he should sit and comfort her, stand and watch, or leave. Maybe she wanted him to leave.

"My love," he said. "I don't know what to do."

"It's okay," she said, fast and hushed. "Sit down with me. Sit right here."

He took the bench, vowing in his mind that he would stay even into the late morning if it was the right thing to do. If only he knew what that meant. If only he could stop thinking.

I I

Murron Leonora Teinetoa
No Country for Old Men in Starbucks
December 9, 2007

HE'S SITTING AT A WIDE AND UNSECLUDED handicap table by the window seats, sipping something very hot and reading a newspaper. Judging by the towering height of the stack, I know it's not the *Chronicle*. True to the West Coast intellectual inferiority complex, they don't sell anything else at the South Bay Starbucks but the *New York Times,* so must be. I smile at Richmond when he spots me, and he nods once, looks back down at the paper, not at all casual in his cobalt-blue jacket, startling black turtleneck, beige designer slacks, and beautifully shiny leather shoes.

Wealth sometimes seems to be no more in substance than a fashion statement, but I'd be lying if I said that he didn't look nice, and gentlemanly, and that it didn't somehow extend, true or not, to who he is as a person. That this promise of public display is, on its face, a hint of the lavish private parties and pyramidical hedge funds achieved only by the throwing down of an absurdly fat stash of money. Anyone can see that he's very sure of himself, even here on the rugged ethnic East Side of San José, where he must look like a target to all the slack-jawed tweeks and dark-eyed dealers amassed in the smoggy heat less than ten long yards from us, Darwinian depravity and American extravagance divided by a tinted, shaded, air-conditioned window.

I know I'm being picky, but I find it disrespectful, even rude of him, not to hold me here with a friendly smile, or easy eye contact, especially given my absence from his family, or vice versa. He's saying, at least outwardly, that the worlds-colliding article he's reading takes precedence over common courtesy, that he's going to find some random gem of data in the two seconds' time it takes me to reach the table.

I see this kind of stuff at work too often, and I've never really gotten used to it in all my time there. I work with journalists, Professional Opinions, newspaper people whose sense of self-import is legendary. But the era of Henry R. Luce and William Randolph Hearst is long gone. Those kinds of people don't exist anymore, or at least not as ostentatiously, like the egomaniacal five-star generals of yesteryear.

"I think we should move."

"Hello, Murron." Still reading his paper. "Do you want anything?"

"No," I say. "Should we be sitting here?"

"Sure. Why not?"

"Oh," I say. "Was just wondering about the table, that's all."

"What, this?" he says, waving off the international blue sign with the white wheelchair in the center, finally looking up from the article. "Don't worry about it. No one's here. Sit."

I'm not sure I want to argue just yet. Before even sitting. Seems small-town and somewhat unnecessary, at least until the moment when the significance of this designation comes into play, but it bugs me that there are a half dozen other tables he could have picked and he took this one. It seems a very *male* thing to do, an overt challenge to the way things work. Not the proletariat challenge looking up but the aristocratic challenge looking down. Caesar dismissing his minions with one prolonged lion yawn. Which, I think, is probably worse. The social unrest coming not of desperation or need but of whim and privilege. But maybe the near emptiness of the place put his social conscience to momentary rest. After all, I've been to desolate strip malls in northern Santa Clara where ten consecutive unused handicapped spaces meant you had to walk half a soccer field from the closest legal parking spot to the door of the Hallmark store.

He covers the sticker with his newspaper, a hardly subtle statement that he's both staying and not worried about the rules. "I'll be the first to give up my seat if someone needs it, okay? Come on. Sit down. We have some important things to talk about."

"Okay."

He finally gives me real eye contact. "Great paper, huh?"

"It is," I say. "They have a lot of money."

"Ever think about getting out there and writing for them?"

"No."

"I think you'd be great. There's nothing like New York."

"True," I say, "but it's also a two-way street."

"What do you mean?"

"Just that if nothing's like New York, and I'd agree with that statement, then we're necessarily different."

"Hmmm. I'd say it's a matter of quality, though, wouldn't you?"

"That's some of it, for sure. Great writers out there. The sheer numbers usually mean a great output. In whatever field. But it's also a matter of writing what you *know*. The question of the native authority of a storyteller, and the people who criticize her."

His eyes are narrowing into slits of skepticism and so I decide, somewhat reluctantly, that I'll go deeper than I normally would into this issue, one I've spent serious time pondering, and that always seems to arrive by complete surprise, like an annual book award. Despite reviewing scores of New York novels and story collections annually, I vigilantly believe in the fictive power of the West Coast of this country which, like New York, is beyond comparison. Plus, I know my constituents out here who read my column, and I like that I know them. There is the old reliable lit-loving crowd at City Lights Books, which has somehow survived, like its nearly nonagenerian founder, Ferlinghetti, this terrifying gluttonous century between a second-story fire escape and Chinatown, and there are the bright- and sometimes cross-eyed youngsters over at 826 Valencia who, whether it works or not, always seem to have a unique trick up their sleeves. There are the yuppie families up on Nob Hill and the flocks of streetwalkers in the Tenderloin and, now and then, there are even a few curious suits in the Financial District. It's not that I don't think I could compete with other critics in New York. Even Michiko gets one wrong now and then. No. It's that I'd lose myself. Anytime I've pondered a life in the Big Apple, I've had an apocalyptic zombie nightmare of me wandering displaced and emaciated through the labyrinthian streets of Manhattan, thirteen days of lonely anonymity in a bustling city of millions, lolling tongue in grotesque salivation for a single square foot of belonging. Something in my center, near my heart, magnetically pulling me to the western edge of the island where I keel over and die facedown in a bubbling froth of sewage. I feel grounded on the West Coast, and also at my best, and I hope it reflects, naturally, in my work.

"Have you read Stegner's *Where the Bluebird Sings from the Lemonade Springs*?"

"No," Richmond says. "I haven't."

"He talks about the power of a West Coast tale and how it really can't be processed anywhere else."

"I'll have to pick it up."

"Definitely. You know, Hemingway and Steinbeck tried to live and write in New York City. Did you know that? Neither did too well. They left before they'd even settled in. Hard to imagine George and Lennie looking for the rabbits in the Big Apple." This does not make him laugh. "I'm just a critic, you know, but I know where I'm supposed to be."

"Well," he says, straightening his issue of the paper as if setting it up to be framed. "I guess there's some merit to that. You're a Stanford girl, I know, but New York's not for everyone."

His tone says that since I don't think I'm good enough to be out there, I'm *not*. It's somewhat annoying. I mean, we're in a Starbucks in East San José, the center of central California, thousands of miles from America's metropolitan mecca, and he's drawing the conversation, and me, *east.*

"I'm not going to New York."

"Okay. Well, if you ever change your mind, I know some people out there who I—"

"I won't be—"

"—could introduce you to."

"—changing my mind."

"You a McCarthy fan?" he asks.

"Yes," I say. "One of his originals before he got famous. *Blood Meridian* is a masterpiece."

"I just read *No Country for Old Men.* Another masterpiece."

I'm not sure if he's trying to share or instruct, but I disagree. "Well, McCarthy is so good even his average efforts are better than the best effort of others."

Despite his encouragement to abandon ship for literary New York, he doesn't like that my carefully chosen words are a carefully chosen contradiction.

"What do you mean exactly?"

"Well, in *No Country for Old Men,* it's sort of like he's now bemoaning the very world of violence that he brought to narrative fruition. No one in the history of American literature has set out to beautify violence and death more than McCarthy. He'll spend five pages describing two seconds of a beheading."

"Well, that's war."

"No. That's *combat.* There's a difference."

"Maybe you need to be a little older to appreciate what I'm saying."

"Maybe," I say, nodding. "And maybe you need to be a critic to criticize literature."

"You're pretty invested in books, aren't you?"

I say nothing. There's an insinuation behind the question that I don't like.

"And how is your son?"

What a transition! "He's doing fine. He gets out of soccer practice at six so I can't stay too long."

"Changed your mind yet about that?"

I hope he isn't asking what I think he is. It's already been a bad start and why make it worse? "About what?"

"Keeping him from us."

"You have a funny way of putting things."

"Are you afraid that we don't like indigenous islanders?"

This time it's my turn not to laugh. I don't want to argue with him yet again, but we're talking about my son. My son. "That's not the point, but let's say you don't, okay? How would I *know* one way or another? How would I know *anything* that really matters about you people?"

"Well, us people came from somewhere, too," he says. "You know, Mom and Pop faced a whole community of bigots to get married. I'll bet you didn't know *that*, huh?"

What do you say to a question put so insultingly?

Did I know the history of northern and southern Italians vaguely enough to appreciate sectarian tensions in a strange new land in the early twentieth century?

Why, yes, I did.

Could I imagine that it was unforeseeably difficult for Antonio Constantino Felice to marry Maria Serafina Capone in 1941?

Well, in fact, I could.

Did I, as a bastard child of the Felice clan, ever hear about the town-hall fight in downtown Pittsburgh once the folks wed?

Actually, your own son once told me about it, asshole.

Yes, that son.

"Of course," I say. "But it's different than the organic bigotry of this country."

"Meaning?"

"Well, I guess I mean that rivalries tend to dilute once you cross a big enough ocean to come here. Like that scene in *Godfather II* where they all stand up on the boat when they're passing the Statue of Liberty. Remember that? It's a beautiful scene. They all take their hats off, too, like a chorus line or something. Sometimes overseas enemies even team up in America." He's rolling his eyes. "No, really. Pakistanis and Indians in an Apple cubicle. Guatemalans and Michoacanos on a Ford assembly line. One of Lokapi's cousins recently married a Tongan. Tongans used to eat Samoans." He neither laughs nor smiles. He's waiting. "Literally eat them."

"Okay, Murron. What's your point?"

"Well, it's the old stuff that started *here* that really counts. Where whole peoples were ruined." Now he lifts an eyebrow, as if my theory on prejudice is pure bullshit, and so I say, "Yes, that stuff, those peoples. Never heard of the five hundred smashed tribes? Sambo Crow laws?"

"Jim Crow—"

"It was a joke."

"Look." He sniffs and frowns, repositions in his seat. "Life is tough, Murron. For everyone. I imagine that Mom and Pop would say that bigotry is bigotry."

"Well, if they would, they're wrong. The way you're putting it, everything's the same."

"Mom and Pop fled the state in '45."

"They didn't flee for their *lives*," I say. "If anything, they fled from their own respective *stories*. There's a difference between getting a new start and being a dozen terrified steps ahead of the noose. I mean, how else do you get a Malcolm X—"

"Malcom X?"

"—from a Malcolm Little? Yes? I mean, what are we talking about here?"

He smiles and it's totally disingenuous. He's bothered by my words, and it's funny. He acts like his frustration is supposed to matter to me, like his transparent attempts at being surrogate sugar daddy are what I have been waiting for all my life.

"Let's bring the conversation back home," he says.

"Back home?"

"I don't want to talk about some revolutionary for black America right now, is that okay?"

"You're free to talk about anything."

"Thank you," he says.

"I believe that was the whole point of that black revolutionary guy."

"Listen, Murron. Slow down, okay? I guess I'm just trying to tell you in no uncertain terms that I support your right to raise a son without the father around."

"And I'm telling *you*," I say, "that your support, while nice, has no *place* in my life. Let's drop it. I was a mother for eight years before our conversation, and I'm gonna be a mother for another eight no matter what we agree on, okay?"

"Murron." The grave tenor in his voice and the quick look to the ground where he shakes his head mean, I think, that we're going to have it out some more. "Do you know what it's like to lose a son?"

"No," I say. "But I know what it's like in reverse."

"Not that your missing father, my brother, is any of my business."

"Well, now we're getting somewhere."

"You know, I don't think I've ever met a more cynical woman in my life."

"Passive-aggressive people bring out the worst in me. It's why I have very few girlfriends."

"You've just compared me to a woman."

"Well, yes, I did. I did just that. Sorry. I can't stand the catty stuff women do to reduce another woman."

"That's pretty funny."

"Do we want to stop this stuff then? I don't mind changing the stage set. At least the tone. I can do it. I want to."

"Yeah. Sure. It's just that I can't believe you're the same sweet child I used to send boxes to."

I can see the image of myself as a scrawny girl sprawled on the kitchen floor of our trailer, his UPS box of Lazarus's wartime memorabilia spilled across the tile like cat litter. I can smell the first ammonia bite of my mother's coal-filtered Lady Lee vodka, enviously watching her children fiend on the relics of a missing man. "You sent one box."

"Murron, you should open yourself to other opinions."

"And you didn't even have the right to do that."

"Guard against defensiveness."

"And sending a box to us doesn't mean you *knew* me. Or *us*. Jesus. This is just a simple matter of critical thinking."

"Fault me all you want, but I just wanted to do a good thing. Just like now. Try not to think about yourself for a moment. Please. Let's think about your son."

I can't take his piety anymore, his certainty of self. He's like the stereotypical Seventh-Day Adventist at the door, peeking in the blinds, sounding the horns of judgment.

"Why would you advise me about parenting?"

"Well," he says. "Maybe you could learn something from my own failures as a father."

I suddenly realize that I don't know anything truly pertinent about Richmond's life except some of the more isolated and prominent details, which are necessarily distorted by virtue of their isolation and prominence. I know that, like Lazarus, he was in Vietnam during the war, that his son died of AIDS only a few years after I'd met Richie in Paris, that he made a fortune in stocks.

"But what makes you think that we share the same problems?" I don't want to be ruthless, but he's given me no choice. "I mean, do you even know what a Samoan is?"

"Why should I care about that?" he says, smiling.

"If you really want to get to know Prince, you're gonna have to learn something about the people who raise him on weekends and vacations."

"But where am I? This is my native country, yes? I've earned the right to be an American, haven't I?"

"I asked you one question and you ask me three. I really don't know what you mean by 'earned.' Maybe we all earn it in our own way."

"Well, I did go to Southeast Asia for a year."

"Uh-huh."

"Nothing compares to war. I know. I was there, okay?"

It's about him, what the war made *him*. Not about others, the bigger picture of our story as a species, how people other than himself—maybe, just maybe—truly suffered. He's possessive of his tale, persuasive Alpha Storyteller, and he thinks he's got the market on suffering. It's either uninformed or selfish, but either way, it *is* American. He's right about that.

"Yes, it's safe to say war is our most trying circumstance."

"For you it was a circumstance," I say. "For others, it's life."

"Murron. Are you going to give me a civics lesson today?"

"Well, for a man who deals with numbers to ignore numbers—"

"You're not talking to my brother, Tony."

"—when they apply to human beings seems strange. Numbers don't mean anything until you put the human story to them. In this case, a million Vietnamese dead—"

"I also went to a good school, Murron."

"—and another tens of thousands dead in a border war with China—what's that have to do with it? I don't care where you went to school."

"It's very impressive that you attended Stanford on your own dime, something to be proud of, but I've got you by almost twenty-five years. A long time ago, I went to an Ivy."

"That's great," I say. "How do you know that doesn't make you antiquated instead of wiser?"

"Well, let's just say I've been around, huh?"

"I think we should drop this." I have no idea what "this" is, but I'm still willing to give it a try. "Let's remember what we're here for."

"Yes," he says, smiling, "let's do that."

"What *are* we here for?"

"Well, we sure would like to meet Prince," he says. "You should bring him down here sometime."

"Jesus. Pleeease."

"You can't protect him from the world forever, you know?"

"I agree, okay? You can't hide a kid from the world. It's not right to create a hermit. As near as I can tell, you're the only one who's suggesting I'm doing that."

"Well, sometimes it takes family to point out truths we need to hear."

"I'm telling you that I'm not sure you're even family, do you *get* that?" This hurts him. I don't care. Sometimes it takes strangers to point out truths we need to hear. "And on the flip side of your argument—"

"I'm not trying to argue."

"—why should I put Prince in a situation where he could be abandoned? He doesn't have to worry about that with his father's people. And then what real value do you or any other of your siblings serve if the one sibling I come from doesn't show up to the party?"

"Laz is like that with everyone, not just you."

"I don't care about *me*! I'm talking about my *son*!"

"Calm down."

"I'm talking about his *grandson*. And I'll tell you something else. It doesn't bother me one bit that he wouldn't show up to a party of yours." He's hurt again. I don't care again. "That's right. You're an adult. Get over it. By the time we're eighteen, we've hurt as many people as have hurt us. Or at least we're starting a list. I'm talking about a kid with a clean enough slate to reverse all this shit 'Laz' and people like 'Laz' have created."

"People like us have created."

"Yes," I say, taking a deep breath. "That, too."

"Well, I don't really see how a kid seeing family can hurt, but okay."

I get the sense he said "family" on purpose. Forget the fact that he's never met Prince. He feels like his right to his own words means his own words are *right*. This is the stupidest and most pervasive kind of intelligence out there.

"Soooo," he says, the teeth behind his lips gritting, making skin dimple around his jaw, "I heard you gave Mary Anna a hard time."

"Who did you hear that from? Mary Anna, maybe?"

"You know, Murron. You've been telling me about how we're not family and why your son is better off not seeing a horrible influence like me, and yet here you are making executive decisions about my mother's health care."

"Actually, I haven't made any decisions."

"Maybe you should stay away from Mom's for a while."

"If I do, it'll be my own choice, and not anyone else's."

"I don't want to make this any more of a problem than it has to be, but why shouldn't I be a little concerned here about your intentions?"

"I have no idea what you're talking about. I visited a woman in a bed. She happens to be your mother. A nurse was overdosing the woman, your mother, on morphine. I asked a question about this. One question. Nothing more. I'd have thought your sister, and you, would've thanked me. Instead, she called my mother to bitch me out behind my back, and now you're interrogating me."

"Well, I didn't quite hear it like that. I heard you were pretty vicious."

"You should maybe pool your sources."

He looks out the window at the indigent people he'll never understand because he'll never get close enough to them. He's making me wait again. I glance at my watch. He pushes the paper over to my side of the table, as if there's a payoff for a covert deal within its formerly coveted ad space, and I must say that it's the phoniest falsest symbolic gesture I've seen since Gabe's adolescent skater buds ripped holes in their jeans at the knee.

"What I'd like," he says, "is for us to get on the same page. I think we can do that. How about you?"

"Well, who knows? I guess."

"You guess?"

"Okay. I hope. How's that?"

"I just mean, are you with us, Murron? Are you with me?"

Even with all the evidence to the contrary, the mathematical impossibility of a planet combusting with seven billion egos, I'm stuck
with the literary affliction of hope. So perhaps it's right that I'm sitting here on the long communion table of the handicapped. I'm with
him. Why? Because I'm for *everyone*. "Sure I'm with you, why not?"

He looks toward the door and says, "Well, good. Good. Think we
covered it all, huh?"

"Are you with *me*?"

"So let's keep our heads together, okay?" he says, standing. "Got
some other things I gotta take care of so I think we can get going, huh?"

"Okay."

"And whenever you have some time, take another look at *No Country for Old Men*."

He smiles and walks off.

I don't want to think about the horrible exchange we've just had
and so I sit there and think of his parting words instead. I'm aware
of what people think about me and my books. Why would someone
take such great offense at their devaluation in this day and age? Why
would anyone argue over the words of someone they've never even
met? How strange? How backward?

Maybe it is. But I have an answer. Apropos of this coffee-talk debate
I've just endured. Despite its obvious lesson, despite the irony, I crave
the good conversation. The prime soliloquy from the premier talkers
of the species, their three years of soul excavation for my three-week
dive into their narrative. Not just for perfunctory reasons. Not just
out of habit. But to find a bead on wisdom, to work a thread on why
we're here, what we're doing. I'll be quiet, as I should. I'll take it in,
if I can. I feel the knifepoint at my chest, but I'll listen. The smart
people out there, the ones like Richmond, are supposed to get others
to pocket the blade.

But he's given up, it seems. No longer interested in the posterity of
a book's promise. He's got other things on his mind. Just like he said.

12

Richmond Lincoln Felice
Flight to Montparnasse
April 13, 1993

EARLY IN THE WEEK the sickness made itself known again, his son spitting up anything they tried, the cream of mushroom soup, dry bread, water. He'd shrunk so badly that the powder-blue gown draped his body twice over now, quads thinner than the ankles.

Richmond was still here in his place at the bedside, cringing internally at the indecision he felt about feeding his son—better to get some food for this last burst or expedite an ending that was certain—when his son said, swallowing to clear his throat, gathering energy, "Bach . . . was like Faulkner. The furthest west . . . he went was Kassel . . . and the furthest east Dresden. All he needed . . . was . . . to see the view from his house . . . to make music. Bach ruined it . . . for musicians . . . three centuries . . . running."

He sat up, almost happily. Yes, he wanted to talk with his son right now, express excitement with this mention of Faulkner, whom he'd called the "American Shakespeare" so many times. ("Why? Makes us laugh, makes us cry, makes us sit quiet, makes us feel small and big at the same time, makes the provincial ethereal, little stage of theater to big stage of life.") Excited to talk because he now thought maybe he'd had some influence on his son. Not the genetic traits and features mapped and decoded all the way back to conception, but the stuff of substance, generated thought which he so valued, the post-womb cerebral world he could never share with anyone, the world you supposedly could change.

And yet if ever there was a time, he knew, for a Felice to shut up and listen, it was now. The same way he'd watched the histrionics during spaghetti dinners in Big Victor. Which meant wider-eyed, murderous opinion tied to the post. He'd learned late in his fatherhood, but he'd be damned if he'd suck any more life out of his son.

"The toughest thing . . . about music," Richie continued, blinking and swallowing at the same time, "is that the best . . . has already been done. Without dispute. Anyone . . . anyone who argues against this . . . knows nothing . . . about music. No one . . . can top . . . Bach. No one can better . . . Mozart . . . either."

Now his son coughed and hacked, the force of it lifting his back off the bed, and he was already holding out a Kleenex before his son opened his eyes. Even this small battle with phlegm pained him to watch, the constrictions of his son's throat were like seeing, the first time, an epileptic in the throes of the disease. Richie didn't move even one finger to lift the Kleenex to his face.

"Plenty of people . . . still play classical. No other music . . . requires the skills you . . . need in this craft."

He nodded silently at his son, holding his own words to his chest like a closed book.

"But what does . . . it matter? Not current . . . you see? Vernacular . . . is outdated. Like being the best . . . at swordplay."

He'd always loved his son's, which were his wife's, eyes, blue-green like the inside of an abalone shell, and now they beaded on the ceiling with borderline delusion, desert-starved intensity, the only comparison he could think of given how few calories his son had taken in these past few days.

And yet Richmond had never heard the problem of ambition in the modern age put better. He was witnessing clairvoyance of no other kind, the human mind preening itself for one pure statement, energy spent, without reservation, on this last attempt to connect. He stayed quiet at the bedside, desperate in his heart, all of his being committed to remembering, forever, the portrait of his son peering in vain through the blockade of steel and glass and drywall above them both, above them all, to assess some far-off star in the ether.

"So it sounds beautiful . . . but only a few . . . know what it means. What they're . . . hearing."

Richie was taking him away from the stench of the bed, the son guiding the father to common ground, and he thought now on the problem of Pound's maxim, which he remembered verbatim: *Make it new*. But he'd witnessed "newness" at a reading after Vietnam. No one had taken the stage of the Berkeley auditorium and the mike stood there dormant for a too-long string of minutes and the anticipation forced upon the crowd by the performer's absence irked Richmond, seemed false, apoetic, a waste of his time, and then like a weasel from its hole someone popped up in the middle of the crowd and said, "Pill counting. One. Two. Three. Pill counting," and then sat back down. That was the poem, that was the show, the poet's recitation.

Leaving in a fast walk before everyone else, Richmond had thought, Pound's maxim dies here.

"Yes." He decided to talk. "I see. Like poetry."

"Worse . . . than a problem." A conundrum, thought Richmond. "How do you . . . produce something . . . new"—The goal of every artist, he thought—"without betraying . . . the monument . . . you love? How do you connect . . . to a truly . . . contemporary audience?"

"Everything is torn down," he managed to whisper. Nothing changed, and yet all was destroyed. How could that be? thought Richmond. "Isn't it?"

His son coughed and waited for something that didn't seem to come. "I remember . . . the first time I heard . . . Duran Duran . . . at a concert. Snuck off . . . against your orders."

Here his son paused, as if driving the punishment deep into his father's heart. If that doesn't matter now, his lesson went, what else doesn't matter now?

Richmond looked down into his lap, this price for truly sharing with his son no price, he thought, no matter. False pride should die in the company of death, doormat to departure.

Clean our feet going out, he thought, if we didn't clean them going in.

"I liked being there . . . to break the rules. Stupid adolescent . . . shit. But you know what, Dad? Before . . . the first song ended, I started to hate . . . Duran Duran." *Oh, my son, my beautiful son!* "Just couldn't stand . . . them, and I rushed . . . to the Davies . . . to see Pinchas Zuckerman . . . do Brahms." *I love you! I agree! It's true! I took you there when you were five!* "And I knew . . . something else then. We kids . . . ruined music. That opinion . . . made me a bigger . . . freak . . . with my friends . . . than being gay. A glamour show . . . meat market . . . no talent Pop-Tarts . . . sham . . ."

He wept now with no thought to control himself, the tears reaching his lips and dropping away to the floor, trying to smile as he looked up so his son would keep talking, make the conversation stretch out like a yawning child in the bed awaiting the father to be tucked in, readying for the unknown world of sleep.

"I'm fucked. Have always . . . been fucked. Not talking about . . . dying. We all die . . . we're dying right . . . out . . . the womb."

"Yes," Richmond said. "Of course. You're talking about the art."

"Knowing the truth . . . about yourself. What you can . . . do. I'm good enough . . . to know . . . I'm not good enough . . . to matter."

He realized that he could say nothing to the contrary, the fatherly instinct to reinforce the child, to encourage, wholly futile. Somehow they had gotten beyond that. They'd reached a truth that was outside the proud realm of father and son, that could get at the orphan, the widow, the savage, a condition fostered best by either side of death.

Death, he thought. The only word devoid of ego.

"Can recognize . . . what I can't do. Just can't . . . get it. What do you . . . think, Dad?"

He was so startled to be asked his thoughts that he sucked in his bottom lip, an old tick from childhood that hadn't resurfaced for decades. This, he knew, was his chance, as close as he'd ever come to a blessing. He dove blindly into his own thoughts as if they were a deep pool at the falls and said, "Me neither, son."

"Huh?"

"I can't get there either." He was crying again, but he stopped at once. "And you're right, son. My God, you're so right. When the kids became its principle consumer, music became a matter of the glands. Not the heart, not the soul. It got silly."

His son swallowed, nodded.

"Started somewhere around Elvis, what do you think? Your uncle Anthony just loved him. By the time the Beatles came along, there was a full-on sea change. And now it's too far in motion. Assumed, marketed, finished. A serious contemplative musician is done before the first optimistic pluck of the strings." He waited and then said, "Is that right?"

His son smiled on the bed. After a few moments, he heard, "Dad. Don't get . . . sad. Okay?"

"I won't," he said with firmness, almost anger. Not at his son, but at himself. "By God, I *won't*."

"But I have . . . to sleep."

"Okay. You sleep, my son. Yes, you sleep."

He wanted to abide by his son's request to not get sad and so he didn't think about how fast his son went down, the immediate consummate claim of dreams, but instead let himself ponder their official agreement, that music had been finished before either one of them were born. He began to think for the first time that maybe no one went for the big stuff anymore because of this. Wasn't just social lethargy or cultural decay, he thought. Wasn't just individual weakness. Finally, it was also the futility of the exercise. There was no referee now, no one knew what was good anymore, his country a breeding ground for unqualified banter. His son wouldn't see the onslaught of mediocrity in this country that he, the father, loved so dearly, the giant that couldn't help itself.

His son slept deep now and he went out of the room to refill the supplies, hand lotion, towels, water, and when he came back into the room, his son had not shifted in the least. It felt as if he were returning to a still shot, a portrait in the gallery, the only difference in content whatever you'd brought, however you'd changed. He sat again and then he saw it under the bedside lamp, his letter sent from Paris this past week. With its every sentence still fresh in his mind, he reached out for it nonetheless, if for no other reason than to see the letter as his son had here in this room, relive a moment in his son's skin.

My Dear Son:

On a flight to Paris. Got a layover in New York for a couple hours, then off to the continent you love. I love it, too, you know. Have always enjoyed Europe over the years. Any chance to see it, I took it. Once even went with your uncle Anthony. Can you believe that? Almost forgot until this letter. Or maybe I forced it into the back of my head somewhere, hoping it would flush out with other shit in my head. I've done my "tour of duty" with him, and then some. One of the most ironic things I'd ever experienced: your uncle Anthony rambling on about the treacherous "Frogs" and how it didn't take them half a century to forget World War II and "how we saved their asses." All as we sat there in a French bistro on the Left Bank. And sipping champagne no less! The only thing that saved us was that the place was empty and our waiter didn't speak English. And then I guess also that Anthony didn't speak French. Fortune by omission, uneducation, something like that. I think I drank more liquor than I ever have in my life on that day.

Remember when we walked the Capri coast back in '83? I can still see you walking arm in arm with Mom. I purposely stayed

*behind, you know, so as to watch the two of you together in the
sunset. That beautiful Italian sunset. Never seen anything like it
since, probably never will again.*

*We have something in common, my son, more than we'd ever
have thought, I think.*

He'd written the letter on the plane in less than an hour, legs
spread wide in his spacious first-class seat, and then laid down on
his first-class bed and slept. He'd skipped the meeting of the board
of directors to catch his flight on time, not worried at all about what
he was missing. They'd go on and on about budgetary restraint and
fiscal discipline, keeping the purpose of business ("Profit!" he could
hear) at the heart of decisions made, those core company ideals of
Paine Webber that he, managing the five most successful offices on
the West Coast, always kept in mind. It was one thing to do what you
wanted with your own money, but one had to demonstrate the utmost
respect when handling the money of others. This was the discipline,
the morality of his vocation.

He was on his way up the corporate ladder of Paine Webber, and
now he was on his way out of the country, for a three-day weekend,
where he'd arranged to purchase a phone booth in Montparnasse
and have it shipped back to America. He'd pulled some strings,
which meant he'd paid a lot of money, for this transaction to
happen. During Richie's best days in Paris, which were his first,
his son had called home from this very phone outside his studio.
Richmond had sworn to remember the warmth, part fear, part hope,
in his son's voice until his own last days. And now he was going
to bring a memory home for everyone, set the past-tense story on
their backyard patio, as if its fire-engine paint and foreign inscription (LE TELEPHONE) could put out the blaze of their present-tense
story at Kaiser Hospital.

The ship set sail yesterday, he thought now, and so I can tell him
tomorrow.

This excited yet saddened him. It was as if they'd saved all the tender moments between them because it was only now, knowing what they knew, that they could appreciate each other. And now this earlier discovery about art at the bedside of his son: *By God, we'd had things we agreed on! Music was finished!*

He smiled now, recalling his boy's eyes the first time he'd leaned the cello between his knees, the disdain Richie had for the first-prize ribbon won for best solo recital. As if it were an insult, beneath the four-note suite he'd just sawed, roughly, into their ears. At the age of three, his favorite phrase came out with a slight tilt of the head, blue-green eyes boring into Richmond's soul, prelude to all philosophical matters: "Why?"

Many times he'd wanted to walk away and teach his son a secret. Which meant, seek only that which you can handle. The boy wasn't even seven when he was asking Richmond pointed questions about the existence of God and the purpose of war and if it was true that the planet had once been covered in ice. The topical maturity didn't scare Richmond as much as the boy's casual attitude, like he'd known that his father was sensitive to these issues and could answer another time if it better suited him. He could wait.

Their life was lonely in those early years, and his wife would feed on the praise of their son. He let her have this, taking in each high mark with private reservations, wondering for the first time in his life if there was another side to intelligence. He wondered what it could do, if un-tamed, if too raw, to a family. He'd let relatives at birthday parties and counselors at conferences and teacher's aides at parents' night ramble on about Richie's smarts, word by laudatory word, feeling a vague pride that was something like the dumb loyalty of a professional sports fan, but preoccupied beneath the surface with a single conversation that had occurred between father and son on the backyard lawn, the soccer cleats his boy had worn netting butterflies, how the spikes punched out holes under the apricot tree, and how his accusation of disobedience met the answer: "Actually, Dad, it oxygenates the dirt."

His greatest fear was that they'd never have a real conversation, the stoic, respectful, man-to-man kind he'd always favored, so rare with his gregarious siblings. Early on his son had seen through him. When Richmond first heard the challenges to his worldview, it was like he'd been ambushed by a wild animal on an oft-used jogging trail. Fight or flight, blood or sweat. The illusion of the happy family shattered by an epithet: "capitalist." It was the vitriol in his son's tone, in the way he'd use the word to sting and accuse and simplify. Richmond had always associated the word with absolute positivity, he'd prided himself on being a "capitalist," which meant someone who earned his keep. Now in his own home, he was disparaged by the term.

He never acknowledged his son's argument that the decline of culture, which so deeply troubled him, had likely sprung from the same free-market system he so deeply admired. In short, that mediocrity made money, lots of it, and those in the business of making money were complicit in the dumbing down of America. Of Madonna in the brain, strip mall in the vision. His belief in culture was only truly tenable, his son had once told him, if he was willing to be broke for it. The gold standard of culture now, what mattered to people, was what sold. His son had once said those very words. He'd written them down, hidden them in a laptop file at his office.

The thing his son had missed was that he'd quit the art for *him*. His own devotion to the free-market system had sustained their family through the years. Poetry couldn't do that. Whatever happened internally, however ugly, was the just price for this step. It had also kept him alive, replacing the God he'd loved as a child, all while feeding his wife and kid. His responsibility, at some point, became impasse. He couldn't see why an adolescent, however gifted, however sharp, had the right to question the provider. It hadn't trickled down from the top, domestic Reaganomics. He'd given his son a river of provisions, had flooded his life with a clean safe space, the best schools, a healthy and diverse diet. Richie had always gotten whatever he'd wanted, however much, and why ever. Anytime Richmond reached this point in the mental argument, he would begin to feel resentment, for the attitude, the easy naiveté and biting words, the naked attack on his work, which, in turn, was the purest form of ingratitude.

Then before anything had been solved, half a decade had passed and he was on a plane again, trying to beat back time on a first-class flight to Paris. That was the one rule he could always come back to: time, whatever it was, moved too fast. The remembrance of things past clashed so badly with Richie's present condition that he could barely restrain himself from gathering the rail-thin legs into his arms and crying into the scabbed platform of his son's knees.

And so he stayed quiet, deathly quiet, as his son swam on, he hoped, with his beautiful thoughts about art.

And then the part of him that didn't believe in sitting on a solution, that couldn't wait, that couldn't accept that there was nothing he could do about a situation emerged into the fore of his brain with a proposal, one he knew in his heart to be sound, the best business proposal he'd come across in years. He would, of course, apologize. He wouldn't mention it to his wife, who was the buffer between them, even now. He had to get it out, he had to say it right. The most important speech in his entire life would be one loaded word, said with the kind of reverence he'd held for God as a kid. This was his son, this was the end of his dream, this was something that took courage, he felt, of the highest order. No distance anymore between what he should have done and what he did. Carry around no such thing as what he should have said. Because he'd have said it.

His son coughed.

"Are you all right, son?"

"Hey . . . Dad," he said, the lips' microscopic movement, an attempt to smile. "Still sad . . . are we?"

"Son, listen." He closed his eyes to gather the right thoughts and opened them on his son asleep again, already, the frail jaw open so wide Richmond could see a bottom molar capped in quicksilver, once braced by a draconian retainer. Oh my son, he thought now, compassion that he hadn't felt then for a teenage trial already done. My poor, poor son.

He'd tried to save him. He'd contacted a friend at Paine Webber who'd been a pediatrician at Stanford Medicine before joining the business. He got a few good names and then over the course of several days, he called each of these men during skipped lunches in his office, the door shut and locked, Amadeus dropping his raindrops from the sound system overhead.

He'd sold his shares of IBM and paid for the operation, a fairly risky surgical procedure that vacuumed the fecal matter gathered in a torn crevice of his son's anus, a fissure caused by unnatural pressure on the lining, and then a few months after his recovery, they got the news. He, the father, didn't even know what AIDS was.

Maybe it wouldn't have come if he'd known of its existence. If he could have taken the connective tissue of its story into his system. But his son's life, as he understood it now, had threatened his own.

He remembered the week after the coincidence in the city, the silence in the house, his wife's pleas to be open-minded, his reluctant thoughtless reassurances. How she'd interrogated friends on the phone and found their son at a community center in the Mission, how she'd reeled him back home with tearful clichés of the mean streets outside being cold, the sanctuary home, warm. How she'd promised to talk to his father.

Richmond heard her out. Everything she said, he'd suspected even then, was right. Still he shut himself off, stayed at the office until traffic died, read old books he hadn't come across in years. The notes in the pages like back-alley whispers from a version of himself long dead. He questioned his own wisdom, he tried to pray. The hours like days, heavy with the threat of he knew not what. She cornered him once in the kitchen pantry and said he had to eliminate his moral predisposition, his aim to succeed, to please others. He should strip away everything inside him except the fatherly rite to protect, to guard, the good rush of blood she'd seen at his birth,

rocking the infant for the first time. Don't worry, she'd said, everything will come back.

"You have to forget what you think you know."

Finally they'd found one another, alone, at the top of the stairs. They
took each other in, not without kindness, and then his son started to
laugh. It hurt, but he was grateful. The laughter was a prediction, an
oppositional force to work against.

"You don't want to know anything about it," his son had said.

"I can handle it. I can."

"You can't handle it!"

Again: "I can handle it, son."

"Yeah?"

He nodded, and looked away briefly. He felt like a child inside,
learning, too fast for his system, something his system would reject
anyway. He felt boxed in by life, but who, he was beginning to think,
wasn't boxed in? Live and love in it, or leap the box and find yourself
in a brand-new one.

"Okay, Dad. I meet johns in the men's bathroom."

He'd nodded, whispered, "Okay." He didn't know what johns were.

"I jack them off in the stall."

He'd wanted to say at once, "Don't destroy yourself, we can get
through this, there are ways," but he said nothing. He couldn't look at
his son. He felt as if he had a million answers in his arsenal of answers
and not one would work here, rectify, bring estranged father and son
together for however long they had left on the planet. He was about to
say these very words when the image of his son in the defiled public
place seized and overran the most diverse, proactive, judicious space
in his brain. He thought now in his tired speechlessness that maybe
his brain was actually more one-dimensional than he'd always thought
("The test of a first-rate intelligence," he'd always quote as a youngster,
"is the ability to hold two opposed ideas in the mind at the same time
and still retain the ability to function"), that especially under torment its
circuitry underwent a simplification of function, a process of mediocrity

over which he felt powerless, and yet which he one day could well look back upon as a fundamental character flaw: typical Felice tunnel vision, the fulfillment of the latter half of the quote, Fitzgerald's, he now remembered ("One should, for example, be able to see that things are hopeless and yet be determined to make them otherwise").

"It's a trap."

"What are you talking about, Dad?"

"You can't do it. Can't get it. No matter what. A preparation for something that never happens."

"Are you even listening to me, Dad?"

"Of course I am, of course. Of course! Jesus Christ. What do you want from me? Go on, son. I'm listening."

"Won't even look at me, Dad? Disgusted?"

"I want to hear it all, okay? All of it. All of it! Give it to me!"

"Fuck you, Dad. You're a fake. A hand shaker."

The words stung. So much for the crusade of the strong. He thought at once of his wife waiting in their room, hoping, he knew, for a situation solved. For peace. He couldn't deliver on either goal, but he pushed past his son and started toward their room nonetheless, readying himself for a new discussion, new terms, the coming together of minds.

"Ha! I knew you couldn't take it!"

He kept walking.

"I suck 'em off, too, Dad! Hear me? I let 'em fuck me in the ass!"

He couldn't help but stop. His knowledge of the photograph on his left made him now feel the exact opposite of what he'd felt that day. Early summer, '79, the family portrait on the clean grass, the rare sun cutting through the dense green of Golden Gate Park, his boy smiling, in love with life. His wife's gentle tremors in the risk of their proposition. Himself, confident, ready.

What we can't handle, he thought, is beauty. We can't handle hope.

He turned and walked toward Richie, his posture deliberately upright, determined to defy the prophecy, to not give up. He took in the rib cage and then the thin and bony shoulders, knowing that it didn't have to be this way. That's why he'd worked, for chrissake. That if it was this way now then it was this way always, and nothing in our fucked-up lives was worth doing, not even the taking in of the first breath at the shock of light.

All it took, he now believed at his son's deathbed, was a lifting of the eyes, the deep contact between bodies hungry for love. That's all it took. A little courage to let another story in. He couldn't do it then, but he could this time. He'd made room for his son in this room, where they were face to face again, sort of. He would defy his own stance on the marble staircase, when he'd reached out to put his hands on his son's shoulders. Before he could pull in the frightened child, he'd let pity give way to fury, and pushed out with all his weight and story behind him, the boy tumbling off the highest step like a package of bones wrapped in skin, Richmond Lincoln Felice already in terrified downward flight after his son, as if he'd meant to catch him before the crash.

"Please forgive me," he whispered now, holding the skeletal hand in his own, pushing his knees into the side of the bed, as if trying to needle his namesake into waking up, sitting up, standing, walking. "Please forgive me."

But the eyes were closed. His son had passed out, either for the hour or for forever, the same vast, cursed plain of a bed as last night. Afloat somewhere between exhausted and dead. Now the senior Richmond fell, too, to the sweet lure of losing consciousness, almost against himself, chin on chest, thinking as he went down into sleep on the meaning of the word "past." Who tightly mastered its chain, who yanked us upright when the legs were weak? He felt the nothingness take him home and once or twice in the hours he rolled his head to the side, his son's gaunt silhouette so incomprehensible and lovely in the maze of shadows that he went back down again, and when a bug crawled into his ear and penetrated his brain, its hard-shelled, flat-lined, primordial call brought him back from the deep. He didn't know how much time had died while he'd slept, but the word would elude him no longer. Perfectly defined by the unending beep of the machine. He'd live with the present of his son—*past, done, gone*—from here on down.

The Felices
Summer Vacation at the Grand Canyon
August 8, 1956

The boys climbed out of the backseat of the station wagon, one by one, in various contortions of stretch and yawn. They looked like cats getting off the couch. They were in blue jeans and boots and V-neck T-shirts rolled at the sleeve in mimicry of James Dean. He'd been dead for almost a year. Now they shook out their long arms and bowlegged legs and jumped up and down on their toes, a kickoff team before the first whistle of the football game. Their father secured the car and their mother rocked the baby, their only living sister. This was the time for horseplay. They half-shoved and half-headlocked one another, kicking at pebbles and spitting at feet, calling each other names forbidden in any other circumstance, and in the blinders of light sport of this fraternal nature they did not look around, almost as if they'd forgotten altogether why their father had driven them across the great American Southwest in the first place.

At any rate, they'd beaten sunset.

Their father back in the car said so: "Coupla minutes, at least three or four. I told you if we didn't stop in Needles, we could beat it. I told you."

Their mother held baby Mary Anna in her arms and she didn't listen to him now in the same way that she hadn't listened to him for the last six hours. In the same way that she hadn't listened with other infants in her arms. When he was too simple in purpose, when he went too far in diatribe, when he forgot about his blessings. Sometimes his words would flow past her ears like a warm and dark ocean stream, millions of words like microscopic plankton, thousands of sentences like schools of fish, an unending soliloquy upon which she'd float on her maternal raft without complaint, watching for she knew not what until she saw it.

And now she was quiet, mother and children quiet. They saw it. Trying to place themselves in it, this inescapable stretch of earth, trying to take in the totality and somehow calibrate it. Knowing even in the doing of this that it was impossible to take in. That a picture could only capture some paltry fraction of image. He was nearing them, looking at them and only at them, saying, "I'm the best driver in Southern California, that's all there is to it," and then stopping. His feet, his plug, his breathing. His wife nodded. Whatever he'd talked about for whatever reason meant nothing in the grandeur of what they now beheld before and above and around them. What they had come for.

"Oh my God."

The buttes were of course miles away and yet they seemed proximal enough to touch, looming like giant shelves before the Felices. The sensual time lines on the monstrous face of the rock front were discolored at this late hour, beige and off-brown and almost dim from the dying light of sunset.

He read from the bronze plaque on the wooden railing: "The earliest evidence of human presence in the Grand Canyon goes back ten thousand years. First there were the Anasazi, later the Puebloans, the Paiutes, Cerbat. Vásquez de Coronado ventured here in the sixteenth century in search of the Seven Cities of Cibola. U.S. Army Major John Wesley Powell led an 1869 expedition through the canyon on the Colorado River. His studies advanced the science of geology in the area. The first pioneer settlements arrived in the 1880s, following the promise of copper mines and other natural resources."

They'd all been listening but their eyes were elsewhere. The sky was growing. So vast and omnipresent that it seemed to sway almost, its spectrum of yellows and oranges undulating like a lava lamp. It was as if they, the Felices, had been jettisoned onto this precipice of igneous rock to partake in nothing more than an exercise of appreciating the scale of life, the infinitesimal nature of their being, simple calculations from this ethereal platform which jutted out and over the deep cut of the canyon below. They were as close as they'd ever be on this earth to the heavens, the air cool and clean and undamaged, no artificial light anywhere to be seen.

And then came the splashes of purple and blue, little tide pools spinning and claiming the light, the dark hue a reminder of the ancient, weathered, and terrifying story before them, stark on the horizon.

"See that. You see that?" He was nodding fervently now, having a conversation with himself again, ignited by the idea of this place. "That's the proof, the God-loving proof. It's worth it. Every minute of the damned thing is worth it. Because that's the American dream right there, folks. Before your very eyes. Up, up, and away we go! Only a few people know this truth. And we're in on the secret."

His wife and their boys beamed up at him. Now he was talking. Pointing toward the rivulets of the buttes like a claimant of yesteryear, a colonial pioneer of the western tale, as they stood there on the terra firma of the cliff.

PART III
Johnny

13

Murron Leonora Teinetoa

Scrapbook of Anthony Constantine Felice Sr.

January 4, 2008

I'M THE FIRST HERE and my goal is not to be the last. To get in, get out, go home. The place, Dolphin Mortuary of the Greater Bay Area, is run-down worse than Elysium Fields, cracks in the walls and pavement, spray-painted tag war across the parking lot. I still don't get the credo at the head of the building: *Live. Live and die like the Dolphin.*

Yes, they capitalized "Dolphin."

I'm here for a man I'd never met before the last few hours of his life when he'd already lost his senses. He didn't know me from the nurse. He didn't know me from his wife in the next bed. Didn't know his wife was *in* the next bed.

This was less than two days ago.

I open the photo album on the center table and see something, immediately, that I admire. At least in photos, he's an optimist. He's looking at the camera in Pittsburgh as if the next place, Upland, California, will fill every empty dream he's ever had. In Upland, ten, fifteen years later, he looks at the camera the same way, the shoulders of two of his kids, maybe Lazarus, maybe Richmond, palmed on either side, their tilting heads hugged into his waist. He's a dreamer, I can see, anyone can see. He's addicted to hope.

It seems so out of place, so unsilly and old world to mourn here at the Dolphin Mortuary, but this is death, after all, isn't it? However much you try to spin it, whatever amount of money you saved burying this man in a bizarre house of business like this, you can't take away that he's been taken away, is gone, and won't be back.

I look up at my brother. He nods, glances around speciously, as if he's in a house of mirrors where some distortion of yourself is about to scare the shit out of you. I half-smile. It doesn't seem illegal in this strange funeral home to smile.

"If we leave now," he says, "no one'll know a thing."

I grab his hand, pull it into my chest. "You've gotta sign on to something in your life, big bro. Might as well be this."

"They never signed on to me."

"At least look at the pictures."

We take in the display table of black-and-white photos curling at the edges: young worker in the coal mines, young father playing catch with his sons. There's a scrapbook that says SCRAPBOOK in glittery aluminum confetti. I don't reach out to open it because this seems a violation of some sort, but not Gabe. In ways, he's still the rebel kid on the skateboard I grew up with. It's like he has this voice inside his head that says, "Don't jump it, don't do it," and in order to give the words no legitimacy in his system, he jumps it, he does it.

"Jesus," he says. "Come here, Mur."

He's dragging his finger across the titles of newspaper articles from the sixties and seventies, pasted in puzzle-piece assemblage to cheap, yellowed, acid-stained cardboard. When we were kids, Gabe and I used to sketch dinosaurs and birds on paper like this. It doesn't take very long to see that these headlines are the same in substance: "HOW TO BE A MILLIONAIRE BY 40," "THE FASTEST RICH TEXAN EVER, H. ROSS PEROT," "IN THE MORNING I WAS BROKE—IN THE AFTERNOON I WAS WORTH $250,000!," "10 QUALITIES FOR SUCCESS." American entrepreneurs making it big, highlighted in glorious cutouts, these fellow countrymen found the pot of gold at the end of the American rainbow. This collage is the celebrated proof that anyone, especially the owner of the scrapbook, can strike it rich on the lotto ticket.

There are no articles, just headlines and photos. It's like he personalized the possibility, extrapolated a dream from the hard proof of each story, but cared nothing at all about process or method.

"Weird, huh?"

"Makes me sad," I say.

"Didn't he go bankrupt or something?"

"I don't know. Maybe he went bankrupt before he cut out this stuff."

And then there are other headlines unrelated to money but stoking, perhaps, some private hope of being this, of trying that. Ultimately lost in the daily tide pool of fatherhood.

"Ma said you were with him at the end, sis?"

"Yes."

"For how long?"

"Happened fast. He was there for two and a half days and I—"

"Two and a half days?"

"—was with him—yes. I was with him for the last seven hours."

"Ma said they moved him into the same room as Mary?"

I shrug helplessly and turn my palms up, as if to say that it's stranger and more insensible than the scrapbook, isn't it?

"Holy shit."

"I came in Monday evening—"

"To visit Mary?"

"Yeah. I had no clue. Mary and I were playing cards for an hour. He was over there the whole time, the curtain drawn. When I was leaving, I saw his name by chance on the door frame. I went back in. Mary didn't know I was there. She didn't know *he* was there. Yeah. I'd walked right by him the first time, thinking he was just the latest roommate of hers about to die."

"Jesus."

"Which is exactly what he was, I guess."

"Man."

"He kept talking to himself about gumball machines."

"So it was real bad, huh?"

"Seemed like it was. I tried keeping him quiet for Mary's sake, but he wouldn't stop giggling at some shape on the ceiling. I was afraid that he'd say something she'd recognize. Now that I think about it, could have been anything."

"Just his voice."

"Exactly."

"Fucked up."

"Honestly, Gabe, it was one of the times I didn't feel right being there. I don't want to be here either."

"Yeah." He looks around, shakes his head. "Pretty sure this place sucks."

"Thought about pulling the curtain, but I wasn't sure what she knew. Or if she could take it. I honestly would've left if someone from her family came."

"I'm sorry, sis."

"Mom watched Prince so I could stay through the night."

"Shit, I'm so sorry."

"I didn't mean *you,* Gabe."

"You want to sit down, sis?"

"I do."

We take two foldout seats in the rear of the chamber. "Mom coming?"

"She's with Prince."

"You wanna know what's cool?"

"Hmm?"

"She sounds so healthy now on the phone."

"I think she's doing really well. Believe it or not, we're good roomies."

"Oh, I believe it. I always knew you two would make out all right."

"You're stupid, Gabe."

"No! I'm serious. Fuck AA, Mur. You're the one that saved Ma, you know that?"

"Probably Prince more than me."

He rubs my shoulder. "You're just being humble. You know how much I love you?"

"Better be a lot, big brother."

He hugs me and asks, "Didn't want Prince to see this stuff, huh?"

"What do you mean?"

"You know, death and all that."

"Do you forget where we live?"

"Noooo."

"By the way, you should visit every now and then."

"And get shot for being a white boy?"

"It's bad, but it's not that bad."

"So just stabbed then?"

"You could be an undercover wigga for a day."

"Well, I'll holla atcha then and we gon' do this, a'ight?"

"You're stupid."

I stroke his Tolstoy beard, kiss his sallow cheek. I miss him, my big brother with the fast-draw wit who will never get married, never have children, never quit his Sonoma Valley punk rock band. He'll never "sell out," he's quoted as saying in some free Xeroxed zine from Berkeley, which means, if I understand it correctly, that he'll never allow himself to succeed. This because success means mainstreaming, he says in the clearly unedited article, and as the mainstream is "solely run by corporate suits without souls," he'd have no choice "but to crawl into a hole and die." He'll be forty this year. He still sleeps on the couches of friends, I've heard, and still gets free drinks at dives in the Tenderloin.

"Did you eat lunch yet?"

"Just had twelve ounces of water and wheat, sis. Three of 'em, in fact. Figured I'd need it to get through this shit."

"You could sleep on *my* couch, you know?"

"What is this? An episode of *The Twilight Zone* or something? 'Return to Childhood in East Sonoma'?"

"Prince would love to have you."

"Hey," he says, "despite the rumors, I'm not homeless, sis. I've met my monthly rent for a pretty long time now."

"I know you have. Sorry. Anyway, I didn't bring Prince because I'm not sure if it's good that he get to know these people yet."

"Sounds like it's more about you than him."

"I wouldn't have come myself if that were the case. I'm trying to keep open-minded about it."

"What did Lokapi say?"

"Not that it's any of your business, but he agreed."

"How is Lokapi?"

"Prince is softer-hearted than me, and he cuts right to the chase of a hug."

"What do you mean?"

"Well, once you let him into your house, he loves you forever."

"Yeah."

"I'm not so sure it's the same with them."

"I feel you, sis. Prince is vulnerable."

"How's your music?"

"Oh, I'm in it. All the way out. How's the paper?"

"Ah. It goes, I guess."

"What's the matter?"

"I don't know, Gabe. I love books more now than I ever did, but I wonder sometimes if I went into the right field, you know?"

"You mean the money?"

"No, no, no. I had this conversation with Richmond."

"Lazarus's big bro?"

"Yes."

"That musta been weird."

"It was, sorta."

"Did he offer you a job?"

"How'd you know?"

"He offered me the same damned thing a few years ago. I guess his wife told him she saw me on a binge in the Mission and he—"

"What was she doing there?"

"Lotta yuppie places there now, kiddo. Mixed in with the ditches on the walk. Anyway, he called me and said he thought I had what it takes to be in the business. Can you believe that? Misunderstood squared. I quit my band to run stocks and they'll lynch me. Anyway, he said to swing by his office, but I never did."

"I don't know."

"Weird, huh?"

"I don't trust his philanthropy. Yeah, it's weird. I have a reason to be suspicious of nepotism."

"We."

I take his hand. "Well, the conversation kind of bothered me. I just mean, I don't know, I—"

"I'm not sure I recognize my little sister. Is this a smattering of doubt?"

"No, no. It's me. I mean, sounds stupid, I get it, but I feel like I should have a few things figured out by now. I don't know what I want to do with my life, Gabe."

"I have a suggestion."

"Feel free to say any—"

"I think I know what you need, sis."

I'd like to start fulfilling, and therefore eliminating, my needs. "What?"

"You don't know?"

"No! What?"

"Shit." He looks over his shoulder. People are pulling into the lot. "Sorry, but this ain't my gig."

"Gig?"

"I'm outta here."

"You're bailing on *me*?"

"Gotta go."

"You bum."

"I'll call you, 'kay?"

I shake my head but smile. "Okay, big bro. Another day."

He bounces up and spins back toward me, the old tradition, the last question. "And good old Laz?"

"I left him a few messages half a year ago."

"You're a better person than me, sis. Not to mention way better than *him*. Galaxies better. Ciao."

An elderly man in a wheelchair comes in as Gabe leaves. He's surveying the place, a deep frown on his face, almost of consternation. A middle-aged man walks at his side, and a teenager follows. Not completely sure, of course, but they look like grandfather, son, and grandson, their knotty southern Italian hair darker than their eyes.

I've never seen them before, not even in photos. They look determined in their purpose, somber to the person, almost as if it's their father who died at the hospice the night before. Each are in dark suits, hair tight to the skull. In that flash of self-doubt where I feel the urge to fill it with words, I so thoroughly understand the fact that they won't speak, are not *here* to speak, that I just say, "Excuse me," and move to the corner farthest from them.

Out the dusty window I see Richmond pulling up in his four-door Mercedes sedan, so crystal clean it looks like he just drove the machine off the lot. The car *is* classy, and maybe that's the point to Richmond, the point *of* Richmond, however many lives it consumes, however many houses it could pay off, quality usually costs money. Behind him, a sports car pulls in, Mary Anna and her girlfriend. A cherry-red, two-door convertible, the glamorous opposite of the establishment. They park on either side of an unmarked gardening truck, the tires flat, temporarily out of order.

In the late 1970s Lazarus used to drive a truck like that, landscaping the wild yards of his fellow Americans to pay rent. As a girl, I kept a photograph of his utility truck in full-body portrait on my dresser.

He's not in the picture. Was probably taking it. The truck's at the curb of a small corporate outfit in the Silicon Valley, the rakes and picks and black cylindrical tubing of blowers suspended across the skeletal frame of the bed, the handle end of a single high-powered mower extending out of the cover of garbage cans and brooms, his prized machine, which he'd gotten, according to my mother, by shirking monthly payments *to* my mother.

I watch Mary Anna and her girlfriend walk through the doors. They're both gowned, symbiotically, in matching outfits. Mary Anna's bright yellow blouse seems to be some kind of simulacrum of the sun, her girlfriend's dull gray blouse meant to be a simulacrum of the moon. The sleeves of both tops lined with laces, frilly snippets of leather. Richmond, looking down at the ground the whole way, enters alone.

"Thanks so much for coming, Murron," Richmond says, tapping my shoulder cordially but with obvious reservation, best expressed, I suppose, by his not stopping to talk. He moves past me fast as a politician, ready to greet the only other people here to honor his father.

"Marco. Luca. *Come sta?* So good of you to make it. And who's this? Your son?"

The boy nods. The elderly man says, *"Dov'è Maria?"*

"She's sick, Marco. Can't make it out here, I'm afraid."

"E dov'è Rebecca?"

"Oh. My wife couldn't make it out either, Marco."

The long, drawn-out silence says it all.

Mary Anna asks, "So who is this, big brother?"

"This is Mom's cousin Marco. His son, Luca. And . . ."

"Marco," the boy says.

"Easy to remember!" shouts Mary Anna.

"Yep. They flew up from L.A. You did, I'm guessing? You flew, yes, Marco?"

The silence again, the kind with meaning.

"And how long," she asks, "is a nonstop flight from San Fran to L.A. these days? Let's see. Hawaii is five hours, Chicago—"

"We flew in from Sicily. We'll be flying out in two hours."

Mary Anna says, "What do you mean? Why would you leave so soon? You just got here, right?"

"Our flight landed an hour and a half ago," says the young man, his irritation slightly traceable, tight in his throat. Not irritated, it seems, by the trip to honor a dying cousin's husband, but at the interrogator's gumption to ask the question without pondering the answer. The tiresome irony given over, too often, by presumption. The young man, in his words, is covering for the old man in the wheelchair. The disgust on his weathered face makes me drop my eyes to my lap. I won't look over again.

Mary Anna and her girlfriend walk by me. As if I'm not present to honor her father, to listen to a few stories about his life. Despite our differences, I'm weirdly affected that she doesn't find it minimally necessary to greet me. In the void of this place, the gesture stands out, a giant middle finger, and suggests bigger dysfunction, deeper paranoia. Because the grudge about my "intrusions" should now matter less, by exactly one half. He's passed, after all, that's *why* we're here, and there's still one left out there to care for after the ceremony. It would seem, logically, that she'd at least be curious to hear his last words from the one person who was at his bedside during the end.

Strange, but I didn't begrudge *her* for not being there, even though she lives less than fifty miles away.

"It's a little early, but I think we can get things started," says Richmond. "I'm sure Tony won't mind. Or he shouldn't mind, anyway. Anybody who wants to will get a chance to speak." He looks directly at me, and I don't like it. "My guess is Lazarus won't be with us today, am I right?"

Everyone turns toward me, or it feels like that anyway, and I lift my eyebrows and hold them there, hoping I won't say what I feel, which is "How would I know?" But that would be the start to playing the game the way they play it.

"Well, we can be assured that John won't be here, anyway. I'm Richmond, a.k.a. the 'good son.' I'm second in the brood, ahead of John, which makes it easy, I guess, to be the 'good son.' Just don't do anything the guy behind you does."

Mary Anna and her girlfriend giggle at this joke, but I don't hear a sound from Marco and family.

"You know, I was in New York for a board meeting one summer, can't remember the year, and they asked us what we admired about our fathers. I was caught completely off guard. Shocked that they'd ask such a personal question. As I sat there listening to all these flattering stories about fatherly love and sacrifice, I realized something. The reason the question bothered me so much was that I didn't have an answer. I didn't look up to my dad as a child, let alone as a man, and this was maybe a problem.

"Can't remember what I said that day to ward them off, but it occurs to me, right here, now, that I ought to sort it out to make things right. And that's why I came today."

He's paused. Someone's here, right behind me. "Come on in, Tony. Hello, Darlene. Take a seat."

Anthony politely removes the black cowboy hat from his head, props it upright in his lap when he sits, strokes his hair straight, front to back, three times. He seems so nervous, so angry. His wife is with him, holding his hand tightly.

"Glad you're here, Tony. So I was saying. Dad wasn't a soldier, no. He not only never neared combat, he wasn't even issued a uniform. Was 4-F in the war, had a bum knee, I think it was. Maybe a bum ticker, can't place it at the moment. So, anyway, just couldn't for the life of me find anything to share with any of those New York big shots."

Richmond talks with both hands, moving them back and forth like a magician. When I really think about it, I've been especially vulnerable to this kind of alchemy of expression, all the way back to childhood, and so I put a question to myself: Where is he going with this?

"And then later in his life, when we came along, he wasn't a good businessman. In fact, he may have been one of the worst businessmen I've come across in my career. Never got close to owning Big Victor. Yeah. Sorry to spoil the surprise, everyone, but the old man paid rent on that place for almost three decades. Found out a few years back when I had to overhaul Dad's debt with a lawyer friend. And the grove—no—the grove was just a co-op, sort of like a time-share or something, that lost money every year until it finally went belly-up. I think the folks owned less than two percent of it.

"And yet he didn't quit his dream, never did, however disastrously he went about pursuing it. The old man was always hot on the latest harebrained scheme to make a fast buck. I could barely hear him out when we'd talk about the market. 'Take your time, old man,' I always said. 'Look around for a minute.' He never listened. You'da thought *he* was the stubborn Sicilian, and not Ma. The last thing he was excited about was this pyramid hustle for rental houses in Tahoe. Vegas? Ah, it doesn't matter. He paid the price for those choices. Boy, did he ever. The shame of bankruptcy, the feeling that you can't earn your own bones, must've been hard on the poor guy.

"But all here would agree, I think it's safe to say, that Dad was a dad. Wasn't he? That's exactly what he was, huh? Jeez. He was a *dad*. He was made, we'd all agree, to be a dad." He nods, hands clasped in front of him with what, I'm guessing, is supposed to illustrate wisdom discovered. "Goddamnit, he was a dad. Tony?"

If Tony says anything, I can't hear it.

"He's going to keep it to himself, Rich," says his wife.

"Okay. Suit yourself. Mary Anna."

They hug at the head of the room, and hard as I try to fight this type of easy indictment, mostly because it usually springs of cheap American materialism and the cattiness unique to my gender, I can't believe she's wearing what she's wearing today. She may as well have worn a clown outfit. She hops up the single step of the plateau and shouts, "I am my father's daughter!"

Wow.

Then she goes into a shuffle dance, a kind of hobo's jig. Her two index fingers are cutting the air in front of her, like the pincers on a bug, as the girlfriend and Richmond both have a laugh. I don't think that Tony and his wife, or Marco and his family, share the idea about the freedom of funereal expression, that everyone has the right to mourn the way they want to mourn.

I'm not so sure I believe it myself.

"Marco," says Richmond, leaning forward in his chair, head turned toward his in-laws, "would you guys like to say anything?"

I'm hoping they don't. Mary Anna is still dancing. It can't be good.

"No."

Thank God.

I start planning my departure, the fastest path out of the Dolphin Mortuary.

"Okay, folks." Richmond is addressing us with his hands again, his sister finally sitting, her eyes rimmed with tears.

"Oh!" she shouts. "Oh!"

Richmond reaches out and pulls his sister to her feet, positioning her in the crook of his arm. "If anyone would like to join Mary Anna, Keri, and me for lunch, we'd be happy to have you. I think we'll be going downtown?" She nods in his chest, then suddenly pulls away, as if his attempt to console her is not only a mistake but an affront. "Well. Yep. A really fine buffet at Gordon Biersch. The summer mussels are exquisite. Thank you so much, everyone, for coming. Thank you."

The queasiness has predictably started and I know that if I don't get some air soon, it'll all come up. I stand and nod at Marco and family, who don't nod back, and head for the exit. I reach the lobby. Just three steps from safety, I hear my name very politely intoned, and so I turn.

It's Tony. "Hi," I say. "I'm very sorry for your loss."

"I just wanted to thank you," he says, "for being with my father in his last hour."

I nod, not sure what the right words are.

"That was good of you," he says. "Damned good."

"Okay," I say.

"I want you to know that I believe you have a right to be there. It's family. Just like *John* has a right to be here. They were wrong not to invite him. He's still a son, isn't he? Or what the hell do they mean by calling him a son of a bitch? And then to give an elegy like that, listing Dad's failures through the years—"

"I did wonder what—"

"—was just shameful."

"—the purpose of that—"

"Yeah, it was on purpose! Of course it was!"

"I didn't say it wasn't. I said—"

"Everything Richmond says is calculated. That's who he *is*. Hey, I didn't need to learn about Dad not owning Big Victor. Why would you bring that up now? How could you put your own father down like that? Why would you do that? *Why?*"

I take a breath of air, and then try to shift back and get some clarification of an earlier statement. "So they didn't tell your brother about the funeral?"

"No."

"What about Lazarus?"

"Oh, no. They invited him, but, well, I'm sorry, but, you know how Lazarus will . . ."

I say nothing, let his fumbling die out. "So then did you tell John yourself?"

"Yes, I did."

"And where is he?"

"Couldn't make it. Said he had a casting call or something ridiculous like that." He rolls his eyes, then pulls out an envelope. "But sent this. Wanted me to read it up there in front of everyone, but I couldn't do it after Richmond's profane speech. Didn't want to be even three feet from that scumbag."

I open the letter, and it's a poem entitled "Me Mudder." Scan it really quickly and am left confused. Why would a son send a poem about a mother's love to his father's funeral?

"You might appreciate that, actually," he says.

"Appreciate what?"

"What Johnny sent. I'd guess that it's right up your alley."

"You mean because it's a poem?"

"Oh, I thought you worked at the newspaper doing—"

"I do."

"—books for them."

"Yes, I do. I review books. Mostly novels. But, anyway, did John mix up who died or something—"

"Oh, that's just John. Always wrong even when he tries to get it right."

"Maybe he thought—"

"Weird, huh?"

"—that he could—well, yes." I hand it back, shrugging. "It is strange."

"It's Irish."

"Yes. Brogue."

"What?"

"You know, the dialect. They call it—"

"What?"

"—brogue."

"What's that?"

It's like he can't hear at the same time he's talking. "Oh, it's okay."

"You say it's not Irish then?"

"Well, ah, it's not important right now."

"Well, Murron, why did you mention it then?'

"Shouldn't have—forget it, okay?"

He steps back in panic, as if hordes of brogue-speaking Gaelic heathen are attacking, and I turn to find Mary Anna and her girlfriend standing there, the contrast of the sun and moon blouses like a test for color blindness. His response is so odd in a man his age, but it's also unquestionably honest.

"Murron," she says, circling me to stand where Anthony formerly stood. Gone with his wind. The speed with which these Felices come and go is scary.

"Hi. I'm sorry for your—"

"Murron, don't you ever talk to me like that on the phone again, do you understand me?"

Her lips are sucked back into her gums, a leftover glower of intimidation from our shared simian roots. It's wasted energy on me. If Gabe had stayed, he could have told her why, exactly why, she should hire someone else to pick her battles.

"Why would you bring that up here? Have you lost all sense—"

"Oh, yeah, yeah, sure. That's right."

"—of decency in that stupid yellow outfit of yours? What are you, twelve? You look like Big Bird. And that *is* right. I'm right. It's your father's funeral."

"Yeah, yeah, you sure got a lot of anger issues, don't you?"

"Me? *Me?*" In one second, I'm looking at the bright yellow insult of her back. She's marching off from a dispute that she'd yet again started, shaking her head at the savageries of my follow-up, her mute and petite girlfriend in tow.

Apparently, Richmond witnessed the exchange from afar because he's sucking in his own thin lips, looking down at his feet while slowly moving for the exit. The shun of disappointment heavy in his clear refusal to give eye contact, in the departure without any salute of civility. I find it just a tad funny how readily he's willing to view me as belligerent, as the folly-bound youth who doesn't know better. How fully he gives his sister a free pass.

I wonder why it's become important to me to try to see the whole thing the way he sees it. How he's played that trick on me, to prioritize his vantage over another's, even my own. He's a paradigm definer, which means he doesn't disagree with *me*. I disagree with *him*.

You're no longer with us, he's saying in his silent, monastic, possessive retreat out the opaque door of the Dolphin Mortuary, and for once, he's exactly right.

14

Johnny Benedetto Capone
Afternoon Drink at Blinky's Can't Say Lounge
April 28, 2004

Now HE LAID his seventh shot of coal-filtered vodka on the fake vinyl counter and nodded. No one was there. He knew this. He nodded again nonetheless. It was just after the early afternoon crowd had left, that profitless stretch of layover when the owner washed glasses and collected quarters from the country-western juke and the unlevel pool table, tidying the place as best he could until the same crowd dragged itself back in for happy hour at five. His name was not Blinky. No one knew who Blinky was. The new owner, Dax Castenada, was gearing up for the silver anniversary of Blinky's Can't Say Lounge, and so he said, "How 'bout barbecued dogs? Get one of the girls to strip out back?"

Johnny looked around and realized that the question had not been directed at him. Dax was talking to himself, doing the numbers. He quelled the insult to his vanity by shooting the vodka in a clean but violent act, the illusion of royalty gone in the motion, his arm jerking in sporadic, gut-generated twitches. Then he reached over and firmly grasped the bottle of Ketel One, which he used to drink when he was an actor in the porn industry, and poured into his shot glass until it spilled over the rim. He lifted the glass and

French-kissed the bar, sucking in as much as he could, his goatee sponging with the spilled alcohol.

"I saw that, Johnny."

"Saw squat." He dropped his quivering forearm and slurped at his skin. "Got no proof. I'm innocent, Your Honor."

"There's the joke of the year."

"How long," Johnny Capone asked, "has Johnny Capone been drinking here, Dicks?"

"Today? Too long."

"Nah."

"You mean since the first time through that door?"

"Yeah."

"Too long."

"Amen, my son."

"Oh, now you're a priest? What happened to the Mafia bit?"

He let the question sit for a while, sipping the Ketel One, taking pleasure in the tang. It didn't bite your tongue, it nibbled. He liked that idea, he wanted to patent the phrase.

"What happened to the porn star?"

"Why haven't you given Johnny Capone a free drink in this bar?"

"Gave you a dozen."

"Dozen, my ass."

"Your word meant shit, Johnny. So I stopped."

"You're a prick, Dicks."

"Backatcha, Don Corleone."

"It's Capone, man. Johnny Benedetto Capone. Get it right."

"Forgive me, Godfather. I'm just a lowly bartender."

Dax laughed at his joke. Johnny wasn't impressed. Sure, Dax was big from the human growth hormone he'd gotten from his "dogs" at the gym, but one day Johnny was going to collect from Dax. Something useful, like a pile of cash or a lump of coke, a dime sack of weed or an ice pipe. Maybe an hour with a hooker, he couldn't say. Would depend on his needs that day.

He'd already stolen a ton of money from the patrons. Dax had no clue. Yes, he was making himself known at Blinky's Can't Say Lounge. He'd only been drinking here for nine months, but they already had all kinds of names for Johnny—STD Stud, Scarface—the pronunciation laced with chilango Spanish. The one that stuck, though, the one he really loved, jibed with his botched Catholic rearing. St. Dick. Brilliant. He'd added to his legacy by drawing a saint on a cocktail napkin, the stick figure dragging his giant phallus behind him, as if it were the tail on the devil grown out of control. Someone appended the inscription "blessed art thou amongst women." Dax had pinned the portrait to the bulletin board behind the cash register, direct center of the bar, as if the mock image on the flushable item held the pullies of this place together.

Johnny looked up at the mark of his fame and said, "Hey."

"What's up."

The foreskin and scrotum of St. Dick were covered with boils and scabs, and the word "Toxic" had been inserted between "St." and "Dick." "Who did that?"

"Did what?"

"Someone disrespected the art up there."

"What. St. Toxic Dick? You wanna add some color, Godfather?"

"Take it down, will ya?"

"That's all right. I like black-and-white portraits just fine."

"I'm gonna—"

"Course you're welcome to come back around and remove it yourself. But then I'd have to uphold the rule about customers staying on that side of the bar."

"You've never helped me once, Dicks."

"All right. Let's ease up now, huh? Want another shot?"

A trick question. Johnny sat quietly. If he answered yes, it was an admittance to the fact that he'd stolen the shot of Ketel with which he was presently only halfway done. If he answered no, then Dax could say, "Well, since you don't like Ketel, let me take that from you."

So he downed the Ketel already in his possession. Now if he had another shot coming or not, the first was already getting processed in the winding serpent of his guts, irrevocably, irretrievably, bye-bye.

He looked up, said, "Yeah. Pour. You owe me for keeping that fucking illicit drawing up."

Dax pushed the shot glass toward Johnny. "Suck 'em up, ya big loser."

Sipping on the shot before the gesture could be reversed, Johnny counted Dax as a friend. If he could slide a free round today, he could damn well do it tomorrow, too. Dax was living large with the proceeds from the HGH sales, but he always acted broke the minute you asked for something. Johnny admired that. Dax drove a Hummer, he had not one but two houses in the Inland Empire, he wore more jewelry, Johnny told him repeatedly, "than a South Central spearchucker," he twice a month took weekend vacations to Bangkok to fuck underage girls for ten bucks a pop. The indigent attitude was an act. Johnny used to play it himself when he was pulling in dough as a stable boy in the industry. Everyone had their hands in his pockets, either for his big cash or his big cock.

Those were the good old days, Johnny thought, before anyone really knew about the girls in Thailand.

Mexico City was his preferred place to tap young pussy, early Reagan all the way up to early Bush I. He had a liaison named Culito who set it up on the straight for real cheap. And it wasn't like now. In the easy eighties, you didn't have to worry about some meddling 20/20 investigation peeking into the room and putting your straining, mid-thrust mug in the living room of every American. You were protected around the world. Nobody fucked with an American citizen. When that goody Richmond had asked why Johnny took so many trips over the border, Johnny said he was going to "dip his chip in some of that good ripe Mexican salsa." Bitchmond wasn't the only one who could be poetic.

"Best in the world," Johnny said now, kissing the filthy ends of his bloodless unsteady fingers. The trademark line, even the gesture, came from their mother, stirring the pot of her famous spaghetti in Big Victor's kitchen.

"And in that Big Mama apron," Johnny said. "Who the hell would pass off a gift like that on their own mother?"

"What'd you say, Godfather?"

"Nothing."

"If you didn't say nothing, keep your mouth shut, would you?"

1961.

Mr. Goody, Bitchmond, had gotten the apron on his pilgrimage to Italia, the one where he'd decide if a life in the priesthood was truly what he wanted deep down in his teenage soul, the whole trip paid for with a scholarship from the Sisters of the Upland Carmelites. Johnny had never had one of the sisters, couldn't even remember them really, but he'd bet a million to one that their famously uptight piety translated into tightness in all the places where tightness mattered. Johnny had to hear all through his childhood about some spinster on the western coast of the boot who'd stitched the apron in question by hand, a fact Mr. Goody was careful to mention in a speech to the family obviously practiced to perfection on the plane trip back, so organized were his hallowed words, la-di-da-di-da, like a list of mixed drinks on a menu, the apron authentic all the way down to the god-damned ball of string.

Why would I care about that? he thought now. Why would I spend a minute thinking about that? Fuck it.

He never thought about this shit in the muddy discharge of the dripping bush, hadn't pondered a damned thing as the popping mortar flashes neared in the inchoate nightmare of night, hadn't reflected as firelight dashes of flying bullets whistled near death past his ear, so why should he start now? He'd hated the apron on sight, and actually stole it the same night, depositing it in the garbage bin on the side of Big Victor. He retrieved it the next day when he witnessed his mother weeping for having misplaced it, cursing her own stupidity.

Before the week was done, he'd stolen three articles from Bitchmond, including the pendant of St. Peter bought at the Vatican gift store and blessed by a country priest at the register, which Johnny sold to a pawn shop in San Bernardino. Anthony confronted him in the bathroom they shared, and when he denied all involvement, or even knowledge that such a pendant existed, his oldest brother said, "Wait here."

Anthony came back in seconds with Lazarus. Johnny could see that Lazarus didn't want to be there. Lazarus never wanted to be there.

"Tell him what you saw."

Lazarus said, "Come on, Tony. It's over."

"It's not over. He denies it."

"We don't have to beat it into the ground. What's Rich say about it?"

"Who cares what Rich says?"

"It's *his* stuff."

"I'm asking you, Laz! What the hell did you see?"

Even today, right now, Johnny didn't forgive the twelve-year-old Lazarus his answer. Back then, he'd thought he could count on Lazarus as an ally. Sure, he'd picked on the little guy, but overall he'd been pretty nice. Or he must have been nice since he couldn't remember a single argument between them. Lazarus had never come to Johnny once with a question. Despite being younger. Almost as if he'd been warned ahead of time. Anyway, the beating Anthony gave Johnny that day didn't mean a thing. He took beatings from that idealistic prick a dozen times before the age of twelve.

Fuck Tony.

He looked over at the door of Blinky's. All year long, even Christmas, the bar was open from dawn until two in the morning. Sound waves of city sirens whined their way through the doors, dying in the din of the jukebox crooning "Family Tradition" for the third time that hour. It wasn't that a punk like Mr. Goody wouldn't set foot in a bar like Blinky's. It was that he *couldn't*. Would damage his highbrow system. Down here the air was congested, the dusty pollution afloat in no perceivable direction, faint yellow light almost caught in the pit of Fifth Street, trapped like water in the sewer.

He stood and walked to the door. An Impala lowrider crawled like a giant turtle along the street, the subatomic woofers beating the battered pavement with the hammer of old school rap. Lurking packs of bug-eyed tweekers shouted down their devils and demons, toothless mouths twisted in some impossible contortion, racial identity lost in the prunelike grayness of their faces. A lot of shit happened out here in a week. Cats murdered birds and dogs murdered cats and certain Melanesian immigrants murdered dogs in broad daylight, daring anyone to murder them back, even setting up a street-corner spit in full view. They left the toothpick bones in a pile by the spit, entrails withering into membranes thin as paper. The dried blood of the dead gave color to the walk. These goddamned streets stank. The sun pulled it up out of the manholes and sewer lines, as if the acids of all the earth gathered here to be processed in the viscera of Los Angeles, the municipality known as Skid Row to the lucky who didn't live here, the Nickel to the fucked who did, or Central City East to the police who patrolled it.

"Pigs," said Johnny. "Pigs with badges, broke pigs, cannibalistic pigs. Brown island pigs."

A teenager in a beanie and a Dodgers pullover bopped right by Johnny, paying him no attention.

Teenage pigs, Johnny thought.

He headed back into the bar and could see the outline of a woman near his seat, humpbacked, low to the ground like a snowman. She had a Hefty bag ballooned at her feet, and even from five yards, Johnny could see the lesions on her face.

"Tell me something new," he said. "We all get butt-raped by the reaper. That includes the ladies. Boohoohoo."

He took his stool, two down from the woman. They were the only patrons in the bar. Someone had to say something. He stayed quiet. A minute passed. She stood with what sounded like much effort and took the stool next to him. He still didn't move. To prove his indifference of her presence, he leaned away from her putrid odor, ass now lifting off the stool, and farted.

"Cocksucker!"

That was a new name. The spittle had hit the side of his face like pellets of rain. It may have been intentional, but he wasn't sure.

"Do you know who I am?"

"Cocksucker!"

Then she stood up and moved back to her original stool. He sat there without the least interest as to exactly which of the scores of bag ladies frequenting Blinky's she actually was. He decided to watch, consciously watch, the television. It was on mute, but that didn't matter. He could read the captions for the deaf. He wasn't a dumb-ass bag lady.

They were talking Iraq. Its comparable features to Vietnam. Johnny wasn't interested. He didn't know which president first sent Americans to Vietnam, just like he didn't know who'd sent him in '67. He didn't know which president pulled us out, he didn't know which one had restored business relations, even though it was only one administration back. They all weren't worth a drop of horseshit, Democrats and Republicans both. What he knew was that he liked watching this host put his guests in their place. Just loved it. Especially those faggoty prima donnas next door in Hollywood. Seeing the man thrust the dagger of an index finger into the personal space of the guest gave Johnny a sexual charge he rarely felt anymore, the blood-red Irish face of the host furious, as if he were about to jump the table to get at someone's throat once they cut to a commercial break.

"Whatcha watching?"

Dax. Cutting limes.

Hope the pig slices a finger, observed Johnny.

"I said, whatcha watching, loser?"

"O'Reilly."

"The fuck you watching that fuck for?"

"Do you mind turning the volume on, Dicks? My rude-ass bartender is talking right through it."

For once, Dax did what Johnny asked. An O'Reilly staffer had found the house of a judge who'd let a statutory rapist off without prison time. The bright light from the camera's helm seemed out of place in the softness of early dawn. The judge was in his bathrobe and socks and the shock on his face did not dissipate from the beginning until the end of the interview. Shanghaied in the somber hour when all Americans, judges and criminals, could be found wherever they slept.

The judge kept repeating, "Who?" and "What?" He couldn't manage to say anything else.

Johnny said, "O'Reilly's got the eye for the ladies. Just loves the cupcakes. Blond cunts. Lawyer cunts. Cunts wrapped in gold chains. Diamonds in their ears bigger than apricots. Gotta respect 'im. Gets all the cunts on his show. He tosses 'em softballs."

"So what's he going after the judge for? The girl was fifteen, man. The boy twenty. Five fucking years."

"O'Reilly wants to fuck every one of 'em. I can see it. Can hear it. He could've been a star in the industry."

"What industry?" said Dax.

"Coulda been the next Johnny Capone."

"Toilet fresheners?"

"Only the best. Only the best."

"This O'Reilly's a prick," said Dax. "Fuck him. I bet he's banged a half dozen broads in his outfit. Now he's busting on this kid that scored some prime ass. What's he, jealous? Cause he can't get it going any longer? Everyone of us be thinking the same thing. Shit."

Johnny said nothing. He looked over at Dax. Still cutting limes. Still ten attached fingers.

"If I'd crossed paths with Britney back in '97," Dax went on, "I wouldn'ta given a flying fuck, bro. No hesitation. Straight hit it. Oops, I did it again. Every morning, noon, night of the week, man. I'da used all my charm on that fat piece of ass. Spent all my money. Treated her like a princess."

"Dicks," Johnny said. "You got it all wrong. Pussy is pussy. It's what *we* got that matters."

"Cocksucker!"

So she was still there.

"Careful, Mabel," Dax said, pushing out his hands, thumbs tucked into the palms. Like a kindergartener playing shadow games of barking dogs on the wall. "You don't want to lose a finger now, do you? No man or woman gets away with disrespecting Don Corleone."

"Capone," Johnny said. "Johnny Capone."

"Daaa-da-da-da, da-da-daa. Daaa-da-daa, da-da." It was the melody from the soundtrack of *The Godfather*. Dax played his air violin, Mabel got up and waltzed around the room. "Johnny Bonedtheghetto Corleone's gonna put your hand in a meat grinder, Mabel."

Nothing he'd heard was worth his royal ears. Surrounded by fools. Johnny stirred the contents of his shot with an index finger, very precisely brought the wetness of it to his lips, as if it were mysteriously deep, or, just as he'd been facetiously accused, *Godfather*esque. The self-insistence to reverse the mockery almost beyond his control, predestined, a matter of order on the universal grid of polar forces.

Once, after an on-set scene took half the day to get done, Peter Entry had told him, "I will give you something, Johnny. You're no quitter. That's for damned sure. But then neither was Nixon. Two gluttons for punishment. Both in a bag of bad skin. Both L.A. bastards. Come November, sounds like you should run for something. President of the Swinging Dicks. On the Straight-Shooter Ticket."

And where was dear Peter now? Johnny thought. Six feet under. With a pulled plug. The last wrist scar he'll ever have. Who had the better bag of skin now? So he was right about the quitting.

"Was dead right," he said to no one in particular.

The jukebox started into a Merle Haggard track and then stopped, mid-howl, seconds later. Johnny lifted his leg again and farted in the direction of Mabel's performance. Because the juke had died, it was louder this time. He looked over at Dax and said, "You wanna hear some truth?"

Dax wiped down the bar with a white rag, blue-striped, wet, and said nothing.

"Well, I owe this to my dear mother. She taught me, you see, to respect my elders. You're just a kid, so you don't know about these things. Now, this respect I give to anyone. Anyone. Including elderly bag ladies who smell like shit."

"Cocksucker!"

"And you do know why they smell like shit, right, Dicks?"

Dax was still wiping, no indication that he'd heard the question.

"No?" said Johnny.

He looked to his left, then at Dax in front of him, but not to his right where Mabel was now sitting again, breathing hard from her solo waltz. Looking up at him with spite. Anticipating an insult. "No guesses? Okay. Well, let me just tell you then. They smell like shit. Because they *are* shit."

She swung a handbag out of nowhere and it connected in the dead center of his ear and he fell off the stool to his hands and knees, writhing in laughter. He was loving every minute of this rare chance to set things straight in the world. Even if the cost was a lumped head. Hierarchy, that's what it was all about. The world a place where everyone had to know their place, or be taught it. He managed to get to his feet, not looking at his attacker. She could stab him in the gut and he still wouldn't acknowledge her.

Dax had come around the bar. A little too slowly for Johnny's tastes, but at least he was here. Dax was careful not to touch Mabel. "Gotta ask you to leave, Mabel." She looked at Dax with as much inquiry as her worn face could summon. "No permanent eighty-six, Mabel. Can come back tomorrow."

She looked at Johnny, shouted, "Cocksucker!" and then shuffled out the door.

Satisfied with the results, Johnny returned to O'Reilly. Already in the middle of the third segment of his show. The No Spin Zone. A picture of a man with a pillowcase over his head occupied the right side of the screen. The corners of the hood pointed out at either side, loose fit, eyes cut out, a kind of indirect KKK allusion except the hood was black, not white. The scene cut to a group of American soldiers gathered around another hooded man in positions of mock rape, the captors smiling up at the camera without apparent reservation, peer approval obvious in the striking casualness of the posers. A guest on the show stated that it was the same prison where hundreds of designated enemies of the Iraqi government had been tortured and executed in the eighties. Four men and a woman were being prosecuted. One of the MPs, an acne-ridden young man with a skin-tight shaved head, was from L.A.

"Fuck," said Johnny. "Can you believe that? Can you believe my shit luck?"

"What's wrong?"

"Will you get off your ass and mute this damned thing?"

Dax reached up and hit the button without looking. "What's up?"

"You know who that prick up there is?"

"The skinhead?"

"He's no skinhead."

"What is he then?"

"My son."

"You never mentioned a kid, man."

"I haven't talked to the prick since he was nine years old."

"So how do you know he ain't a skinhead?"

"No son of Johnny Capone is anything but one-hundred-percent strapping Euro-American male, that's how."

"I believe that would be the skinhead credo."

"Will you please shut the hell up? He's half Mexican."

"I thought you said you'd never touch one of my people."

Suddenly Johnny winced at a needling sensation in his abdomen. He'd counted two new bruises this week. He was sure he hadn't collided with anything. "Turn it up."

He didn't need to open a book to know which southern third of the continent claimed half of his son. But why should he expend the energy of cleaning up his statements in a bar like this, to a man like this, in a city like this, in a life like this? Why should he address any accusation of denial? And then, when had accuracy or truth ever helped him? And finally, even if either accuracy or truth, at some point in his life, had indeed helped Johnny without his knowing it, still, again, why would he care? For he would've already gotten what he'd wanted in the first place.

He held out his swollen hands. They were shaking worse than ever before. It wasn't so much full circle, it was just bad all the way around. Johnny saw no pity in Dax's face, a déjà vu moment.

Yeah, the sun also rises, but on what does it shine?

"So what's his name, G.I. Joe Capone?"

"I'm in pain, man. Real pain."

"So what? Been ten years then?"

"Since the kid?"

"What else are we talking about?"

"Yeah. Ten, eleven since I seen the little rat. Maybe twelve."

Dax looked up at the screen. "So if you didn't care then, why do you care now?"

"I don't. A long story. About my brother."

"What, he raised him or something?"

"Are you kidding? Does that kid up there look like a week-kneed faggot to you?"

"He looks like a skinhead."

"Shut the fuck up with that shit."

"He looks like a skinhead who don't give a fuck."

"My brother's a prick."

The caption was on fire. They were going to full-on prosecute, starting with the son of Johnny Benedetto Capone. "He looks like a skinhead in big trouble."

"Good old goody-goody Richmond."

"The rich one?"

"They're all rich. Except the damaged MIA. Lazy Laz. Who knows where the fuck he's hiding."

"I lose track of your brothers."

"I'm talking about that pious asshole. Richmond. Bitchmond. Just can't stand him. Never fucked up in his life. Never done a damned thing wrong. Always got a fat wad of bills in his pocket."

"Depends on what kind of bills, man."

"Well, Johnny Capone had him on this one."

"Whaddya mean?"

"I beat Bitchmond with my son."

"Don't get it, man."

"'Cause his son's six feet under. From taking dicks up the ass."

"Dead?"

"AIDS."

"Still don't get it."

"My brother has some kind of weird fascination with military service, see? Goes back to my other prick brother. Bedtime stories about the Alamo. Probably still reads 'em, the fucking dump truck."

"So you're saying you beat your brother 'cause this kid you don't even know joined the army?"

"And his kid didn't."

"Jesus."

"And can't. Not anymore he can't."

"You're a cold character."

"It's about offspring, man. That is what the makers of this rich-as-fuck real estate care about. My brother ain't got anyone to give all his millions to. Boo-hoo-hoo."

"Freezing."

"Tell me you don't care if I live or die, Dicks."

"As cold as they come."

"Heard it, man. Save it for someone who cares."

His plan had gone into action beautifully. At the beginning, anyway. Calling his darling mother and sharing the news about Jaime's enlistment. How excited she'd been, dropping her standard "wonderful"s and "beautiful"s into the conversation. How eager she was to hang up and get on the horn, as he knew she would, to let his lame siblings know that the patriotic torch had been passed. To *his* son. Let them call him, or his son, a bastard now. The Felices had achieved intergenerational success through the progenitive gold of Johnny Benedetto Capone.

He'd wisely left out minor details like the boy's Hispanic last name. Let vicious dogs and sleeping secrets lie. He'd left out how Jaime had been picked up for possession, meth and heroin, in the Eighth Street Basin in East Upland, how the deal cut in Judge Judy Brown's private chambers was that military duty wiped both the crime and the probation clean, how he'd specifically gone into a branch of the service where combat wasn't required. He'd conveniently skipped how someone had missed certain facts of a druggie civilian history proscribing even the filling out of an application in the first place. Either lost by chance in the rope-thick red tape of the army's annals or ordered top-secret down the line by brass with very big brass balls. How the irony of Jaime Manuel Ramirez arresting *anyone* had not been discussed until now, an afternoon hors d'oeuvre for the hard-hearted, soft-headed Americans feasting at the table of the twenty-four-hour cable monsters.

Now someone pointed out that he'd religiously played *Grand Theft Auto* right through the bulk of his high school years. It was all over the screen, on the main part of it, on the subheader. O'Reilly's guest was breaking the fact down, rendering expert psychological advice. "This very important fact is like a peek into the mind of this very damaged individual," he said, grave eyes on the camera, and America.

An ex-girlfriend verified that he'd threatened to kill anyone, mother, cop, judge, girlfriend, who threatened to take his "*GTA* away." "I became an ex at once," the ex-girlfriend said with considerable pride. The flashing caption sprinted along the bottom of the television screen, as if the letters themselves were trying to escape the lascivious eye of the nation.

"You're famous, Godfather."

"Turn it off."

Dax reached up and thumbed the power button. "Not too many Skid Row winos get indexed on Fox News. Their kids neither."

"The goddamned thing's ruined."

"Cheer up, man. You've joined the ranks of O. J. Simpson, Bill Clinton, Scott—"

"Ungrateful prick."

"—Peterson, Drew Peterson, Saddam—"

"Gave him the world, man."

"—Hussein, Osama bin Laden. Who else? Your macho amigo Geraldo Rivera."

"That s.o.b. s.o.b."

"What's the first s.o.b.?"

Johnny's wolf eyes burned. "Bastard."

"Come on. Take it easy, man. You had more than a hand in it, no?"

"Nine years of work and sacrifice."

"So you *did* raise him then?"

"What's the difference? I signed over half my paycheck to his cunt mother. For a fucking decade."

"Who's the kid's mother?"

"Some cunt from the industry. Used to fuck her off-set. When I lived at the Aloha."

"Uh-huh."

"Same old story. La-di-da-di-da. I told her, 'That's real funny. I didn't know you could have a baby in your ass.' Just my luck. The one time I fuck the cunt in her cunt she's got an egg waiting. One time. I said, 'So what do you want me to do about it, Cherry?' She told me what she wanted. In Spanish. I laughed out loud. Then a judge told me. In English."

Dax said nothing.

"Yeah, man. I told the judge, 'I ain't giving a dime to a kid that ain't mine. Tell that translator to let her know.' They ran a paternity test the same day. You know, when I was physically present. Fucking prick bailiff followed me around for two hours. Even stood outside the stall when I took a shit. I wasn't taking a shit. Making him work, earn a buck. His dirty money from the state. The rest is just bad history, man."

"So she raised the kid by herself?"

"She bankrupted my ass, man. Called a year ago to get more money. I told her to go to hell. She told me all that shit about the kid I never wanted to hear. Said this is who the kid is becoming. I told her, 'Do a better job then.'"

"That's not the way to look at it, Johnny," said Dax. "You're acting like an s.o.b., to use your terminology."

"Only Johnny Capone," said Johnny, "uses Johnny Capone's words."

Dax was around the bar now, wiping down the stools. "Why you always talking about yourself in third person? Like you're some big shot or something?"

"The kid fucked Johnny Capone up. First when he showed up in the world. Now this."

"He don't even know you."

"And that bitch took all my money."

"She raised your kid, man."

"Yeah. She done a hell of a job, huh? Little prick can't even keep his fuckups under wraps. Goddamned Mexi-cunt."

"Hey."

Johnny felt himself being lifted from his seat. As if by magic. As if a high gone out of control. He couldn't tell it was bad until he tried turning in the momentum of his body rising. He felt caught in the clutches of a pure animal force and though his eyes strained from the monstrous weight pushing his head and neck toward the ground from behind, he thought he saw out of the blur a smile on the painted face of Mabel the bag lady and he thought, You rabble-rousing whore. Clap-ridden. Cunt dead of. Seduction.

He rolled his eyes up as far as he could and found the betrayal of his half-ass Brutus in the Blue Ribbon bar mirror, Dax Castenada shrugging him off the chair as if he, Johnny, were the resistant object to be twisted in some backwoods Scottish strength competition. The jeering crowd wanted his neck broken, spine snapped. But none were gathered. Mabel the bag lady wasn't here. No witness to whatever was about to happen. Dax Castenada had Johnny Benedetto Capone pinned like a donkey in Blinky's Can't Say Lounge.

"Let. Go," he managed. A whisper. Couldn't do anything but whisper.

"Sorry? Did you say something?"

"Please."

"You ever look up 'Castenada,' you stupid fuck? Huh? South of the border came this s.o.b.'s mother, you mutherfucker."

"I."

"Did I hear something outcha dirty mouth, you bitch?"

"Can't."

Suddenly he had air again but couldn't stand upright. He'd been released. The muscles around his lower back weren't working. He knew there was pain way down beneath the nethers of benumbing drunkenness. That tomorrow in the cotton-mouthed morn of hang-overville he'd feel it. With the early sun burning into his leathery, malformed, grotesquely pockmarked face. He'd always hated his face, still did. The way the skin peeled now when the psoriasis built up, like the rind on rotten citrus. With days like this, it could only get worse. The face and the hatred both.

His head was hanging down by his waist, like a horse about to chew grass, yet he couldn't lift it, couldn't move it. He wondered in his own ignorance of physiology if his neck was broken. He rolled his eyes toward the polluted light streaming into the bar through the door. Dax was there. The door closed. Locked. The shadiest bar on Skid Row dark. Dim with the promise of something not right. Dax came back and was breathing like an asthmatic struggling for air and Johnny saw the eyes widening into a kind of controlled madness and with it the broad-jawed mouth locking into a trap, and he whispered, "I thought. You were my friend. You said—"

The punch to the ribs doubled him over again and when the kick connected in the pit of his gut Johnny dropped to the ground for the second time in ten minutes. This one was different. Something was dawning on him, something important, but he couldn't get it. Maybe it was the pain from within, wherever pain came from, maybe it was the final beating of a lifetime of who knows how many beatings. Whatever it was, he wanted it as sincerely and truly as he'd wanted anything in his lifetime of beatings, and so he reached out with his quivering hand across the filthy floor of this dive bar. He didn't get it. Never got it. The cold, vacuous, same old story of Johnny Benedetto Capone.

He looked up, breathless, maybe for mercy. It was too late. He somehow felt the steel-toed boot crash into his body before seeing the actual kick. And then he watched his beating for as long as he could, the back-and-forth action of the boot like a chime on a fast-forwarded clock about to break for good, meaning break forever, now feeling his gray-wolf eyes fluttering shut at each jolt, and then a faucet releasing a flood of liquid through his bloated gut, pulsating, rushing, soothing, like warm bathwater cleaning out the dirty innards of his body.

15

Murron Leonora Teinetoa
Calling Forth of Lazarus
January 10, 2008

WE'RE PACKED INTO the spacious, air-conditioned, Air Force Academy-stickered interior of Tony's monstrous Ram truck, abiding the fifty-five m.p.h. law to the very mile, on our way out to find Lazarus in Madera. The plan, as Tony suggested, is to surprise Lazarus. That way he won't have time to disappear after a warning call.

I can tell that Johnny likes the mischief of showing up on someone's doorstep without invitation, as if we're going to walk in on Lazarus with a woman. As if that mattered. We've all seen what damage sexual relations have done for poor Lazarus.

So the plan sounds sound to me. I've tried everything over the years to get ahold of him, and since nothing ever worked, it not only means I have no claim on solution but also why not? I mean, I couldn't get Lazarus out to Prince's baptism, and I called him half a year ahead of time, once a month all the way up to ten minutes before the water dip.

They've been arguing for hours. I deserve a medal of some sort for listening. For just *being* here. These people are crazy for money, insane to pocket a buck, and except for Richmond, they have no ears. Of course, Richmond's golden pair only halfway counts since he tunes out with omniscient whim, but at least he doesn't spit when he talks, which means shouts, as if the other person isn't three feet from you.

"What do you think, Murron?"

This surprises me. I don't want to waste my opportunity, if that's what this is, to get into Tony's dimly lit, black-and-white head. I need to know what these people are really willing to do for their mother.

"Well," I say, "neither one of you wants to pay for her care, so I don't really see why you're arguing."

"Hey! I'll pay! I just wanna know why I'm the only one being singled out for it and—"

"Well, this is what you *want,* right?"

"Of course it is! I'm not on *their* side! They've kept me out of the loop from the get-go!"

"Then why does it matter?"

"Why does *what* matter?"

"Why does the money matter? Why are you intent on making sure everyone carries the same financial burden?"

"Hey! Why does it fall on my shoulders to pay for the whole thing?"

I pull in a deep breath, the kind you take before a big jump of some sort. The kind I reserve for children in need of an explanation that I know they won't quite comprehend.

Tony's hard not to condescend to.

"Again. If what you want is for your mother to be moved, then why not do it yourself?"

"Yeah! You got enough money, don't you, big boy?"

I wait for Tony to answer Johnny, however insincere the intent of the question. Almost miraculously, a Felice's words are pointed and pertinent. Anthony barely blinks, silent for once, pondering something far off in the dry and dusty San Joaquin Valley skyline. Maybe this place was meant to inhabit weed- and cud-chewing cows and their rectal chimneys of methane, but we humans don't really blend in around here. This place seems, to me, like a reverse-mass ghost town. Rather than getting deserted as it should, it keeps growing.

"You and your old lady been playing the market for how long? You gotta have a million by now. By the way, how's my old stock doing, big guy?"

"What? That Roto-Rooter thing?"

"The Rosy-Flush Clip-On. Best stock second to GE. Also known as the one Pop dropped the ball on."

"Johnny, you have no right to—"

"I know it's hard for someone with Pop's lofty moral standards to believe, but—*yes!*—you can even make a fast buck on shit. Or as Bitchmond would say, 'excrement. Fecal matter.' Bullshitter."

"Johnny."

"Pop lost me my million, but what's new? We ain't gonna get it back now, are we?"

Tony looks over at me. I've heard enough stories about Johnny to not want to hear this one. It's not that Tony knows this and it doesn't matter to him. It's that he *doesn't* know this—*he can't read me*—and so how could it *possibly* matter to him? When it comes to people— mannerisms, tone, intent—he's an illiterate.

And then, Johnny, well, the first thing he wants you to know is that he doesn't care *what* you think. And that he doesn't, it seems, care about you. Or anyone. Maybe the bad pores and flaky skin mean he doesn't even care about himself.

I look into the rearview mirror and—just like that—he's passed out, faster than Prince after Saturday morning soccer games.

Now he's snoring. "I can't believe," says Tony, "he fell asleep that fast."

I can't believe he's talking about Johnny as if he isn't in the same truck as us. As if he couldn't be faking it. Anything seems like a possibility with him. "Well," I manage. These two brothers prompt an inarticulate, grunting self I never knew I had. "Yeah."

"He doesn't look too good, does he?"

I shrug. Maybe without Johnny intruding for the wrong reasons, I can make some real progress with Tony. "So what are you going to do?"

"About Ma?"

I nod.

"I don't know," he says, "that there's anything I *can* do. I have no say. They've made that clear, anyway."

"That's not true. You do the research to find a better place. I can even do it. Then you make a proposal. I can do that, too. Then when they give the nod, you pay for the move and her care. I don't have a lot, but I can help a bit."

"Hey! Does that sound fair to you? Why should *you* of all people have to pay? Oh . . . I'm sorry."

"For what? I enjoy my visits to see your mother. If I have to pay something to have that, who's to say that isn't just?"

"Let's make them pay their share!"

"You can't make anybody do anything."

"I have four other siblings, or maybe you forgot!"

"Maybe," I mumble, "*they* forgot."

"Don't let 'em off the hook!"

"Listen." It's the editorial voice that I don't like using with other adults. Some view this kind of assertiveness as combative, others listen to it. At the paper, I've got every person pegged on whom it works and doesn't. Despite his reputation, I think Anthony is one of those who will listen. He wants my help. I don't know why, really, but he respects me. "Can I be direct with you?"

"Of course. That's what I like. No one else ever is."

"Look. If Richmond sees you put out for this, he'll chip in to your cause. Why? He'll guilt himself into doing it. And if the guilt isn't strong enough, that's all right. He's not gonna let you trump him in any way. Fraternal rivalry, whatever you men want to call it. He's just not going to allow anyone to think that you know how to care for his mother better than he."

He's quiet, he's thinking. Hopefully. Because he's got no guarantee from the sister, he's got nothing from the brother passed out in the backseat, he's got no guarantee we'll even find Lazarus. Not very good betting odds.

"Just think about it," I say. "He believes he's the moral compass of this family. It doesn't—"

"Hey! I'm the—"

"—matter if it isn't true."

"—oldest brother of this family."

"You have to get his needle pointed in the other direction. Make him reconsider what's right and wrong. Who cares if you have to eat your pride? Who cares about the method?"

"Hey!" He's already forgotten what he apologized about. Didn't hear me. "We're here."

I look around at the sights. Poor Lazarus. "Is this here *exactly*?"

"Madera. This is where your . . . where my brother lives."

Madera, my dear, you are ugly. But ("Hey!" I can hear Anthony shout . . .) East Palo Alto is ugly in spots, too. The difference seems to be that this place has no life. At least in East Palo Alto people are out and about. There's movement. ("You need movement," I hear Gabe jest, "to move dope.") Madera looks like every citizen signed some kind of underground death pact in which, "Yes, I'll live here next to you as long as we both stay inside the house forever."

We park across the street at an abandoned construction site, the vast dirt lot randomly filled with cars. The upright planks look like the skeletal remains, just unearthed, of dinosaurs. Tony takes up two spots, a wiggly spray-painted line dividing the truck down the middle.

"You sure you want to park like this?" I offer.

"Hey! It's not illegal."

"Oh, I don't mean in this place. I mean taking up two spaces."

"I don't want anyone to scratch it."

I can't believe he doesn't know what I mean. It's like he'd be shocked, even damaged, to discover the paint of his American tank keyed down to the steel.

"You know. Like this way no can park next to me, see?"

You can only do so much. If he gets it, he gets it. Not gets the thought but gets the *key*. Can't help him after that. "Okay."

"Should we let him sleep?"

"You mean leave him here alone in your truck?"

He raises an eyebrow, angry at himself for not anticipating whatever it is I'm suggesting. "Johnny. Johnny. Hey! Let's go! We're here."

We cross the dust of the lot, the dried mud caked across the walk and into the gutter, spread two feet into the street. A lot of space between us. I stay on the other side of Anthony, keeping my pace even with Johnny so that he can't size me up from behind. He's been trying to hold me in his stare since we met. He has this giddy mischief in his eyes that suggests he doesn't care about the blood relation, that I'm not *really* a part of the family.

I look over at him and he's right there again, locked on my face, then down to my breasts, up to my face again.

I don't want to be too hard on a guy I didn't know before today, especially a brother to Lazarus, and yet he's something of a creep.

I worry about Prince. It sometimes seems as if my primary job is not to provide for my son but to remind him, through motherhood, of the grace and sacrifice inherent to my gender. And for some reason, it has to be shown, not said. I want to show him that delicacy does not mean weakness, that strength has forms other than power or force, that you can find beauty in the palm of your hand. Over the years, I've tried to keep Prince away from those men of my generation who've already rotted from the inside out, who'd bring him down. The brain-dead video-game zombies, the spaced-out insomniac tweekers, the pants-sagging East Palo Alto playahs, the impotent Internet porno addicts. I've thought of late that if I can keep Prince out of any one of these categories, I'll have done a decent job with my son, and we can worry about lowering his piety levels later.

We knock on Room 109. It has an American flag curtain. The bottom five colonies, I guess, are missing behind the sill. A welcome mat with the w and e rubbed out so that it reads ELCOM. A few tied-up trash bags under the window, the light over the door a single bulb, flickering on and off, bugs the size of Jelly Bellies popping off the thin glass. Suddenly, I feel queasy.

"Lazarus is living large, in't he?"

"Shut up, Johnny," Tony says. He reaches out and cups my elbow with his palm.

"I'm fine," I say, wiping at my eyes.

Tony says, "You sure?"

"Yes. Thank you."

"Cut the dramatics and knock again."

"I said, shut up," Tony says, glaring at Johnny, rapping harder than before. The weak sound of his finger bones colliding with the door indicate that it wouldn't be too hard to break into. He knocks again.

"Doesn't look like he's here, huh?"

We walk off and I peek over my shoulder with something between relief and regret and say, "He's there. I know he is."

"Yeah?"

I turn to make my way back, and suddenly he's standing in the frame of the window, the car dealership flag behind him, in what must be the same T-shirt he was wearing when he visited us in our trailer for the last time. He'd been passing through wine country, three in the morning, Tuesday. Everyone missed him but me, Mom "slam-drunked," as Gabe used to say, on the couch, Gabe at some silly punk concert in the city. I woke up and said nothing. He gave me a key-chain Rubik's Cube, kissed my forehead, said, "Shhhhhh." Then it was morning and he was gone again. I tried for weeks to get the colors lined up, I rubbed the prints off my fingers, but I never came close. The most I could get was one side and half of another.

He's waving me over, and I smile inside. He rushes to the door, the flag falling halfway to the floor without his knowing, and I can already hear him talking behind the old plywood.

"Well, well! Lookie here! What've we got here? Well, well."

I let the smile out and take a half step forward.

"Come here! Come here!"

His face, which was tender and soft in my memory, is crusted over now, lump-scarred and swollen, hard as bark. He's got a few divots in his sallow cheeks and shrunken chin that even the shoddy beard can't hide. His arms are badly atrophied, like a cancer patient's, but he pulls me in with the force of a young man in his prime. The gray hairs are sharp and not soft at all on my neck and he reeks of toxins, but it's worse than that. He smells like an old wet chimney and an old wet cat at the same time.

The sympathy of the child starts to creep in for this man, and as I feel myself losing myself to compassion, I'm held in control by the ancient anger of adolescence, overcome with the old familiar harm of his absence. Just then, he lets go of me with almost a shove and rushes to his two brothers, slapping them both, over and over, on the shoulder. He's a three-pack-a-day smoker, his fingernails hardened brown from the nicotine.

I wonder when he'd lit the first cigarette that sealed him to this chain of repetition. Was he ruined before or after the war?

"Hey!"

"Hello, Laz!"

"Well! Looking good, Johnny!"

"Always am."

"Bullshit!"

"Hey!"

I wipe at my eyes during their brotherly banter. Well, I think, it's good, at least, that he hasn't lost this.

"What brings you two high rollers to the beautiful part of this state?"

"You ain't kidding, buddy boy," says Johnny.

"Shut up, Johnny."

"Shit, I thought I was back on Skid Row with the niggers and spics."

"Which one were *you*?" I ask, thinking of how he would view Prince, let alone his Afrocentric Samoan father, if they met.

"Sassy girl—she's fast."

"You look good, Ton."

"You too, Laz."

"Hey! Come on in, come on! We're standing around like a bunch of penguins."

"A bunch of junkies."

"Shut up, Johnny."

"Come on in, beautiful people, step right up."

It's a good thing he has a flag over the window. Because there's no other decoration in the "living room." Not even a couch or a lamp, no photos on the wall, nothing but a pull-chain lightbulb, which isn't pulled, in the middle of the room. The oriole-orange rug is the long-fibered kind you can trip on if you don't pick up your feet. Gabe and I used to hide pebbles and BBs in the teal rug of our trailer home.

"Oh. So! Well, you know what they say. Gotta keep the bugs and the rodents to themselves. That's what we've got here. It's got running water and a halfway-running sewer line and solid-matter walls, and as far as I know—and, hey, I don't know much—no one—not even those iridescent lab rats you're always hearing those PETA nuts yapping about—has figured out how to meth-astatize. Unless, unless, unless it's some stupid superrodent in one of those sci-fi books I got back there. Yeah, I got a few. L. Ron Hubbard, too. Ever read him? Old sci-fi guy gone religious. Well, I read that shit now and then in between shifts. They're all the same. Who knows, huh? Weirder things have happened on this planet! Yeah. So. Well. You're safe is what I'm trying to tell you. Nothing to worry about in here. Oh boy, Madera's got rats all right, but they congregate out there! You hungry? I don't eat much. You want a beer? How about you? Can you legally drink yet? Are you of age? They drink wine by ten in Italy."

John is heading toward what must be the kitchen. I could legally drink seventeen years ago.

"Laz," Tony says. "You know, we thought we'd come to—"

"I know! I know! It's great, I tell ya, just great. You know what's weird is I was just thinking about you, yeah, because I'd read this article in—ah, I don't know what or where, really, forgot—but, you know, they were talking about how the drinking water in Mount Shasta is the purest in the country. Yeah! That's right. Mount Shasta, California. And so I thought—you know, stupid thoughts—I should drive out to see you and Darlene one of these days and drink a beautiful glass of Mount Shasta water."

It's hard to see this man the way my mother remembers him. According to her stories, she couldn't get him to say more than ten words a day. Either he learned how to talk or he learned to be nervous. Johnny comes back, shaking his head, the smirk not unlike my own child's when he's just heard an adult joke he's not supposed to have heard, but completely gets. He cracks open a beer. "Natural Light, Laz? You're living in style, drinking in style."

"Ah, I don't mind that stuff, you know? It goes in, it comes out, what the hell does it matter, really, you know? I first drank that stuff in the bush. Had a friend there named Le. A Montagnard. Little badass was about ninety-five pounds and just deadly. Woulda never thought it looking at the guy. You'da thought he was twelve years old. But used to just love it, you know? Drink that American piss down like—yeah!—Mount Shasta water!"

Tony reaches out and pats his brother on the arm. "Hey. Okay. So you doing all right, huh, Laz?"

"Yeah! Great!"

"Great," says Johnny, lifting the aluminum can to full tilt, emptying it to the last drop. "Pisswater."

"Well, that's great. We were worried about you, you know?"

"No, no. Nonsense, nonsense."

"And we said, Hey. When's the last time we got out there to see him, huh?"

"Yeah, it's great you came."

Tony puts his arm around Lazarus.

"Queers," says Johnny.

"You want to talk about things, though, Laz?"

"Sure, sure, come on in. Everything's great. You hungry?"

"Thirsty," says Johnny. "You got any real liquor?"

"And so I tell you what I learned—"

"Like a bottle under your bed?"

"—yesterday when I was—ah, I can't remember where—but this guy tells me—oh, it was at work! Yeah! I work with the guy at Thompson Semiconductor—anyway, he says that they're not Montagnards. They're called Degar. And I said, 'How do you know?' and he said, 'Me Degar.' Well! Almost forty years later. I'd been calling them—or thinking of them, I guess, yeah, more like thinking of them—as Montagnards. Name is Kpa. A great guy. Works like a goddamned ox."

"Kapow."

"I hate when they keep their names," says Tony.

"Oh! Wanna see something?"

"Yeah," says John.

Tony doesn't say anything. He seems irritated that Lazarus is fond of this Kpa.

"Stay here a minute, will ya, kiddo?"

I shrug. The brothers walk off and, just like at the Dolphin Mortuary where their father was buried, I don't feel right looking around. I don't wait long. Anthony's back.

"I didn't want you to be alone out here."

"Thank you very much."

We don't say anything for a few seconds. "You know Johnny," Anthony suddenly says, "he's not too . . . I just . . . well, you know, he's not very—"

"Nice?"

"—don't think you should listen to him—no! He's not. That's right."

I knew we could agree on something. "Don't worry."

"He's not a good person."

"And yet he agrees with you about your mother."

"Yes! It really shocked me. I'm still suspicious, you know? What does he want? He's always got an angle. An ally like him, shit, well—I'm sorry to say that—I mean, he is my brother, but he's, well, there are lots of things I can't accept—"

"About him?"

"—about him and—yes, that's right—and I guess I just hope he doesn't bring his, well, you know."

I feel that I vaguely understand enough to say, "Yes."

"Okay, Murron," he says. "Boy."

"What?"

"Well, it's just that—"

"So what's Lazarus got back there?"

"—you can't blame someone—"

"A porno library?"

"—it's very hard to be alone."

"Come on. I can handle it. I've handled it so far, haven't I?"

"Well," he says. "It's an arsenal, Murron. It's guns. A lot of guns."

I nod. Never knew, but I'm not surprised. Again, what do I really know after all this time? My brother, Gabe, wouldn't spend a second pondering the problem. If he were here, he'd join them in the back to pilfer from the stash. "Get something legit from the old man's inheritance," I can hear him say. "Something I can pawn for a case of Corona." If my mother were here, the real-life image of Lazarus all alone with his guns would probably force her back to the bottle.

"I bought one from him a few years ago—"

"What? A gun?"

"—after leftists vandalized my property."

"What happened?"

"Oh, I didn't have to shoot 'em. Not yet, anyway."

"I meant with the vandalization."

"Hey! Why does it matter? Property is property, Murron! Don't I have rights, too? Why do the law and the media and all these leftist operations continue to interfere with our lives?"

"I have no idea what you're talking about."

"Murron. Murron. The Constitution guarantees . . ."

The arguing in the back gets him to stop. And his silence holds, definitely noteworthy. Sounds like a beef over weapon superiority. Then, as if the TV volume were turned up on a cop show, I can hear Lazarus clearly order Johnny to put the gun down because "it's goddamned loaded, you fucking fool," prompting laughter that doesn't feel good to hear after a caveat like that.

Anthony's shaking his head as they both return to the living room, Johnny talking about a terrorist-target scenario he mastered at a firing range in Riverside.

"Hey, Laz," says Tony. "You know, we've got a lot of stuff to talk about."

"Yeah! Be my guest! Talk away, Ton. Anybody can have the floor here. You, too, Johnny. We're still family, huh? We still gotta stick—"

"Laz. Sloooow down. Take a breath, will you? There's some business we need to discuss, money issues."

"You guys need money?" He looks at me. "Oh! I get it! That's why you came! *You* need money!"

"No," I say, thinking, You don't get it. *None* of you get it. "I do *not* need money."

"We gotta discuss Dad's moneys, Laz."

"Hey, hey, hey, I don't know if that's right, Ton. The old man's got a lot of pride—"

"Well, we know the two of you were close—"

"—and, you know, it's only money."

"—and he gave you the rights to a lot of the financial stuff. The will is in your name."

"The will?"

"That's the other reason we came here, Laz. We gotta talk about the moneys Dad left behind. You've got all the control here, Laz. We need to talk seriously now."

"Control? What? Wait," he says, looking from one brother to the other, but not at me. "Dad's dead?"

I almost shake my head but, honestly, I sort of suspected that no one here was connecting. When you can't take the first step in a marathon conversation on the most important thing we face in our lives, how hopeless is the race?

I remember my mother once shouting, "He's *not not not not* coming back, Murron! He can't handle it, okay? Do you get it yet? We're better off without him! *You're* better off! Open your eyes!"

I didn't believe her then, I even thought she was foolish, driven by the standard resentment of the abandoned parent. I feel the urge to leave right now, find my mother, and apologize to her for that one inaccurate thought I'd had almost twenty-five years ago.

Johnny's smiling again at the confusion, Lazarus is walking toward the kitchen. We follow him. He's at the phone. The red light flashing mercilessly. Lazarus presses the button. I'm certain that no one but I sees the small tremor in his finger.

"Fifteen new messages." *Beep.* "Hi, Laz. It's Mare. Hope you're doing all right with this. Try not to think about it too much. Give me a call if you want. Next Wednesday's best. Around lunch. On my way to a *Nutcracker* rehearsal right now. *Learn how to drive, you idiot! Goddamnit!* You take care." *Beep.* "Uh, hi, Laz. Tony. I'm sorry to bother you. Yeah, just thought I'd give you a call. Was worried how you'd take it. Not sure if you're there or not. Hope you're doing okay. We, uh, Johnny and I, were thinking about going out there to see you. Is that okay? If—"

Lazarus hits the erase button. "Shit," he says. "How's Ma?"

Tony shakes his head. "I don't really know."

"But she knows, right?"

"Of course," Johnny says. "She was there."

"What do you mean?"

"Mom was in the room."

"Jesus, Johnny!" Tony shouts. "It doesn't count!"

"You're a real literalist, aren't you?" Johnny says. "No shit it doesn't count."

"You mean she went over there herself?" Lazarus says. "I got an e-mail saying she was dying."

"Sure you did," Johnny says. "Show me your computer."

"Yeah, we got the same e-mails, Laz. We've all been getting e-mails for the last two months."

"So who took her over there?"

"She was in the same room," whispers Tony.

"What do you mean?"

"I mean, Mr. MIA," says Johnny, "that she was laid up in the bed next to him."

"What?"

"Well, that's why it doesn't count, Laz," says Tony. "There was a curtain between them."

"A curtain?"

"That's what the man said. You can thank the *Nutcracker* clown for that setup. Nutcracking ballbuster sister of ours."

"Shut up, Johnny."

"She just loves to—"

Tony grabs John by the collar and says, "I said, shut up, Johnny."

"Easy, easy, easy, Ton."

"So much for allies," says Johnny, smiling, casually unpeeling Tony's hand from his shirt, as if it's the only job he performs on an assembly line. "You got the wrong enemy this time, Kid Conservative."

Lazarus says, "Please, John."

"That's all Johnny Capone requires. A little politeness. His mama taught him that."

"You go ahead. Go on, Ton."

"All right."

"Yeah, you go right ahead. You have Johnny Capone's permission."

"Shut the fuck up, Johnny!"

"All right, all right," says John. "Don't lose your dignity, Your Laziness."

The minor miracle occurs for a second, for two. Three. The silence counted off by the echo of my heartbeat. I guess an urgent directive from Lazarus means a lot to these brothers.

"Thank you," says Tony. "Well, it was real hard, Laz. I mean, when I came in and saw Dad laying there dead, she was mumbling in her sleep."

"Mom was?"

"Yeah. Right on the other side. Bad dreams. Had no clue that he was over there like that." He looks up at Lazarus. "I didn't have the heart to tell her, Laz. I mean, what are you supposed to say: Uh, let's go out on the patio, Ma, so the authorities can take away your husband's dead body? I couldn't even look at him like that."

"Wait. Let me get this straight. So you're saying he died right *next* to her?"

They nod.

"In the same room of this hospice?"

"Without her knowing," says Tony.

"Jesus fucking Christ! How the hell did we—"

"Calm down, Laz."

"—allow this? Who are these people calling the shots?"

Tony looks down and says, "Laz. We been trying to get ahold of you for months."

Years, I think. *Decades.*

"Poor Dad."

Tony's fuming, Johnny's amused.

"What? Is this whole thing funny to you, Johnny? Hey! I mean, what a fucking tragedy! It's your father, too! Been together seventy years to die like that? What the fuck—"

"Take it easy, Tony," says Lazarus.

"—is wrong with this country?"

"He was never a father to me," says Johnny, who can identify irony, it seems, when irony wounds.

"It *is* sort of funny, though," Lazarus says, in his far-off, almost untraceable way.

"How long are we supposed to take—What's funny?"

"Well, we been talking for fifteen minutes, Ton, and I had no clue, you know? I thought you were just here to lay out some numbers, Pop's bills and stuff."

"Well, we *are* here to do that, Laz."

Finally our eyes meet. I want to tell Lazarus I'm sorry about his loss, and yet it seems more pointless than blowing air into a dead body. It doesn't take him long to look down, pull a cigarette pack from the pocket of his pants, lift the box to his face, swat its bottom, catch one in his mouth.

I can't hold out. "I hope you're doing all right."

"Hey, what the hell, huh? Pop lived a good old life, you know? A good guy."

"That's right," says Anthony.

"So what was it then?" He has yet to light up, his ashy lips sealed, the ventriloquist act of the advanced chain-smoker. "Heart attack?"

"Oh, I don't know, Laz. Jeez, I never asked. Do—"

"Jesus Christ."

"—you know, Murron?"

I left the room when all the official documentation was happening. Should I have stayed? What difference would it have made? "Well, I don't know. Old age? I mean, he was—"

"What a bunch of morons."

"—pretty much out of it—"

"Shut up, Johnny!"

"—by the time I got there." His feet were swollen like ripe melons, his skin so dry and scaly I couldn't penetrate the pores with cream. I tried to hold his hand but he kept pushing it away, as if I were a stranger.

Which I was.

"Hey. Well. Yeah," says Laz, the unlit cigarette bouncing up and down on each word. "All right."

"Morons."

"I'm going to ask—"

"Death is death, huh?"

"—for an autopsy report next week."

"I gotta—ah, don't do that, Tony. Let it rest, huh? What do you say? Sleeping dogs lie. Sleeping Pop, you know?" He finally lights up, but the ventriloquist act continues. "Sorry to give you the slip, kiddos, but I gotta leave for work in a couple minutes, all right?"

"Laz," Anthony says, "you gotta smoke in here?"

"A little late for that," says Johnny.

Anthony whispers, "You've got guests."

He means me. That's the best Anthony can do, as good as it gets. This pseudosubtlety misses Lazarus, an eyebrow raised, now slowly making for the sliding glass door to the patio. He's gonna check out from his own house yet again, lighting up as he walks, the twirl of smoke following him to the exit.

"Secondhand smoke will kill you," he says. To seriously ponder the slow-death perils of cigarette smoking. While smoking. After just hearing about the death of his father. "Yeah. Read once somewhere about it being as bad as firsthand smoke. Weird, huh? Nothing gets better from the source to the victim. Weird."

I don't know why, but Anthony and Johnny go with him. The smoke stays behind with me.

"The fellas at work tell me I should go pick tobacco and save myself a thousand bucks a week. Well, what the hell, huh? Ah, poor Pop. So you knew about all this?"

He's talking to me, I think. I can hear him, I can see him, but he doesn't know that I'm not there *with* him on the patio.

"She's not fucking out here!" Johnny shouts.

I shake my head, and Johnny pokes his head inside to get me to laugh, the smile clownlike and grotesque. I give him nothing. He doesn't care, in one direction or the other, about people. Backward or forward, it's all the same to him. Johnny seems to love the drama, the idea that someone, anyone other than himself, is hurting.

We all know the world is easily cracked like an eggshell. The weight of our sorrow and nastiness and stupidity too heavy for the thin mantle to bear. Beyond that, I don't know really what to say about it. And yet I don't wish, for a moment, that I didn't have pain. That would be like me saying I wish I wasn't *me*. I just hope we can recover, that's all, when we fall through the crack into the pit. Johnny and his crackhead kind don't help, that's for sure, the lending of a hand more foreign to him than Arabic.

"You couldn't find dust in a dust storm, could you, Laz?"

I walk past Johnny without touching him, join the three brothers on the patio. Try to abide my own rigid words. These Felices are like a test, each one in their own way, against anything you believe in.

"She's been a godsend, Laz," says Anthony. He grabs his younger brother, my progenitor, and holds him there. "Just done a heck of a job with Mom. Cleaning her, feeding her. Monitoring the nurses."

Lazarus looks up at Anthony, the cigarette dangling like a small branch about to break off in the softest trace of wind.

"Yeah, Laz!" Tony reaches out and pulls me in, kisses the top of my head. Caught between passion and indifference. Presence and absence. Two nuts of a different sort. The smell of nicotine, the smell of Lazarus is gonna make me puke. I put my hand on Tony's shoulder, pull out of his happy headlock.

It's sad how rapidly good intention goes bad.

"You should see Mom when this girl comes in the room! I tell ya, it's just precious. She's brought life to Mom, Laz. It's the best medicine in the world. Can't beat it!"

"Well, that's great to hear." He's walking to the corner of the patio, mumbling through sealed lips, "You know, those endorphins respond at a molecular level. Read that somewhere. Yeah. Positivity works. Even into your eighties."

As if my time with his mother is an abstraction, something he can look up in an encyclopedia. As if there is no question to ask of me, nor of me about my son.

"Why don't we grab a bite, huh, Laz?"

He looks up from some completely private dream and says, "Can't do it, Ton. Told ya I gotta work."

"Well, how 'bout grabbing a burger on the way out?"

"Would love to but gotta run, kiddos."

"What's new?" says Johnny.

"I understand," says Anthony. "Someone's gotta keep the wheels of this country running. Business is business."

"That's right," Lazarus says, extinguishing his cigarette on an ashen slab of concrete. He tosses it into a mound of at least fifty snipes, piled like bodies at the edge of the mass grave. "Haven't been late once in twenty-one years, kiddos. Believe that? Haven't missed a day."

As if he's perfectly entitled to say this in the presence of his second kiddo.

16

Johnny Benedetto Capone
Share of the Rosy-Flush Clip-On
January 8, 1981

HE TOLD HIS FATHER don't listen to them, what the hell do they know.

It didn't take long after he hung up the phone to go on a mental rant against his family. From top to bottom, his siblings had always held him down. He had no use for them and the so-called leader, the bright son. When Richmond had heard about Johnny's business proposal, he'd actually had the nerve to contact their father from a free-market symposium led by successful Princeton alumni. Johnny couldn't believe the guy's balls. Wasn't even out of his business diapers yet. Still parroting some four-eyed nerd's ten-cent theories in the peapod of the classroom. Yet he thought he knew, didn't he, knew enough to make a phone call to California as if he were some big-shot boss on the East Coast, toss in his ten-cent theory on the viability of the Rosy-Flush Clip-On. Wannabe Carnegie, Rockefeller fuckup. The bottom line was that he, Bitchmond, not only had no say in the deal but he had no firsthand knowledge about the device. What kind of a leader was that? His call was the ultimate example of bad business. Pointlessness. Waste.

If Bitchmond had called Johnny, Johnny would have said, "How would you know about this deal, big sister? Don't you go pee-pee sitting down?"

Because it was genius, pure genius. Johnny was amazed it had taken this long for his innovative countrymen to invent the damned thing. They came up with condoms, Johnny thought, they legalized abortion. They came up with VHS tapes. This one was just obvious. How many times did you enter a public restroom only to U-turn at the urinal, your nostrils annihilated by the sour odor of unflushed piss and gobs of blood and God knows what else? Some of those urinals were brown as a muddy football field. How many times did you just walk out and find a park bush to hide behind to relieve yourself?

Too many damned times to count, thought Johnny.

The device would sell because it relied on the one thing everyone could rely on. Human weakness. In this case expressed through indifference, even indecency. That's what guys like Richmond never thought about. Their understanding of humanity was confined to the chamber of the heart where blood flowed cleanly, a current of goodness rushed to the needy body of the world. Their business imagination stemmed directly from this. They thought that money was made by some savior device conceived of altruism, sometimes even love.

"That prick thinks he can reverse the apocalypse."

Short of manufacturing difficulties, distribution issues, matters of the appropriation of capital, and all the standard stuff that went into doing good business, an area of expertise that Johnny had not yet been able to adequately impress upon the country, let alone Los Angeles, the functional premise of the Rosy-Flush Clip-On's success was no stretch for human psychology. Its salable feature was the low level of responsibility men felt toward their fellow Man. In this case, it was literally men toward other men, which of course was all the better since all men were pigs.

This was a matter of personal immortality, Johnny's big shot at the as of yet unclaimable crown of social approval. This was his porcelain god smelling good for once, "as it should," he said, "as it should," thinking of the thousands of times this particular deity had attacked his delicate sensibilities. In dive bars and no-tell motels from Tijuana to San Bernardino, with pull chains, with kick levers, with push buttons, reading grout jokes and bounty-hunting ads and gang graffiti, always adding in the least rushed manner his trademark tag, a giant phallus gorged with blood from the center of the shaft to the mushroom tip, the initials JC across the crest of a cock ring.

"As it damn well should," Johnny Benedetto Capone said.

He dialed up his inside man on this project. He'd seen him on the local television station pitching the product. Johnny had been calling for days. He hadn't been called back once, but that's the kind of guy, he imagined, that Mr. Gillingham was. Mr. Gillingham was busy making money.

Johnny called his father. The old man still had reservations. Bitchmond was a piece of shit.

"Dad," he said. "Who you think you're talking to here?"

His father said nothing.

"This is Johnny. Your third oldest, for chrissake. You think I'd steer you wrong of a good deal?"

The line was quiet for a heavy second and then his father said, "No. I don't think you would, John."

"I don't keep a hot thing like this to myself, Dad. I share the wealth. I'm not your second son. Mr. Goody."

"Let's keep Richmond out of this."

"Well, that's what I'm talking about right there, Dad! That's exactly what I'm saying! Stay out, for chrissake! Keep your goody nose to yourself!"

"John," his father said, "I'm putting all my faith in you."

He didn't like that his father's voice had cracked. The man was forcing the faith. It wasn't natural. "Come on, Dad. Spare the fucking lecture, huh?"

"You know this is all the money we've got?"

"Dad," Johnny said, "you want in on this deal or not?"

"John."

"We're talking about *free* fucking money. It's like robbing a bank legally. Bathing in gold."

"I've been playing the lottery every Friday for the last six years. Your mother lets me take five bucks, John. To this day. Bless her heart. Even on Good Friday she lets me go. I never won. Not even five lousy bucks to make a day's losses back. Now I'm asking you if this is the right thing for me to do."

"Look here, Dad." Johnny pulled his face away from the phone, bent over and mouthed the filter of the cigarette in the ashtray, dragged on it once, and exhaled out his nose. His right hand was holding the phone, his left hand fondling his testicles, his eyes on the clock. He had to meet his dealer in downtown Upland in fifteen minutes. "Fuck Rich."

"I told—"

"Okay then." He took his hand from his crotch and reached out across the table. He slid it into the sleeve of his custom-made Peter Entry Films windbreaker, the one with the miniature nude woman on the chest pocket and the stalker's hood that kept his head warm at late-night bus stops. Then he twisted his torso to work his way into the other sleeve. "We can do this another way. Let's try this. Fuck. What. Rich. Says."

"How do you know, John?"

"Do you want to listen to me for once or not, Dad? I mean, what the hell are we having this conversation for?"

"We don't have many options left, John."

"I should go to someone who appreciates it."

"I hope this is the right thing to do."

"You're welcome. No need to thank me."

"I pray it is."

"Great. So you're in. A great start. Let's do a little better next time on the gratitude front."

"Think of your mother, John."

"I am, for chrissake!"

He hung the phone up. He didn't call back. Nor did the phone ring. He mumbled once under his breath, "Fucking geriatric prick," and then left for his daily rock of crack cocaine.

For the moment, he had $19 to his name. At the neighborhood liquor store, he bought a $12 quart of Ketel One. A few weeks back, he'd told off the owner, a Persian named Cyrus Rohan, for having the nerve to sell candy manufactured in the Middle East. Johnny didn't like that he'd given some anonymous camel jockey x cents of his twenty-two-cent purchase. What's more, he didn't like that he'd loved the flavor of the candy after making the purchase. Despite his belief that everything from that part of the world should suck rocks, the carmelized sugar was subtle as honey, the sesame seeds crunched softly between his molars. One's heart could be stoked by the fire of prejudice, but apparently not one's taste buds.

Johnny had forgotten the exchange. The owner now counted out Johnny's change, his knee rubbing against the two-by-four leaning conveniently against the register, the nail in its end rusted orange.

"Let's go, man," said Johnny. "I don't have all day."

He pocketed his pennies and nickels, opened the bottle's top through the paper bag. He took a swig where he stood, smiling at the store owner. Then he held the bottle out halfheartedly, knowing that there was no way in hell he'd lose a drop of his liquor to this clown. The generic dress shirt was tucked in, the collar ironed, face shaven, hair slicked back, as if this foreign square were an ordinary American.

"Too hot today for the towel, Abdul?" Johnny said, pointing at his own head.

The owner did not say a word, did not move, his eyes on Johnny's hands.

"You look like you're gonna run for president."

"You go now."

"Gotta be born here, Abdul. Your parents, too. Your grandparents. All the way back to Columbus and his Pilgrims."

"Get out, okay. You go away."

"You hiding out over here, Abdul? Trying to look like Mr. Rogers? You had me conned for a minute."

The owner reached down for the two-by-four. When he brought it up to his waist, Johnny laughed aloud.

"Okay! Okay! You crazy fucking jockey! You're gonna get yourself a life sentence if you don't watch out!"

He laughed his way right out the beeping door.

Now he drank as he walked, the strides long and arrogant, the pushed-out chest as spindly and full of air as a box kite, his fat lips wet with liquor and spittle, humming the refrain of "Jessie's Girl." He trekked past office buildings and grocery stores and construction sites, he passed all kinds of people on the street without taking them in, exactly, as people. Admirers, obstacles, slugs. His somatic self started in the center-middle. He made a point to slow down anytime a lady could see the package he carried in the front of his pants, the thought of her inner shame filling his monstrous cock with blood. One woman turned away and looked over her shoulder as they passed each other, but he did not stop. He nodded at the back of her head, smiled, and looked up at the streetlight as if it were a camera documenting his sordid life.

He entered the alleyway behind the Safeway and sat on a delivery ledge hidden from the street. A line of dumpsters to his right, concrete walls to his left. He looked around, he drank, the bottle a quarter of the way done. He did not think on anything. When alone, he often did not think on anything. After a few more drinks, he started to ponder his hookup being late to this rendezvous. "He's fucking late. The prick is fucking late." He didn't wonder if there'd been a mistake about the place or time, if Juan was having trouble on the way over. Because he'd get what he came here for, now or eventually, whether his hookup showed up or not, was timely or late, alive or dead.

He took another shot, his lips pressed to the spout, and saw Juan approaching. He wiped his mouth with an elbow and shook his head.

He didn't look at Juan. Eye contact would be a kind of forgiveness. Forgiveness was weakness.

"Late, amigo. Late."

"Hey," Juan said. He did not sit down. "You wanna deal or what?"

"No apologies?"

"Cut the shit, man. You want in on this thing I got, big man?"

"I came here for an eight ball. You think you can handle that?"

"Small shit. I'm talking about big money."

Johnny finally looked up at Juan. "What do you know about big money, Juanita? You can't even show up on time."

"Okay. You're stupider than I thought, big-talking man. I'll see you on the streets, tough guy."

Johnny stood. Juan was still there. "Well, what've you got?"

"Today's your lucky day, big man. I'm gonna add you to my sales team."

Johnny shook his head no, but inside he already felt good about the prospects. "Like I said. What've you got?"

"You put in a small investment and you'll get your money back five times over, man."

"To do what?"

"Sprinkle some A1 blow on those bitches you saying you know in the industry."

Johnny hadn't acted in a Peter Entry film in two years, but he still knew a few of the older starlets who'd been around since the good old days. The young pussy, the good stuff, he knew less and less about, but he'd give this hustle a shot if he could just get around Entry. The man had virtually blacklisted him from the entire Southern California adult industry, although Johnny was sure he could do gay porn if he ever had a switch in predilection.

What's getting a BJ but a mouth and a tongue? he thought. You don't like it, just close your eyes and change the channel.

And if I wear the old wolf mask, no one'd know a fucking thing.

"I get you in there, it's worth more than five times over, and you know it."

"No. I *don't* know it. I don't even know if you're really in there, big man."

"Oh, I'm in. Don't you worry. Johnny Capone is nothing if he ain't in."

"Start you at seven or eight G's. You do something with it and we'll renegotiate numbers, cool?"

Johnny thought the offer over. If he could get the twelve G's in the mail by the week's end, he could roll the bulk of it over selling blow. "You got that eight ball?"

Juan handed it to Johnny. He unwrapped the foil and put his tongue on the middle of the rock. "This flower power is an advance on our partnership, Juanita."

"I'll swing by your place in a few days to pick it up."

"Come Saturday."

"Still at that motel?"

Johnny nodded.

"All right."

"That's right all right," Johnny said.

"Cash, big man."

"Who you think you're talking to?"

"All right. See you then, big man."

He went home and convinced his father to front the cash to buy a hundred shares in the Rosy-Flush Clip-On. His father said, "John, we'll talk again, son." Two days later, he picked the envelope up at the manager's desk. The check was for $12,000, the combined lifetime savings of Mr. and Mrs. Anthony Felice Sr., egalitarian investors in each of their children. They were still in the dark about their third son's new surname, Johnny Benedetto Capone, and so had inscribed it to John Felice.

He showed an old ID with his former name at the Western Union and cashed the check, losing a 3 percent cut on the service fee. He took to the streets with $11,640 in hundreds and twenties in the

inside pocket of his overcoat, trying to figure a hustle to get the 360
bucks back before he got the blow from Juan the next day.

On his way back to the Kindly Cactus Motel, he bought a brand
new VHS recorder at Radio Shack. Then he caught the bus out
to Adulterers and tried to find every movie he'd made with Entry
Films. None of the tapes were alphabetized or even dated and so he
had to look through the entire category labeled Straight. He'd done
twenty-two scenes in all, thirteen films total, but he found only two
on the shelves. Luckily, he had a big part in each, and could get off
on himself pretty easily. At the register, he picked up a pair of anal
beads that he liked to use on himself while masturbating, and then
walked out of the store with his newly bought goods in a flaring, logo-
less, smut-black trash bag.

At the Cactus he sat down on the edge of his queen-sized bed
and, fighting his own instincts, thought about his life. Yesterday was
gone and forgotten, tomorrow on the clock's winding arm awaiting
its chance to be likewise forgotten. He'd cut a deal tomorrow, but no
one could tell him it was any different from today. Not his fool of a
father, not his ex-boss Peter Entry, not the cleanest-souled Quaker
with the dirt of the earth under his nails. You made your bucks,
you kept the swine away from your bucks, and then you died. That
was life. If anyone showed up for the funeral, it didn't matter to
you anymore, did it? And if they were stupid enough to throw down
some cash for your posthumous ass, you'd get buried. And if they
said a few good words of fiction, it probably had more to do with
themselves than with you.

He drank another shot of the Ketel and then flipped through the
TV Guide. *As the World Turns, Dallas, CHiPs.*

"Bitches and bikes," he said, his taxed mind sputtering into a
memory that hadn't yet died like the rest.

The summer of '64, just caught stealing a bike downtown by a
businessman named Boddington, his father half a minute from delivering a straight right to his upper cheek that would blacken his eye for

a week and a half, his mother now jamming an index finger into his father's chest, commanding, "*Abbiate capito cosa intendo, Antonio!*"

"In the American," his father said.

"You will *not* put him out on the street. If you throw him out, I go with him. Not one of my children will ever go hungry! *Non uno dei miei figli!*"

"I said, speak in the American!"

Yes, she had been the only one who'd ever loved him. All the way back to childhood. She'd iced his black eyes when he was a kid, she'd stood at his side in the dean's office when everyone damned well knew he'd said it, he'd done it, she'd introduced him to an angel named Anna when he'd gotten back from Nam, she'd made every excuse for his failures, to family and nonfamily both, with startling conviction. If someone had ever shown her an ad for a Peter Entry film with her son's name and mug at the promotional crest, she wouldn't have believed it.

She had the true faith, she believed good would triumph over bad, she did not know who her son was.

Johnny took a deep breath, coughed as if there were a furnace in his lungs, then rubbed at his burning eyes. "But maybe she knows what I can be," he said.

With her in mind, he could do this thing right now. With her in mind, he wouldn't cut corners this time. He counted the cash twice and said after each tally, "That's Mom's cash. The eleven G's is Mom's cash. Not mine not mine not *mine*. Not that prick father of mine's neither. Not anybody's but Mom's."

He stood up and made his bed. Wiped down the cracked mirror over the faucet, cleaned out the needles of glass collecting in the drain. He walked down to the office and asked to borrow a broom. Back in the room, the bristles dragged across the plaid rug like a rake across thick grass, the dust clouds rising and settling with each stroke. He shaved, he took a shower, he got dressed. He poured the pint of liquor left in the bottle directly into the sink, wincing as the vodka swirled down the drain, clear and quick as water.

He lay down on the plank-stiff bed and did his damnedest to think about his mother. Somehow he did this successfully enough to fall asleep and, as usual, he did not dream. He awakened with a hangover, the sunlight boring into his face. Not knowing how close his subconscious mind was to being reclaimed by the images of dereliction, overrun by the porn stars and dive bartenders and heroin junkies and motel clerks and correctional officers who constituted the crux of his adult life, he sat up and swung his legs over the edge of the bed.

He didn't move for minutes. Terrified of what he was about to do. It was Saturday morning and he had no game plan about how to get the thing done. The idea as impossible as heaven. Finally the knock came in the early afternoon, and it scared him. Still he did not stand. The stripped brass pole of the curtain rod had been ripped out of the wall and pinned diagonally between the corners of the naked window. Juan stood there now in the frame, swinging a McDonald's bag lightly into the glass, a smile on his face.

Johnny Capone shook his head and closed his eyes.

There was a steady knock and he opened his eyes and looked over at the window. He stood, went to the door, opened it a crack.

"It's a no-go, amigo."

Juan said nothing.

"We'll try this another time."

Juan smiled again, leaned against the cheap wood, head down, and walked by Johnny into the room. He put the McDonald's bag on the bed and went back to the door, gently nudging Johnny aside. The lock clicked and he said, "Got the shit in the Quarter Pounder boxes. Two of 'em. The Big Mac and fries are your bonus. So you sit down and eat. Get to work whenever you want."

"You can't come in here like this." It was almost a question. Juan was already inside the room. "I can't. No more. Can't do it."

"Too late," Juan said. "Sit down."

"My mother once told me to—"

"Just take a breath, big man."

"I can't remember what she told me."

"She told you to make money."

"She birthed me. Raised me. That's what my mother did."

"You high, man?"

"Can't do this, okay? Let's try again another day. I have spoken."

"You have *spoken*? What kinda funky shit is that? Lookie here, man. Do we gotta do this the wrong way?"

"You gimme a few weeks."

"I'm leaving with the eight G's whether you hustle that blow or not, big-talking man. Your mother told you not to get into wrecks."

"A couple weeks."

"Not me any longer. You know that. When you say it's gonna go down, I tell someone else what you said. You can talk to that someone else if you want. But you better bring a bulletproof vest."

Johnny fell back onto the bed and curled into a fetal position.

"Hey, man."

He pulled his knees into his chest.

"You just nervous, all right? I seen it before. Take a look where you're at, man. You one step away from being a junkie.

"Listen. I'm your guardian angel. You don't know what to do with your fantasy, that's all. Well, this here is the mutherfucking moment, big man. Right here. The big money sitting right there on the big man's doorstep. The superstar life, all you ever dreamed of."

Johnny looked out from under his elbow and grabbed at Juan's hand.

"All right," said Juan. "Take it easy, all right."

He got up, retrieved the cash, gave it to his dealer.

"You done good, big man. Just stay out the Swamps. That's my territory."

The day passed into evening. By dark, he was higher than he'd ever been in his life, the coke the best he'd ever snorted, the decision obviously the right one. The room spinning like a carnival ride, his cock

harder than a steel rod. With blow like this, he'd get more than the
asking price on the streets. He took a walk around the complex and
by the time he realized he was doing it, morning had come.

He sat down outside his motel door and closed his eyes. Flies buzzed
across his face, landed on the tip of his nose. Again, he dreamed of
nothing. When he opened his eyes, it was as if he'd never slept. He
had no clue what day it was. Finally he stood and went inside the
room and felt nothing at all when he found it completely turned out,
the bed flipped, mattress and pillow cut, his clothes scattered across
the bathroom floor, the bag of blow gone.

They'd left the television. It was flipped on its side but still plugged
in. One of the tapes had been crushed under the weight of the TV,
but *Little Red Riding Hood Rides the Big Bad Wolf* had survived. He
rewound the tape, didn't bother righting the screen. He stripped down
to his underwear, watching himself in Goodwill wolf garb crookedly
enter some random woman's backside, trying desperately now to get
hard. The shot didn't show enough genitalia for his present-day liking. Puritan standards back then, half a decade of liberty later. It was
hard to keep it up past the halfway point. He found the anal beads
draping the rim of the bathtub like a necklace, climbed inside, stuck
them one by one up his ass, and passed out.

He awoke again in the haze of his highness, curled into the tub
like a snake. He stood and the beads came out and rattled on the
porcelain. It was now Monday evening, but he didn't know that. He
swerved across the room, threw on his pants and went down, shirtless,
to the manager's office. She told him there was only one key per room.

"Many times there is the stealing here. Every *semana*. Even cars.
Killings, too. I change *la pinche* sheets and there is blood everywhere.
I no lie."

"You beaners all stick together," he said.

"What jou say, *cabrón?*"

He walked back to his room. He stood in the middle of it. The phone,
a black rotary, rang out. It shook violently with each announcement,

like a bomb about to explode. He didn't pick up. A few minutes later, it rang again. For some reason, he didn't go near the stand. As if the bell were merely a wind chime catching the light wind of the storm to come. It rang straight through the next hour and the repetition seemed to make the chime grow, exponentially, into a brass bell inside his head. Still, he avoided even looking at the little black box. It could blast out the gray matter of his cranium for all he cared.

Because he knew what it was after all, knew who it was. He was no prophet like that punk brother of his Richmond, but he could read the signs. Despite the blow just stolen on his watch, despite it happening when he was no farther than fifty yards from the scene, maybe even laid up against the room, despite just now realizing that the whole thing had been planned as far back as their meeting at the Safeway dumpster, Johnny Benedetto Capone was street smart.

He left the room, went slowly down the complex staircase, lowering himself into the world by intervals of collapse, his head still spinning, and picked up the first *Los Angeles Times* he saw. He sat on the very doorstep upon which he'd found the paper, his head hanging like a sunflower long dead, and opened it without looking around.

Just like he'd predicted, there it was. The blaze breaking out and burning up the banks. In under a week's time, the Rosy-Flush Clip-On had doubled its worth, earning investors a nice lump of cash. His father rang in again.

"You son of a bitch," he said. "You goddamned son of a bitch."

17

Murron Leonora Teinetoa
Blackjack at the Ohlone Indian Casino
January 15, 2008

We come up the parking ramp of the Ohlone Indian Casino and
Anthony says, "This is it, right? This is it?"

"Yes," I say, looking down at the note in my hand. It reads, *Hey, kids!
Meet me at the tables! Ohlone I.C. See you there, kiddos—*

"This is the place?"

"Yes," I say. "This is the place."

We didn't know what I.C. was. I felt stupid and angry at the same
time. We waited outside Lazarus's apartment for Johnny, but he never
showed up. "Some ally," Anthony kept saying. "Some ally." At a single-
pump gas station in a one-cow town called Avenal, the attendant
pointed toward the desolate highway and said, "Yeah. Blackjack. Slot.
Money. Sookie-sookie."

So we followed the road out past cows cows and more cows, and
now here we are, an hour and a half later, making our way into what
must be, judging by the full capacity of this garage on a Tuesday night,
a gambler's paradise.

A puritan's hell.

I'd thought that maybe our conversations would improve without
Johnny potshotting them, but Tony's too uptight to relax, as if he thinks

he's got an enemy around every corner. It's tangible, his nervousness, and I find myself feeling bad for his uncertainty in the present, his obsessive connection to yesterday. Somehow it seems uniquely masculine, just as, I suppose, my feeling bad for him seems uniquely feminine. I don't care for these gender parameters, but it's sad to see someone unable to enjoy whatever bit of life is left.

We're already on the fourth floor and I say, "There's one."

"Hey, I need two," he says, visibly concentrating like a sixteen-year-old at the DMV exam. He stops at the speed bumps and then proceeds, inch by inch, over each one. You would have thought that anyone driving a tank like his around would be prone to carelessness, or even displaying, now and again, the brute force behind the engineering design, but not Anthony. He's so particular about staying within the yellow lines, keeping within two miles above or below the speed limit that you want to reach over and spin his wheel off track for a second.

We finally find two spaces on the sixth floor of the garage, which is the roof, open-aired to the starless sky above us. It's not smog out here in this valley that blocks the constellations. It's dust and dirt, the stuff meant to be under the heels, hooves, and paws of this valley. I step out of the truck-tank and get all the confirmation I need.

"You need a surgeon's mask to breath out here."

"Am I straight?" he shouts. "Hey! Am I *straight*?"

"Straight as they get."

"*Straight*?"

"Yes. Yeah. Yep. Straight." Jesus.

"Make sure you lock your side."

I close the door. After he hits the button on his key chain, it locks automatically. The horn gives one fast beep after he does this, and he says, "Did you lock it?"

I take in a deep breath. "The door is locked."

We take the elevator down and the quietness between us is so absolute it's almost hostile. I focus on the electric numbers and hear the infinitesimal whine of the car's rapid descent down the cable line. Anthony's standing there in the golden glow of the elevator doors with his fingers laced in front of him, rocking back and forth on his heels, little-boy awkward in my company.

We reach the starred floor, which is underground, and are fed onto a moving walkway. The thousands of lights up ahead assault the shutters of the iris. We're embarking on a 3-D trip into the randomly firing synapses of a schizophrenic's brain. I blink once or twice to clear my own brain and Tony has stopped walking.

I head back and smile reassuringly.

"I feel bad," he says.

"Oh," I say. "It's not a sin in this century. I believe it may even be a credit."

"No. I left my wallet in the truck."

"That's okay." I'm afraid he's about to confess to something I don't want to hear. Despite standing there, we're moving toward the manic electric buzz of the casino. "I have money."

"No, I . . ."

"At least for an hour or something."

"I did it on *purpose*. Darlene told me not to spend one dime here tonight."

"Well, I won't tell if you won't."

He doesn't smile. Too late. We're on the floor. We're in the brain. The rows of machines shine all the colors of the spectrum. Like nothing I've ever seen before, these are the slots. Stares that could burn a hole through the screen and get at the green bills behind it, cherries and apples and numbers. Right arms pumping up and down like cable car conductors'. The adult arcade, carnival of greed, the zoning-out zone. We've arrived, but it makes no difference. No one cares about anyone's arrival here, and I think at once of Prince, how I don't want him to ever be so wounded or desperate or indifferent or covetous that he'd wander into a place like this on a Tuesday night, wishing his life away on a false promise.

Now I see Lazarus at the far side of the room, Prince's would-be grandfather, seated like his wayward, checked-out brothers and sisters, still unshaven, same shirt, an unlit cigarette poking out from behind his ear. He's draped by a morbidly obese young man whose layers of arm rest on the machine like a baby hippo, dark rings of sweat centering Lazarus's far smaller head. He's watching the dizzying shuffle of fruit like some Kool-Aid drinker on the brink of instant heaven.

We stand behind him for a few seconds.

"Hey, Laz," Anthony says.

His friend, the young man, taps his shoulder and says, "Lazarus."

"Okay," he says, not turning from the screen even a quarter of a revolution. "Hold on."

He gets a lemon, a cherry, and a seven, says, "Hey, hey, hey, welcome to life, huh?" and spins his legs around. "You guys will do better. I know it."

He stands almost dizzily, catching his balance by pressing money into my hand at the same time he's tucking money into Tony's chest pocket. It's five hundred-dollar bills.

"Let's go," he says.

"What's this, Laz?"

"Let's have some fun again, huh, Ton? Like old times' sake?"

"Johnny couldn't make it, Laz."

"Oh, he made it."

"Madera?"

"Let's have a good run tonight, huh? For Pop."

"Okay," says Anthony. "But where's Johnny?"

"Well, he made it *here*. And now he's *gone*. Oh, well. Just like Big Vic, huh, in and out all day long! Well, I say more machines for us!"

"How the hell did he—"

"He's not here. Who cares?"

"You guys fought, huh? That goddamned Johnny. He can't ever keep his mouth—"

"Ton. Let's not talk about anyone who isn't here, huh? Unless it's Pop. Let's go toast Pop at—"

"*Hey*! I'm all for Pops, too, okay? But where the hell is Johnny? We waited for him almost an hour outside your door. You fought him because he left us there, didn't you, Laz? How many—"

"Ton!"

"—times do I gotta tell you, you can't change that guy. You just gotta—"

"Ton! We didn't *fight*, okay? He got his five hundred bucks and spent it differently, all right? Let's go. The clock's ticking on this night. You look great!"

The last is to me.

"What'd he spend it on, a hooker? What a waste of money. He's a waste of an ally. I don't care if he's on Mom's side. What's the use? He can't even—"

"Tony! Who cares who he left here with? It's his right, *right*?" This appeal is to me. I don't nod or shake my head. Don't blink. I don't trust where this whole thing is going.

He gives his friend, whom I'd forgotten about, a hundred-dollar bill and says, "Okay! Let me show everyone around the place, huh? Well, not you, Big Al. Big Al's royalty *aquí*. But come along, come along. The more the merrier, huh? That's what Pop used to always say."

Big Al doesn't smile or say anything, but I can't think that it matters. Anthony's jaw tightens. We follow Lazarus's lead, me first, Tony after me, Big Al filling in, entirely, the rear. Despite the noise, I can hear the fabric of his sweatpants rubbing together. We pass the poker tables and the players hunched over their fanned hands, curled palms hiding the knuckles, the tight green felt divided into lucky numbers and deadly columns like a diagrammed star system. Lazarus greets the security personnel, shouting, "This is Anthony and Murron and, well, you know Big Al!" and they both nod back.

Lazarus walks like he's not moving forward of his own volition, it's like he's constantly being sucked into the next second. And rather than fight it, he's decided to go along with it. He's missing resistance. I want to help him, get him to turn to us and stop, but I know better by now. Despite the proud pronouncement he just made, despite the money he gave us, we're not completely *here*. It's like he thinks that nothing in life—his life, anyway—is predicated by choice. That whether we drove all the way out to this casino or not, he'd be on this same path to the same bar with the same feet beneath him.

The same story behind him.

At the bar, he orders three shots of Patrón and says, "Do you drink this stuff?" I shake my head no. It's not a lie. He just left out a preposition. I don't drink this stuff *with him*. "A pop then? Juice?"

How can I partake of spirits with Lazarus if I can't have a drink with my own AA-honor-graduate mother?

"I don't drink either, Laz."

"Right. Yeah. You know, I love teetotalers! Well, how about a Shirley Temple, you two? Those are great. Pop used to order them for us at the steakhouses. Yeah, 'member that, Ton? Oh, you don't like this place, huh? Well, you're right to think that. This place is no good."

I think he's talking to me. If he is, I honestly don't know what to say.

"No good, these places. Don't ever let the kid come near a show like this." I'm assuming he means Prince, although I suppose he could mean Tony's son. "Unless he goes the mathematical route, I guess, huh?"

The drinks come. I have no clue what he's talking about.

"You could win on poker. If you had it up top." He taps on his forehead. "*Rain Man*, huh? Counting toothpicks. Even pinochle. Great games."

It's a game, I think. Not a career, not a future.

It's a drug.

Now Lazarus's friend is looking back and forth at the brothers. I think he wants to make his single a double. To chase his shot with Tony's shot. He's waiting for something, wiping his forehead with the top of one hand, and then again with the other. The sweat returns, unflustered, to his chafed and stretched skin, beading at the edge of his bulging chin like a drip system for the garden. It drops into a layered fold of his neck, and as he cups the two shots for himself, the liquid floods the upper hem of his shirt, sudden blue in one small move, no longer gray.

Tony sees none of it, looking around the casino like a Secret Service agent.

"That's the spirit, Tiny-o! Well! Here's to Pop, huh? One down the word pipe for the old man. Salud!"

Not the slightest trace of wincing from either one, the burn of ingestion long gone, and he reaches out and pats my shoulder, turning to face me directly, his nose mine, his eyes mine, and nothing else. "Yeah! You look great, kid! Just fantastic!"

"Laz, there are some things we need to talk about."

"Come on, Ton. You got your share. Why don't you—"

"What do you mean—"

"—lighten up, huh?"

"—my share?"

"Let's go play a hand of blackjack."

We walk together to the table, Anthony keeping a few feet from the group, sulking—I'm guessing—at this lavish and wasteful enterprise. I'm not sure I disagree with him but, then, I don't know how successful we'd be asserting ourselves. Lazarus is always missing, yes, Lazarus in his cave, Lazarus on the road, Lazarus not where he's supposed to be, but lest we forget that Lazaurs does what he *wants*. The freedom to be commitedly uncommitted. Pity not Lazarus, I say. Pity the person who can't do what she wants. I don't think I've ever known anyone who's been so adamant about getting his way, and has gotten it, without complaint from reliant parties who've grown, without choice, no longer reliant.

Damaged but independent, I think, seeing my mother in her nightgown on the floor of our East Sonoma trailer, cross-legged, cross-minded, photo album open on her knees, bottle resting against her groin, the shot of her and Lazarus on the hood of the now broken-down

Mustang in his Madera garage that he promised my brother for his sixteenth birthday. Too many years later, weary but still here.

Lazarus leans his thin body over the edge of the table. There was a day when I'd have the recurrent dream of being given away by Lazarus, of having my unsure hand asked for. My girlhood fantasy followed me into womanhood like a stray cat, spurned, hungry for a meal, not knowing at all what to do with affection.

We were at the starfish tide pools at the Monterey Bay Aquarium when Lokapi said, "Your father's a punk."

Just like that, absolute certainty. The fight that ensued was horrible. I must have called him every variation of "asshole." What's most hard to process now is that I lied all the way through it, knowing he had a perfect right to be angry at Lazarus, who'd never returned one of his half dozen calls asking for my hand.

Prince's father is a good man. Today when I dropped Prince off at Lokapi's house, he gave me his entire two-week paycheck. It was a little over $600. He works an honest job at St. Vincent de Paul loading used furniture onto moving trucks. I gave it back to him and said, "It's okay, Kap. We're good this month."

"So am I," he said. "Take it."

"We're doing—"

"Us Teinetoas got a roof over our head. That's all that matters, Mur. Please."

"Okay."

A few years ago during a weekend without Prince, I had a panic attack that I was losing my son to his father, and so I talked to an attorney in the city. He said, "You've got thousands of alimony dollars coming your way. Just gotta file the paperwork." I walked out and never went back.

Maybe I've agreed to keep the courts out of Prince's life because I'd lose to his father in a custody battle. Maybe lose *badly*. When you take away the job at the paper (one that could, I'm constantly reminded, be very easily taken away) and the fact that I birthed Prince (a sixteen-hour ordeal that doesn't seem like much in the context of Lokapi's grandmother, fourteen babies in nineteen years, sixteen when counting the stillbirth and the tubal fetus), I don't have much to show for as provider. No village behind me, no lineage of a family tree. I don't really know what's up ahead. In a recurring nightmare, I'm barely hanging on to the same name as my son.

The blackjack dealer is more emaciated than Lazarus. He's a Southeast Asian, probably Vietnamese, colorful dragon heads and dragon tails running the length of his veined wiry fatless arms. In our neighborhood of EPA, just about every other male is "sleeved." A few weeks after his seventh birthday, Prince said he wanted to get a *pe'a* around his waist, a tattoo reserved for high chiefs in Samoa. I told him, "It's illegal in this country." The next week I went and lasered off the rose on my lower back, anticipating a civil rights argument I'd lose to a second grader.

The dealer has no desire to be here except for the same reason as his players. This is what people will do to themselves for money. To be here or not to be here, that is the question. I suppose the self-persecution can sometimes be helped, sometimes not, but there has to be a line, somewhere, between killing yourself out of choicelessness or extravagance, for need or desire.

Lazarus busts.

"Hey, hey, hey," he says, the stacks of black chips collapsed by the dealer's annoyingly prompt ruler, a thousand dollars of plastic swept away in a perfectly straight line to the kangaroo pocket of the new owner.

"Laz," says Tony. "We should talk."

"Okay, Tony-o! What do you got for me, huh? What's the big fight tonight?"

"Well, what did you mean back there by my share?"

"Tell me who the new enemy of this good country is, Tony-o! Gimme your shit list of libs, your hit list of lefties! Who's tops, huh? I want the biggest threat to the Union, big bro o' mine! Is it Gore? The EPA? Streisand? The entire fucking Middle East?"

"Hey! What are you picking on *me* for? I just asked you a question!"

"Yeah! Your questions have got no riddle to them, Ton. They're easy to hear, easy to *hate*!"

"Riddle? We got real issues here! We gotta—"

"Gooood blesssss—"

"—figure out—"

"Amerrrrrica!"

"—how we're gonna pay this thing, goddamnit!"

"Land that I loooove!"

"Hey! Goddamnit, Laz! We didn't drive to this hole in the desert to hear you sing!"

"Hole in the head, it's a hole in one! You think I don't know whatchu want, Ton? You think I don't know your cha-ching heart. That cash register in your chest. You bleed green, don'tcha? Huh? Huh?"

Anthony goes quiet, as if he's been caught with national security codes by some Eastern bloc gestapo. Watching these Felice men try to communicate is like watching a two-legged dog try to stand.

"Yeah. Well. I'll pay for her bed. Will you, Ton? Will you? How much—"

"Hey! That's not the *point*! I—"

"—money you got tucked away, huh, Ton?"

"—don't want your money! Hey! That's *none*—"

"—of my business, right? Huh?"

"That's right it's not!"

"Never once heard you say how much you got stored up, Ton. And so answer me—"

"Hey!"

"—how much?"

"That's *not* the *point*!"

"Cut that wrist and let me see—"

"Hey!"

"—the green blood flowing!"

"Hey!"

"Open your damned accounts up, Ton, and pay it. You go right—"

"Why should I be—"

"—ahead and I'll follow you, okay? Just pay for the whole damned thing and I'm there. Don't worry—"

"Hey! Why should I be the only—"

"—about a goddamned *coalition!*"

"—one paying for her care?"

They're chest to chest now. No one but me noticed the dignified retreat of Big Al, who nodded once at me apologetically, then waddled away. I feel so lonely and foolish in the middle of this floor of avarice that the visceral rumble returns like an evil friend, and soon I'll have to use the bathroom. I don't know how it happens, but they both look over at me.

"I'd just try to remember where I'm at," I say. "This is a public place where people can be publicly arrested."

"Well, she's right, she's right, and—"

"I know—"

"—I'm sorry."

"I know. Me, too."

"What the hell, huh?"

"So ashamed."

"Hey, I love you, brother."

"I love you, too."

"Jesus."

"Awww."

Of course, they're hugging. Peace without resolution. It'll come back again, without warning. Without reason. As I think on their problem, my stomach calms. I came here for Lazarus, yes, but I'm leaving this place for his mother. I had a wallet photo of Prince cut out, and I was going to talk about his grandson's dynamite left foot on the soccer field. How he might want to see a game sometime, that Saturday mornings at Stanford are just gorgeous.

But the truth is I wouldn't be alive if I didn't know better, deep down, where it hurts. Somewhere along the line of a life, I guess he gave up the ghost. I don't know if he was a war hero in a far-off land, but I know he's a coward here on his native soil. Unlike him, I witnessed it firsthand, I was *here*. No burning sensation down the throat, no burning tears in the eyes. He taught me that tonight. From this point on, whatever sliver of himself he gives me—*to hell with what I want*—I don't need.

18

Johnny Benedetto Capone
Last Shot at Peter Entry Films
March 22, 1979

It was seven in the morning, Friday, the season of fertility.

He splashed Old Spice on his deeply pockmarked cheeks and neck, across the dyed-black hairs in the concave pit of his fragile chest, he sprayed again over his groin area, and then a few strokes up and down his flaccid penis. It did not respond. That did not matter. It would come along all right. He wore no underwear for a reason. That way there was always a public response, which got him off. The looks of shock from men and women both, the locked jaw of lust from women and queers both, he especially enjoyed seeing the eye of envy from little-dicked men coveting what he had in his pants. Poor mice, they'd never know what it was like to be *the* man. When strutting down Santa Monica Boulevard with his heavy package swinging freely between his legs, he felt like a pitcher warming up in the bullpen.

He came down the staircase at the end of his complex, the Aloha. Today he was wearing, without underwear of course, a white polyester suit like the one he'd seen Travolta sport in *Saturday Night Fever*. He'd "honky-conked" his naturally curly hair back with Vitalis, the grease holding it in place through sun, wind, rain, and other meddling elements. At the bottom of the steps, he casually snagged the newspaper sitting on the manager's doormat. He tucked the morning issue of the *Los Angeles Times* under his arm and walked on. The media was always spouting the same predictable crap about life, so why did anyone need to read it? If the original story was crap, and then the copy of the next story was still crap, what did that mean in real terms except that the recycling industry was a top-notch scam making a pretty buck on crap?

Suddenly it struck Johnny Capone that he was actually doing the manager a favor by lifting his copy of the *Times,* and this thought prompted him at once to stop, wind up, and whip the paper back toward the manager's apartment. It clapped loudly against the door. He'd been aiming for the window. The door opened, but he was already around the corner of the building. He stood under the shadows of the awning of the parking garage, adjusted the Ray-Ban shades he'd "liberated" from a set last month, fired up a Marlboro, dragged and exhaled through his gritted teeth, snorted at the idiocy of someone opening a door so freely to the hostile world, snorted again, flicked the lit snipe a few feet behind the muffler of a neighbor's Pinto, looked around one last time for anyone else he'd have to set straight, and headed out to the bus stop.

This was Los Angeles, the West Coast, the great suburban sprawl. This was the sunny Southern California he'd grown up in, but Johnny Capone liked to think about New York, a big city he'd never visited, *the* big city, when he was walking. Johnny loosely held his head as if there weren't a single muscle in his neck, his imagination narrowing New York regionally to the Bronx, the time frame to the morally gray era of Prohibition, all this despite having the same name of a gangster from Chicago. When confronted for an explanation, he was quick to point out that his maternal grandfather, who was from Pittsburgh, and whose family had disinherited the name in the forties for the same reasons of infamy that he'd taken it in the seventies, was a Capone. So it was in pre-Prohibition 1918, as a young Al displaced in the Bronx, that Johnny Benedetto Capone traversed 1979 West Hollywood on the hunt.

He got to the bus stop and didn't sit. He stood coolly in the spacious shadows of the Longs on Firestone Way, as if he were merely there to fulfill the illegitimate end of trade in a legitimate drugstore. Ten feet back from the curb, he didn't want to be seen. It was embarrassing enough that an actor of his caliber had to shack up in a place called the Aloha, a residence that his creditors seemed committed to avoiding. That was good, anyway, or at least acceptable. But the bus stop was a bad place, full of rotten memories. Like that time those two teenagers in a cherry-red convertible Ford Mustang entered his life and fucked with it. He'd never gotten it out of his mind.

He'd seen them at the corner of Santa Monica and Minx. He didn't know it, but he'd stood from the bench at once and turned toward them as they approached. He looked like a peasant awaiting the king's carriage. The girl in the passenger seat was beautiful, and though the majority of her body was hidden behind the shiny slopes of the Mustang, he knew she was very tall. She had pronounced Nordic features, summer-white blond hair, a spaghetti-strap blouse hooked over wide, copper-skinned shoulders. More than tall, this girl was probably statuesque, the very image of the ideal he'd created and coveted since childhood, and what was painfully worse about the setup was the young man driving the car. He had one arm extended in front of him, wrist on the wheel, the other arm wrapped around the girl, and somehow, even as he sat, he was leaning away from her, his strong jawline twisted slightly to the side. Not because she repulsed him—Fuck no! thought Johnny—but so that everyone could see the kind of girl he was casually escorting through the city. He could do with or without her. The pure true confidence. He was the boy that Johnny, ten years his senior, had always wanted to be.

It wasn't, like everyone said, just the simple innocence of an adolescent outlook. Of not knowing about life, of inexposure, of a shortage of information. Johnny knew better. This, what the boy had, was the American dream. The hot girl, smoking car, natural good looks, the right attitude. And the money, wherever the hell it came from, you had to have the money. That never changed, wherever you were in life, however close to the end.

Johnny stepped to the curb, still watching. The Mustang slowed visibly and, in an instant that brought him out of his reverie, was right in front of him. She was smiling like a Miss America contestant. He was confused. They pulled alongside the walk twenty yards beyond the bus stop. She twisted in her seat, facing him from the breasts up, and waved him over like a Miss America winner. He walked forward with absolute obeisance, as if her beauty-queen gesture actually meant something and, more, as if it meant something in regards to *him*. He didn't look over his shoulder, he didn't look around. For all he knew, he was alone in the most populous city in California.

He'd almost forgotten about the driver. He got to the door of the car and suddenly thought about the very important issue of eventual riddance of the boy. Not riddance in the Mafia sense, although if it came down to that, he knew the right people for the job. And that went for anyone out there who shortchanged Johnny Capone, not just some smart-ass teenybopper. But what he meant was replacement of the boy. A flippant yet coercive shove off the cliff of American life. You got a little scared on the way down, scraped your knees a bit in the fall, but if you survived you had one more story of self to make your dick hard. Which was, after all, all that mattered, the axis of a sprung cock, upon which the world had been spinning since the beginning of time.

The important thing was that he could give the girl liquor, lots of it, and the boy couldn't. Not legally anyway. And he could give her more than a secluded make-out point in the Hollywood Hills, that dark starry sky covering the city like a nightcap, yeah, yeah, yeah, he'd seen it already, and the word for the view of the valley was "overrated." Warm bed, sweaty sheets, that's what you needed. Even a barren-walled studio at the Aloha was better than a teenager dry-humping you in the backseat, Mustang or jalopy. He could get her the best coke in the city, clean white powder fluffy as snow, he'd score garbage bags of pot. The kid had no clue about it. He could give her an existence without the constant irritant of parental authority. *He would be the authority,* he would be the happy sugar daddy patting his knee to mount. Sure, he would have to get some kind of hustle going to be her steady supply, but he knew the right people to get it lined up. Those two variants of "green"—cash and weed—would keep her dizzy, and returning. Who cared about cause and effect? It was all good, a damned good dream for Johnny Capone. He couldn't afford to let this opportunity go to waste.

He smiled confidently at the girl and the girl smiled back, matching his confidence. He saw deviltry in her eyes and, liking it terribly, he came forward at once. The world at last was here to be had. At the door of their car, he reached out for the shiny handle, feeling alive, clean. He nodded at the boy with just a trace of cockiness and the girl's smile widened into wild laughter. He froze for a second, the engine growled deeply, and he knew he'd been duped. The Mustang roared off, and the girl, twisted yet again toward the rear of the car, issued two slender middle fingers at Johnny. The driver, the boy, was in the same posture of adolescent certainty as when they'd driven into Johnny's life seconds ago. The only difference now was that his left hand, propped lazily upward like a signal to turn left, added a third middle finger to consummate the insult.

He'd never even touched the car.

Something else immediately set in Johnny's mind. He would never get a shot to avenge himself against the bastards, this in a city of three million people. There were at least eighteen different high schools in the proximal area and, anyway, those two weren't the kinds of kids who endured the boredom of primary education. So he couldn't do anything but eat the insult and counterbalance their gesture by slashing the tires of every Mustang he came across in the Aloha parking garage over the next few months. This he did, under the cover of A.M. darkness and with the internal courage stemming directly from a hallucinogenic state of mind.

And, still, here he was, four years later, at the same bus stop, with the same lint and nothing else in his pocket, in a worse financial situation, the same city of dead angels. This urban bubble of discharge and smog. To think he'd come back from Amsterdam to be here in a West Coast city of American shit.

The Line 12 was now approaching, a double bus today, one of those new deals connected by a midsection that swivelled and compressed like a Slinky toy, and Johnny Capone emerged out of the shadows of the city to ride it. He flashed the driver, a Mexican, his bus pass for the month of March, walked down the aisle past a half dozen passengers, all, as near as Johnny could tell, Mexicans, and sat in the rear corner, legs splayed wide across two seats.

These Mexicans, he thought. They should be sitting back here where I'm at. Either that, or they shouldn't be on the fucking bus in the first place. Shouldn't even be in this country. Fucking beanerniggers. What do they contribute to this place? What are they but fillers of space, occupying bus seats that Americans like me could fill? Shit, I'm just like that Rosie Parks, a little old lady with not a single ally on the side of what's right.

He should have studied when he'd had the chance. He should have taken his exams without cheating. Yeah, yeah, yeah. He should have never dropped out of high school, gone off to that stupid war. He should have read a book now and then like his shining star of a brother. Then he could have made a pretty buck or two.

He shook his head at the thought of Bitchmond, looked out the window at more Mexicans, shook his head again. He didn't want to think about anything that would put him in a bad mood. He had to perform at the shoot, earn his dollar just like his goody-goody brother did on scholarship at that East Coast snob pond for guppies. He looked around at the freeloaders, welfare babies, socialist-system rejects.

Did any of these people *work*?

"You know, like a broom, a-mee-go," he said aloud. "Scrub the dirt out of my shirt, camp-ren-dee?"

Well, he had to bust his ass this morning. Like any American. Get it up and growling by ten A.M. in the velvet-carpeted living room of his asshole producer, Peter Entry. The faggot behind the camera. The endless close-ups of Johnny's balls and asshole were proof of Peter's faggotry. You were supposed to focus on the woman in this industry, you were supposed to record every inch of her inside and out, and then add one thing, which Johnny had in gargantuan portion, from the male end. That's it, that's all you needed from the man in the equation, and that's just the way Johnny liked it. He was a stud, a slinging monster phallus, a walking cock. You didn't have to get a close-up of the stud's face, his chest, stomach. All you needed was Johnny Capone's hard rod.

Looking out the window again, he played a game with himself where he tallied the number of girls he would fuck, including the Mexicans, and lost count at fifty.

He said, "I'm an equal opportunist," and laughed at himself loudly, daring any of these foreigners to shun their better instincts and gaze upon him. No one did, as if a warning had been given by coyotes at the border.

He got off on Silver Lake and Sunset and commenced down the street in the same way he always did: Al Capone, young, on the rise, the Bronx. No birds congregated on the telephone wires above him, very few trees lined the neighborhood. The sunlight fell almost reluctantly upon this Los Angeles neighborhood. Johnny Capone's swagger loosened, his chest expanded.

He came to a modest domicile, tinted windows, rusting gutters, the roof sprouting a modern city of antennae, clay gobs speckled across the bright orange face of the house like acne cream. Someone had started the project of repainting the walls but had stopped. Johnny crossed the dirt where the lawn would have been, spit across the porch into a flowerless garden bed, opened the door, walked in.

On her bruised knees, Sherry Cherry's head was bowed, and she looked like a stalk of grass bending in the breeze.

Unbuttoning his white Travolta trousers, Johnny said, "Hold that thought."

No one said anything. There was one blinding light coming from the corner of the room and someone refocused it on the cleavage of Sherry Cherry. Someone else snorted and said, "Nice o' you to be on time, Johnny, the century's over already," and Johnny said, "Am I *naked*? Are you fucking ready for me? No answer? Nothing? Shut the fuck up then and *shoot*."

Johnny stepped into the light, as naked as he'd said, and stood so that her head was parallel to his groin, heavy scrotum dangling like fruit in her face. The slightest movement of his upper body made his penis swing. That's how big it was. He was thus very generous with this movement. He swayed once or twice like a Hare Krishna on a street corner to increase the momentum. Though he was an hour and a half late, he made everyone on the set continue to wait, which meant in real terms that he forced everyone involved in the shoot to ogle his monstrous member. The moment she looked up at him, he clutched at the discolored roots of her hair and pulled upward, as if she, in no uncertain terms, were an it. Inanimate. A handbag, luggage. She rose off her knees like a sputtering phoenix and he responded slightly, which was considerable in itself, but still not enough to carry the scene, or justify a full-body shot. He was nowhere near capacity.

He heard, "Cut!"

Sherry Cherry said, "Let go."

Johnny was holding his costar by her hair in midair suspension, looking over with anger at the light. Out of it stepped the producer/director/sponsor of *Close Encounters of a Lewd Kind*, Peter Entry.

She said it again, twisting her face upward, "Let go. Please!"

Johnny dropped her down onto the floor.

"Take your time, Johnny," cooed Peter, "You wanna take a walk or something? Go drink some prune juice at Vic's."

"No, fuck no."

"I got some oysters in the office."

"I don't need any fucking oysters. Let's roll it."

"You sure?"

"Sure I'm sure. What the fuck is this? Ever heard of coitus interruptus?"

"All right."

"Shoot the scene."

"Johnny," Peter Entry said, "that's my line."

"Well, *say* it then."

Peter Entry shook his head and disappeared backward into the light. "Let's roll it."

They lined up again. This time she refused to be on her knees in the way he desired. The hair on her head was tangled and disheveled like a neglected foster child's. She reached out and shifted half of her weight to her hands. She was in the position casually called "doggy style" in the industry. He watched her stare at his weak knees. They were wobbly, thin, lined with in-grown hairs.

This change in setup was keeping him soft. Her hair running down the middle of her back made him softer. He wound it around his fist like a rodeo rider—tight, hard, unremitting—and pulled her upward. She resisted. He saw a tattoo on her upper shoulder that all that hair had been hiding. It was a makeshift dollar sign, enclosed by a makeshift Superman crest.

Shit, Johnny thought, the world was made of bucks. The old man had been right about that at least.

Now he had to get it up and in, that was his duty, his vocation, how he made a buck. The last thing he wanted was to think of his fucked-up family. Because of all the people out there in need of a dick in their ass, he hoped they, *especially* they, his family, were down on the pads of their knees, one by one, lined up like daisies in a garden. Everyone but Mom, bless her soul. The assholes, they had no right, no right at all to judge him for his job. Who the hell did they think they were? All his life he'd had to listen to their bullshit, their sermonizing, their nonstop weighing in on crap they didn't ever know crap about.

If it wasn't for Mom, he would've forgotten about those people long ago. She was the only thing that kept him around, curious now and then, wondering what was going down with those jerks. So maybe she was the one to be angry at. Without her, he could've been clean of all their infectious shit. He couldn't think it enough: *Shit.*

Couldn't say it enough: "A family of shit."

"Cut! Cut!"

He held her there in midair, unexcited, yet panting. She was jerking away from him, like a bad fish on the line, but he didn't move.

"*Cut!* I said, *cut!* Let her the fuck go, Johnny!"

Johnny Capone tossed her forward and walked off the set.

He went into his dressing room, which was nothing more than Peter Entry's daughter's room during her annual supervised Christmas visit. He leaned on the lavender Hello Kitty nightstand and pressed his face toward the pink-framed mirror. He had devilish eyes, the opposite of this stupid cat. He hadn't seen himself from the neck up in months. He shaved without looking at himself, he popped pimples on his chest in bed to avoid reflection. What he hated most was the shape of his eyes. From the bridge of the nose, the eyes slanted noticeably upward, as if there were a polar force centered at the bottom of the nostrils pulling down. They were thin across the iris, and creased into tight folds of skin pointing at the temple. If he drank too much the night before, the corners of his eyes would fill with fluid in the morning like a beaten boxer's. Well before he'd ever started using, they'd been clouded in a milky swamp of yellow. As a boy he'd constantly been teased about having "nigger eyes." All he could ever say to his tormenters was that the descriptor didn't stop there, and "did you want a private peek, you little-dicked jerk-off?"

He pushed himself up and turned his face away. He walked over to the phone and dialed. They hadn't talked in over four years, and so he was shocked to have remembered the number. Suddenly she was on the line, a bigger shock. So she still lived in that run-down studio in East Hayward, or she had kept the number. He had no idea. He wasn't sure he cared, but here he was.

"Hello," his sister said. "Hello?"

"Hey," he said.

The silence came and, with it, the torture of guilt. Though he hated the silence, he stood there in it nonetheless, as stuck, dumb and empty inside as a scarecrow. He didn't say anything for some time. Finally he mumbled, "Hi there."

She hung up the phone and the torture ended.

"Fucking bitch," he said. "I ain't apologizing for shit. Fuck her. Just curious kids, that's all we were. Stupid kids."

He heard, "Sorry, but that's it, Johnny," and looked up into the mirror. Peter Entry was standing under the bridge of the door, smoking his customary post-shoot cigar.

"Sorry, man. Gotta get you to pull out. Lou's gonna finish off your scene."

The suggestion of replacement sickened Johnny, but why did it have to be the twenty-two-year-old kid? Didn't they appreciate that Johnny had Lou by better than an inch in girth? Lou had the Southern California credentials of bronze skin, barrel chest and no brains, but what irked Johnny Capone most was his Hollywood face. Everything from the almond-shaped eyes to the chiseled Anglo nose to the effeminate, down-turned mouth was perfectly symmetrical. No hideous or even modest scars, not a visible blood vessel. Johnny was sure he used eyeliner to accentuate the blueness of his eyes. And he hated Lou's attitude, which followed some bullshit line of progressive equality whereby his role as the set stud was no better or worse than her—the bitch's—role. Which, Johnny reasoned, was no more than lying there and exerting a few timely, titillating moans, a signature phrase like "Ride me, cowboy" or "Give me all o' whatchu got." In short, Lou had no figurative balls with the bitches, didn't even use the word "cunt" if prompted. Not even when *they*, the bitches, used it.

Therefore, Johnny concluded, Lou himself was a cunt, to be fucked, figuratively, like any other big pussy.

And then there was that stupid name of his: Louie the Largeness Monster. Who the hell would take on a name like that? thought Johnny Capone.

He didn't bother hanging up the phone. Johnny Capone's philosophy was, What's done is done, who cares?

He said, "Louie the Littleness Monster gonna be in diapers, ace?"

"Come on, Johnny."

"When I was his age, you know where I was at?"

"Johnny."

"You know what it's like to be a kid in the bush of a hostile Southeast Asian country?"

"Didn't you go AWOL?"

"I got more medals than—"

"I don't care, Johnny. I don't care if you ran. Can't we just get this done with no problems?"

"You think you can get one over on me and I'll sleep right through it, ace? I knew you were a piece of shit from the start."

"All right then," Peter Entry said, extinguishing the cigarette in a flesh-colored ashtray shaped like a woman's ass. "No insult taken. But I don't see the point in continuing any business together. Let's just terminate it right now, okay?"

"Fuck you. I'm gonna terminate you."

The producer said, "Look. I can't put your fucking mug in the shot, anyway, Johnny. You got skin like a grater. You seriously limit my range. I gotta use shadows and fucking angles ad nauseam. And it ain't just that, man. It *ain't* just that."

"I'll be back to finish you off before you finish this ten-cent flick."

"Scare someone else with that fucking fake Mafia shit, Johnny. I heard it already, man, heard it."

"I'll take out everyone on this set."

"It's *that* right there, man! Right fucking *there*! That's why I don't want you in my films! You're an evil bastard, Johnny! Are you listening? Fucking evil. You bring bad energy to this place. I mean, what the fuck's anyone else have to do with this shit? This is *my* set, *mine*. I make the decisions. What the fuck does Lou or Sherry have to do with this? But I believe you when you say what you think, man, I believe you. If you did have the balls to go through with it, which you *don't* despite that swingin' dick, you'd throw every innocent person into the mix. I believe that."

"I'm talking to a corpse, fuh-get about it."

"Best get off my set. 'Cause I won't call the cops, man. You'll wish I called the cops."

"You're gonna learn something about respect."

"Uh-huh. Sure. Get back to that no-tell motel you live in."

"I know some people."

"The only thing you got in common with Capone is a bad case of syphilis."

Johnny made his way out of the room. The accuracy of the last comment set into his stomach, virally, and with annoying sting. So he would stop by the old crew to pass along the torch. There was one more scene being shot, one more chance to get even.

He stood in the doorway, watching her lazily grease an orifice with one hand, twirling the stretch of a red satin sheet between the thumb and index finger of the other. The sheet was stained purple in oblong, amoeba-shaped spots. The walls, in theme, were also naked. He knocked on the frame of the door and the woman immediately covered herself to the neck, as if she, L.A.'s own Luscious Angela, were a damsel in distress.

"Gotchu some kerosene?" he asked invitingly.

"What's that? Some kind of Indian lube?"

"No, baby. Gas. It's gas."

"Um, I haven't ever—"

"Better getchu some, honey. For after the shoot."

He'd made her bleed on last week's set, and hadn't bothered to stop. Afterward he'd told a joke to a camerman about "the slippery benefits of V8."

"Gas?" she asked.

"That's right, baby. Gas. Your costar told me yesterday he's got a bad case of—"

"Get the fuck out of here, Johnny!"

Peter Entry was standing in the doorway of his office, which was firstly his bedroom. He had his hand on the grip of a steak knife sheathed in the leather pocket of a construction belt, obviously a stage prop of some sort.

"Leaving, boss." He eyed the producer's waistline with amusement. "Nice getup. You think you're John Wayne or something?"

The producer pulled out the knife and pointed it toward Johnny, one half of the blade glaring silver, the other dead black. Then he started to walk forward, slowly, as if in a midnight dream, or a scene from one of his own films.

"I'll see you again," Johnny immediately said, trying, as if there were such a thing, to expeditiously saunter across the floor. He stopped at the exit and turned to the girl. "'Member what I said, seen-your-rita. Don't forget: Ke-ro-sene. It'll torch any critter you got hiding out in that beat-up pussy of yours."

He went out the door, not bothering to shut it, and stood in the smoggy face of promise of the infamous city of angels. Everything he could ever imagine was happening right there in front of him, but his eyes went to one image and stayed. Across the street, little girl skipping rope on the driveway, feet double-Dutching to the count. She couldn't see him, colorful pigtails whipping back and forth across her joyous face. His heart missed a beat. That might have meant a lot to someone else, but not Johnny Benedetto Capone. He took pride in his steel-hard insides. He said seven words, "That fucking bitch *knows* she liked it," and that was it.

The Felices
Vision at the Upland Independence Day Parade
July 4, 1955

*They weaved their way through the crowd of the Upland Independence
Day Parade, the boys anxious to spread across the lined-in-flags walk of
Third Street and claim it, baby Mary Anna in the custom-made carriage,
a marriage gift first honored upon Claudia Adelina Santacanale in the
Sicilian village of Sinagra in 1862. It survived Garibaldi's call for Italian
unity, right through World War I and the death of all the Santacanale
men but three, it fled Mussolini to cross the Atlantic in eight days, finding
its way into the cramped quarters of Enrica Santacanale Capone, who
actually had it blessed by a priest. Then in the Pittsburgh town hall five
years later on the infamous wedding day of her daughter, Maria Serafina
Capone, the hand-carved artisan's project handed down one last time.
The carriage in transport yet again, bouncing about in a bullet-shaped
trailer over the Continental Divide, Victory-declared summer of 1945,
with the newly wed Mr. and Mrs. Anthony Constantine Felice and their
firstborn, Anthony Jr. Now permanently residing on the West Coast of this
country, twelve straight years of service escorting the five Felice children
during infancy, the wooden wheels logging more than a thousand miles
in the up-and-back trip to downtown where the library and post office
were, where the Monday farmers' market and Tuesday sewing circle met.*

Now he walked beside his wife with his own family talisman propped sharply on his head, just as his father had taught him, the bequeathed wool fedora leveled at the center of the brow, brim line even all the way around. They passed the newly constructed pizza place, Jack's Magnificent Pizza House, they passed Margie's PX with the candy in the window and the soda fountain in the rear, the crowd as loud as it would ever be in the town of Upland, even after it would grow, like all SoCal towns, into a polluted, congested, strip-mall city of the late American century.

Today the boys carried tiny American flags, the kind one puts in the penholder on the desktop, and they wore matching red, white, and blue collared shirts their mother had ironed the night before, and, truthfully, without question, even a parade a fraction in size of the present affair would titillate the patriotic hearts of this family, would incite the loyalist fervor in each to cheer that much louder. As it was, the whole town of Upland was present, standing on the downtown walk three and four rows deep, flag-waving children on the shoulders of their fathers or perched on benches, necks outstretched to catch the latest float. Or they were in the parade itself, commemorating some beautified thread of the rich fabric of their country, the firemen, the Little League team, the nurses' union, the masons, the office of the mayor, the veterans. The veterans last, always last, bringing up the rear.

He stood there at the curb of the Upland Hardware Store with his family, this good and simple man, taking in the victory of the day, trying to stay focused on the event's purpose. A father of unsurpassed hope for his children, a husband of frustrated fidelity, a son of the Great Depression, a laborer of the Pittsburgh steel mills with the mottled, bone-dry, cancerous skin to prove it, a fiscal conservative with welfare in his near and far future both, a Chapter 11 signer-to-be twice in his unillustrious "career," an irony too hard to bear to the last day of his life and so not talked about, ever, this was Antonio Constantino Felice Sr. He had his hands in his pockets, smiling down on his sons, and then looking out at the sharp-eyed, angular-browed, round-faced members of the VA.

He was not a soldier. He believed he could have been one. His brother had gone, the Pacific theater, toward the end of the war when it didn't count. He, Anthony Sr., had been a rugged football player before dropping out of high school in 1935, and so he knew he was tough enough. If it had anything to do with that. He wasn't sure. He'd never been there. He'd always had bum luck. Had been stopped at the gate by a man with an X-ray in his hand, a stethoscope around his neck. It was the old story: a bad body, a misshapen issue. Even in World War II, a ticker the size of a grapefruit was enough to keep you homeside, as they used to say. 4-F Felice, his brother called him.

He could never find the right deflection away from the issue of his uninvolvement. The lottery game of the economy, the recent aggressions of the North Koreans, the comic brilliance of Milton Berle, and even an impression now and then, making silliness of his story, having fun with himself—none of these methods made him feel truly manly in that deep region where the demons of shame have always taken residence. He was worried that the story he'd pass on to his children was insufficient, maybe even fraudulent.

He watched the Upland Junior Princess sitting between two Shriners, the men in their little red hats that looked like giant maraschino cherries, she in a purple taffeta dress pinned and sewed together the night before by her mother, the best seamstress in Upland, the girl now smiling down on the crowd from the rose-bedecked backseat, resting her gaze upon him so kindly and without threat that his own eyes started to water, an allergy, he'd say, if caught by one of his boys.

The veterans were claiming the street in their somber but proud way, and he started, with caution, to think about something. Not disrespectfully, not against them. He was for them, always for the veterans. Maybe it was a revelation. Whatever it was, it made him close his eyes in the dead heat of a dry summer and consider himself as a man, meaning most precisely as the living carrier of tale. Maybe there was courage in the ordinary life. Not as much of course, not as concentrated as in death. But it was a kind of death, maybe. The internalization, the swallowing of the

*sense of self for another. Ensuring that your story was nothing more than
a structure for your children to walk upon, solid in its singular purpose,
a staircase to their desires, their destinies.*

*He looked down at his boys, one almost to his shoulder, even the
youngest taller, by now, than his hip. A hand-in-salute shading the eyes,
another mounted on the fire hydrant, the younger two rock-scissor-
papering on the curb. They weren't his cover from the shame. But they
were his reason to be a man. If ever they'd challenge him, on a graduation
day perhaps, over a choice of college, for a girl, he'd come down from
the throne of ego and make himself last, smallest, least. Rather than go
on in his fluent Italian, he'd speak broken English in their home, he'd
sign his name Anthony and not Antonio, he'd allow their Americanness
to blossom, he wouldn't push his aged European conscience upon them.
No old world tête-à-tête with the new world. He'd try to live up to that.
Let the covetous part of his heart and brain die, that barren field always
sown with dead seeds, anyway. He'd give in to his own empty role in the
story. Would kill it off like the enemy for his family, a vision of duty on
this Day of Independence.*

PART IV

Lazarus

19

Murron Leonora Teinetoa
House Hunt with Anthony
March 2, 2008

NOW HER DARK EYES, which I've always known, brighten as if she's at that last moment of shimmering light, and hold me right there where I'm standing above her, having just forced the brush through the pure gray bed of hair in another harsh stroke, the dry and wiry follicles catching in the bristles like refuse in a broom.

I feel panic because it's difficult, in some stage of consciousness, not to think of anything but death in this room. It's in the air, it's on the sheets, it's written across the walls like graffiti. Even the flunkies can read the message, even the unfeeling know what drives this place. She's on roommate number seven in the next bed, the longest-lasting thus far other than herself, a frail schizophrenic dead-silent woman having taken her husband's place. On the check-in chart at the front desk, Mrs. Eunice Phelan hasn't had one visitor during her stay here.

"Are you okay?" I whisper.

"*Sí*," Mary whispers back. "I am fine, honey."

"Were you having a bad dream? Should I get the nurse?"

"No. No. Sit down. I was having a good dream."

"I'm glad."

"Open the drawer."

"This one?"

"Right there. You see them?"

I unroll the rubber band around the photos and postcards, unfold a news clipping gone yellow and brown, meet the eyes of her four boys just enlisted to serve. Lazarus, for once, is looking right at me.

"Those are my good dreams."

"I see."

"My mother used to say *che bedda*."

"Yes. Beautiful."

"That is what you are holding."

"Well, we should put them up," I say.

"No!"

"No?"

"No!"

"Okay. But can I ask why not?"

"I put them in the drawer to keep them safe," she whispers. "Anyone can take them from the wall. There is no other way to save them."

I don't say, No thief would be interested in your photos, Mary, but instead, "I understand, Mary. Very valuable."

"You can have them later."

"Okay," I say, not wanting to think about what she means by "later."

"And save them for me, *sí*?"

"Save them."

"Do you promise?"

"Yes," I say. "I promise."

"But I want you to look at the photos now, and then you put them back in the drawer. *Si tu vuole*."

"Oh, I do. I very much want to see them."

"Well, that right there," she says, her eyes blinking, "was just a *wonderful* day. My boys were the talk of the town. The mayor visited our house. I made him lunch. A tuna fish sandwich."

I nod, smile back. "And what's this here?"

"That's a sunset at the Grand Canyon. Our Mercury wagon. Summer 1956."

"I can't believe you remember all the dates and details, Mary."

"Oh, I remember them all. Anniversaries, birthdays, christenings. April twenty-second, 1970."

The day I was born. "Yes."

"See, honey?"

I shuffle through photos of the Felice kids at Little League games, the Felice kids at a theater, the Felice kids at the races, the Felice kids at the beach. Always, unbelievably, in the same group pose, almost delirious with happiness. Positive energy squared, tripled, quadrupled. The pictures do seem exactly like a dream, given this place, something unattainably passed.

Almost, despite the hard three-by-five evidence, untrue.

"Where is this one?" She and her four boys under an olive grove in front of a lovely church.

"That is the Carmelite Mission in Upland. My favorite place to be. I prayed for all of my family there."

"It's beautiful."

"I prayed for you."

"You look beautiful."

"No more."

"Oh, you're as beautiful as ever, Mary."

"The mission, honey. That's what I mean. No more. They tore it down."

"I'm sorry."

"I miss them."

"The boys, you mean?" Those days?

"Anthony," she says, without inflection.

My heart sends out the inner signals of concern, waiting in between beats for whatever's next. I can't bring her husband back, I'm not even sure it's right to bring him *up*. My place here at her bedside has been dubiously defined from the very beginning.

"What's that?"

"Anthony." This time barely audible.

Just as I figure out what she means, *who* she means, and that she whispered it because it's a sound, it's a name, to which she's been reverent her entire adult life, I hear her oldest son, the Anthony she bore, down the hall, speaking in that loud volume of the Felice men and women where everyone in a fifty-foot radius fully hears their business. He would really appreciate, he announces, if they'd keep "an extra eye on my mother," if they'd go "beyond the call of duty," and that "here's a couple bucks" to ensure the request.

I worry about divinity, if it's still a concept with meaning. I don't know what could be more divine than a mother's love for her child, in this case a sixty-four year old son, whose voice is getting her to shift the middle of her body and sit up, lift her head off the pillow, look toward the hallway. When he puts his head in the door, the long Italian nose, *my* nose, punctuated by the genuinely childish smile, she says it again, this time with the grim possession of her race, the passion of her motherhood.

"Anthony!"

"Hey, Ma!"

"Come in, honey. *Veni ca.* Come in."

"You're looking good, Ma! You know that? Just beautiful!"

"Oh, stop it. Come in, come in."

"Hi, Murron," he says. "Can we talk outside?"

"Sure, but—"

"Oh, she doesn't mind. Do you, Ma? We'll be right back."

"What's wrong?" she says.

"Nothing at all, Ma." He bends over to kiss her brow and she closes her eyes, smiling. "We're gonna step out on the patio for a quick minute. Be faster than a speeding bullet."

"Okay, honey. You go on."

"You're so cute, Ma. Just adorable."

The day is the same as half an hour ago when I'd come into the room, overcast and bleak, colorless, the smell of polluted groundwater rising.

"I've done a lot of thinking," he says, sliding the door shut, "and I want to thank you."

One sentence from him and I'm suspicious. Not of him, exactly. He's too simple to be duplicitous, he doesn't have the passive-aggressive acumen of Richmond. I suppose if you took out the politics, he'd be more like his sister, obvious like a hurricane, full of one purpose.

"Thank me for what?" I say.

"Well, I'll just ask. Do you want to go with me to do some house hunting?"

A strange question, an event nearly impossible to envision. There is a matter, here, of marital priority. However strained or ancient she may be, this is his wife's job. Anyway, I don't want to go. In fact, I can think of a thousand things I'd rather do than help Lazarus's eldest sibling select sleeping quarters. "Please don't take this the wrong way, but I don't think we share the same tastes with that kind of stuff." He looks at me as if I've betrayed him to the police. In his case, the PC police. "What's wrong?"

"It's okay," he says. "It's okay. I just thought you'd be interested in finding her a bet—"

"Oh!"

"—ter place."

"You mean Mary! You mean your *mother*."

"Yes."

I nod. "Sorry. I'm so sorry. Yes, I'd love to go with you."

"Great!"

He doesn't spend a moment pondering the confusion. This means a lot, I think, in the way that how you walk means a lot. He's already back inside the room, telling his mother that we've got urgent business to attend to, but that we'll be back soon, so don't worry.

"We can stay a bit," I ask. "Can't we, Tony?"

"You two go, honey. Have a wonderful time."

"Okay, Ma. We love you."

"I love you."

I pat her legs under the blanket. "I'm coming later this week, okay?"

"All right, honey. But I don't want you going through any trouble to get here. You have some fun, you promise?"

"Yes," I say.

"You're young. You don't need to be in here every day."

"No," I say. "I have plenty of fun with you. Let me put your photos away, Mary."

"Bless your heart." I smile, close the drawer. "I knew that I could trust you with these, honey."

"Of course you can."

"Bless your heart."

"See you Friday then."

"Okay, honey."

He's at the nurses' station handing Marietta money. Licking his fingers and separating the bills so she appreciates the exact amount she's getting. A deposit on the credit of his mother's life. Two other Filipino nurses are noting this exchange very closely and, I'm sure, will be extorting him next week for all he's worth. This is America, the farthest reaches of Western civilization, and here we are bribing the natives to care for our dying.

"I give them two dollars," he says, as we walk toward the exit, "every time I come down from Shasta."

"I know. I saw."

"You don't think—"

"I heard."

"—I should? I'm parked over there."

He walks with the hurried angst of a green soldier, thoughtless and dutiful, with the kind of forward progress that more than hints that someone from a different clan could get hurt. His mission, I'm assuming, is to get his mother a better, cleaner, bigger bed somewhere, and this seems, if not outrightly honorable, at least defensible.

A defensible war?

"Well. I don't know." I'm a fast step behind him. "It's up to you."

"That means you don't think I should."

"No, I didn't say that. But you know, I'm just saying, if you're going to do something, why not do it all the way?" To avoid confusing him, I forgo my desire to suggest that he visit with his mother longer next time. If you're going to come here, I want to say, try to stay awhile. "And then there's the matter of tact. You should be a little subtler in your intentions."

"What do you mean?"

"What do I *mean*?"

"Yes."

"I mean, two dollars won't get them a Big Mac, Tony."

"*Hey*! You gotta start somewhere! I'm not responsible for their welfare!"

"We're talking about something else. Getting your mother what you want her to have."

"Hey! This is—"

"Our whole reason for being here."

"—not a charity outfit we're running."

"No, it certainly *isn't*," I say, and as we pass the parked cars, I'm forced to tune out because I've spotted it right there in the corner of the lot, can't miss it really, his one-man, noncommissioned tank ball-hogging two spaces. I can't believe he would have me, a single woman with a child in my charge, sit in his truck with its new accoutrement. We stand before his tailgate, and he doesn't get it. Thinks we're still on the topic of his mother.

The truck's changed with the seasons, yes, the political seasons. The viciousness against brethren and sistren started some time ago, the demeaning of the enemy next door, twenty-six months before the day we Americans vote on the executive seat, nearly half a presidential term, by my calculations. It's not just left and right, it's also step forward and step back. Two years at 1600 Pennsylvania Avenue is a long enough grace period for the hounds these days, if you don't get the thing swung around by then, nice try, good-bye, get out. You lead the people of this country with your head thrown over your shoulder, unsure of whether you're winning the race or fleeing the torch-bearing mob.

Already Anthony is on the front lines of his party's call to duty, the first sent, like a marine. If the posterboard duct-taped across the tailgate of two nooses filled, respectively, with the heads of Hillary Clinton and Barack Obama doesn't get us shot at, I'm sure the words underneath the horrid images will.

"Jesus."

He joins me in looking down at his truck, then over at me, beaming now, pulling me into the lunacy of his infantile decision. I mean, he literally took time from his day to sketch this abomination, tape this abomination to his truck. And then he decided to start the engine, drive five hours south to the Silicon Valley, forty minutes south of the progressive mecca, my workplace, the city by the bay.

I'm sure the twelve minutes it took him to get through San Francisco must have sounded glorious to his ears, like the car horns of Judgment Day.

"Huh? Huh? Great, huh?"

The same free and unaware smile I'd seen in the doorway of his mother's room. Hope and hopelessness dancing their toe-breaking tango again.

"Uh, I think I'll follow you. I've got to get home to Prince just after this, anyway, and—"

"Oh, okay, no problem," he says, and I can see that he believes me. He can't imagine, at least not initially, that I'd think anything but what he thinks about a poster with the words VOTE 'EM RIGHT TO THEIR KNEES IN THE GALLOWS!

I guess if I have to dig for some goodness beneath this nutty entreaty, it's a quasi-generous act to assume that you're a loyalist to his cause. That you start out, that is, as his friend. That if you say nothing about your political leanings, you must *naturally* be with him. He hates them, and he doesn't hate you, so you obviously can't be *with* them.

It seems like such a pure, true, and lonely way to live.

"I was thinking we could ride together to talk about this place, but—"

"Well, we can talk there, I'm sure."

"We could talk at your apartment, too."

"Oh, no, no. No."

"Gotta work, huh? Well, it can't take that long."

"What can't?"

"Oh. I just mean your work, Murron, that's all. Don't take it personally!"

How can I? Someone at the paper once told me I'm like a precocious grown-up who writes book reports for idiots.

Still, at least Richmond thought my choice of vocation, while futile, was somewhat charming. This brother, it seems, thinks literary criticism is *silly*. The one with the murderous cardboard on his truck thinks my work is silly.

"Anthony, I didn't say anything about books or any—"

"So it's the kid then! Can't blame ya, Murron."

"What do you mean? I told you before that I've told Prince about your mother."

"Well, what's the big deal then?"

Talking with him is like building a highway on sand. One step in that architectural direction and you've opened up a whole host of problems you couldn't possibly imagine but will discover, week by week, the project constantly sinking in on itself.

"Look. I don't want to mislead you. If you come into our town with that truck, you won't *leave* our town."

"Oh, yes, okay. *Ohhh*, you mean—what a *shame*, huh? Well, that's all right. I've been through that before. In Mount Shasta. Slashed tires, eggs, vandalism."

"I'm not talking about your truck."

"*Really! Hurt* me? Ohhh, you mean a *fight* then."

"A fight?"

"Like they'd *attack* me. They'd come after me. Jesus. First Amendment? I mean, that's *illegal*! What's this world coming to? Really?"

I look at him in the same shocked way people look at me when I tell them (reluctantly) I'm a literary critic. Serious? They can't believe someone could be so removed from society as to read books for a living, let alone make a buck off it.

So he would have East Palo Alto—the highest per capita murder rate in the country for two straight years in the early nineties, where Norteños and Sureños, Bloods and 415s, and all kinds of friendly ethnic gangs habituate, sling, perish—witness this decision of his?

The lips on his Obama caricature are dangerously puffy.

Serious?

"Rush says that the double standard on race will be the downfall of this country and, you know, he's been saying this for years. No one listens. I try to tell them. Won't quit until the day I die. That's right. Rush is right! Ditto! Have you ever heard his sketch on the happy Negro? The Left has no clue about who they're helping, if welfare for the masses is—"

"Tony."

"—good for America—What?"

"Don't mean to be rude, but are we going house hunting or not? I'm sort of on a schedule. Have to get my son to soccer practice—"

"Oh, okay! Why didn't—"

"—with several happy Negroes."

"—you tell me?"

"Just did."

He finally gets it. He was just made fun of. I'm sure his deity, Mr. Limbaugh, would appreciate the irony. And now I get the supercilious, class-conscious nose raise that Richmond was so constantly, and expertly, negotiating. So at least they have *that* in common, if just for a moment: shared arrogance, the only tribal trait left after the civil war.

"Well, okay, okay. We can talk about this later, huh? Because if you think for one second that I'm a racist!"

"Tony."

"You know I adopted a boy from Korea, don't you?"

"Your son."

"Well, what's that say? Hey, I'm no—"

"Tony."

"—racist! It doesn't make sense! How can—"

"You're rambling, Tony. Was just a joke."

"Okay, okay. Well. Okay. So. Let's see. So you'll follow me then, is that all right?"

I'm already walking off, my stomach grumbling. "Sure."

I pick up the cell phone and dial home. The valet watches me start my car. This available service seems like a throw-off of some kind, a facade to prevent inquisitive minds from peeking inside the facilities of the Elysium Fields Hospice. *Within* the walls is what matters around here.

I pass the valet's tarp-covered booth, the kind that topples in a mean wind, and the valet winks, the zits on the edge of his nose like a bad rash. His work pants, even while he's working, are in the sag so common in the South Bay it's more middle-class than gangsta, the hems dragging on the walk, his boxers visible. The dollar-sign design on lacelike fabric, the green S's in silver-and-gold trim on a bright white backdrop, all of it reeks of rotting cheese in the larger scope of things.

"Hello?"

"Hi, Ma. You wouldn't believe what I just saw."

"Oh, no. What'd they do now?"

"I feel like throwing up."

"Where are you?"

"Leaving the hospice. Tony put a new poster on his truck."

"Oh my God. I don't think I want to know."

In the rearview mirror, the valet is pointing at his drawers with both index fingers, reminding me of the dollar's meaning. Yes. He comes up all day, he's a walking bling machine. Despite their accordance on greed, I don't think the valet and Anthony are on the same team.

"Just tell me something good, Ma."

"Something good? Oh, well. Okay. Yeah. Prince and I are working real hard, baby. His fractions. He's so cute. And determined."

"That's great."

"Are you coming home?"

"Not yet. We're going to find Mary another place, I guess."

"I knew it, I knew it! I told you Richmond would come around. It's not like—"

"It's Anthony, Mom."

"—him to— Oh. Well. *Really?* Well, you know, that's good, too. Yes, that's just fine. But, honey, whatever you do, please don't—"

"I won't, Mom. Won't listen to a single word, promise." I leave plenty of room between his truck and my car, even at the stoplight, no association at all. In the next lane two kids about Prince's age are laughing and pointing fingers, their father shushing them from the front seat. "Won't read a word of it either, Mom."

"What's that, hon?"

"Nothing. I'm just trying to stay focused, you know?"

"Yes, honey. That's good, very good." She's worried about me. "Stay focused."

"Just got a little thrown off."

"I have faith in you."

"I know you do, Ma. Feel better already."

"Are you and Mary still doing okay?"

"Oh, yeah. Definitely. In a weird way, helping her has helped me."

"Well, you're such a busybee, Mur."

"No, no. It's more than that. More than something to *do*. I feel more centered now than ever caring for her."

"That's fantastic, baby. Really happy. So where's this new place?"

"I don't know."

"You know, they have enough money to put her up in a mansion."

"That's what I suspect. But no one will say anything."

"Tightwads. Started with their father. He loved money."

That pathetic scrapbook. "Yeah," I say. "Well."

"What's money for—"

"To bury."

"—if not to bury your own—well, that's right! I agree!"

"We agree. Who'da thought, huh?"

"I did, baby. I *really* did."

"Ma?"

"Huh, baby?"

"Don't you worry about Gabe and me house hunting for you someday. Don't spend even a second thinking about that, okay? Okay?"

"I won't be a burden on you two again!"

"You never were, never are."

"You saved me, Murron."

"No. Gabe and I—"

"Yes, you did!"

"—love you, that's all."

"I know!" She's sobbing into the phone, choking on her attempt to get it under control. "Oh, don't worry, baby. Prince has seen me bawl when the tulips lose their petals. He knows I'm hysterical half the time."

"You're funny, Mom. I'm not worried."

"Oh! Almost forgot! I love you, too!"

"Okay, Mom. Calm down."

"I am!"

"Would you please tell Prince he's a little magic man?"

"I will. I do. *Here*! Tell him yourself."

"Hey, you little magic man."

"Hi, Mom."

"Can't wait to see you, hon."

"Me neither."

"We'll grab a gelato together when I get back, okay, hon?"

"'Kay, Mom. Be careful, Mom."

"I will."

"Are you driving?"

I know this one. "Yes."

"Dangerous, Mom. Let's not talk."

"Agreed. Let's not talk, magic man."

"Love you. Here's Grandma. Don't talk too long, Grandma."

"He's gonna show me how to husk a coconut, can you believe that?"

"Yes."

"I'll let you go, baby. He's tugging my blouse. God bless you, Mur!"

"Okay, Mom."

"I can't help it! It's what I want to say."

"I know. Say whatever you want. Will see you in a bit. I think we might be here, anyway."

"Okay, baby. Bye."

He's making sudden stops in this bumper-to-bumper five o'clock traffic, looking over at the buildings to match the address he's holding in his hand. He doesn't use his mirrors, either one. Has no clue about the monster peeking into the slit of his wound-up, tightly held world. They want to kill him out here. The sign is bad enough, but the driving caps it.

Everything skids to a stop half a foot from his bumper. My belt slings me back to the upright position, fast glance in the mirrors. The horns like angry geese. Jeez. A second-slower response would have been a fender bender. *Be careful, Mom.* A deep grateful breath for my son's looking out. I have to pay attention to the road. I don't want to even imagine what kind of litigiousness Tony would wage in the immediate aftermath of me rear-ending him.

The would-be Democratic nominees fill my windshield in their would-be nooses. He hasn't moved an inch, totally unaware of what just happened, brake lights as red and distorted as the lens of 3-D glasses. He's looking over the digits, glasses at the tip of his nose.

Finally he lets his foot off the brake, resuming his place in the race with no urban urgency at all, so legally under the speed limit it's probably illegal. Amazing how fast this city transitions from ghetto to gold. Unlike East Palo Alto which has the polluting divide of the 101 to demarcate truly opposite realities, the socioeconomic patches of San José seem variant, so without pattern that you tend to miss the sights. As if the shifting landscape means you're not in the midst of something long enough to process it. And yet it was just three minutes ago, I think, that we passed an obvious hot spot for tweeks and burnouts, a barren run of taquerias and pawnshops, only to now be passing some of the most lovely Victorian homes in this or any city, vast lots with spaces of green on either side, the tree life of this neighborhood bustling, strong-bodied oaks, ghost-white birches, the wide empty street shaded over from one side to the other.

He stops in the middle of the road again, looks down at the paper in his hand, up at a brick-trimmed colonial house, nods, points over at the property, head over his shoulder to find me, the truck-tank immediately rolling forward. I nod just to get him to turn back around. I'm afraid he's going to hit a fire hydrant, or test the grit of one of these beautiful trees.

I keep nodding. I understand. I get it. That's the place.

I pull quickly past his left flank to park, and he earnestly watches me do this. I take the space a house down so he has two spaces for himself, the way he likes it.

"I'm gonna park across the street," he says, a few decibels shy of shouting.

I don't bother pointing out the obvious fact that not only is the street virtually empty, and more spacious than a soccer field, but these people are rich. They've probably got a worse case of paranoia than he does, a simple matter of sky-high insurance premiums on vehicles from West Germany.

I wait at the walk and watch him go through his ritual of security, the once-around, the cursory check for scratches, key marks, dents. A pressing down on a loosened corner of duct tape, the conceivable threat, even in this neighborhood, of his mock-execution cardboard being entirely ripped off.

"Where are we?"

"University Avenue," he says, glowing, walking, waving me along. "Isn't it great, huh? Isn't it *gorgeous?* Do you just love those Victorians or what? I grew up in one, you know?"

"I know. You showed me the picture."

"Big Victor."

"Who's that?"

"Oh, that's our house, I named it when I—"

"I know, Tony. I was kidding. Don't you remember? You showed me—"

"We really beat the dust in that house. So what do you think, huh, what do you think?"

The winding walk is beautiful brick, the grass some of the best sod I've seen in a while. Not a weed to be found on the front half of the premises, the bushes manicured, you can see, professionally. No signage either, which for some reason I somewhat like.

"It looks nice."

"Nice? They don't make 'em like this anymore, I'll tell ya."

"Well"—a safe question—"how'd you find this place, anyway?"

"Used to work down the street."

"You used to work around here?"

"Yep. That's right." He's excited by my question, maybe because he thinks I'm impressed by, or interested in, his early capitalistic pursuits. I just don't understand why we nearly collided in midday traffic on a major city street he should have already been familiar with. "When I was starting out in stocks."

"Like Richmond."

He nods. "Who do you think got him into the business? I set up his first interview with Paine. Never thanked me. Not once. The guy made his first million and never thanked me. Can you believe that?"

"I don't think that—"

"You know, I remember when his boy got rejected from the school down the street."

"Bellarmine Prep?"

"Yeah, that's it. Just a great school. We had lunch the day he got the news. His wife was furious. 'They've got some nerve,' she kept saying, 'turning down my son. Who the hell do they think they are?' Like she was royalty or something. Hey! They have their standards, too. I bought him a beer and we talked a bit about it." We're on the porch now, and since he doesn't, I reach out to press the doorbell. "Who'da thought it, huh?"

"Thought what?"

"That twenty-five years later we'd be here trying to find my mother a decent place to stay. Hey! It's *his* mother, too, isn't it? She changed his diapers just the same as she changed mine."

I nod. It's true.

"She sent him to Italy to do pilgrimages when he was fifteen. All because he maybe wanted to be a priest. I remember. He mumbled it at dinner. Everybody shouted, Wow! Hey! Pretty neat! She absolutely went crazy about it. Did you know that? We sent him off at the Ontario Airport and picked him up three months later in the same spot. Yeah! He didn't get to that Ivy League school all by himself! Someone fed him, clothed him, kept him safe! Hey! What are we talking—"

The door opens and I know he's still ranting because I can hear the sounds but not the words, the way you hear bubbles underwater. The gentleman, a young and strong-framed Filipino, says, "Hello," nodding at the both of us.

"—and now it's time for those sons of a bitches to change her diapers, to get their hand—Oh. Hello! Anthony Felice Jr. Nice to meet you. Yeah, we were just talking about the reason we have to come here in the first place. But I'm sure you hear stories like this all the time, huh?"

We walk into the foyer, which is clean and high-ceilinged, exchange pleasantries. I notice at once the lemony scent, a trace of Pine-Sol. This is good, even if done ahead of our arrival. His name is Rubelle. Anthony says, "That's a strange name," and Rubelle only smiles, as if it's a question he's asked every day by his clients. He has five. Luanne, Tilly, Thomas, Martin, and Charles. Until last week, he had six. She passed in the early evening, her daughter at her side. He, Rubelle, misses her. Mildred Patterson, from McMinnville, Oregon. Talked so lovingly about her native Yamhill Valley, Oregon wine country, that Rubelle booked a trip to see it this summer with his wife. Her old space would conceivably be Mary's new space.

Anthony says, "Awww, that's very touching, Rhubarb," and then, "How can you leave these people?"

He's unrattled, which, again, is good. "I have a staff, Mr. Felice. My younger sister, Liz, is the co-owner of the business. And our cousin Felinda puts in another twenty hours a week. We've been doing this for four years now. It's been a good experience."

"A good business," says Anthony, nodding.

"Yes, it is. I think that when you take care of people, they take care of you back. In their own way."

"Which means money."

"Well, yes, it does, Mr. Felice. We're lucky—"

"By God! You're good Americans! You're—"

"—to have this house—"

"—not Filipinos! You're more American than my siblings and—"

"—in which to run our business—"

"—they were born here!"

"—but they're equally lucky— Excuse me? Oh, I was—"

"They've burned their birth—"

"—born here. Oahu. But you—"

"—certificates!"

"—were saying, Mr. Felice?"

"He said," I say, "that you're *his* kind of American."

"Hey! That's right!"

"Well, I've seen some of the alternative homes, Mr. Felice. I've worked in some of those places. It's tragic."

"Tragic! That's right! They're slum landlords!"

"Would you like to look around, my friends?"

I have to detach from these two soon because, after all, someone else's life is on the line, and I want neither the soldier's anger nor the salesman's spin to affect my evaluation. I can get the facts later from Anthony, who's going off now on how the American Left has created this situation, how his siblings have lost their values. It's almost as if, for Anthony, the principle of the offense supplants the real person. That it's the cause, not his fellow soldier, that he fights for in the field. I've never been to war, but this seems staggeringly naive to me, a reduction of the experience. I sort of understand, when confined to this topic, Richmond's condescension toward his older brother. It's almost as if death, to Anthony, is merely a medium through which you meet the enemy, battleground plains about to be bloodied by the other side's latest political iniquity.

"Excuse me," I say, "but I have to use the bathroom."

"Okay. No problem, ma'am. It's just down—"

"I'll find it myself, thank you."

"Oh, she's smart like that, Mr. Rhubarb. You should see her with my mother. She's like another nurse and I can't . . ."

I go first to the kitchen to give it a quick glance over, the kind my mother taught me when I was a girl, where you look for necessities first, accessories second. It looks great, I must say, better than adequately stocked. I open the fridge door and see the condiments and juices neatly stacked on the shelves, the milk and eggs a few days from their expiration dates, no rotting fruit or vegetables in the bin, no yellowing leftovers. I read the plaques on the sill above the sink, their adages of HOPE IS WHERE THE HOME IS and WE ♥ EACH OTHER seemingly perfect in theme, and there is a small crucifix overhead, middle of the entryway arch, the kind with the little stick-like body of Jesus centering the four corners.

I hear chatting. I follow it out of the kitchen, passing hallway furniture that is homely but not run-down, colorful photos on the wall of field trips to the San José Heritage Rose Garden and a walk along the Guadalupe Creek Trail, a signed studio photo of Irish balladeers called the Geriatrics of St. Patrick, each frame free of dust and symmetrically hung, a glass case from ceiling to floor with board games and dominoes and decks of cards inside it, plus a shelf of paperbacks, mysteries and romances, another shelf of DVD classics like *The Magnificent Seven* and *Casablanca* and the original *Willy Wonka & the Chocolate Factory*, Prince's favorite.

"It's a great movie, isn't it?"

"It is," I say, turning toward the voice, which comes from an elderly man who, I'm assuming, is either Thomas, Martin, or Charles. He's hunched over in too many areas to quantify, but he's got a lot of life in his eyes, which are taking me in fully, though not anything like the valet. I guess "fully" in this case means appreciatively, as one looks upon a piece of art. It's not at all accurate, of course, not just because his face would change dramatically if he found me retching on my knees in the bathroom he uses, but because, it often seems, one of the principle problems for many aging men is an utter loss of the ability to judge beauty, such that it's merely the young who catch their attention, and as 90 percent of the living women in the world are *younger*, nearly every woman is *lovely*. So the compliment, while sweet, essentially means nothing.

As if the space between us is just an echo chamber of strained intentions, a sphere of lost gestures, a grid of badly fired impulses.

"Gene Wilder," he says. "Wow!"

"He does a great job, it's true. You know, my son didn't like the Tim Burton version, and I didn't say one word to influence him. That's a victory of taste, isn't it? Hope for the next generation."

"Yes! I have hope for them! I do! They can be good people, too. I have no clue who that Tim So-and-so is. But—"

"That's a good thing, I'd say."

"—I know what kind of phooey is out there. Yes I do! This is a *good* place. Bring your loved one here, sweetheart. Rubelle is a *good* man. His wife took the others to a lawn-bowling tournament. They can't play. They *watch*. Too old to play a geezer's game. Yes, sir, I have been to plenty bad places. Only the VA hospital treated me better. We're going this summer to see the San José Giants game this—"

"You're a veteran then?"

"Yes! I was a gunner for one of Patton's divisions. Do you know who Patton is? He's—"

"Yes. I mean, I guess—"

"—a real son of a bitch. And that's—"

"—I know the historical Patton."

"—why he's famous, see? A great leader. A real—"

"I guess I don't really know him."

"—son of a bitch. No one will get famous *here*, sweetheart. Rubelle has no ego. I never met a Fil-i-pi-no before. I still don't know why the hell he does this. He says he's a good Catholic and he's this and he's that. I *used* to be Catholic. Parents are Polish. I guess I'm a *bad* Catholic. Well, he's *crazy* to do this work! You know how he got this place? There was a lady he cared for who *left* it to him in her will. Thelma Clinkenbeard. She was richer than the dickens. He never knew until the lawyers came a-knocking a week after she passed. Yes, sir. A true story. Her kids never came around until the *end*. One of 'em got here too late. There were only two. Somehow she knew what they'd do before they did it. Makes me real sad. I should calm down."

"It's okay."

"I don't want to give him more work. That's my *goal*. The one thing that keeps me going. When I go, see, I hope I just go . . ." He lifts his hand up very slowly, and snaps his fingers. "Like that. He's done a lot for us. I love him like my own child."

"Do you have children?" Even as the question comes out, I truly regret it. I've broken the journalist's two-step law: expect the worst, and look for the worst. Too easy to turn off your disaster meter getting charmed by a genuine-hearted old-timer, a cruel and stupid irony.

"Well," he says, "I guess I don't, do I?"

"Oh, I see."

"It's okay, honey. Like I said. A bad Catholic."

"Hey!" Anthony's back. I say, "I have a son—"

"Hey! Mom's just gonna love it!" He's bouncing with elation. "What do you *think,* huh? What do you *think?*"

"It's very nice," I say, nodding. "Anthony. This is, well, I don't know your—"

"Thomas."

I want at once to disarm Anthony from his embarrassing machismo. He's too upright, towering over Thomas like an older brother. It's harmless, I suppose, in a place like this, but far more foolish in a place like this. "Anthony Felice Jr."

"Well. If you're gonna say your whole name, I better say mine. Tomek Znajomy Mackowiak. My parents were from Warsaw."

I'm hoping Anthony doesn't make a Polish joke, but he appears to be struggling with placing Warsaw on the European map. The charming elderly gentleman's mood has soured. He doesn't like Anthony's energy, I think, the way it drowned him out.

Strained intention, lost gesture, misfired impulse.

To bring peace to these two, I'll mention war. "Thomas, uh, Tomek, is a combat veteran."

Anthony looks at me and then back at Tomek. "For us?"

"Yes." I'm worried I may have missed something in the story. "Right? Patton, you said?"

"Third Army. Infantry. Forty-three to the shutdown."

"Hey! Well, thank you very much, sir, for your *sacrifice!*" He's shaking Tomek's hand a little too hard now, losing his male inflatedness. Deflating, I guess you could call it. "You're a good man!"

Anthony keeps going: "Well, we like the place just fine, Thomas! We sure as hell do! Boy, I'll tell ya, this is a top-notch outfit, to use a saying of your old boss, the good general. Yeah, I've—"

"You are only aware—"

"—got a lot of respect—"

"—of the fairy tales of war."

"—for Rhubarb and his business model here. Hey! I think—"

"Sonny," Tomek says, reaching out and grabbing Anthony's wrist.

"—Mom'll have— Yes? Thomas? You said something, right? You go right ahead. You want to say something? Go on, Thomas. No, no, no! I insist! You can do it. Go ahead."

"Thank you." Tomek tosses Anthony's hand like a farmer spreading seed, and turns to me. "You tell your grandmother she's welcome here anytime, all right?"

"Hey! I will! We will! Thank you very much!"

"You have a beautiful child."

"Oh, no," Anthony says.

"You take care of your people!"

"You don't understand," Anthony calls out, but Tomek's already walking off, shouting, "Take *care* of them! Take *care* of them!"

I smile, but Anthony's unfazed by the confusion. "Hey! Well, that's it, huh? Can't get much better in the personal-testimony department! This is the place."

"Yes," I say. "I agree."

"Yep. I've got it all figured out. Very doable. Now I just gotta get everyone to chip in their fair share."

"What?"

"To monthly payments, you know, and it's a done deal."

Strained, lost, misfired.

20

Lazarus Corsa Felice
Recall of the Hell Hospital
October 6, 1997

LETICIA LOOKED UP from the floor and saw him in a cutting out-line of sunlight, the vision so plain and invasive that she felt for the powder-blue drawstring sheet, patting her hands along the floor like a blind cripple who'd fallen from a chair. No, this was no longer the padded-white hell of the hospital, she was in her own room in her own run-down one-bedroom apartment, and finally he'd come. Oh God, she loved even his faceless frame, the thin shoulders, the long middle of his body, the bottom hems of his jeans flaring wide and steep like a ski slope.

"Do you want me to stay or go?"

"My love," she said. "You've come back."

"Ma, I gotta know if you got any savings tucked away. Murron and I gotta put some money together for this place. Rent's three weeks past due."

Now she realized her mistake, the same one she'd made, in in-termittent spaces of time, for nearly three whole decades. This one had been slipped into her consciousness like the knockout pill in a neglected drink at the bar.

"They never did for me!" she shouted. "Not one damned thing!"

"Who? The doctors?"

"Jesus Christ, Gabe!"

"Come on, Ma. I don't even know what you're talking about."

"Oh my God! My God! My God!"

"Don't sweat it, Ma." He was whispering, as one did at the death-bed. "Take it easy."

"I am not sweating."

He nervously chuckled. "It's cool, Ma. You want me to stay or what?"

She shook her head but not at him. She was looking at the window curtain, which had been drawn for over a month now. Every day she wanted to raise it, and every day she didn't.

Murron walked into the room.

"Okay, I'm out, Ma. You take care."

"Thanks for coming, child number one," said Murron. "Sure stayed long. A whole five minutes."

"I'll be back, sis. Don't sweat it. Late."

It was not anywhere near the closing hour of midnight and yet Leticia felt as if she'd died several times that day and come back, despite herself, to the same life each time. The heaviness in her heart seemed to seep across her sternum and compress the surface of her lungs, straining, impossibly, under the weightlessness of oxygen. The pitiless vapor, she thought, the gas that doesn't kill you. Was the inner torture merely a creation of her own cruel brain, was this the final stage of human reverie, did the amateur pastels of childhood picnics in fields of mustard and lavender finally end in nightmare? The last vision a black screen into which, she knew, even the fiercest atom of light could not penetrate.

Her husband had never been and her children were gone. Every-one off to themselves to live their lives. Away from her. Sometimes she looked at all life wherever you found it as an absolute guarantor of ruin, a chain of tales that embodied dysfunction even when the links were purely opposed, that wealth would ruin you, poverty ruin you, kindness ruin you, viciousness ruin you, strength, weakness, callousness, sensitivity, each and all of them containing the same disproportionate force of story, each and all the same end, the next link welded shut and trapped unto itself. That the only recompense was no recompense: you can pass along your own ruin, too.

Murron stepped forward and stood over Leticia, both hands perched on her slender hips like trained birds. Leticia's ragged head hung as if there weren't a single muscle in her neck. She looked up without lifting it, her eyes flooded in the collapsed damn of damnation, and felt the same kind of shame she'd had confessing premarital relations to the priest. And now she wanted to beat out this curse in her daughter's eyes, the insult of reverse roles, the arrogance of answer where there was no answer, and so she howled like a beaten child, the fingers of her tired hands clawed to the bedsheet.

Murron slapped her across the cheek. Harder than the one time Leticia had slapped her daughter in the park, breaking her life vow of pacifism. Harder because it was deliberate, not reflexive. Punitive, not restrictive. She shook with these revelations, arms, legs, head, her jaw locked firmly into place. She looked like a ventriloquist gone berserk in the absence of the puppet. Insane with the weight of story. She opened her mouth for air and out came the full effect of every decibel, her voice crackling like the flash of raw meat in a pan of hot oil. Now she punched at the air and beat her chest, she fell to a ball on the floor, going quiet in the collision. She reached up to the top of her head as if discovering it for the first time and ripped at the roots of her hair. So much of it came out that she howled again. She reached up for more hair and Murron dropped to a knee and pulled back swiftly on her elbow.

"Gabe!" This time it was Murron, trying to lift her off the floor. Gabe rushed in and said, "Here, Mom. Take a sip o' this."

There was a thin line of blood coagulating in the mat of her hair. Blood on her hand. Suddenly she was calm. Gabe pushed the can at her with the confidence of solicitation that she'd never had, and she put the beer to her mouth as they both knew she would, and drank. It was wonderful. She didn't look over at Murron. It was Keystone Light.

When she was done she followed her son to the kitchen, squinting at the leftover light of noon. He pushed aside rotten fruit and boxes of Chinese food and spoiled milk.

"A case minus the one you just pounded, Ma." She carried it back to her room, telling her daughter in the doorway, "Please please please just get off to yourselves," avoiding eyes, pushing past.

She closed the door softly on the world outside her room with all its threat of narrative light, the alluring lie of story.

She slid down where she stood, back to the wall, and pulled both knees to her chest. She angled her shoulder against the door and tried not to think about her children or the staff at the hell hospital. The beer would help. Beer was her prayer and sleep was her angel. She popped a can and drank it down, breathing in through her nose, harshly, like a winded horse.

Even in the nothingness of the dark room, the past never left you alone. Richmond had once said as much to her decades ago, the stupid certainty of youth in his eyes. As if he could overcome the backwash of history, his own or anyone else's. He was young, yes, but she was younger, easily intimidated by his arsenal of referenced books, the ten-dollar words that seemed so odd coming out of a teenager's mouth. She could never tell him about her problem with ambition, how she mourned the poor souls who got squashed in his path to glory, how no one escaped the jaws of death. She wondered if he was the same now. If the end of his son's short story had emboldened his cause, made him stronger. Or had he been brought to his knees behind the locked door, worshipping at the altar of shame like everyone else?

The past, he'd read to her from a little red novel, is never dead. It is not even past.

She could still see the cloth choked so tight across the cover that anyone inside the book simply had to be dead. As she lay there taking in the oxygen-poor air of the room, the only words that came to her head were "adze" and "dying." She couldn't see the name of the book. Not only had she forgotten who'd written it, she couldn't name five novelists. Well before Gabe and Murron had reached adolescence, she'd stopped reading. In the same way she'd quit the Ladies Club in town. Both the books and the women brought her spirits down in different ways. The beautiful stories, woven together like some rich Grecian tapestry, made her sad. The women, chirping like evil birds, made her sad. The beauty and ugliness of the world made her sad.

Why had that damned line from Richmond's book come back into her life except to create more misery? If not for her, then for someone else?

She popped a can of beer in the dark and took in the contents in three swigs.

Once she'd written in a journal: No one alive no one dead not anybody you will ever know has negotiated the chasm between this and the next moment.

It had taken her six hours to write from first word to last. She believed in the message. She'd ripped the page from the journal and kept it in the Bible her mother had given her as a girl. Almost nine years now as a bookmark. But now she couldn't find the note and it felt almost as if she'd lost a child conceived not of her belly but of her head, and this thought scared her so much she crossed herself out of habit alone and wept, waiting in the relentless dark for death.

When she'd first worked at the Santa Rosa Homeless Center in the seventies, cooking meals and cleaning beds, she'd found solace in the goodness of a deed, how each guest fulfilled by a single meal was one less body in need on the streets. They came through the doors, one by one, like parishioners hungry for anything that would save them from damnation. This stoked the Samaritan inside her. She loved coordinating the meals more than anyone else at the center, putting her own personal touch to a heavy starch like mash and gravy, cooking healthier than code but within their laughable budget. She'd keep her counter shiny as a new city, all to give her guests one clean place to congregate in a life of filth, an immaculate hour to remember what was, or what could be.

Miracles were not only possible, Leticia believed, but necessary.

Sometimes she'd let her role at the shelter take her mind to the ends of delusion, which meant thinking of these people she knew nothing about as her own children. She loved to ladle her homemade tomato soup into their bowls. One year, she'd gotten sixteen organic farmers in the valley to donate their unsold dairy every other week.

Colleagues warned about burning out, whispered to keep their operation in perspective. Articles about the victims of crimes were presented in professorial tones over a cup of coffee. Cops barged into the center reciting rap sheets like poetry, leaving with not one but three of her supposed children in cuffs. She never listened. She even posted bail when she could.

She was putting money in her purse at the shelter. Not literally, never that, but figuratively. Goodness, she believed, bred goodness. The world was one big flower, and it was inside all of us. Even her. All the good things that could possibly happen could happen to anyone, and here she was desiring only one visit from goodness to her doorstep, a rosebud of a gift that would save her from herself.

Because of course she loved him. Had never stopped where it mattered. Anyone who knew her, which meant her children, knew this. She admitted it to no one, but she always believed he'd return. Like an old habit you thought you'd lost over the years. Yes, he would appear on their trailer doorstep smiling, presents for the kids mounted to his chin like that silly but beautiful scene from *It's a Wonderful Life*. She'd seen it a hundred times, wept a hundred. But in her dream film, he'd drop to his knees in the dirt. She'd do what not one friend would advise, put out her hand and raise him to his feet, say, "Stop after one sorry, my love. It covers all we've lost. Not just our loss, but *yours*. I know now that you see what you've lost." She'd kiss him at the base of his neck, stroke his scruffy face, and say, "We have to mind the time. There's still daylight left. Let's live our life together like we were meant to."

Nothing ever changed without a gentle reminder of love's power, a potion that worked on the tiredest of hearts. It was as if her own weakness of spirit was, conversely, the very ground in which a tiny kernel of hope grew best. When she didn't think of her life, when she didn't weep at her loss. Out from the ground of her mind it came, stretching toward the sky like a rope-strong vine willing itself into existence. Flowering upward and outward for weeks, months, years, until she had to look up from her shame and claim it.

A thousand times the dream flickered open and shut like an old camera lens and then, mid-eighties, early summer, consumed her yet again. She saw the new smog gathering orange and pink in the valley, she heard one conversation with a homeless veteran at the shelter. He wore his unit patch on his jacket and she recognized it. Said a word or two about why she knew this fact, right there in her tie-dyed SEEK PEACE IN BERKELEY T-shirt and broken-buckle sandals, and he said, dead-eyed, "Never seen Birkenstocks so beat up, lady," and "Yeah, I know 'im."

Lazarus lived in a trailer park in Milpitas, he said. During the day, he manned an assembly line at a software manufacturer called Macintosh, worked the graveyard shift at a 7-Eleven in East San José. Had recently been jumped over a piece of beef jerky, insisting at the door that the three kids pay like everyone else. She was proud of herself for staying quiet. The man was referring to him in the present tense, and that was enough. Didn't make the evening news, the man said, which meant, she knew, that he hadn't been hurt bad. Smoked like a chimney, looked like shit, and the statement scared her as she considered the haggard source. Didn't talk at first but eventually, when started up, when he trusted you, never shut down. Was single.

"Not true," she nearly blurted, covering her mouth at once.

Without visiting, she could see the layout. On the floor in a corner of the trailer was his bed, a Salvation Army mattress, the military-issue blanket scrunched into a ball. Two pillows, one long as his torso, the other square as a couch cushion. When he slept, he'd slide the smaller pillow between his legs. No fresh food in the fridge, empty cans rimmed with cigarette ash atop anything constituting a surface, a small pile of T-shirts and tighty whities and stretched-out socks in the top drawer of a cheap dresser, nothing else inside the plywood drawers. Not one decoration on the wall save a plastic Coca-Cola clock he'd bought at a rooftop auction benefiting the Upland Little League. Stuck to the sink mirror by a gas station magnet was a photo of his arm-in-arm team on some random Vietnamese hill. And somewhere in the trailer, hidden under a stack of World War II books and encyclopedias, was a cigar box with her love letters inside it, tied up with a bow, in perfect order by date, unopened in fourteen years.

Untouched. She knew that, too. He wouldn't go near them. And yet she feared that the key to their future was held in those talismans of the past, laughter at a line, conversion in a paragraph, marriage by the end of the page. She'd find contentment with the notion of his solitude, her soul satisfied by the image of him patching up the siding on a neighbor's trailer, a nail between his teeth, pencil between his ear, whispered bar of "Folsom Prison Blues" on his tongue.

Now she lay there on the floor in the darkness of her room, giggling at this stupidly hopeful memory as if she were thirty years her junior, the prom-bound Upland High School graduate-to-be, the girl with sunflowers in the waves of her hair, she was this, yes, she was.

"Gorgeous," her mother had said, rolling her bangs into curls. "Just gorgeous."

There in the dress passed down from her sister, sequinned, strapless, peach, her thin shoulders browned from watching the Felice brothers surf the high-tide break at Huntington Beach. He'd actually combed his hair that day, he'd miraculously been on time, maybe even early. The neighbors spying each step up the walk, his smile lifted to her in the bedroom window, skittle hop at the porch for his audience.

She came down the steps utterly in love with her life. He kissed her on the brow and shook her father's hand confidently, like a boy on his way to war who'd come back a man, which meant nothing more to Leticia than a boy who would stay with her wherever he went, and opened the door to the Mustang. He'd paid to have it specially waxed that week in a Los Angeles dealership. They drove into the young night holding hands across the gearshift, a three-hour evening of doo-wop songs and spiked punch from the conception of their first child.

"My Gabriel," she said. "My own son."

Now she rolled to her bloated stomach to crack open another beer. She reared back her head and drank, neck arched like a scorpion whipping up its tail. She lay there for minutes in her own indigestion. Facedown, as if dead. No footsteps on the other side of the locked door, not a birdcall outside the shut window, she stood slowly for no other reason but to punish herself with the labor of drunken exertion.

She bent down and lifted the mattress to a vertical position. She leaned against it to rest, and then extended her weary arms. The mattress fell, heavy like a human body. She dropped to her knees and felt around for the lone letter he'd written from the war. His pissant testament from the place that ruined him. Ruined her. The children. Finally her hand found it, dry as a dead leaf, and she wrapped it around a can of beer like a mug holder. Her kids had gone through it, her friends, her support group, the fingerprints all mixed in untraceably, the envelope soiled as a doormat.

She closed her eyes and recited: "Dear Leticia. This war is hell on your insides. Sounds cliché, I know. But the whole thing feels wrong. The other day the lieutenant got fragged for telling one of the guys to dig a trench. Fragged means killed. By one of your own. On the sly. This over a fucking hole in the ground. A man's life, his whole life. Everyone knows who did it, no one says a word. Not me either. Am I a coward? I don't want to get fragged. I'm transferring out of this unit soon as I can. Gonna find a tighter-knit, smaller team, you know? They see more action, and maybe that's bad, but you can trust the guy next to you. Heard stories you wouldn't believe. Seen some things, too. Wonder about my brothers. I want to come home to you but can't just yet."

He was on the other side of the globe. What could she do but wait? And grow. She surrounded herself with people who believed in her dream.

The fertile soil and good sun for the growing bean in her belly. In the course of several months, a hundred people she'd never see again had kissed her belly. That's what she meant. That was beauty. She'd spend her days floating through the collectively willed peace like a dandelion in the wind, she'd close her eyes and attune her ears to the sound of a neighbor kissing his school-bound son on the cheek, she'd take a song's refrain and turn it into a greeting, "Hello" replaced by "Try to love one another."

Everyone filled with wonderment of a better life the earth over. Of love reigning at long last in every land, even Vietnam. Across every ocean, even the Pacific. For every living soul, even the untouchable father of her child.

He came home after the first tour and heard this spiel on a Monday evening in the Upland Bookstore. She was reading him a poem from the movement, she was excited by the words that she didn't deep-down understand. He didn't make one comment about the poem, he didn't ask one question about the birthing of their son. She'd gotten through those nineteen hours in the hospital without him, which meant with her mother at the bedside recounting Leticia's own birth. How her father, long dead of cirrhosis, had passed around vodka and cigars to the staff before her mother had been dilated five centimeters. She held Gabriel in the cradle of one arm, the poetry book fanned open in her free hand. Her life would be like this now, ambidextrous, heavy.

"We are so happy," she said to Lazarus, closing the poem on itself. She reached for his lap and pulled at his hands, already nicotine-stained at nineteen. She placed them to the rapidly beating heart in their baby's little body. "So grateful that you made it back okay."

Eight months later he enlisted for a second tour which, in her book, meant that he wasn't okay. Like something in him had died over there and he was going back to get it. Not a note of regret in his announcement, a fast kiss on both brows, her own and their year-old son, both parents unaware of their next child already inside her.

"I forgive you," she said now, talking to the letter as if it were human. As if it were *him*. "We are all trying to forgive ourselves for being alive."

Searching for that one place. The graveyard to bury the sorrow of one's past. Put it to rest forever. Making the past past, killing the caveat of that novelist. Because of course the promise of a collective peace had meant, by reduction, the personal peace. That was the truest test, the terms brought directly to one's own heart.

I need the numbing, she thought. I was built to feel.

"Sounds like a cliché to me," she said, and laughed herself into a crying fit. "A fucking cliché."

She ripped the letter in half, quarters, eighths, over and over until she held a hundred shredded strips of it, the only hard evidence of his love but confetti now, which she tossed into the air, and let fall upon her head and shoulders like rice at a wedding. "I got fragged. Do you know what that means? Killed by one of my own! Fragged over a hole in the ground called Vietnam! You put a bullet in my heart. You cut the artery in my neck."

The last time she'd broken to the liquor, they'd fired her from the shelter. Clinton about to be voted in, Fleetwood Mac song on the overhead at the rallies. They'd sent a letter through the mail citing repeated violations of the sobriety code. The news a lit match to the dried wood. Because it wasn't one thing, it was all things. It wasn't her own life, it was every life she had taken into her system. It was the bone-thin children of East Africa, it was a fistfight in the shelter. It was war in Latin America, it was poverty in the streets. It was pollution, it was cigarettes. It was a hole in the world's center, it was a hole in her heart. She didn't wait until late evening, she broke the bottle's seal in the warmth of her bed and nipped at one-hundred-proof rum through sunlight and shadow, Swanson microwave dinners and the five o'clock, eight o'clock, ten o'clock local news, right until the sleep came down upon her again.

Her life down the mouth like this, leather skin and leopard liver, children grown and gone, discussing your future in the hospital hell with a doctor you've never taken in sober.

Sober.

The unaltered vision. The terrifying realness of self.

She had to go way down into the pit to pull out a memory from the far back past of sobriety, her liver still virgin of chemicals, the days of rapped knuckles and forced catechism, uniforms and worn knees, austere and structured God of her childhood. The words of a Carmelite nun at the mission, something she hadn't believed then. Not at all, not barely, the hokey stuff from some ancient grapevine place that wasn't California.

"Happiness, my dear girl, does not exist on this sphere."

Yes, she thought now. That is right. That nun is dead and she is right. Woman to woman. That bride of Christ is dead right.

She could never recite the Beatitudes to the word like she could a Hail Mary, but they'd always been her favorite part of the Bible. She hadn't known why until now. Thinking of their meaning seemed to give her license to take another breath by a universal dream. If there be such a thing. If she'd been there on the mount with him, cross-kneed and starry-eyed in the shade of an olive tree, she'd nod at every word: I am poor in spirit, I've been the very embodiment of meekness all these days.

"I will try to find a tiny bit of rightness out of the wrongness of my life," she said now, plainly and simply. "I have no need to connect the last and the next. I will not waste my life, I will not seek happiness."

Of the consecrated names she could remember, she said every one very slowly, savoring each consonant.

"Mother Teresa. Martin Luther King Jr. Mahatma Gandhi. Bobby Kennedy. I thank the dead for their lead. I thank Christ, who suffered more than anyone."

She stood with conviction and hope and the kind of desperation she'd felt when Lazarus had promised her a ring after the war, the scary charm in his eyes, the purity of naïveté that she'd always loved and hated, now looking down at her forty-eight-year-old feet like the last-chance leap into her life, courage on the steel rail of the bridge.

She opened the drawer of her bedside table, found the framed picture of him filling up his Mustang at the downtown Texaco—Upland High School Prom Night, Dreams of Tomorrow, 1967—and pressed her thumbs into the center of his heart. She lightly bled on the cracked glass, but did not think of her pricked skin, or if there were shards that had penetrated deeper than the naked eye could see. A mother and a licensed nurse, she knew by now that foreign objects would be repelled by the body.

Maybe not with grace. Not painlessly, she thought. But in time it will all come out.

She turned on the bed lamp, opened her jewel box. She reached for her rosary. It wasn't there. Hadn't been for a long time. She dug under Apache beads and various lockets with pictures of the kids and all kinds of yarn and thread twisted into itself on the velvet lining and found the crucifix her father had worn, at his own insistence, in the end. She kissed the inch-long body embossed across its center.

"I forsake him. I forget him."

She dropped to her knees and prayed. Dear God, I understand that I have the right to be with no one but you. That is the contract. I am meek and I am poor in spirit but I am not nothing with you.

She wrote on her hand the only Latin she remembered from her childhood: *Sine tuo nomine nihil est in homine.*

She walked out of the apartment with the trash bin in both trembling hands. The blood from her thumbs dotted the hard plastic. She tossed in the frame and it thumped at the base of the dumpster, the glass crackling with finality. She had no tears. Was dry of tears. She went inside and took the box of Keystone Light to the kitchen. Poured each can into the sink and then sat down at the living room table, intent on calling Murron later that night. When put to the chopping block of her daughter's twenty questions, she would say, "If I'm right, I'm saved. If I'm wrong, it won't matter then, will it?"

She would announce her victory to all in her life by apology, beg for forgiveness through the tone of every said word. She would carry her cross sober now, and she would say it too, commit herself to life by the witness of another, the pressure of a loved one, but first she returned to her journal, an honest start to the old tradition.

It's tougher to live than to die, she newly wrote. But I am ready.

21

Murron Leonora Teinetoa
Boiling Water in the Room
March 12, 2008

HER LAST ROOMMATE, the eighth in five months, died a day and a half ago in her sleep, and so now I watch the latest homesteaders move into their half of the room, as I lather lotion into Mary's lovely Sicilian skin. She's fallen asleep from the rubdown on her hands and forearms, and maybe that's good. Even so, she twitches now and then, like she's responding to an electric current in the air that we, the walking, can't feel, but will feel someday, the minute we lay down.

They're very efficient. Movers of every age, from children to the elderly, they enter and exit with bags and boxes in a desperate haste, the kind you see at an outdoor market. They're all related, these newbies to the Elysium Fields Hospice, the extended reaches of a Vietnamese family. It's as if I'm not over here at all, let alone Mary, as if our assigned rear of the room exists in another sphere of health care, as if I have no need, whenever it comes, to use the door they've monopolized to leave for home.

I merely smile at them because each of us, wherever we come from, whatever we are, will be setting up camp at death's doorstep someday, and then, also, I don't think they speak English. And although I eat *pho* and *bo kho* in Chinatown every Friday with a group of editors, I don't speak a word of Vietnamese.

Seems like there's always some kind of problem sharing space with someone, even if you love that someone. I remember Gabe pinning me down, twisting his torso to perch above my face, and farting. The shouting matches, the mean-spirited pranks, his endlessly flashing skater friends.

And yet there was laughter, too, lots of it with my brother, especially when he'd tell stories about the other families in our trailer park. He was hilarious. I've always thought he could have been a great stand-up comic. He'd pull his pants up to his chest and mimic our neighbor Silas Branzen, "Silly Silas," calling in his children—elucidating why we were actually blessed by Lazarus's absence from our lives. How no kind of late-night hug from Daddy was worth that kind of embarrassment in public. Gabe, relentless Gabe of my childhood, our austere prophet and loving jester, drill sergeant and protector, administrator of familial tests to process pain. He used to make me laugh so hard I'd pee myself. And then I'd rush to the bathroom and get ambushed by tears as I'd change my soaked panties.

Sometimes I'd awaken in the warm early mornings of our lovely valley and wonder about the strength of our cohesion. "The Good Triumvirate," Gabe used to call us, Leticia and her two children. I didn't want to lose the little we had, which in sum was our broken-down trailer, a few photos of Lazarus, and each other. And then Mom, as if they were lovers, had her hidden and unhidden bottles of vodka, always the generic coal-filtered kind. I once called her a cheater for getting her consolation from liquor. I really did. I was scared. I had an ulcer by the age of seven. The doctor didn't understand until he looked at my nails, chewed down bloody to the raw flesh, pink and tender to the touch.

It took leaving Gabe and my mother for me to really learn how much I loved my life with them, how existence between the extreme ends was more or less good, certainly survivable, sometimes banal. Like anyone's life, I suppose, in this lucky country. And then when I had Prince and chased away Lokapi, it was like I forgot everything I'd learned, like I'd returned to the old familiar stretch between the childhood poles of happiness and hope and peace and of sorrow and fear and anger.

One of the children says, "Where you want this?"

"Oh," I say, looking at what he's taking out of the shopping bag: a Coleman camping stove. "Well, I guess—"

"*Sura cura lon, danh tu.*"

Obviously, he wasn't talking to me. I wonder if it's a policy violation in this place to cook your own meals. On the ceiling, I find the fire detector behind the television, wait for what feels like minutes for the tiny green light to illuminate its forgotten, dust-rimmed corner of the room. I'm disappointed in myself for never checking the battery before.

A middle-aged woman in a business suit says something in Vietnamese—a directive, I'm assuming, since the child, without nodding, moves instantaneously. He unplugs the lamp on the desk, which makes their half of the room a bit darker, and then carries it into the hallway, the base of it resting on his shoulder. His mindful posture and committed eyes remind me of Prince approaching the batter's box at home plate, pensive, duty-bound. The boy returns in seconds, lifting the Coleman stove to the desktop, squaring it, still not looking over at me or at Mary, then reaching down to light the burner, his brown hands deft and free and as knowing as two birds on a branch.

By God, they're really going to cook in here.

I find myself again in indecision. I'm reluctant to share this bit of information with a nurse because, again, I'm concerned about the long-term price of such an act. It doesn't take much of an imagination to conjure the possibilities of abuse and dereliction by any average human being with a grudge. Someone who'll amicably shake your hand only minutes after spitting in the soup. Wherever they come from, whatever they are, no one likes being told on.

"Excuse me."

The boy does not look over. A smaller child, cute girl of five or six, rushes in and stops at his side, tugging his elbow. The woman walks in carrying a mini-refrigerator, her chiseled forearms lined with veins. She drops it in the corner, their bedridden relative unfazed by the noise. Her eyes are glazed over with the weight of looming death, or maybe the system invasion of morphine, and now I remember a frightening lineup of Eastern Asian opium addicts in an article or a book I'd read, their skin as dry and gray as this poor woman's.

Already she's starting for the door, and I say it again, louder.

"Excuse me."

"Eh?"

She stops, turns to the boy. I'm waiting for anyone to acknowledge my presence. I take a step forward to force the issue. The boy says one harsh word and the girl vanishes. Now the woman and the boy huddle like two gossips in a playground and I want to say, "I'm not dangerous. I'm not mean. I just want to be fair. You're sharing this room, see?"

Only the boy speaks, fast and serious commentary in their native tongue, lifting his eyebrows at me without looking at me. She nods and looks over, smiling, shaking her head.

"No, no, no, no," she says. "You hungry, eh? You *hungry?*"

"No, I'm actually—"

"Yeah, yeah, you hungry."

"—not hungry."

"You like *pho,* huh."

"Look."

"Very good. We make it ready for you real hot real good too." She pushes the boy out at me. He still won't meet my eyes. "He make it good for you. Best hot. Very good."

I lift my eyebrows in disbelief at life's twists, the way it can wrench your arm behind your back, the way it can make perfect sense even in ESL. I say, loud enough for the boy to clearly hear, "You don't have to cook for me. I don't make any decisions around here."

"Yesssss," she says, stepping forward, stroking my arm, "you like noodle, very good for you. Make you strong. Okay. I come back."

She's out the door, and then before I blink she's with us again. Nodding at me with a smile so drippingly lurid, I look down in embarrassment and then over at the boy, who's already cooking, which means boiling the water. She's setting up on the bedpost a bamboo box smaller than a human hand, her relative's lifeless head inches away, and then she looks over at me, smiling, and flips the swtich.

"*Ding dun gun cua. Ding dun gun cua. Ding dun gun cua.*"

Over and over, a Buddhist ditty of some sort, the vertical toothpick in the middle of the music box going back and forth like a metronome.

"*Ding dun gun cua. Ding dun gun cua.*"

The new roommate has fallen asleep in her bed, and Mary has not awakened, so the contraption seems to have worked. For now. Still, the tune seems to threaten something, like a real-life high wire, the dividing line between instant exhilaration or eventual death. In this case, instant soothing or eventual suicide.

Prince had toys as loud as this, toys worse than this actually, the kind of maddening device that would blast out a five-minute guitar riff of "American Woman" if you accidentally dropped it, or stared at it wrong from the other corner of the room. I'd ask myself questions about the "appropriateness" of so much sound, reviewing DeLillo in the early evening. I'd mutter, "Yes, yes, yes," but not too loud lest I contribute to the racket. I honestly couldn't decipher if the problem I had was with Prince or with myself.

Was it white noise or had I become outdated? Was I objectively opposed to the song's dumbing down of my son's little-boy brain or subjectively bothered that I was an American woman without a man? Was I maintaining a standard of expression for my son or jealous of Prince's vast and generous and always growing patrilineal network, which had gifted the musical chopper, amid a dozen other presents, for his fifth birthday?

I know, when I stop in the middle of the day over a sentence gone bad, that I'll never provide for Prince what I want, that it requires the lining up of the moon and the sun and a thousand fickle stars to even start his life the way I'd want it, which is to say with a big family on both sides.

But this delineation could be another high-wire line.

By the time you figure anything out, it's probably too late, the ancient tragedy of the species. Maybe a child is nothing more than a living, talking exacerbation of this problem, a recurrent reminder of your own failure to have applied the proper remedy, been guided to the right light, to have said no when you should have, and yes, too. Sometimes the things that should make the most sense make the least, and yet somehow you must believe in order because not to believe would be like a tacit submission to the parental horror, the very real vision, of your child drowning in amoral chaos.

Now I watch the boy with admiration because I don't know what else to do. He's so nimble and purpose-driven that he achieves, it seems, the kind of sustenance fish get out of constant movement. Oxygen through the incessant present tense, to not look back, to not ponder death, to not die. Then it occurs to me. This poor drooling thing propped unconscious on four stacked pillows could be his mother.

He won't stop moving, she won't ever die, his jaw clenched tight.

All kinds of questions you'd never ask yourself occur in the face of pure commitment. Does one's absolute rights, those rights connected to all people who've ever set foot on this planet, wane in proportion to how unvisited one's bed is? *A heart is not judged by how much you love*, the Wizard once said, *but by how much you are loved by others*. If no one comes to claim this woman, why should any complaint, which will arrive as sure as the storm behind the clouds, matter? That is, matter to the doctors, the nurses, the attorneys, the lawmakers. How does the childish desire to serve at all costs measure against the adultish lobby to *have* at all costs, here, in this place? Whose swinging elbow vying for space has the right to last rites? It seems to me that the boy, who's setting up a cot now, dropping into the webbed cocoon of its interwoven string, tucking his chin into his chest, and daring an agent of the adult world to remove him—this boy deserves, somehow, to have what he wants.

"Hey," she says. "Hey."

Mary's talking in her sleep, scratching the tip of her nose, as she often does in the first phase of REM. It makes me wonder if she has the same response to different dreams, or if she has the same dream each time. Or she could just be perpetually itchy, the physical state creating her mental world. Maybe her mind is infested with insects, the incoherence of a foreign language translating into an annoying buzzing sound.

I don't know what to do with these people and their Buddhist metronome, foldout cot, and Coleman stove. I do know, however, that since I admire what they're doing, Mary should have the same loyal vigilance from one of her own. I'll be back. I stroke Mary's forehead, fill up the plastic cup with water, cover her naked feet with the sheet, take to the hallway. I pass half a dozen relatives of the new roommate, and none look up or stop talking. I'm not three steps past them when the stench of feces and urine surrounds me. So strong it feels like the air is thicker in the hall where all the odors of the Elysium Fields Hospice gather. I switch to breathing through my mouth, but the first intake of oxygen makes me gag, and I rush for the hallway bathroom.

The key is missing, someone's inside.

"Oh, Jesus."

I catch the first thread of hacked spittle and close my eyes to focus on something beautiful like Prince in his p.j.'s during Saturday morning cartoons, curled into the couch, those wavy locks of copper hair, and I hear the door creak open at the same time my stomach freezes in its regurgitative revolt, the frustration I know to be on my own pale face not apparent to the man who emerges from the bathroom, Anthony Constantine Felice Jr.

He's fuming about something.

"Did you *see* it? Did you *see* it?"

Obviously I have no idea what he's talking about. As usual. The inroads to Anthony's head are clouded over with anger again, and I can't see anything. "No."

He reaches into his back pocket, and I walk past him and clean my palms on a paper towel. As I turn, he hands me a piece of paper, folded over in no conceivable pattern. I look up at him and he says, "Open it, open it."

The cracklike creases indicate that he's thrown the paper away once or twice before retrieving it, presumably to read again.

"Go ahead," he says. "Read it."

"Let me out of the bathroom."

"Oh, yes, yes. Sorry."

I nod and silently read,

Anthony—

First, allow me to apologize for my inappropriate words regarding your sulking at Pop's service. It is not my, or anyone's, place to judge how someone mourns. Please forgive me.

I look up. "This is good, isn't it?" I scan to the bottom of the letter for the name. Richmond. "He's apologizing."

"Did you read it?" he says. "Did you read it? Here."

I hand him back the letter and he reads aloud right there for everyone to hear: "'Anthony. Allow me to apologize for my inappropriate words regarding your sulking.' My sulking? My sulking? Huh. 'Your sulking at Pop's service. It is not my, or anyone's, place to judge how someone mourns.' Goddamned right it isn't, you son of a bitch. 'Please forgive me.' Huh. You think I'm crazy? Fool me once, fool me twice. 'I hope you don't think, however, that—"

"Anthony."

"—my apology means I've changed my mind about—"

"Anthony!"

"—Mom's health care.' What?"

"I'll read it myself, okay?"

"Where? How about over there?"

He's pointing to the exit and the flanking bench, the two patients sitting at either end so medicated they don't seem aware of each other's presence. "That's fine."

"Did you read the e-mails? Did you see my e-mails?"

"Everyone did. You guys CC everybody, right?"

"Well, I guess it's a legal matter, huh?"

I want to say, I imagine that's where the problem starts, but don't. I don't know why I feel so reluctant to be didactic with Anthony, to not lecture him about the things that are so obvious. Part of it, I suppose, is that I feel bad for him. And at least, for what it's worth, he's engaging in a form of sharing. Unlike Richmond. But also I just don't like wasting time and energy and words on conceptual issues he'd dispute to the grave.

He'd say, "Hey! The problem starts with them! They've been abusing this power-of-attorney stuff for too long! They've corrupted its usage!"

And then before you know it, ten minutes have passed, my eardrums are sore, and we're that much further from the original point.

"Excuse me, sorry," I say to the two women, and drop down between them. Anthony stands above the three of us. "I'm gonna read in silence, okay?"

"Go right ahead."

The two women say nothing.

First off, let me say that I have grown weary of the e-mail food fight we've had over the last few weeks, and feel that it is beneath us as a family. I'm disappointed. Name-calling has never solved anything. The problem is merely compounded. My belief is that e-mails are very dangerous because there is a dissociative tendency at play where one feels less responsible for one's words than in person. Perhaps it's because a one-on-one conversation, or even a conversation over the phone, forces the participants to be, at minimum, considerate. Let's not hide behind the virtual screen any longer, huh?

Let's all stop the food fight.

I think you're missing a basic premise of good business. Let's discuss the problem before offering solutions. I didn't know you were hostile to the type of care Mom is receiving before I read your e-mail, Tony. I may be a pretty successful guy, but I'm no mind reader. Let me assure you that you were not excluded from anything. In fact, I called you, and even Johnny, several times to keep you both updated. I encouraged Mary Anna to do the same.

So why didn't you, or even Johnny, call me directly, rather than sending out a flurry of angry e-mails? You see, I was being presented with a solution to a problem I wasn't sure existed. I know I haven't spent as much time with Mom as you, Tony, but I have taken you seriously. How can I not have? You've been as serious as a nuclear war from the outset.

I specifically asked Dad just before he passed if he was concerned about the issue of moving Mom. He assured me that he was not. I asked him several times. I received the same answer. "No." But I knew he was somewhat delusional and so I asked Mary Anna about the issue. While I cannot share with you the terms of our discussion, or even Mary Anna's answer, it is very simply not my place to enforce your preference over Mary Anna's, and most certainly not over Dad's. I would direct you to the standard law book when it comes to the legal integrity at stake in protecting the power of attorney.

When Richie died, I accrued over a million dollars in medical costs, and so the question of Mom's care must be addressed all the way out to the worst-case scenario. After Pop's disastrous handling of money and the bankruptcies over the years, a decision of that magnitude cannot be made on emotion alone.

It's no secret that Mom is losing it. This may hurt you, Anthony, but when I last spoke to her, she was recalling her dog from Pittsburgh, Rex, and how much she missed him. It doesn't mean that we should send her off on a ship of fools, but obviously everyone needs to identify what's appropriate to do with respect to her condition, not to what we ourselves feel, or hope, or believe in politically.

A whole range of associated issues need to be worked out before we get to a solution—move or anything else. But I haven't been sitting in front of the fire brooding about your involvement, Anthony. More than anyone in this family, I've been damned lucky to have a good life and have a hell of a lot to be thankful for. Equally vital is the idea that I've pretty much always believed it's preferable to try to do something good than to stew about things. Hope you'll understand that this includes caring for my mother.

I don't know that I will ever agree that a move is necessary, but if you want to make a proposal, give me a call. If you can make a case, I will call a meeting. Let's just all agree to put the anger aside because—as you may or may not believe—it rarely resolves a difference of opinion.

Hope you're taking good care of yourself.

Rich

"Well, what do you think? What do you think?"

I can't believe the ease with which the successful revise history. "Well, it's—"

"You know, I've never given Johnny any credit over the years, and I don't think he deserves it, you know, but he used to always call Richmond a bullshitter. The one thing he got right, I guess."

"The thing is, who cares in the long run if he's not being *honest*? Who cares about pride, you know, in the bigger—"

"Hey! That son of a bitch—"

"—picture of what you can get for your mother."

"—is a liar!"

"I think you should forget the passive-aggressive stuff and look at the letter as an opportunity to get her out of this place. Be passive-aggressive back. First step is to forget the accounting of how this went down. He left certain things open-ended. It's a huge chance."

"You're right. I'm going to write that bullshitter tonight and set him straight."

"No!"

"What?"

"You're not listening."

"Hey! Why the hell should I listen to him? He's got—"

"I don't mean him."

"—a lot of nerve throwing out his leftist lies and . . ."

I know what he's angry about. Who likes when anyone brushes up their sins in hindsight? He'd be angrier if I shared with him the conversation I witnessed between Dr. Patel and Richmond after Mary's successful blood transfusion in October. How Richmond had bulldogged the doctor into agreeing that Mary, like anyone, could die the next minute, how he'd used his dead son's hopeless situation to justify the position, how he'd nodded at Mary Anna's advice to keep the details from the other siblings, including Lazarus. And yet I think I should try something else altogether with Anthony. If my full disclosure will ruin his chance to get what he wants in the end, and I, too, now, really do think it a better end, why would I share anything with him?

It's not about Anthony's anger or Richmond's passive-aggression or Mary Anna's outright lies or Johnny's amorality. It's not, still not, about Lazarus's absence.

"Let me write the letter for you," I hear myself say. "It's about Mary, not you guys. I know exactly what to write to get the move."

"Hey!" He pats me on the shoulder. "Hey! Thank you! The pro! Thank you!"

22

Lazarus Corsa Felice
Enrollment at Università degli Studi di Palermo,
  Sicilia
March 19, 1987

WHEN HER ONLY DAUGHTER came home from varsity volleyball practice and said, "I need these papers signed," Leticia McCluskey casually reviewed them, blinked two or three times at the seriousness of their contents, looked up at her daughter's resolute face, and in what was surely the most important moment of her motherhood second to giving birth said, "Wait here—I'll be back," and in the tie-dyed shirt and Birkenstocks she'd been wearing the length of an entire week, left for what she swore in her mind to be a short drink (meaning no more than three) at the Sonoma. On the walk over, she couldn't keep from thinking about how this latest problem had been created by someone who hadn't been around her child in years.

"The MIA," Leticia said cynically.

At the bar she ordered a shot of house tequila and a twenty-four-ounce can of Foster's, popped the Foster's, shot the tequila, chased it with the Australian lager, looking sideways at the flat-topped barkeep.

She said, "Thanks, Scooter," and then took the Foster's out the door without the cover of a paper bag.

Leticia crossed the street to Plaza Park, a designated public spot where the city council of Sonoma had made it legal to drink years ago. Was a big story in the papers. The city's resources, the city clerk had said, were better spent on more serious issues than a wino tripping over himself in front of Readers' Books.

Drunk in the very park of dispute, she had forgotten to vote on it.

Up the street she saw Darren Condin, a good, broad-shouldered man whom she used to date when they were neighbors in the trailer park. At one time, Leticia had thought that she could have loved Darren Condin, a surprisingly gentle man's man who used to barbecue tri-tip on the trailer commons in the early Sonoma evenings, who religiously followed the Pittsburgh Steelers and their "hard-nosed, working-class ethic," who insisted, even when no one was on the site to catch him, of putting in an honest day laying pipe and cement. Never punched in late, never punched out early. He'd been so strong in the heart and the hands that she'd felt less like a lover than a daughter. Not loving someone like her father, but loving the man her father had never been.

She watched him round the corner of Napa Street and suddenly remembered that he was younger than she was.

"By three years," she said.

No kids. He loved hers. Was so kind, thought Leticia. Once bought Gabe a skateboard. Not a cheap plastic banana deal from the fifties, but a solid wood board, aerodynamic like a shark, wheels on the pavement loud as boulders crashing down a mountainside. Darren taught him to do an ollie. Took Murron out on Halloween and filtered through her candy for anything suspiciously wrapped. She'd never thought of it herself. Listened to Murron talk on her father's made-up heroic exploits until his ears were burning. He was the first man to disprove Leticia's lifelong fear of machismo. He delivered on the code she'd been hearing about since childhood but had never personally witnessed, one that seemed to be the exclusive purview of Hollywood sitcoms: Ward Cleaver, Mike Brady, Cliff Huxtable. She'd finally found a man who could protect her, yet not harm her. Who would be there. If they'd decide he could be there. There was a lot to consider. She was a single mother. She didn't feel like she deserved him. She treated her time with Darren Condin as if it were, for her heart, a kind of vacation away from a broken home that sat in the direct center of a drug-addled slum.

She wasn't sure that much had changed since then.

About a month ago, she'd heard that he'd lost his job after standing up to the site foreman about the mistreatment of Mexican workers. Sounded like Darren. When they'd dated, he'd been so excited about their truly Semitic stories, how they'd crossed the border at great risk to their lives, eluding coyotes and the border patrol, how they outworked Americans for half the price, and then mailed back their paychecks to a family of nine in the destitute state of Michoacan, their barren home town surrounded by guerrillas and dust clouds. How they slept six to a room at the SoNoMotel, how the construction job was one of two jobs, the other being in the early morning at the Sonoma Grill flipping jacks and frying eggs. "And we work hard out there, Tish. Bust our asses. These pint-sized guys pack a punch, I'm telling you." How they shared everything at the lunchmobile, which was called *El Truco,* invited gringos like himself to join in for a warm burrito of *chorizo y huevos,* the tortilla filled to the folds, insides lined with Tapatío, fragrant spices dripping across the catch of foil. A habanero pepper to mince on in between. It was his, they said with a translatable nod, all his. Eat up, brother. *Comes, hermano.*

Sometimes on Friday nights, they'd decide against a movie and walk to the public library instead, all so Darren could listen to the Spanish cassette tapes in the language room, the headphones dwarfing his head like giant earmuffs, his Latinate pronunciation so poor and redneck she'd lift the *National Geographic* over her face to giggle. He tried hard to connect, he really did, and she'd also liked that about Darren. He was idealistic like her.

The problem was that Darren Condin included single mothers in the realm of the sufferers. She knew he cared about her, but she wasn't sure how much of it was an act of charity.

Four and a half years have passed since Darren, she thought. Almost half a decade of my life. Evaporated like a puddle of water in Death Valley.

Her memory had been affected by the drinking so that she saw things now in isolated flashes, sometimes linear and vivid with color, all kinds of young and unscarred faces forced into the scene like a collage of candids in an elementary school yearbook. Her children in the spilling waves at Santa Cruz. Herself on the knee of her father, his own grimy face absent, taking in the Southern California sunset on the verandah. Neighbor children, Mexican children she'd never met, innocent faces lost under the calorie count on the sides of milk cartons. Though she wasn't certain if her conclusions about the images were accurate, the idea that her mind had attached color to the pictures made her feel, accurate or not, as if there were some promise out there. Promise for herself, Leticia McCluskey, and her own, Gabriel and Murron Felice. Her heartbeat resonated throughout these flashes, the blood hot on the elusive tail of hope.

Other times her head was filled with bordering plains of black and white, perfectly touching yet perfectly cut off from one another. As if the border could be broken down with one lucky neurotransmitter making it successfully over the wall. As if half of her mind was shouting to the other, "Do you remember this?" During the hours without color, which came in her sweat-drenched sleep, which came when she staggered home from the Sonoma in the cut of shadows under the elms, which came at first light while sifting through the thousands of black-and-white digits constituting the *Sonoma Times* morning edition, she could come upon one image that, as near as she could figure, was herself: an island of broken concrete, drab, unmapped, sustainer of no life, beset in the middle of a dark, cloud-drowned sea.

"A sea of Foster's," she said.

She sat down on a bench in Plaza Park, Darren having disappeared around the corner forever. She finished the last of the Australian lager.

It didn't help her memory. What it gave to her, peace, it took away just as easily. It was a cycle. That was a fact. Her daughter was right. Her son, who never said a word about it, was also right. Yet she just couldn't get at the reason Darren had left. Things seemed to be going beautifully between them. Well, she wanted to know: Was that right? Was that fact? Had he *loved* her?

After she'd realized that Lazarus wasn't coming back from wherever he was, she'd taken the advice from some of the ladies at the shelter to go on a date, just get out a bit. In 1981. If only she were a writer, she could tell the sordid stories, the unimaginable perversities.

One man she'd met at a convention for Christian fellowship had asked her to defecate on him. She'd never heard of this. Actually hadn't thought it *possible*, in the same way night couldn't be day. This was less than an hour into a dinner at Wendy's.

That wasn't the only man she'd walked out on. They tested her level of empathy all the time, almost as if she wore a sign to the dates. One man told her that his mother didn't deserve the warmth of a fart in a freezing wind. His exact words. She waited, didn't put him to the test of interrogation. She couldn't remember his name now, but she could see his beet-red face, red like lipstick, red like the fires of hell to which he'd damn his own mother. He said as much.

But there had to be something, she thought, some explanation. She went on several more dates, hoping to get at his wound. The anticipation of discovering his backstory was greater than her desire to protect herself from danger.

Their dates would start with his talking, be composed of his talking, and end with his talking. She didn't have to ask a single question. When he'd talk, she'd dream about midday picnics in rolling fields of wild mustard, visual alchemy like the kind she'd seen in coffee-table books about painters from France, a sun-drenched luncheon with her children or anyone who could love like she could love. It was a dream. Never Lazarus in the dreams, not as Lazarus had been, nor as Lazarus was, or would be. As if it mattered. Dreams were made of people and people came from real life and so dreams also sprang of real life. That was the ascension from the physical to the spiritual that so few people really understood.

You had to *be* there for the dream to have meaning. In real time. On the watch, she'd thought. No other way into the heart.

Plenty of ways out of it.

So she'd waited some more and finally the confession came. They were somewhere in Sonoma since—like the other grounded, unimaginative, cheap men she'd dated—he'd never taken her anywhere outside the city limits.

"She gave the money to my brother," he said.

"The money?"

"I got the house. Fucking shack wasn't worth twenty thousand. You ever heard the term 'screwed'? Yeah? Heard of it? Know what it means? Yeah? Yeah? Well, yeah, that's me."

"And what else?" she asked.

Very gently. The way she used to ask Gabe about the reason he'd killed mockingbirds in the gully with his BB gun, broken a window with an obviously aimed and not misthrown baseball, stolen a bar of chocolate from the liquor store with a handful of quarters in his pocket. With the idea that her kind countenance would extract from him something deeper, worthy of her concern, her heart. With the idea that the lesson being learned would begin with a response to confession that the confessor, surprised, unspurned, wouldn't get from anyone else. That after the confession, another bird would be spared, another window unbroken, another liquor store owner could close out a hard day even. The old story. That beneath badness must be goodness.

"What do you mean *what else?*"

"Oh," she said, stumbling, "I just meant she must've been bad in your childhood, too, huh?"

"No! That's the whole point. She was a great mother. Lived for her kids."

"I'm sorry, I don't—"

"And then she leaves us like *that*? I got two-to-oned in value, see? What a joke."

"Maybe she—"

"No. There is no maybe. What else? Come on. That's all you gotta say: What else? I'd say that's enough, wouldn't you?"

She nodded and said, "Yes. That's enough. Good luck."

She went home the long way, under the lights, rapidly and without looking over her shoulder. She feared that he wouldn't take the insult walking, and then when she got home safely, it was obviously because she wasn't important enough for him to follow his natural predatory instincts. Even the mad care enough to commit the crime. He didn't care.

And then Darren came. She didn't know exactly when, or how much time had vanished between that walk home and Darren, she didn't even know if there were other men in between, but next came Darren. That was the important thing.

She wondered what Darren's advice would be now. She imagined he'd say it was a stage, maybe, a way for Murron to find her father. Yes, she'd say to him, someone she'll never find. You've got to be there to be found. And yes, he'd say back, that's true. But she still has to give it a shot. She'll come back, don't you worry, babygirl. Your sticking around will mean something when there's more perspective, okay? All right.

He was like a village elder from another age, an old soul in a strongman's body, the sage sought out by many but whom few could be. He was simple and good and maybe he was good, Leticia thought, because he was simple.

In the Felice family, Richmond had always been the source of advice. But his goodness was maybe trapped, she thought, or eaten alive by intelligence. His goodness was always being fed upon by outside parties. But then, admittedly, she didn't know him anymore. Except for the stupid package he'd sent the kids, the grandstanding letters and transparent attempts at wisdom, she didn't know him. He wasn't there either. None of the Felices were there. She'd been abandoned, too. Not just her daughter and her son. She was first, and then her kids by extension. They'd left her with these children bearing their name and half their looks but no claim on a story. Not a trace of legacy.

Leticia should have known this flight to the Mediterranean would happen. Right when Murron had hung all those generic posters of Florence and Naples and Rome on the walls of her tiny room. Somewhere around the spring of her sophomore year at Sonoma Valley High. The cassette tapes of English to Italian that she'd mail-ordered from a company in Chicago called Berlitz. The Italian flag blanket bought at the weekend flea market with a month's worth of saved allowance. The shrinelike picture over the closet mirror of that pop singer, Madonna, half-naked on a peasant-maneuvered gondola in some polluted offshoot of Venice.

She tried to converse with her daughter. During evening meals in the candlelit end of the trailer that was their kitchen, Leticia would mention the Beat poets of the fifties and sixties like Ginsberg and Kerouac, thinking that the splice of a borrowed sermon she remembered Richmond giving on the topic of contemporary poetry would softly push the dinner discussion away from the money-driven eighties, back to when movements had meaning. Even if the meaning was wrong, it didn't matter, she said, because at least they stood for *something*. Could you say that about this Madonna, honey?

But the talk about the just cause of mass protest, civil rights, and the Age of Aquarius only pushed her daughter further into the past, several centuries back, to another era she knew nothing about save the random facts of artistic beatification she'd learned as a Catholic over to a continent she'd never visited, and certainly never would visit. Not because it wasn't beautiful and meaningful but because she had no money, and unless she struck the lottery or robbed a bank, never would.

Between bites of macaroni and cheese Murron would talk about a conversation she'd had with her cousin Richie, whom she'd yet to meet, and how he'd said that no one in the world could compare to the Italians when it came to a cultural contribution to the arts, that if you took the Chinese, the French, the English, and most especially the Americans and added them all up you still wouldn't get a Michelangelo or a Leonardo. Murron was taken with her cousin almost as much as Leticia had once had a crush on this same cousin's father. And now with a lifetime of being badly unread, so badly that the last book she'd finished was *To Kill a Mockingbird* in Mr. Habiger's senior English class at Upland High, Leticia didn't know how to respond to a statement that sounded so suspiciously untrue, or to ask if that kind of ranking was even possible, simply listening to her daughter ramble on, not sure if she was more proud of her daughter's ability to talk without reservation or more ashamed of her own incompetent silence, her daughter transitioning to another theory of Richie's, who'd said that the Germans, musically speaking, came very close to the Renaissance Italians with Bach, Beethoven, and Mozart. She could only nod, her eyes on her daughter's red, white, and green bracelet, and say just above the hushed volume of a whisper, "Richie sounds a lot like his father."

She should have known Murron would leave when she'd started leading her statements with "Richie says." "Richie says" that she should visit Italy someday. "Richie says" she should attend college in Milan or Rome and see culture while she can, see beauty when it was still around. That he wouldn't trade his "trips to the continent" for anything. "Richie says, Richie says." As if it were a stamp of authentication in a pint-sized kitchen in a pint-sized household in a pint-sized town that Richie himself would never condescend to visit.

Now her daughter was walking through the park, her dark eyes searing into Leticia even from a hundred yards, carrying the passport application in front of her, as if it were burning her hand and she were about to drop it. Walking as all the Felices walked, bowleggedly, the space between the knees so wide that it looked painful even on a seventeen-year-old girl full of vigor and steam. The limbs loose and slender, held together in tenuous cohesion.

Leticia felt a deep affection of the kind she always did watching one of her own cross into the next realm of life, for that's what this was, a crossing, and then in the realization of what it meant in real terms, of being left to die, the breath in her chest froze in shame and nervousness. She couldn't move. She sat there as if paralyzed by the image of her daughter's long body, letting the moment consume her from the inside out, unprepared for even a single minute of the irreversible, undiluted solitude that would be hers to sit in. She couldn't keep the anger out, not even as she knew it was pushing a bad thought into existence.

What the hell did Richie know, that kid? Did he ever think that "trips to the continent" were an extravagance some couldn't *afford*. Well, maybe he did. Maybe he knew. Yes. Maybe his real question to my daughter was: Are you aware that my Big Daddy has a lot of money, little broke trailer-trash cousin of mine?

"I asked you to sign this."

"I told you I'd be back, Murron."

"I knew you'd come to the park. You're so predictable."

Leticia watched Murron scan the transients strewn randomly across the manicured lawn. Unshaven, exhausted. It was as if they'd each died in their own unsolvable misery and no one in the town had bothered to bury them, not family or friends, not city authorities.

"This place disgusts me."

"Be quiet, Murron."

"Such an embarrassment. I can't even walk around town without worrying what my friends will see. Why do you think Gabe left, Mother? I mean, don't you *get* it?"

"Please, Murron. Remember we're in public, okay?"

"Me? *Me*? Why don't you abide your own words? You've been in the public eye for my whole life! This is a town of seven thousand people, Mother."

"It's more complicated than my failure."

"This is worse than your failure, Mother. This is disaster. Apocalypse."

"You're so young, Murron."

"Young! I ate peanut butter sandwiches for a year, Mother!"

"You both are young. And there's still a lot of life left. Don't let this be the only way you feel."

"You're insane."

"Please, Murron. Let me share with you how I see it. Gabe loves his music. I think it's good that he follows his dream. If he makes it or doesn't, he's living his life. He'll learn either way. He's a young man. He's got it in his genes to fly from the nest."

"So it's a matter of genetics? Is there another factor in common here? What is making all these people leave?"

She waited in the sting of the insinuation and said, "Everyone pays a price."

"What did I ever do wrong?"

"It's not about that, Murron."

"Why do I deserve this? I just grew up thinking I could have a normal fucking childhood someday. Like everyone else. I didn't do a damned thing wrong."

"I didn't mean we pay the price for our *mistakes*, Murron. Jesus. You talk over me and I lose what I want to say."

"There's something else influencing your amnesia, Mother."

"I meant that we all pay the price for being *alive*. For just taking a breath."

"Excuses."

"It's not just about you, okay? Can you see that? Who doesn't have some huge bag of tragedy to lug across town?"

As suddenly as her daughter rolled her eyes, she remembered why Darren left. It was a meal with the three of them. Just the children and herself and the big question. He'd given it to her earlier that day in a petite bouquet of roses on the doorstep. Now she was giving it to them over a platter of Samson's fried chicken and Tater Tots. Murron said she'd run away, would leave forever if it happened. That they'd never see her again. Gabe told her, Shut up, you little fool, he's never coming back, get over it. But whether Lazarus was never coming back or not, she couldn't do it to her daughter. Gabe stood up and said, "You're both fools then." She wrote a letter. Couldn't face Darren with the truth of her backstory. She said he'd be a great father someday, a wonderful husband, I'm sorry, I love you.

She looked up at Murron as if she herself were the daughter, vulnerable, in need of guidance, hoping for the giving of something. An end at least to eye-rolling cynicism, the opposite of peace. She yearned for the kind of grace one found between new lovers, the quaint image of interlaced hands in the sealed-off garden of yesterday, an idea she'd been holding onto like a pillow since early childhood. Back then she of course hadn't yet found love, but somehow she'd known a truth about it that couldn't be taught, like a child who knows that it's safe to build a sand castle on the beach, even as the edge of the drowning sea is only yards away. And later when she did have love, she didn't have it for long, she wanted more, she wanted to stay. She'd thrown up her arms. Not to give up. She'd fought, she'd struggled. Like that same child being elbow-dragged from that same beach, her sand castle far from unfinished.

"Please look around. Please think about what people go through."

"You were talking about this town, Mother."

"Everywhere, Murron. I'm talking about *everywhere!*"

"No, Mother. Not everywhere. You were talking about a town of losers, Mother."

"Murron."

"And now I'm leaving this town of losers. Starting with *you.*"

"You have to stop this. Please stop. This self-pity stuff takes up half your brain. The other half is anger. If you don't quit it now, you never will. Please, baby. You'll be like this the rest of your life."

"Okay, Mother. You teach me then. Go ahead. You tell me why I'm leaving. I want to hear your answer. Do your job as a mother."

She stood up, grabbed her daughter by the collar and said, "It's all right if you leave, okay? It's *fine!* I don't care if I'm alone! I love you here, I love you there! Do you *see*? Same with Gabe. No matter what you do. I love you. I . . . *proved* it! Can he say that, Murron? Where is he? Where is your wounded hero, huh? Mr. Wonderful, Mr. Barrel-of-Laughs? Where is he? Where the *fuck* has he been for the last nineteen years?"

"If you were the mother of my children, I'd leave, too."

"He's an MIA, Murron, that's what he is. Missing in action from his life. For the rest of his life."

"You make fun of it, Mother."

"For all he's worth, he might as well have died there."

"I can't believe you just said that."

"He did die there." She closed her eyes and said, "Will you tell me where you're going at least?"

"La Università degli Studi di Palermo."

She opened her eyes. "Where is that?"

"Where your would-be husband's mother was born. Don't worry. You won't have to pay a dime. You see the words 'academic scholarship'?"

"Just give me the paper. You don't have to stay here any longer than you want."

"I wouldn't be here if you weren't here, Mother."

Leticia took in her daughter's dark tortured face, the Latinate features, the extra flesh of the nose, a Felice trademark. Murron hadn't considered in even the shallowest terms the irony of her own statement. Yes, she *was* here because Leticia was here. Absolutely correct. Correct here in this park, correct beyond the bounds of this town, correct in Palermo, wherever the hell that was. Correct anywhere in the world. This outburst was a matter of limited planet time. Or so Leticia hoped, prayed. If there was a man out there who could stand her, one day her daughter would be a mother. And the child, boy or girl, would bring her daughter one more reason to stay alive. And maybe she'd remember in the downtime of her own maternal trials what she, Leticia, had done to keep her alive as a girl, fed and housed and loved, yes, but also leading her by the hand to this very bridge of freedom she was about to cross, however blown out, however badly in shambles, the bridge and the escort both. And maybe someday when Leticia was at her lowest, Murron would kiss her on her own tortured brow and whisper, "I wouldn't be here if you weren't here, Mother."

And she wouldn't care. If she was there on a bed with soiled sheets. She wouldn't turn her daughter away.

Murron surveyed the ground. "Never again, Mother. Not one more minute in this dump." She'd been focusing on her mother as she spoke, shading her face as if the sun were out. It wasn't. The gray clouds had set before they'd even said a word. The early spring wind picking up.

"Okay, Murron. Okay."

"Not another minute in the presence of these losers."

"I said, shut your mouth."

"They turned downtown into a sewer. Who the hell would visit this place? Why don't they get some cops to come out here and—"

Before she knew it she'd slapped her daughter hard across the cheek, even as Murron was in the middle of pulling the paper from her sweater pocket, the words, whatever they would have been, flying out of her daughter's mouth on the back of spittle already spreading wildly through the air, the spray yet tracked by Leticia's unsober eyes in the slow-motion shot of a dramatic film as Murron's own eyes sponged with shame, the tears dying on the slopes of the lashes in what she knew to be a willful act of punitive restraint, Leticia was writing her name on the line under the words "Parent/Guardian Signature," saying, "I love you I hope you find happiness you're a beautiful lovely wonderful girl wonderful and don't listen to anyone who says otherwise even over there if you need me you can call anytime don't forget, okay please okay, baby?"

"I won't be calling, Mother. I don't think you'll be around to pick up, anyway."

"Murron."

Her only daughter walked off.

She sat down without really knowing it, the transients unawakened by the scene. Stray vines from an adjacent garden of Japanese wisteria slithered up between the wooden slats of the bench. She was literally sitting on beauty, smashing down the givers of oxygen. In her thirty-seventh year, nineteenth as mother to Gabe, seventeenth as mother to Murron and pseudo-widow to Lazarus Corsa Felice, she knew, for what it was worth, that she was wholly right on the point that her daughter was young and that, yes, even in the wine-flowing valley of Sonoma, it was hard to stand in the harsh winds of mid-March.

She stood at once, though quite slowly, found an unoccupied space between a man she recognized and a man she didn't. She got on her knees. The wetness of the grass awakened her slightly, but she quickly fell back to the comfort zone of reverie, patting down the bed of grass with her fluid-filled, blistered dry, nail-bitten fingers. She used to tuck in the kids at night in this very way, wondering what was up ahead of them as fatherless children, of herself as husbandless wife, even of the world at large with all its missing parts, conscious of a lump of sadness in her throat, a vision of dread. Then for what must have been the fiftieth time that short year, she lay down without reservation in the historical section of Sonoma's Plaza Park, where the dogs and the drunks had been pissing and shitting since the Ford administration, the chilled sky above covered with layered quilts of cloud graying dark like nickel, thinking that sleep the kind the dead sleep was a most lovely dream from the stained ground of her lonely life.

23

Murron Leonora Teinetoa
Terms of the Correspondence
March 13, 2008

I FINISH THE LETTER at my bedroom desk, the door closed to Prince and Mom in the living room, and at once I proceed to read it aloud, the old editor's habit, ready, with the disinterested empiricism of a surgeon, to cut or add what I must.

"Dear Richmond—

"In the spirit of moving forward for Mom, I want to thank you for your letter and the time you took to write it. I also appreciate your apology. That said, I tried to set aside any personal differences between us and confine my letter topically to those issues that have affected or will affect Mom's care. Please don't mistake that for an avoidance on my part of certain issues you mentioned. As it is, I realize that we'll probably always have a difference of opinion when it comes to the way in which certain things developed, and that those differences shouldn't prevent a bridging, where possible, of other differences paramount in relation to Mom's care.

"To begin, Rich, I have some fundamental problems with what you deem an accredited opinion. While the type of caretaking Murron and I have been engaged in over the last couple of months does not require expertise in a given field, we've learned important truths regarding Mom's care merely by being there. It does not take a mastery of human physiology to identify, and then do your best to meet, the rudimentary demands of Mom's care. As a former soldier on the front lines, you can appreciate more than most the schism that often exists between those in the field and those experts calling shots from afar. I have never claimed to understand the corpuscle's role in the body's circulation, but I can read the signs shown by my mother when she's hungry, happy, sad, when she needs changing, when she wants me to leave. I defer to the expertise of the doctor when it comes to the empirical workings of Mother's system, but I can read things that he of course cannot, and won't ever.

"Notwithstanding her qualifications as a career physical therapist, Rich, Mary Anna is not a medical doctor. To Mom's detriment, that fact became grossly apparent very early on. Mary Anna has been repeatedly in error as to the decisions and judgments she's rendered regarding Mom's situation. Consider that she went from stating explicitly to the family that Mom's system is 'shutting down,' going as far as orchestrating last good-byes for Dad, extended family members, and the like, to then admonishing us in the last run of e-mails that Mom could 'live as long as six, seven years.' She never acknowledged the 180-degree turn in her position, that her present stance was mine to begin with and *precisely* the point of dispute. You can imagine how I felt when, even as a 'shutdown' was occurring, Mom made very real improvements in very strict medical terms: though her weight has fluctuated, she continues to take in upwards of 1,500 calories a day with no coercion; she has a 130/70 blood pressure; her vitals are consistently intact. To give you a recent example of how misinformed Mary Anna is about Mom's situation, I'll refer you to her last e-mail, from late January, where she stated that she would 'allow Mom to sit up if she can take it.' Rich: we've been pushing her around in a wheelchair at her own request since early December! Sometimes four or five times a week. And as far as 'sitting up,' she's been engaged in that 'activity' of her own volition since her arrival at Elysium Fields.

Mary Anna does not know this, among many other things, because, first, she has not been there enough to know and, second, her source of information (the hospice nurse) is unreliable due to her commitment to fill beds. Combined, Mary Anna and the nurse spend less than ten minutes a week with Mom, if that. Despite Mary Anna's professional acumen and workload (which I understand inhibits her ability to visit), the time she has spent with Mom gives her an insufficient picture of the typical fluctuations in a typical day for Mom.

"No disrespect to you, Richmond, but I don't believe you know, either. I strongly dispute your statement that 'Mother is gone.' As I've spent close to one hundred hours with her in the last few months, I, along with Murron, have witnessed a wide range of biographical recounting from Mom, in often staggeringly acute detail. At times, it has been misplaced on the spectrum of time, yes; occasionally, but not regularly, it has been convoluted by a mixing of different periods in Mom's life."

A knock at the door. It's my mother. Prince would have just walked in.

"Almost done, Mom."

"Mur, baby. There's something you should see."

"Is it urgent?"

"Well, no, baby. It's not. I mean, it is for someone else, I guess, but not you. I mean, not *us*. Not me either, but it sure breaks my heart."

Something sad in a third-world country she's read about, maybe the latest Sudanese atrocity. My mother's bleeding heart is daily cut apart by my industry, wrecked and recovered in twenty-four hours. She's a good person, and if I can get one question out of the way, I will comfort her as I should just afterward, at least be an ear to her very real woes. "Is Prince all right, Mom?"

"He's fine, baby. Oh, don't worry. I'll show you when you're done."

"Okay. I'll be out in a sec."

"Oh, baby. I'm so sorry."

"Don't worry about it, Ma. I'll be out in a sec, 'kay?"

"Okay."

". . . But it has never affected her ability to speak to the factors within her immediate realm—our presence, her needs, the events on the television, the noises in the hall, the disposition of certain nurses—nor has it diminished her instinct to be maternal, to express concern for us in our lives, ask about other members of the family and even concerning jobs they've undertaken, where they were, when they were coming to visit, etc. She has gone from initially not eating when family was not there to accepting food that was fed by family to presently feeding herself without any assistance at all. She speaks with clarity and reads the subtitles off the television with no problem. She is observant and sharp. She beams when family is there. The preceding details should 'tug at your heartstrings,' at all of our heartstrings, especially when you consider that Mother has repeatedly expressed her desire to 'go home.' She constantly asks both family and nurses when she will be leaving. She's not talking about leaving life, Rich. She means Elysium Fields. She knows she's in a hospice, or a facsimile thereof, and she does not want to be there. She is aware of her setting insofar as it is not 'home,' and as there are plenty of places that would satisfy Mom's understanding of the word, it is my hope that we can come to a meeting place.

"Not to backtrack, Rich, but I was given a death notice, more or less, for Mom. I immediately drove down to visit her with the understanding that she was on death's doorstep and I wouldn't have another chance to see her. All I started with was what I'd been told over the phone. Only in the ensuing week did I see very real evidence to the contrary, and that evidence has piled up over the last few months. Are you aware, Rich, that over that time frame Mom has outlived eight roommates, including Dad, each of whom died in the room there with her? *That speaks both to an undesirable situation and the likelihood that Mother is not in the same category as her terminally ill hospice peers.* Conceivably, if Mom lives another year, she could have twenty rommates die on her. We can do better for our mother, Rich. I'm saying this as both a son and a brother, appealing to our shared desire to do what's best for Mom. I could provide you with dozens of examples regarding the shoddy conditions of Elysium Fields, but I'll just share a few: 1) Mom was repeatedly told to 'shut the fuck up' by an earlier roommate; 2) there are schizophrenics next door to Mom who shout epithets and vulgarities at the nurses on schedule; 3) On a recent visit, I saw three roaches scatter under the hallway rug. There is more, much more, but these are a few of the lowlights I've witnessed, and will continue to witness, independent of the *Consumer Reports* piece on hospices across the country.

"In reference to your letter, Rich, Elysium Fields *is* the worst-case scenario. You spoke to a need to address the costs. You must have either missed or dismissed the e-mail I sent out about how economically feasible a stellar alternative like Thelma's Place truly is. The proprietor there, Mr. Rubelle Cristobal, is firstly a businessman so, as you know, it behooves him to run a tight ship. Murron and I have both seen the place. Mr. Cristobal is nearby to supervise; he lives in a house directly across the street. The price of this superior care would be approximately $2,400/month. It offers an infinitely more homey environment and more intimate personal care than Elysium Fields. It is a real *home*. She would have home-cooked meals; the benefit of a 1 nurse/2 patients rate of care with five housemates; she would have thoroughly hygienic corridors; she would be in a safe neighborhood (South Willow Glen); she would have her own room, where the constant noise of a roommate and the roommate's family would not keep her awake. She would not have to listen to other patients shouting curses at the staff. There are bimonthly field trips taken by the house should she wish to go, and there is a spacious wheelchair-access yard to enjoy. In addition, she will lose nothing that the hospice has to offer with respect to medical care: a doctor can be summoned just as quickly; medication will still be administered; and Mother will be cleaned regularly. I would like to take this opportunity to personally invite you to see this home for yourself firsthand. It's important that you have an intimate understanding of the place, which has thus far been discussed in dismissive terms. If you are pleased with it, I would be happy to look into all the details, and would of course share all information I come upon.

"It's my belief that the daily visits from Murron and me have helped Mom tremendously, but I'm not naive enough to believe that they've been the only influence. Anyone knows that staring at the same wall around the clock cannot be good for you. Just the same, it's clear that Mom is not as close to the end as was originally suggested. I know that we can do better for Mother, Rich, and I look forward to talking to you soon about it.

"My very best to you and yours,

"Anthony.

"We've got it. That's it, folks. This is the one."

I feel good right now. Probably because the letter has real purpose. I don't feel silly about this. I am grateful. Why should I think something is silly just because it's obvious? That's the code of charlatans and fake intellectuals. Yes, the obvious can be offensive and often very American and certainly predictable, but sometimes the obvious can also be *profound*. And maybe even necessary. I'll leave the abstract world and its theoretical value to the novelists, but purpose to me means connection with real people in a real way, and that's what this is. That's what Mary is, a real person. In decline, sure, but still there.

I don't want purity on a mountaintop, the thin air dizzying my brain. I want to give it an honest shot down here in the valley. I don't know, maybe the pen isn't a sword, but when its usage is controlled and purposeful, a well-written letter can weaken the inner fortitude of any sovereign, and I know this. Maybe nothing will happen. You can't say. There are all kinds of real and figurative swords out there pricking at a person's insides, but when your spun phrase can make someone frown with reconsideration, it's a beautiful thing to witness, and always justifies the effort.

It's not hyperbole to say that it justifies one's life, too.

I print the letter, fold it, walk into the living room. Prince is dribbling his indoor soccer ball across the kitchen floor, flipping it from one foot to the other, letting it roll halfway up his shin, and then looking over at me, his athletic feet still in skillful locomotion.

"Jeez, Prince. That's fantastic."

"Juggling, Ma. Coach Mulitovic taught us."

"He's the one that played for the Earthquakes?"

"Yeah!" The ball pops up head-high and he leans underneath and catches it with his upper chest, lets it roll down his arm into his hand, and pulls it into his belly, hugging it like I hug him. "He gave me this. Look!"

It's a soccer card of the coach in his early twenties, a goalkeeper for the former Socialist Federal Republic of Yugoslavia, World Cup, 1972. The Cyrillic beneath the English looks, linguistically, as exotic and decorous as the spires on Eastern Orthodox cathedrals. I can see in his eyes the youthful intensity of male desire that sustains, and ruins, the world. A fire, I think, honest and natural, maybe unavoidable. Conceptually noble, potentially dangerous. But unlike Dowd and her cheap and simple-minded conclusions about dating the other gender, I don't know if men are the source, or the circumstance, that makes the world worse, and I don't know if we women are any better. When it comes down to it, I'm afraid for and afraid of men and women *both*.

And when I see a book entitled *Are Men Necessary?* on the shelf at Barnes & Noble, I take it personally. It doesn't require much extrapolation to conceive of *Are Boys Necessary?*

Is My Son, Prince, Necessary?

"It's very good, Prince. Your coach looks like he knows his stuff. I want you to listen to him about the game, okay, hon, you listen, but whatever you do out there, I'm proud of you. You're just doing beautifully."

"Yep yep yep. Thanks, Ma. Grandma thinks he's crazy—"

"Well," I hear from behind, my mother in her rocker, "he's—"

"—but I like him, Ma."

"—kind of intense."

"He's my favorite coach ever!"

"Okay, hon." My mother is bursting with a story, her cheeks practically trembling from the suspense. "Just remember what I said. It's *only* a game."

Prince shakes his head and turns away, and this subtlety, just slightly, hurts my heart. He thinks I don't understand the game because I'm a woman. What it means to take the field, what's at stake in a striker's penalty kick, the contract of competition between future young men. That it's serious, serious stuff.

"Mur?"

"Huh, Mom? Yes?"

"Hon. Would you like to see this now?"

"Oh," I say, walking over to her window spot, arms crossed. "Yes. I'm sorry. I forgot."

"Thinking about Lokapi?"

"Is he coming over *now*?"

"It must be tough for you, baby."

"Oh, that's right! He said six."

"I can show you this later."

"What the hell. I'm not going to get ready for Kapi. That's ridiculous. He'll pick up Prince and he'll leave with Prince. That's it. So what have you got there?"

She points at the screen of her laptop and I have a premonition by the drained look in her eyes that it's a personal, not international, story I'll find. Just as I'd predicted, the screen shows Mary Anna's e-mail address, iker4u@gmail.com, and the standard Felice CC of every relative, and then what must be Anthony's address, rushisgod23@aol.com.

"Jesus," I say. "I can't read it."

"Baby, you have to. It's crazy. *They're* crazy. I can't believe what they say to one another."

"How did it start?"

"I guess Tony went into Mary's hospice room and found a Vietnamese family making noodles in there. Does that sound even *possible*? I mean, I think he's kind of paranoid. I know I shouldn't be saying that, honey, but he was always a little, I don't know . . . confrontational. And you know what else? I shouldn't tell you this, but once I borrowed five hundred dollars from him when your . . . Lazarus was in Vietnam, and he put me on a payment plan the next month! I was pregnant with Gabe, baby, and that greedy capitalist jerk charged me—"

"Mom."

"—five percent monthly interest."

"I know the story."

"Sorry, baby. I just can't get over it, I guess."

"I know. But you're right. Here. I should see it."

Sometimes you know enough about a correspondence, or even a book, by the way a person chooses to write, the epithets used. Anthony is, according to Mary Anna, a "vicious thug," a "right-wing bigot," an "angry zealot," a "medieval homophobe," a "chauvinist pig." "Anyone," she writes, "who aligns with Johnny has got some serious problems."

"What do you think, baby?"

"I guess I've got some serious problems. Although I don't think Tony and I aligned with him. I think he just picked the side that would push the most family drama. He loves turmoil, I think, loves to see people in pain."

"Johnny, you mean? Johnny?"

"Yes," I say. "Did you think I meant Tony?"

"Well, I don't know."

"Tony's his opposite. He's a bit of a sap, actually. He's very honest. It's just that the stuff he's honest about doesn't square sometimes. And he *is* a zealot. I mean, I don't know. Where's the line between being a believer and a zealot? Anyway, what did he write?"

"Well, baby, I'm a believer, but I don't force my—"

"I know, Mom."

"—positions on others."

She scrolls down to his letter and adds, "I don't believe in that," and as I read words like "ashamed" and "abdication of duty" and "grotesquely misnamed shithole of a hospice," I find myself agreeing with the zealot, at least on the only point that matters, the issue of dispute.

Why is this woman whose children have millions of pooled dollars still in the same room in a hospice heading *Consumer Reports*' List of Disrepute?

"Did you read Rich's letter to Tony? Mary Anna pasted it into her e-mail and CC'd everyone."

I shake my head. Tony read it to me, Mary Anna read it to everybody else.

"I don't know, baby, how she knew about Rich's letter if—"

"He *gave* it to her, Mom. That's the only way. Richmond let her read it before he sent it to Tony."

"Oh."

"Or they wrote it together. But I doubt that, actually."

"Why, baby?"

"She's not too bright. He puts out the arguments, she shouts out, 'That's right!'"

I don't know how the infinitely complicated problems of the species can ever be resolved if these selected samples can't somehow keep it together. Save the world? As difficult a suggestion as God in the modern age. But maybe God, or his twenty-first-century simulacrum, is needed to cap the monstrous egos of those "successful" people prone to hiding, altering, and disseminating data, Gestapo police in their own small-minded minds, of their own sickly circles. It's as if to some, the subterfuge and revision of information are more important than the actual story, the story like a frightened, chicken-boned, hair-on-end mouse trying to carry the world's load across a barren, shorn, wide-open field. The poor little animal won't stop, but it won't make it either.

"I don't need to read Anthony's letter, Mom. I agree with him."

"Honey, you—"

"The substance, Mom, not—"

"—should read it."

"—the delivery. I don't have to read it. He's going to lose," I say, smiling. "That's how I know I agree with him."

"Honey. I just don't want—"

"—me to get hurt, right?"

"Oh, honey! The anger is so terrifying! Look at this: 'I'm tired of carrying your baggage around, you misanthrope right-wing pig.' 'Sounds like you want to kill me, baby sister. That would be the second family member, by my calculations.' 'That's slander, you son of a bitch.' 'Better slander than murder.' 'Are you accusing me of killing our mother?' 'I'm accusing you of confusion and I quote: Mom's systems are shutting down. I have been assigned power of attorney. Since Mom is no longer with us, all questions should be directed to me. A murderously bad Freudian slip, Ms. P of A.' 'Try looking in the mir—'"

"I got it, Mom."

"Oh! They're just slinging more and more mud!"

"Well."

"I don't want you to get hurt."

"Dad!" Prince sprints from his room to the door.

"I'm all right, Mom. What hurts hurts the same every day to me. With or without these people in my life. The story never changes."

"You don't believe that, honey."

"Of course I do. I'm sorry. I don't mean to offend your Twelve Steps or your Ten Commandments, and I'm happy you have them, but it doesn't change the way things are. The way people are."

The door is wide open to the things. To the people. I can hear the soles of Prince's shoes skipping down the concrete stairs, and the thought of him tripping and scraping his knees brings me back around to the conundrum. That all of me cares about my son, and thus all of me refutes the premise of an impossible world.

My mother's right, but just barely.

"Don't worry, Mom. I won't back down." I hold the letter up. "Was gonna throw this into the trash when you started in on their lame debates, but I'll keep trying. Mary's worth the long shot of her children shutting up and actually doing something with themselves. I've gotta catch Prince, okay?"

"I love you, honey. I'm sorry."

"For what? You didn't do a thing wrong. I love you, too."

The air outside is cool, the day sunny, a soft Bay Area wind sweeping through the complex. I step around the trash collecting on the steps, floating debris tickling my shins, the leaves and candy wrappers and God knows what else carried and dropped, carried and dropped, like a magic trick.

Prince is mounted on his father's shoulders, drumming the top of his head with his knuckles, his smile so wide and sincere that the scene looks like some late-night infomercial encouraging single fathers to step up and be single fathers. As I near, I think about retreating into the shadows of the corridor, but they spot me.

Lokapi casually but quickly flips Prince upside down and over, then bounces him three times on his feet, finally letting him go when I'm near enough to touch.

I'm here, right here.

"You okay, Mur?"

"Well, yes. I guess."

"Something's wrong."

"No, no. I'm fine. I am."

He nods. "Prince. Go sit in the car, little brother."

This is what made me love him, the constant caring, why I opened up way back when. The paternal radar for what's wrong. I've always admired his gentle but stern command with our son.

"You can talk to me. Come on. We can still do that, right?"

I look at him, take in his eyes. "Just sort of drained. A lot of drama today."

"Work?"

"No. I mean, it's stress, but I'm used to it, you know? The cliff and all."

"So is it Lazarus?"

"Sort of. I mean, no."

"It's his family?"

I nod.

"I thought you haven't talked with them in a while."

"Well, not those ones."

"Is it that crazy one again?"

"Which?"

"I don't know," he says. "I don't remember. They just all sounded nuts."

"Well, I think they are."

"So what's their problem?"

"I don't know," I say. "They won't take care of their mother."

"Your grandmama?"

"I guess. I met her for the first time in the hospice. So I don't know. She's Lazarus's mom, but he's never there either."

"That reminds me, Mur! You 'member Aunty Tali?"

"Of course I remember her."

I loved her. The third person I mourned after the divorce was Aunty Tali. First was Prince, second was my mother. Aunty Tali would have told me to take care of myself first and then I could handle other people. That I had to be kind to myself. She was always saying wise gentle things like that. "Rest, honey. Come here. Sit down with me. *Nofo i'a.*"

I never saw her stand. In the late 1990s she'd had a stroke, which left her paralyzed, and the cousins and uncles and aunties and sometimes people I'd never seen before would take shifts caring for her. They'd come in and rotate out like nurses on the clock. She'd been propped on a bed in the middle of the living room for three years when I'd met her, the invalid's throne, and she'd weigh in on family decisions from those as mundane as which television show to watch on Monday nights to the weighty stuff like money concerns. Her youngest daughter, Malia, was nine when she'd lost her movement. When I left the Teinetoas', Malia was sixteen.

"She said to say hello to you."

"Oh my God. I am fond of her. I genuinely am. What a beautiful lady."

"Aw, Mur. You making my insides go soft."

"I'm sorry. I don't mean to. Don't pay any attention. You guys have a great weekend, okay?"

"Come on. Mur."

"Oh, Kap."

"I'm right here."

I used to wonder what kept him around through multiple crying fits when we first started dating. Then later, during our marriage, the vicious attacks on his hopes and accomplishments, the nearest domestic object hurled with all my strength at his sturdy body. He stayed through it all, and then when I recovered, I told him to hightail it, to leave forever.

"Daddy!"

"*Filemu, tama leikiki.*"

"I'm ready!"

"So go sit your backside down then. *Fa'akali lea i le kavale.*"

He turns to me.

"So you wanna talk, Mur? I'm listening."

"You sure, Kap?"

He nods.

"Well, I don't want to talk about them anymore—*all right?*—except to say that they reminded me of how so important it is to not be afraid. I just mean if it means something to you, then you have to try. I trust you, you know?"

"What you talking about, Mur?"

"Oh, well, you know, I just was thinking that, you know, crazier things happen every day out there, all over the world, really, than two people who really love each other getting back together."

He looks away once, then back at me, nodding. I'm not sure if it's accordance or pity.

"Because, I don't know, life is over so fast, Kapi!" He takes my hand and pats it so softly, I can't help but cry. I can't help but want to stop, too, but that's not going to happen. I can feel it. Not soon, anyway. He'd hug me, I know, if there were no long-term threat to the act of rendering comfort. He's worried about me, but he's worried more about our son. With the setup now, there's no way anyone, not even I, can intrude on that priority. I wipe my eyes on a sleeve and say, "It's like everyone doesn't want to think about this because the magnitude of it will knock them off their feet. I miss you. I can live without you, but I don't want to, you know?"

"Mur," he says. "I love you, too."

"But you can't live with me."

"I can," he says. "I did."

"Maybe things will have changed by now, who knows? I'm not trying to convince you of anything, Kapi. I'm really not. You know how bogus it would be for me to say that to you. I'm just saying there's another side of things. I mean, I'm almost forty, Kap. Life really is affected by time passed. Time lost."

He shrugs, eyebrows raised. "Don't know, Mur."

"But maybe."

He nods at the car. "But it's not just us anymore, you know?"

"Yeah, I know. We have to be sure. I don't know if there's such a thing, but we have to be sure. His life is at stake, right? That's what you're saying."

"No." He steps back. "That's not it. What do you mean, his life is at *stake*?"

"I just mean we can't let him see the way I can . . . be."

"You're a good mother. That's all he knows. You're the best mother I know, Mur."

I start crying again, and this time he pulls me in. Our mutual fuck-it moment, putting caution to the wind yet again. It feels and smells like home, nostalgic and familiar, our rooftop capped with the pressure of this crazy American story.

"I'll stop," I say. "I'll stop."

"Well, you know, I didn't want you to leave, but you *told* me to. Said you hated me, that I was no good. That's okay, Mur. Because I hurt you like I did, too, you know? But there's a lot of other stuff, I guess."

"I know."

He reaches out and strokes his palm across my face. "You're the most tender woman I know, but you're the toughest, too."

I smile. "I don't think so."

"Of course you are. The police couldn't calm you down, my mother and father couldn't. 'Member?" He chuckles recalling this, from that deep-welled Polynesian region of voice I'd never heard before we'd met, sincere joviality derived of a lighthearted self-regard. "I was embarrassed by your toughness! You didn't have any respect for the order in my family."

"I'm so sorry."

"You know what I kept thinking? They're gonna have to tie her down or something. Take her away. Like that movie you love. What's it called?"

I've just been compared to Blanche DuBois. "*A Streetcar Named Desire.*"

"Yeah, and then they took *me* away. Funny, yeah?"

"Oh, God. I'm really sorry."

"Nah, nah, I didn't mind. Was okay. I'm sorry, too, you know? I watched you, I learned. Once you wanted it blown up, that was it.

No going back. I don't like to say it even now, Mur, but I sorta wanted to get away from you."

"Even in handcuffs?"

He nods, looks over at the car. Prince is watching us both in that wide-open way of kids where possibilities are still kind and friendly and not at all short on promise. I realize that Prince wants what I want. The only difference, I guess, is that I haven't yet earned what he deserves.

"Yeah. I didn't mind staying in that cell for a few weeks. I knew you'd bail me out when you could. You still paying on that?"

"Come on, playah," I say, smiling. "I live in EPA, don't I?" He laughs unguardedly at the phony gangsta intonation of a born-and-bred Sonoma Valley white girl and I take his hand, look up, and say, "We can do it."

"Well," he says. "Just gimme some time, okay?"

"That's what I mean," I say. "I made a mistake."

"It's okay."

"No. There's no such thing as it being okay."

"You talking in circles, Mur."

"I mean, it's either rekindled now or not. But it's not okay. If you get another minute on this planet, the chance to rekindle may be there, and may not. You may take it, and may not. I guess you can forget about it, too. But it's not okay until you've *made* it okay."

"I know what you mean."

He looks at me with the intensity of vision that used to scare me. An old song, a favorite Beatles riff of my mother's about looking through a woman and wondering where she went.

"I'm sorry for kicking you out, Lokapi."

He smiles. "It's okay, it's okay."

"Okay? I just—"

"It's a joke, Mur."

"Oh, sorry. And I am, you know? I so very much am."

He nods. "Me, too."

"You know what I'm starting to think?"

"Hmm?"

"No wound or mistake should outlast a life."

"Some are pretty big, Mur."

"But there's no point if you don't try, you know, Kap? Somewhere someone has got to overcome, or forgive. To redeem. Stop. Go forward. Every angle should be tried. From one side or the other, the more sides the better. And it doesn't matter if you get there, you just have to keep at it."

"You mean Lazarus, huh?"

"I mean him. I mean me. You. Everyone. I even mean Prince, eventually. Especially Prince. I want to endow our son with an appreciation for the immediacy of the moment."

"You sound like one of the elders at my pop's church. 'Cept they use the word 'blessing.'"

"Well, who knows if they're right or wrong about the metaphysics of it? But they're right about what it means to stay."

He nods. "Yeah. Well. It sounds like tough stuff, you know?"

"Maybe. But look at me. I'm trying."

"I know you are. Life means so much to you, Mur. I'm proud of you. But that's a lot of pressure."

"No," I say. "It isn't. Not anymore, it isn't. Because if I say it's pressure, then that's the start."

"What do you mean?"

"It's the first motion of turning away from my life. Of not being there for Prince. Of not being at work on time. All of it. Too many steps in the other direction and this life won't mean a damned thing to me. I know this. I've been there."

"I know you have."

"And I don't wanna go back."

"You won't, Mur. You won't."

I hope not, I think but don't say. "Okay, Kapi. Thanks for the session and—"

"Anytime."

"—what do I owe you?"

"I don't know. Nothing."

I stroke his arm, look down at the ground.

"Just keep being yourself, Mur, that's all. Just keep being a great mother."

"Thank you, Kap."

"And keep your head up?"

"I will."

He nods at Prince in the car. "You done a fantastic job, girl, with that boy right there. He's a straight champ. See you Monday," he says, and then walks away.

Prince practically jumps across the gearshift onto his father's lap, and they play-wrestle for a few seconds. Eventually Prince settles into his seat and Kapi nods at the belt. Prince listens to his father, even when he hasn't said a word, clicks it right into place. I'm happy about that. He listens to me, too, but differently. There's usually a slight pause, a pondering, after my directives. Sometimes it seems that he tolerates me and adores his father. Which could be the burden of the single parent who, five days a week, keeps the child fed, schooled, disciplined. All the serious stuff of a rearing, the stuff the kid needs but doesn't like. And yet I know it's hard for Kapi, too, that he's lost a lot from his side of divorce, and that he'd trade some of the fun time with Prince for, say, a serious "man-to-man" talk about a slipping grade.

He starts the car, rolls down the window, and says to Prince, "Say good-bye to your mom, little brother," something he, Kapi, has never forgotten to do himself.

"*Tofá soifua!*" Lokapi's family used to shout these very words to us when we'd leave their house. Good-bye and God bless. Prince's accent, as near as I can tell, is flawless. "I love you!"

"Love you, too, baby. Have fun. And be good, okay?"

I haven't watched them drive off together like this in a long time. I Iave always turned back to my half of a life—the separation, for a weekend, from my son. He's gone now to a world that I somewhat know, or remember, anyway, but lost entirely on my own.

24

Lazarus Corsa Felice
Arrival of the Package
July 23, 1982

A PACKAGE FROM RICHMOND came.

She watched Murron sprint into the living room and drop to her knees like an Eskimo child gazing upon a fire in winter. The hunger reminded Leticia not of her own real, irreparable, ever-present wound but of her children's collective desire, even Gabe in his young-man denial. Of the Cream of Wheat mornings and Top Ramen nights in their modest, two-thirds-government-assisted home in the indigent trailer park in East Sonoma, the deafening and absolute void of grown-man presence within its stripped walls, of grown-man sound, of grown-man action, grown-man thought, grown-man smell, the by-product manifest of a man—a real man, thought Leticia—who'd be there for his kids because he couldn't help or fight against it. A man who called his kids his very own, who tethered their panicky souls to his hip, who got them out of their own terrified, unilineal heads, someone in whose eyes they could see themselves.

"Doesn't look big enough to fit a man," she whispered. "Gonna have to send the box back."

Mr. Might-As-Well-Be-Dead Lazarus Corsa Felice, unraised from his combat grave.

And now her daughter started to chirp like a caged and needy animal and so Leticia shushed her as if she were a rowdy guest at a wake, went into the kitchen and poured a popper heavy on the Safeway-brand tequila side, and then shot it. The harsh burn in her gut made her wince. She was just as confused and excited as her child, and it bothered her.

"What do we got, Ma?" Gabe said, walking past her into the living room.

Her children were now waiting in silence, worried, she knew, that the tiniest erroneous sound would usher their mother back to the downtown Sonoma bar she'd just left. Leticia knew this, and though listening to Waylon and Willie over a one-dollar highball at Dave's Happy Hour was just what she needed, she felt that the box's potential promise meant she had to stay.

"Mama!" shouted Murron, jumping from the couch onto the floor.

She worried more about Murron than Gabriel. He was casually tough about Lazarus's absence, which he'd taken, by nine, to calling "the situation," but Murron longed for her father almost bodily, her fingers always curled to clutch at his belt loops. She'd cried at school watching the handheld, Daddy delivery of kindergarten classmates, she couldn't sit through half an episode of *The Brady Bunch* without asking, "Where?" "How come?" She was a high-strung kid, and she learned, at five, to begin every inquiry with "We need." It was a bad start. Special occasions like this drove her to a crazed pitch. She was long-boned and stringy-haired and she bruised as easily and permanently as a peach. When the momentum of a moment seized her frail body, Leticia foresaw collapse, hospitalization. Either for her daughter or for herself.

Limb straps and white walls and force-fed medication.

"No," she said to Murron, trying to calm her. She didn't need to anticipate Murron's question. The first question, the only question. "It's from your father's brother. Not your father, Murron."

"I told you," said Gabe. "Lazarus don't send shit."

"Gabriel."

"Lazarus don't send anything."

Why she wanted him to say "father" or some variation thereof suddenly mystified her. Why should he? He's a smart kid, he knows what's going on. Why should I protect that asshhole from his son's judgment? She pushed the issue no further. Instead she said, "When you cuss like that, your sister takes it all in."

"Where does it come out, Mama?"

"Your ass," said Gabe, shoving his sister.

"Gabriel! Will you stop it damn it!"

"Sorry, Mom."

She'd stopped herself from saying, "You're as callous as your father." She felt horrible for thinking it. She didn't believe at all in the heredity of personality, the soul, the spirit. The most important things, she knew, were forged in the white-hot oven of one's heart. No guarantee could be made about their academic and financial success, but she would bet the little she owned that her kids would turn out to be good, decent, love-filled human beings. No child of hers would be superficial. She simply wouldn't let it happen.

And yet she couldn't deny that Gabriel was callous. At thirteen, she thought. He's thirteen! He'd turned his internal pain into a funhouse, poking his mocking fingers at everything within reach of a comment, projection of a predictable sort that was hiding his little-boy heart from the pain of examination. And the sentiment shrank the longer it was tucked away. A thousand days from now, how much harder would it be to get to him?

"Gabe," she said, stroking the back of his head, "you look handsome this morning."

"Hey, hey, what can I say, my lady?"

Pathetic. The pattern between mother and son had become childish banter in a playground, Leticia's round at recess with the bully. He wouldn't stop the antics until she'd give in to the lunacy, and he could see her visibly giving in, trembling lip, burning eyes. She hated their ritual, but she also knew in a twisted way that it ended with her son saying, without having to say, that he loved his mother. That that was enough, anyway, to coat the pain of her life for a few minutes.

"Maybe Daddy sent it through his brother."

"Doubt it," said Gabe.

"Mama. Did Daddy send it through his brother?"

"No."

"Told you, Moron. Stop living up to your name. Murron the Moron."

"Gabriel, would you shut up?"

Gabriel was in a squatting position. These days he seemed to prefer the ground-level vantage. Now he stood, yawning, and sauntered out the door, snagged his Powell-Peralta skateboard from under the mailbox, then roared off down the street. She hated that she hadn't said a word, that she'd watched her son peripherally, that she knew what he was doing because they'd acted out this scene too many times before. Maybe it wasn't a matter of preserving energy like she always said. She was tired, yes, but she was *always* tired. She didn't believe she could corral her son any longer. That's what it was. He was like a rogue state that had gotten too strong, the bond with the host nation broken. He did what he wanted, but she was still afraid for him. The difference was that now she was also afraid *of* him. His independence frightened her at a primal level, and this fear, like all the scattered remains of her hijacked inner life, wound back to the missing element in the house, the gray pit in the living room corner of which everyone except Murron steered clear.

Where is he? she thought. Where is the man of the house to put my son's ego in check?

What a joke, a supreme joke. To hell with his cave, his damage. He couldn't happen upon a gathering of this family by accident, couldn't cross paths with these children by mistake. That's how self-absorbed he was, how missing from the world. She'd heard that saying before at a Wives of Vietnam Veterans support group at the Santa Rosa Community Center: *Back in the world*. It meant to a soldier "back home," "back in the United States," away from the sweating, malaria-ridden jungles of Southeast Asia. It meant "back in the world with the people who love you."

And whom *you* love, she thought now, squatting on the same square of rug just vacated by her son.

You had to love them, too. It wasn't a one-way deal, even during the horror of war. Even through it. You owed them something, too. They waited for you like monks, they nightly prayed for you like monks. They defended your name from nineteen-year-old fraternity punks decrying a war you yourself didn't believe in in your heart. Your coming "back to the world" meant your coming back to *them*. Meant living with them. Staying. Being around. Because this is what you thought about in the cold dead winter of war, this is what kept the mind alert and the heart alive with hope, this was a part of the formula. If you lived taking from it, you lived giving back.

None of his people, thought Leticia, looking at Murron's Roman features, none of them want to say it.

Especially his staunchly loyal mother, Mary, and the wiser-than-all-getup Richmond. But she could say it because she lived it. Mary's damaged son Lazarus Corsa Felice, their fun-loving brother Laz, this family member of *theirs* was nothing but a weak-willed truant, probably a transient, probably dead. And, anyway, who would know the difference? If he was a burrito vendor on a street corner in the Mission District, if he was a millionaire investor in the splendor of Pacific Heights, if he was a casualty in a supermarket heist, who would even know or care when it mattered?

You're born into this world of problems, thought Leticia, but you're born into this world. Someone out there needs you, wants you, keeps track of your heartbeat. Every second of your life is owed to somebody else.

She believed this and she was infuriated and amused that his brother was trying to make up for Lazarus's absence.

This ark of a cardboard box making up for a dead covenant.

She wished she'd never met him. But then she'd never have her children. Maybe his older brother would have loved her. She'd had a crush on Richmond first. Back when they were just kids, romantics prone to the high ideals of the young. She'd stumbled on him reading poetry in the Upland Public Library. He'd croon the lines of Rilke and it made her desire him and fear him both. It didn't take long for the fear to win out and the smallness of her own heritage to take over. She knew Richmond was the kind of person who made his dreams a reality. If he ever stopped crooning, his smarts would expose Leticia for what she was. When he took her to Big Victor to meet his favorite brother, Lazarus, she thought, Here is my equal. Here is someone I can breathe around.

She didn't understand then what she did now: He didn't bring us together. He dumped me on his brother.

"Mama! Can I? Can I?"

What could she say? The kids had gotten to the package first. Gabe had come back. He, too, had the right to recovery. If there was such a thing. She went outside to light up on the porch and watch through the window. Murron ravaged the box like a famished orphan. Poor girl, she thought. Beautiful girl. Even Gabe, she could see, was excited, however much he tried to hide it, pointing his sister along, squatting down beside her. Poor beautiful boy.

They pulled out a camouflage jacket whose shoulder width, she saw, was precisely that of her ex, a crumpled boonie hat of his head size, a framed photo of Lazarus in Southeast Asia, black tar or whatever they wore over there smeared all over his face. Murron was pressing this photo to the window now, and she nodded back at her daughter, trying to smile, but seeing in the reflection that she was only squinting.

He looks like he fell, she thought, face-first into quicksand.

He came back from that place tapped of bravado, deprived of oxen. He was no triumphant combat vet, the kind she'd seen in the John Wayne and Rock Hudson films at the Upland drive-in. He was a broken man. Like a child, full of fear and uncertainty. Couldn't look her in the eye. This encouraged her. She could take care of him. She was certain of it, was maybe built for it. She was excited.

She waited for him to notice her. To say something about the place he'd just come from, the damage he'd carried for his cause, but he spent two days with the family and then left for two weeks. She had no clue where he went. He said nothing. She almost didn't want to ask. What she feared she didn't dare say to him. This because she didn't want the idea introduced, if it wasn't yet there. That if he didn't stay any longer, that if he didn't try to see them for what they were, his own personal saviors, then he'd lose himself to the solitude, maybe even get addicted to it.

She wanted to say that he wasn't the only one who'd endured. She'd been faithful to him in the dim suburban evenings where a highball and *The Ed Sullivan Show* kept her warm inside. She'd created a dreamworld where death didn't exist, she wouldn't hear of it, no. Because if death existed and Lazarus was at war, a battleground bullet could claim him, and they couldn't transfer, together, to the other dreamworld he'd promised her someday, a five-minute ceremony at the courthouse in downtown Upland.

Before she could ask where he'd been, he was off to a second voluntary tour with the same team of men he said he loved so much, and could never leave. So she returned again to the world of pretend, a term whose life expectancy, if she was lucky, would be not a minute shorter or longer than 365 days, this time with an infant at her breast. She watched the same shows, nursing virgin versions of the same drinks of the year prior, asleep no earlier than midnight in the same low-end neighborhood of husbandless wives.

"Look at Daddy, Mama! He's got mud all over his face! Oh, jeez, he's silly! Can we put it up? Yes! Can we, can we, please?"

"You can put it up in your room, okay? Gabe will help you. Gabe!"

He came out with his skateboard, already wearing the camouflage jacket, the sleeves rolled to his elbows, very cool. He handed her a letter. She was grateful for that, anyway. That Richmond had sealed it, that Gabe hadn't pocketed it, that Murron hadn't ripped it open.

"Watch Murron for a minute, okay?"

"What's a minute?"

"Just watch her, will you, Gabe? How goddamned long could it take me to walk around the park?"

"Depends on how many trailers have moved in."

"Just do it, Gabe. Please, hon."

She walked off. She knew the way Richmond wrote. He could make the hardest drill sergeant drop his face into his hands and weep.

Now she passed the garden of the filthy Branzen trailer and the old lady, Sheryl Lynn, gave her customary greeting from the lawn chair she practically lived in, "Getting better all the time! Gonna watch *Breakfast at Tiffany's* tonight!" holding a Pabst Blue Ribbon out like a torch.

Leticia nodded and put her head down and opened the envelope as she walked. She rounded the south end of the trailer park, reading the letter silently to herself. He'd listed Lazarus's medals and commendations and he'd even denoted, by date, his two tours of duty, the unit he was in, the squad leader, and where, in South Vietnam, his unit has been stationed. Then she got to the last sentence and gasped, repeating two words out loud—"To forget? To forget!"—before rereading the whole sentence.

"I just didn't want you to forget," she repeated, "who your father is."

The son of a bitch, she thought.

These insane people always butting in at the wrong time, giving their two cents without a trace of reluctance. He hadn't asked how she was, how things were holding up on her end. Where was the package and letter when she'd received the breakup note from Lazarus? The one with no address, no words of condolence from the war hero, only legalese and Latin words that looked, combined, like fancy ways to get out of his responsibility. In cold, black, fully legible ink. The natural connection between mother and child, he'd written, was something he just couldn't break. Where were these people when they could have butted in on *her* behalf, which meant her *children's* behalf, why hadn't they given their precious Lazarus a needed berating?

What a fool Richmond was. He thought that poetic sensibilities gave one license to write letters like this, to send packages full of memorabilia. You can't fix my pain, she thought. There was only one way to make things right in her life, in her children's lives, and all the money in the world wouldn't make it happen.

"He should've sent that letter to his brother. Same words, real meaning. I just didn't want you to forget who your children are."

To hell with the mother, she thought. Just be there for these children.

She felt a surge of blood fill her chest, dropping to one knee in the shadows of the fake-looking palm trees. She closed her eyes, breathed slowly and deeply, opened them again. Not a heart attack. Just a rush of torment. She did the work, she kept the house, she made the money, she fed the children, she nursed their wounds, she tucked them in, she drove them home, she baked them cakes, she cried and worried, she killed her liver, she woke up scared, but it was like nothing she could do would buy back what he owned in his absence. The joy of their household in his pocket somewhere, wherever he was, why ever.

She'd lived with a different name than her children, met the pious stares with her head up for them.

Now she stood and dusted the gravel and dirt off her naked knee. The three swaying eyesores she'd always hated still there. Once she'd had a dream where the palms fell in a winter storm, one by one, and crushed the whole trailer park. She hurried behind the trailers to avoid the senseless catcalls of the insane Branzen woman. She wanted to walk, but she didn't want to be seen. She came from behind and stood hidden by a corner of their trailer to watch her son. He was accelerating up a plywood ramp he'd made, skinny legs bent to balance himself on his skateboard. He'd tied the camouflage jacket around his taut waist, the same frame and build of Lazarus fifteen years ago.

"Mama!"

Murron bolted out the front door of their trailer, tripping but catching herself in mid-stride, practically diving into Leticia's arms. She caught her daughter, planting her heels and trying to laugh, too, so touched by the girl's trusting honesty, her unambiguous thrust of self toward loved ones, that tears came, now carrying the girl so she wouldn't have to look into the eleven-year-old eyes that were not her own.

"Wanna come see it, Mama? Wanna?"

"In just a bit, okay, honey?"

Gabe walked over and said, "You all right, Ma?"

She nodded, stroked his arm. "I love you guys."

"I love you, Mama!"

"You, too, Ma."

"I put it over my bed, Mama! Right next to your picture!"

She heard herself say, "Okay," but she wanted to shout, "No! Don't do that! You mustn't do that!"

Gabe said, "You're a little fool, kid," and walked into the house. Leticia knew he would take it down and put it somewhere far from her own portrait, the unflattering picture of Leticia pregnant with Murron on the stately porch stoop of Big Victor. Mary, she remembered, had insisted on taking it, then sending it to Lazarus overseas. She was embarrassed about her body but she'd also thought, Who can look at this and not come home and do right by the mother of his children?

Big Victor, she thought, not daring to look around their trailer. Mary fit so perfectly into that home. Exactly where she was meant to be.

It wasn't just Lazarus. Leticia had fallen in love with Mary and the family, too. Big Victor was warm, the decorations personal and revealing and unashamed. The black-and-white communion photos over the fireplace, each child in the same prayer pose with the same priest, the family trips to Disneyland and the Golden Gate, the boys arm in arm on a ledge of rock in the Grand Canyon, a Sicilian uncle waist-high in a cloudy pool of blood, whacking a shark-sized tuna fish with a baseball bat. Real memories, real stories. The Felices were real people. The wild spaghetti dinners and political histrionics and verbal barrages and tender make-up sessions were so unlike what went on in her own house, she felt drawn there by the repulsion of her inheritance. She came of morbid parents and she shared a room with a morbid sister. Their house was right around the block, another Victorian on Fourth Street, but it seemed as far from her heart as San Francisco.

She was used to keeping ideas to herself, of counting the hours of silence in her locked room. But when she entered Big Victor, the energy consumed her. A Felice had an idea about everything. It was hard to form a clear thought in the Felice household, let alone get a word in, but whenever she'd leave she found herself immediately wanting to return. The standing joke was that the family should invest in a revolving door. Everyone constantly came and went, and they brought stories into the house like groceries from the market.

The first talk of the war came on one of those lovely Southern California evenings where you could see the cut of the San Bernardino Mountain Range miles away. Rich and Laz had brought Chinese food home from Longo's and Anthony was dancing with Mary Anna through the living room, "Don't Be Cruel" on the phonograph. Johnny was in Glendale trying out for a television show, or so he claimed, and the folks had gone out to catch a Ronald Reagan film at the Upland Theater.

Anthony swung Mary Anna off his arm and swatted her bottom. "Skedoodle off to your room now."

"Don't wanna!"

"Go. The big folks gotta talk politics."

She watched Mary Anna take a few steps in the direction of the stairs and slide behind the far end of the couch. Anthony had missed it, big-eyed now about his favorite topic, why the country was prime for a Nixon presidency.

"The same Nixon," Richmond asked, "who lost his run for governor of this state?"

"He's a grunt. A trooper. Hey! He has no quit in him! Trust me. A guy like that learns from defeat. The worse the better."

She tapped Lazarus's knee. "What do you think?"

"Sounds good," he said.

"Anthony. That makes no sense at all." Richmond was smiling, almost laughing. "But if what you say is true, then he'll be the best president we've ever had. Losing California after being Ike's number one man is about as big a defeat as you can think up."

"I can think of worse ones," said Anthony. "Like a Democrat winning in '68."

There was quiet for a second, and Leticia took Lazarus's hand. He did not look at her. His chin was in his palm, his elbow posted on the table.

"I think botha you fellas have good points."

Richmond squinted at his younger brother's suggestion, as if trying to focus on an obscure image.

"Nixon is twice the man Johnson is," Anthony said. "Johnson's frustrated. And he's a liar."

"Tony," said Richmond, sipping his water, reflecting. Leticia had never seen the temperate Richmond drink anything but water. She'd never heard him use a cuss word. When she was told the story about his wish to go to seminary school, she felt as if she'd discovered an essential piece of his psychological puzzle. Anthony Sr., seeing the earning potential in his son early on, put the kibosh on the wish, and Richmond didn't talk to his father. A whole year of composed, indignant, powerful silence. Of nods, shrugs, calculated avoidance. Even if she had known nothing else about Richmond, Leticia would have admired him for the sake of the purity of his boyhood dream. "Your detestation of Johnson," he said, "doesn't make much sense to me. I mean, think about this for a minute, Ton. He got us into the war *you* support."

Lazarus said, "Good point, good point."

Take no stance, she thought, make no enemies in 1967? The most contentious social period of the century, a bulge-or-break test for the U.S.A., and all he could say was "good point."

They had thirty-five years of life evenly split between them and they were both dreamers, but Lazarus was a different kind than Leticia. He was a wanderer, he walked in his sleep, he couldn't impose coherence on his visions. This worried Leticia. If you couldn't make sense of the inner world, how confused would you be in the face of reality?

"What do you mean," she said, "by 'good point'?"

Lazarus hadn't heard the question. Neither had Anthony. Richmond shook his head as if both of his brothers had slapped her. This angered her. She preferred being ignored than condescended to.

"What?" Anthony said. "What? What happened?"

"You really didn't hear me?"

"Hey! Sorry! I didn't!"

"Hey, Laz," Richmond said, lightly clapping his little brother's shoulder. "Your girl's got a question."

"Hey! Say whatever you want! You make your point, Leticia, okay? But you have to agree with me, huh? I mean, you see my point, right? You can't get around it. Right is right, Leticia, huh? Right?"

"Ton," said Richmond, "let the poor girl breathe."

"I'm trying to include her in the discussion!"

Richmond inhaled deeply.

"I'm sorry, Tony," said Leticia, "but I disagree with you. If it makes you feel any better, I still like you. I just don't want to argue."

"No, no, no, that's *fine*," Anthony said, convinced, she could see, that he'd successfully recruit her before the night was out. "Go ahead, go right ahead, Leticia. We want to listen to your argument. We'll listen, right, guys?"

"Well, I believe Richmond is right about Nixon. And I think Vietnam is a bad war."

"What does that mean 'bad war'?" said Anthony. "Define 'bad war.'"

"Well, I don't know." It seemed so clear, so right in the peaceful quietudes of her head. "I guess I mean we shouldn't be there."

"Leticia. There is no such thing as a 'good war.'" He turned to Richmond. "Would you agree with *that,* little brother?"

"Within the context that it's always sad when a human life, any human life, for whatever reason, ends," Richmond said, shrugging, "yes, I'd say you're right."

Anthony clowned in a singsong, pouty voice, "Within the context that it's always nuh-nuh-nuh-nuh-nuh."

"You're right for *once,* I should add," said Richmond.

Lazarus said, "Leticia."

"Hey, Laz! It's all right! Let her talk, let her talk!" shouted Anthony. "This beautiful country is free, haven't you heard? Say some more, sweetie!"

"Well," she said. "The only thing I want to say is that Lazarus has no point."

"Oh, no, no, no. He does, he does. He surprises you, he really does. You've just gotta let him go."

"So let him go then," said Richmond.

Lazarus stood up. "I can't believe you just said that."

"Who? Me?" said Anthony. "Who?"

She stood and faced Lazarus. "Me neither. But I said it. Now I want to know what you think."

"About what?"

"This issue. Nixon. Johnson. Vietnam. Everyone wants to hear your testimony. Any issue. I want to hear you say something, Lazarus."

"My testimony? What is this?"

"You know what I'm talking about, Lazarus."

"A Baptist church?"

"You can't duck out of this conversation. This is too important, too big an issue."

"What the hell are you talking about?" Lazarus tugged on her sleeve. She wouldn't sit.

"Make a statement, Lazarus."

"Okay. You're crazy."

"Something. Anything. Say it."

"Nuts."

"Say it, say it!"

"You want a statement?"

"Yes," said Leticia, her voice shaking. "I do. I deserve it. This baby in my belly wants to know who you are."

Lazarus stood and said, "Okay."

She watched him walk calmly out of Big Victor.

"Come on, Laz!" Anthony hollered. "Come on back, man! Get in the spirit of the debate! Don't take it so hard! It's just ideas!"

"Ah, don't cry, huh, Tish?"

"He'll be all right."

"Yeah," she heard. "Don't worry. He'll write you from over there. I'm sure he will."

This last statement from the family prophet, the author of letters and the sender of packages, the words said with the presumptuous certainty of the parental world of which none of them, not even Richmond, were yet a part.

As it turned out, three of the Felice brothers preempted the draft and joined up the same week. Not that it mattered, but Lazarus signed on first, that very night. To either hurt her, she thought now, or escape her. Same difference. Richmond broke down at a Thursday night spaghetti dinner after Anthony shouted in front of their parents, "Why don't you go to Canada then, you coward bastard!" Johnny got drafted. Three of the four went to Vietnam. All three came back alive, limbs in place, a CIB for Johnny and Lazarus, CMB for Richmond. Anthony went to Germany and didn't learn one German word, returning stateside the same way inside as before. No flag-draped boxes for this family, no body-bagged bodies. They were lucky.

But she remembered now amid her own bad luck in this dead-end trailer park the going-away party at some pizza house in dowtown

Upland whose name she'd forgotten. The boys had gathered for one last round before being sent off overseas. They were rattling on about their favored branch of the military, what units had the highest medal count, shaking hands and patting backs, not seeing in their stoked and hackneyed visions of vainglory Leticia penniless at the juke, her whispering of the titles to herself—"'Jailhouse Rock,' 'Volare,' 'My Funny Valentine.'"—the quiet saunter back to the red-and-white checkered booth. She mounted the wobbly table and pulled both legs into herself as she'd learned in the weekly Cold War prep of second grade, ducking for cover from the bomb. Her nose pressed between the soft skin of her naked kneecaps, eyes on these blind and beautiful Felice boys.

For just a moment in the smallness of self-protection, she asked the question, *Do I really want to be a part of this family?*

The Felices
Jimmy Baldwin of the Upland Little League
July 29, 1954

They arrived en masse at the Upland Little League park and wildly filled the stands. They arrived everywhere en masse. Today they carried popcorn, hot dogs, bottles of Coca-Cola, blankets, binoculars, and all of them wore baseball caps of various major league teams. They were almost all to themselves. The other section was overflowingly full and the Felices didn't go anywhere near it. This was a time to indulge in what the good life in America had to offer. Anthony, an unathletic kid, had made the tournament finals of the San Bernardino County Baseball Fair. They sat next to the only other family in the section, the Baldwins.

Now they rooted for twelve-year-old Jimmy Baldwin at the dirt of home plate, naked in their loyalty to him, the only colored boy in the neighborhood, their adoration of his cuts and swings at nearing glory unabashedly pure. He was one of them, he was an American boy with the promise of tomorrow in the fuzzy bed of his dark brow, he had the most clever way of bunting down the third-base line, and the Felices, in their own naked and impartial hope for themselves, collectively hoped for young Jimmy.

One family, the Raineys, thin-skinned in their own insecurities, now hated the oblivious spectacle of the Felices more than the uppity Negro family.

For the entirety of the season, the Baldwins had been sitting far from the mad crowd of their own volition. Separatism based on comments too sharp and too biting to ignore, the senior Baldwin's pride in his pride of cubs, a decision he'd made dozens of times before and, sadly, even after the Felices would swoop out of his life into the good-tidings year of 1956, one he'd make again. There were still three innings to go in the middle of America's century.

But the Felices, with their crazy, obtuse, incessant positivity seemed to ignore the drag of this backstory. They cheered, shouted, yelled slogans. "Jim-my! Jim-my!" The Baldwins sat tight as fighter pilots in their seats. Mr. Felice talked politics with the senior Baldwin and Mrs. Felice shared recipes with the missus. Mr. Felice, himself a Pittsburgh High School dropout of the Great Depression, was always especially excited and committed during those rare times in life when he could drop conservative wisdom on someone from a lower educational background. She, Mrs. Felice, loved to talk about her world-famous spaghetti to anyone, especially coloreds, who had no understanding about real Italian food. In this instance, both couldn't be more wrong: Mr. Baldwin had a degree in education from Tuskegee University and had studied business under the son of Booker T. Washington. Mrs. Baldwin had mastered culinary Italian by her early teens, keeping house for the sole Mediterranean family in eastern Tennessee, the Albinonis.

Witnessing the manic elation of the Felices, some on the other side— the younger, the less certain, the curious—would wonder for at least the length of an inning why they, their parents, had been that way to begin with. What had happened to them? Was it more than just a matter of what was taught, of what was right and wrong? Was there some deeper failure, or horror, or fear that had nothing to do with conditioning? That went beyond these borders, that was universal? Could time wash away their feelings? Could a home run? That was a seed, anyway, the adolescent questions worthy of sustenance.

Jimmy struck out. Neither side offered applause in the dry sun. The ump dusted the plate in the silence, plastic black mask still pulled down over his white, dirty, stubbled face. The pitcher popped his mitt once and patted the chalk bag on the mound.

The Felices shouted, "Atta boy!" to Jimmy and "Next time, champ!" and "Hell of a try, kid!" Jimmy didn't look back. The Baldwins didn't move. The ump grunted, "Play ball!" and the next innocent-hearted kid stepped up to the plate.

Hope and promise and pain and smallness congested on a Little League field like the mucus of a pneumonic infant.

PART V

Mary Anna

25

Murron Leonora Teinetoa
Motherhood on the Terrace
March 25, 2008

I'M SITTING OUTSIDE HER ROOM on the broken-concrete patio, my week's work—a fine book to praise—open like a hymn across my lap, shades pulled down tight against the buoyant afternoon sun, a nose plug pinching my nostrils shut. I've been breathing through my mouth to keep the stench of the Elysium Fields Hospice away from my super-sensitive olfactories (unlike my stomach, my heart, my menstrual cycle, and the enamel on the backs of my teeth, bulimia actually improved this part of my body), and so far it's worked pretty well. There was a time when the decay of rotting fruit could make me puke. I'm past that now, or it seems that I am, but methane and other noxious gases are a different story.

I've been holding down my meals of late, something I'm both happy and worried about. Superstitious, too. My suspicion is that if I think on it too much, even if the thoughts are promising, the conclusions positive, I am ensuring another round with my insides. I'm relying on the straightness of the slow haul. Also, I'm not yet certain that there's such a thing, anyway, as overcoming all your monsters. You're probably lucky just to keep the beasts in their caves long enough to live a life. Without hurting too many people, without hurting *yourself*.

I don't feel young today, but I don't feel tired either.

There is nothing else on the patio but me, the cheap lawn chair I'm sitting on, and the novel. I shift my hips, and the four plastic legs wobble under my weight. The protagonist of the story is a nameless young man from Boston, twenty-first-century smart and old world tough and completely crossed about his story. He is African-American, he is a father of three, he is trying to be a good husband, and he is beginning to realize that perhaps ambition in all its easy American luster requires, above all, the locked-in tunnel vision of the engineer on the train tracks. The focal point the next immediate moment, what's right in front of you. I like that the novel ends with success. That he gets the money he needs, that he gets his wife and kids back. It was such a surprise. So sturdy in its postmodernist flouting. Dickens made the opposite choice of closure a hundred and fifty years ago, opting for the ending where Pip's great expectations are not only unfulfilled but unachievable. Like I said, I'm superstitious. I hope that the author doesn't opt for a sequel, which would put his protagonist without a name at risk. I want the characters of his novel to be okay forever in the suspension of literary victory.

I peek in and she's still asleep, a few feet from our lunch. At her request earlier in the week, I've brought a beef shawarma from Al-hana's Mediterranean market in San Mateo, the owner there, Abe, promising me out the door that he'd pray for Mary at Mass, to which he was on his midday way. I didn't know anyone did that kind of thing anymore. Or at least admitted to it. And on a Wednesday afternoon, no less. He'd used filet mignon especially for her. I'd watched him proudly slice the shavings from the impaled, glistening lump of meat, and it was so appetizing to witness and kind in gesture that I ordered a second wrap for myself. He's never met Mary. He doesn't even know that she's Lazarus's mother. He doesn't know Lazarus either. No one knows Lazarus. But Abe was tickled that someone Mary's age would try something so foreign, and then actually like it.

I told him about the tragedy, as I view it, of her family, how the Felices and their words of chaotic flight seem to kill all good action, a verbal slam dance beneath the stage of impossibility. There I was, sharing this story with a Middle Eastern merchant, my thoughts flowing freely because for the first time I didn't have to worry about my "anonymity" being violated, which meant exposing how I viewed, ethically, what these people were doing. They were cowardly, selfish, greedy, small. Maybe even betrayers. My personal wound of a fatherless childhood aside, I'd been right all along to want nothing to do with them. The image of Mary lying there alone in the late-night hours of the hospice so moved Abe's Orthodox sensibilities that he vowed to visit her soon, and I believe him. I have no idea how someone so generous stays in business.

Nor do I understand why a stranger will do more than the family for the infirm. If it's just the indifference of Western self-absorption to blame, there should be a mandated statute of limitations on this kind of lethargy. Somehow the indifferent should be forced by an entity greater than themselves—God, culture, the state—to have to care x number days of the year about their fellow man. Or at least be fingered as someone who *doesn't* care.

Mary has awakened. She rolls her head toward the window and, seeing me, nods and shouts, "Come on in, honey!"

I can't hear it clearly through the glass, but I've watched her mouth move to form the same greeting to anyone waiting outside her door, family or friend, doctor or nurse. It doesn't require much to imagine Mary on the spacious doorstep of her Victorian in old town Upland, summoning in the newspaper boy for a glass of juice, dusting her children's kneecaps after a game of chase through the grove, sending her husband off to work with nimble hummingbird fingers.

"Hi."

"Hello, honey. Come in." She twists her shoulders, squinting as her body gradually repositions. Yes, she's old and maybe couldn't walk to the end of the hall, but she can properly visit. "Come in and sit."

"Okay." I remember Abe's culinary kindness. "We can eat, too."

"Oh, I hate the food here, honey."

I don't know who wouldn't. "Well, you know, I brought you some lunch."

"I knew I smelled those A-rab burritos!"

"Yes," I say, giggling and not feeling at all bad about it, "the shawarma."

"Oh, let's eat, honey. I'm starving."

"Would you like to watch TV, Mary?"

"No, honey."

I bite into my shawarma, catching the dripping juices with a cupped palm, and she says, "I love shoo-mer!"

I nod. "Me, too."

We eat in silence. My own Prince has never once done this. He cannot scrape food off his plate without slapping his fork against the tabletop. He's always stomping his feet on a timer in his mind, whistling college football fight songs. He tells stories like the scops I've read about in the old Yugoslavian villages, endowed by the solidity of his sources, what he shares with the audience. "His people," as he calls us, my mother and Lokapi and me, the connection, when added up, to his beginnings. I used to worry about his energy, especially when the ADD trend was spreading wilder than a viral pandemic, but I eventually realized that the best thing I could do was forgo my ancient parental instincts to interrupt, to correct, to instruct. It sounds Hallmarkish, but I read Gibran's poem about the egolessness of parenting. Well, I could do that. I did that. This is a different generation, a new version of our children. Eventually, I learned to love to listen. I'm still worried, of course, but I'm best when guiding my son along his journey, watching for the pitfalls in his next little-boy quest, finding the holes in his little-boy logic. I let him build himself up, I help him build. I catch him when he falls. Sometimes I fall, too.

Last night, he went on and on about a penalty kick he'd missed at practice, how he's worried the coach will bench him for the next game. His heroes Zidane and Landon Donovan, he said, never make errors of this kind. Why he has to do better tomorrow. He's only nine. Mother always says that the stronger he is now, the stronger he'll be as a man, and that's all the better for me. He'll never forget me, my mother's been quoted as saying. A thousand miles from home, years from hearing my voice, he'll remember, at some indistinct but nonetheless essential level, our fried chicken dinners on Thursday nights.

"Honey. You haven't eaten your A-rab burrito."

I see that her shawarma is gone to the last cubed cucumber. "Oh, you're right. So sorry. That was sort of rude, wasn't it?"

"It's okay, honey."

"I guess I'm not used to silence. Better catch up to you, huh?"

"He'll be all right, honey." She pats my hand as I bite into the delicious meat. "Don't worry about him so much."

I have to risk the question. "Who?"

"Your son, honey." She nods at the certainty of her statement. "He'll be okay."

"I'm so worried about him!" I blurt out.

"Yes," she says.

"I sometimes think the marrow of my bones is made of worry."

"That's very hard. A mother's cross."

"How did you deal with it, Mary? Can I ask you that?"

"I remember when the boys went off to the war. The afternoons were very long. September second, 1967. February eighteenth, 1970. That was the last boy home. That was my youngest boy, Lazarus. He went back for a second time, you know?"

I nod.

"Our house, we called it Big Victor." Her eyes widen hearing these words, the flash fire of memory, and she sits up. It's hot in here, the air sticky, and I can feel the skin between my nose and upper lip starting to perspire. I look at the clock. I've been inside this room for a mere fifteen minutes. "We loved our house! Daddy always said, 'We have enough energy within these walls to light a city grid.' What does that mean, anyway, honey? Like the downtown?"

"It means you were incredibly patient."

"Oh, honey. You're doing just fine, too. Don't you worry. You've come to visit me too much. I don't want you here so often. You are a beautiful, beautiful girl. *Che bedda.*"

"Okay," I say. "We don't have to talk about this stuff."

"Honey. I'm going to hit this button. I'm going to have them put me in the chair."

"Oh, I can do it. Remember? I did it by myself at Christmas."

"I don't remember."

She's already hit the little red button on the side of her bed, and I feel no real personal loss in the draining sink of her long-term memory. This because I'm here, after all, ready, if possible, to create another memory. It somehow makes perfect sense that her institutionalized days of repetition at Elysium Fields Hospice will, in turn, blend all the mundane, eventless, familyless days into one. Or at least blend a few into one. Or else bring forth the past to replace the present. I've heard the New Ageists call this coping. Who knows? Maybe for the sake of having lost our wheelchair moment at Christmas, Mary has filled the space with a game of blackjack we'd played last week. Or maybe her mind has held tighter in the past few months to the stories that have always meant the most to her, the stories of her life that have made it a life, the sustainers of her sanity.

"*Sí,* Mary?"

The nurse is here. I nod and smile at her, look down at Mary, and give her the chance for the first response. I don't want to interrupt their social rituals here, the sanctity of their interactions. Even though I've been visiting every Monday, Wednesday, and Friday while Prince is at soccer practice, that leaves at least 165 hours of the 168-hour week that she's on her own, and you can pray, and you can hope for the best, and you can even alleviate your worries by dropping a five-dollar bill on every Filipina and Michoacana and Eritrean woman in uniform you pass in the hall, but, alas, you're not here, and you haven't seen, and so you *don't* know.

This could be a key to understanding the Felices. They just keep stuffing their problems deeper and deeper into the box. And they don't want to know until they *have* to know, until it springs upon them. Which means—too often, I imagine—that it's too late, and it doesn't matter, now, that they know.

"Hi, honey. Come in, come in."

"Hi, Mary. Is this your daughter? *Quién es?* Who is this?"

She nods, sits up again. "This," she cries out, "is my granddaughter! Murron Teeny-toe."

As I'm laughing at her lovely mispronunciation of my Polynesian last name, I'm so touched by the earnestness of her announcement of my place in her fractured family that I hide my eyes from these two women. If she says I am one of her own, then that's what I am.

"Ohhh, hello, hello. Jou know I love Mary, huh?"

"Me, too," I say. "Thank you for watching over her. "

"Oh, no. This is my pleasure. We are like family, jou know?"

"Yes."

"Murron has a son!"

I smile and nod again, looking at the nurse, knowing before she speaks that she's a mother herself.

"*Sí*, Mary. You tell me every day, don't you remember?"

I had no idea. I've talked so sparingly about Prince within these walls. Or that's what it felt like, anyway.

"Want to get up? Is that what jou want, Mary?"

"She always knows," says Mary.

The nurse unfolds the wheelchair in one efficient pop, pushes the dinner tray against the wall with her hip, flicks the brake into place, and says, "Come on, Mary."

I find myself utterly admiring the shamelessness of this dutiful nurse who bends over the bed right in front of me, the fatty skin of her back pushing over the outline of her bra strap beneath the blouse, her blocklike lower back wider than everything below her waist, the thin legs like two sturdy posts propping up a beach house.

"Do you want some help?"

"Oh, no, no." She's rolled Mary upright and is now reshifting her own hips to hoist the weight. Inch by inch, Mary rises from the bed, her frown line screwing down on itself. "We do this thing all the time, sí, Mary?"

"Ohhhh."

"I know it hurts, Mary, but we gotta do it, sí?" Mary's body is over the dangerous divide between the bed and the chair, the near dead and the living. "Get those muscles moving."

"Ohhhhhhh."

"Are you sure she's okay? I can help, you know?"

"Oh, sí, no worry, she's fine." And just as the nurse says it, Mary plops down into the seat, her eyes popping up and leveling like a buoy at sea.

"Let's go, honey."

"She want you. Not me."

"Yes, yes. Thank you. I'll take over from here. The easy part."

"Jou just call me when jou finish."

"Okay. I guess I'll follow you out."

"Oh, no. I clean up this bed and everything else, too. I go fast."

"Thank you."

We roll very slowly into the hall. The other day the nurse said that Mary's heavier by a few pounds, but I wouldn't know it now, the strain on my legs light, something of a surprise. So I guess I *am* getting healthier. The first time we got Mary into a wheelchair in December, I barely made it out of the room before I was winded. We pass the other open doors of the Elysium Fields Hospice, the sounds emitted like the groans and exhalations of barn animals. The shadows at the base of the IVs and oxygen tanks like shades of dirt, darkening incrementally the closer you get to the patient in dead-eyed repose on the bed, the outline of each skull traceable from flesh loss. I try very hard to turn back the literary cynicism, the biting critic in me who's ruined too many relationships in real life, the ice-cold librarian pulling references of comparison from the Dewey decimal system of defeat—"we moved down the bridge and there I saw the chasm's depth made clear"—for rapid transit to the front of my brain.

Why is this lady, four months later, still with these poor souls who will all pass, every one, in less than a week?

At least five people, staff and patients both, have amicably stretched out to say hello to Mary, and her response has consistently been "Hi, honey." Her friends are patients in wheelchairs stationary as fire hydrants, nurses at the nurses' station painting each other's nails, orderlies dumping soiled sheets into laundry bins.

We reach the outdoor terrace, which is somewhat nice, I suppose. There are broad-based maple trees that probably predated the construction of this place by a few decades, the branches woven into one another like nature's own cross-thread stitch, an overhead canopy of shade against the merciless sun. There is a single picnic table in the center of the grass, whose dead yellow blades and deep-rooted weeds don't make it a lawn. There's no one else from the hospice out here, neither staff nor patient.

"This is nice, honey."

"Yes," I say. "It is."

"Did you have dinner with Tony?"

"I did. A few weeks ago."

"He's a beautiful boy. I'm so blessed to have my kids. Aren't they wonderful?"

I smile and try to look away subtly. It's probably better to spare Mary an impulsive response from me. They're not here for her now, so I can at least let Mary keep what she feels about them. I know something, though, that maybe they don't, or they've forgotten. There's nothing I could say about her children that would diminish her love for them, not even her troubled middle child who wrought so much chaos on her household.

My one child, without question, has kept me alive and focused and determined. If I'd been alone for the last ten years, spinning my wheels, blowing kisses to strangers, who knows where my prediliction for self-destruction would have taken me?

Actually, I do know, and I know precisely.

Mary's five kids must have done for her, exponentially, what Prince has done for me.

But, then, that doesn't mean there weren't ever missteps, right? My own mother had said that Mary, like her, had taken to liquor when she was very young and alone with the children, hiding bottles of cheap red wine in the cellar, and later mixing generic vodka into her orange juice at dinner. Everyone in the family knew, but no one said anything. She said that Mary was the proof that even the toughest and most committed lady needed some kind of break from the affairs of the world. The world being her home in Upland, the world being Wednesday night dinners for seven, the world being the day's end before its start. I used to think it an excuse of the worst kind by my mother, citing someone else's sin as mitigatory evidence of her own failure, a batch of snitchery that I would have otherwise never come upon in the real time of a living person with real shame. But now, strangely, looking upon her drooping but nonetheless meaty shoulders in the chair, I'm glad my mother shared this truth about Mary's life. I wish I could offer her a glass of wine right now, an upgrade to the good stuff, the kind from the valley I grew up in. I'd like to work, with Mary, against the easy judgment of others, and let us refute fate. I wish I could offer both women, Mary Capone Felice and Leticia McCluskey, a glass, that we could toast one another's lives, toast our children, lean back in our chairs and lift our faces to the stars in the sky, quietly aware of some maternal rite that we, and not the judges, share.

My admiration for a mother's lifelong internalization of some secret dream away from home has no cap, I think, for I can see in the unformed ethers behind my closed eyelids Mary emerging, say, in the middle of a wide-open city like San Francisco and kicking up her heels every night at Vesuvio in North Beach, or pursuing, somberly, an associate's degree in art at a junior college on the California coast, her instinct for putting a landscape to the canvas fiddled with and either further refined or put to rest for good, or maybe Mary opening the first Italian restaurant in a tiny, quaint town in Waspish New England, her spaghetti and meatballs legendary in more homes than just her own, or perhaps, for even one glorious twenty-four-hour stretch, disappearing from America altogether to return to the homeland of her family line to watch, as I did in my exchange-student youth of the late eighties, the opening night of the *Cavalleria Rusticana* in Palermo's Teatro Massimo.

"I want you to go out and have fun, honey."

I smile, drop my eyes. "I do," I say, but it's a lie. For a long time now, the concept of fun has seemed flighty and infantile to me, a state of mind not to be trusted, one that obstructs rationality and good sense.

But I do think I could use a night out. Lokapi, Prince casually said last week, kissed a woman at the park.

"Honey. I want you to go on a date with a boy. I'll pay for it, okay?"

I smile again. She has no money, but even if she did, I doubt that it would matter. She has no more control over her life than a common prisoner. She's here because someone wants her here. I didn't know her husband because his mind was gone by the time I got to meet him, our seven hours together, but I can't imagine that he, or any husband, would want this for his wife. Especially, as my mother has pointed out, with all the money in this family.

"I am interested, a tiny tiny bit, in a guy I . . . met earlier this week. I think he could be a good guy."

"Ohhh, I'm sure he is, honey. Have a night on the town with him, okay? You two grab a steak or shrimp—shrimp! I love shrimp. You go. I'll pay for it."

"Oh, no," I say, smiling, "we've got to get *him* to pay for it, Mary."

"You're right, honey," she says, as my phone sends its vibrations across my thigh. It's her son Anthony. "You just keep right on doing what you're doing."

"Excuse me, Mary, but I have to use the phone, okay?"

She's embarrassed, and it's cute, and it's sad, and Anthony can wait. "I'm sorry, honey. You go ahead."

"No, no," I say. "I can call back later."

"You make the call now! I won't interfere with your life!"

"Okay," I say, standing. "Excuse me for just a minute."

I walk to the orange cast-iron gate dividing the terrace from the parking lot, watch the teenage valet pump the system in his souped-up two-door Acura coupe, his seat leaned back at a forty-five-degree angle. He's brushing his eyebrows with a comb the size of a toothbrush.

America is in trouble.

"Hello."

"Oh, excuse me, Murron. It's Anthony and I—"

"I know."

"Huh? It's Anthony."

"I know. Your number comes up. Hi."

"Oh, hi. Listen, I'm sorry for calling you like this—"

"It's okay."

"—but the move is a no-go."

The air I take in lung-deep leaves a hot and dusty trail across my tongue and the lining of my throat. I feel sick to my stomach, yet again, and I close my eyes to focus on what's important.

Not me, I'm not the one who runs, not me. Hold it together for the lives I love. I can't afford to succumb.

Not me.

"You there?"

"Yes. I'm here."

"There's no money."

"Where," I ask, "is there no money?"

"Yep. That's right." Talking to himself again. "Lazarus distributed everyone's share and we—"

"—got ours that night." Five hundred dollars.

"—got ours that night. That's right! Five hundred bucks! Was a good thing I didn't spend the money, huh?"

"What a break."

"No money in the end."

My mind wonders in ways that Tony's doesn't. He has plenty of hatred, plenty of passion, can probably count and keep track of his earnings to the last penny better than anyone, but he's hollowed of skepticism. Were there more "inheritance monies" put into the Ohlone Indian Casino than into Anthony's, or anyone's, pocket? Seems possible to me, given my own bankrupt inheritance from Lazarus, as well as *not* possible given their father's real-life bankruptcy, but in either scenario, whoever's to blame, it's definitely not worth mentioning *now*. Let's move forward and try, at least, to collide with the right thing. "But why did we look at that house," I ask instead, "if you didn't—"

"So you want to see the e-mails?"

"—have enough money . . . no," I say, intent on deleting them when I get home. First thing, before they pollute my mind.

"Oh, what am I talking about? You were CC'd, too, and—"

"Of course I was."

"—you can see for yourself."

I know that Anthony won't lie to me. He's a political nut, yes, but he's also impeccably honest. Maybe to a fault. He doesn't have a passive-aggressive bone in his body, just like John Wayne, which is just how he likes it. I don't think, if it came down to it, that he'd lie to save his own skin. My mother calls it Catholic guilt, I call it wasted integrity. If you can't stand to be around anyone, what does integrity matter except on your own personal scoreboard? When does "integrity" become a euphemism for "intransigence"?

"So Richmond never responded to the letter I wrote for you?"

"I didn't send it."

Of course he didn't. "Why did you ask me to write something then?"

"Hey! I can't send that kind of sniveling to him and sign my name to it! I thought you were going to use your business skills to really let 'im have it! Instead, you're apologizing out the gate! We haven't done anything wrong! You haven't either! You've been stalwart for Mom! Don't be ashamed of your position, Murron!"

"Believe me, I'm not," I say. "I'm not ashamed of *that*."

"Good! You're right! *We're* right!"

"So what are you," I ask, "going to do?"

"Well, Rich and Mary Anna said they wouldn't pay for any move of Mom."

Of course they won't. "Really?"

"Yeah! They'd opt out once it happens! Oh, but they sure took their five hundred dollars, right? Those bastards—"

"But they'll continue to pay for her bed here?"

"Murron. Murron."

"Yes?"

"Murron."

"Go ahead."

"Medi-Cal pays for that room. They don't pay a dime, Murron. Didn't you know that?"

Jesus Christ. "You've got to be kidding me."

"Murron. Murron. It's one hundred percent *true*. As long as she's got hospice status, the state pays. Off hospice status, we foot the bill. Yeah! How do you like that? My esteemed brother and sister are socialists when it benefits them. Yeah. The Marxist pond scum don't care if they bankrupt California."

So much for my so-called gift of skepticism.

I recall Dr. Patel. "But could they get a doctor to sign off?"

"Hey! Doctors are human beings, too! You ever heard that scumbag Rich talk? He's smoother than a silkworm! And that butch-bitch sister of mine has been involved in the industry for thirty-plus years! She's gotta know someone out there who'd help her bullshit cause!"

"Her industry is physical therapy. She's not even an MD."

"Hey! You're wrong! Her industry is *health* care, Murron. This is *business*. People make connections. Listen. I'm reading her words right here. Listen. 'Richmond and I will respectfully withdraw from any financial burden of Mother's care should any relocation occur.' Can you believe that? She probably got her attorney to write it. Jesus! What the fuck is wrong with these people? Hey! Do. The Right. Thing."

I look over at Mary and she waves me off, a way to encourage an immediate return to my phone conversation. I'm fine, she's saying. Just fine. I can't think of anything to say to her oldest son except what I already asked. "So what are you going to do?"

I hope his silence doesn't mean what I think it does. "What? Can you speak up?"

No, I can't. But I can be clearer. It's time to directly ask Anthony the big question he's been avoiding his whole life. "How much money do you have?"

"*Hey!*" I put a few inches of space between the cell and my ear. "I'm not the one who created this *mess!* Those two pukes ducked out of their *duties!* Richmond is nothing but a *Mafia* boss and Mary Anna is a leftist *rug* muncher! Neither one has the moral authority to make the right decision! That's right! *Right?*"

"So you're not going to do anything then?"

"What the hell can I do? They put the kibosh on the whole deal." So he's going to leave his millions of mason jars buried in the backyard. I look at Mary. Her eyes are closed. But she's not sleeping. She's sunning herself, the way seals do on the pier. "That's it. It's over."

"It's *over?*"

"Hey! There's nothing more for me to do, Murron! How many times can I let them slap me in the face like this? I'm a son, too, goddamnit, and I have no say!"

"Okay," I say. "Well."

"I'm the oldest—"

"I have to go."

"—child!"

"Good-bye."

I hang up before he can respond because there's nothing else to talk about. I hope he can make peace with his namesake son someday, with his native country before he dies, and with his own problematic military history, but I honestly don't see how any of it will happen if he can't find the solution just given to him. If what he says is true, and I'm sure it is, Richmond and Mary Anna have maintained their strategic plans the whole way through, and are doing so even now. They know their brother better than he knows himself. Because Anthony has been offered exactly what he won't do, at least not alone.

I'm no economist, obviously, but I know that money is valueless if you won't ever foot the bill.

Mary is smiling at me, still, the rear corner of her wheelchair exposed now to the burning heat, the sunlight flooding down through the pollen and pollution. The truth not only hurts, it blinds you. I put my shades on and nod at her, return the smile and hold it, despite the recent news about her beloved children. The only thing that makes sense to me is that she facilitated them so well, built them up so thoroughly as a mother, that they forgot her. They didn't need her. Left her. Moved on. They have their own priorities to tend to, and she isn't one of them.

I was right to keep my son away from the Felices.

I walk behind the wheelchair to push her back into the protection of the shade, and she looks up over her shoulder.

"Mary?"

"Yes, honey?"

"Can I ask you a question?"

"Of course."

"Would you like to meet Prince?"

"How wonderful!"

"Good. That's so good. Can I ask you something else?"

"You go right ahead, honey. And don't worry about anything. I don't want you worrying!"

"I won't."

"You're young! You go have fun. You have your whole life in front of you."

"Mary?"

"I love you, honey."

I lick my lips because I won't cry here in front of her. "I love you, too."

"I have to ask you, Mary."

"You go ahead, honey."

"Do you like this place?"

"Oh, it's fine, honey."

"Do you like the food?"

"It's fine. But I'm tired of wilted peas! The food is horrible!"

"Do you like your room?"

"It's fine, honey. I want to go home."

"Didn't you say this place is okay?"

"Yes, honey. It's fine, but I hate it!"

Not that it's any excuse, but I guess I can see how someone with little interest would view her statements as the deluded and insensible words of an Alzheimer's patient. How can it be fine, they'd ask, if you hate it? But I get Mary perfectly. This time I'm sure. It's a mother holding in, as she's been conditioned to do her whole life, two contradictory impulses at the same time. The place is fine, she's saying, because her kids want her to be here, and the place is rotten, she's saying, because it's rotten.

I know one thing for certain. I won't even finish the question before my mother says, "Yes, we must embrace this chance." And my son, I hope, will eventually learn to get along okay with the adjustment. That's what it would be, for however long we'd have together.

Tonight I will call Mary Anna myself and offer this good woman my bed.

26

Mary Anna Felice
Abstinence at the Estate
July 4, 1998

SHE PROUDLY STOOD on her toes and stayed there for half a minute, posing for no one but herself. She was feeling good, her body rock hard. She lowered herself slowly, bringing her hands across her flat stomach and flat chest and then opening up her entire wingspan, and flexing like a bodybuilder. Again, she stayed like that for some time, the blood rushing to her chiseled arms, uncaring about the old threat of *beware thy vanity,* words of supposed wisdom from a long-dead childhood nun and a geezerly ex-boyfriend, as if he mattered, named Don. She'd heard that his gallery in downtown Hayward had finally gone bankrupt, and she'd called at once and said, "Oh, poor Donny. I'm very very sorry you couldn't make it. If you need to borrow some money, we'll see what I can do for you, okay?"

Keri had gone to the store for some last-minute goodies, and this image of her lover at the door saddled dutifully with groceries made her breathe in deep and think about her fabulous life in the lower foothills of Blackhawk, the richest community per square foot in the Golden State. She bounced and spun, too old to be elegant but young enough to believe the world still fancied her flighty bouts of joy, and came down on her bowlegs, flat and inartistic. She had athleticism but no grace, like an NFL linebacker.

"I'm a ballerina!"

In her sweats and socks, she danced across her state-of-the-art kitchen, courtesy of a threshold of wealth she'd entered last year, the remodeled eating quarters, as her father used to call it, costing $25,000, plus another $5,000 to furnish. She looked out her oak casement kitchen window and across the 1.39 acreage constituting the faux-country yard of her faux-country estate and said, "Shit."

On the way out of the house she muttered it again ("Shit"), right over the hand-laid brick terrace, a speed walk now, past the custom-framed French gazebo, almost a jog, and the twenty-five-meter length of the black-bottomed pool ("Shit shit shit"). Over the years, the person she was about to confront had put in each of these appendages himself, ocassionally getting his wife, Lolita, and their two children, Rosie and Ernie Jr., to help pour concrete. By the fair exchange of a paid wage, he should have known better.

If you cut corners, she'd always told him over the years, you're eventually going to have to redo it how I want it, anyway.

"Stop! You! Hey, you! Stop!"

He stood there, having in fact stopped his work once he'd heard the patio door open, a conditioned response, no doubt, to the number of times she'd come out during his "assignments," as she always called them. He was about half her size, clearly half her intellect, and so he didn't have much ground to stand on when it came to bucking orders. He had to do what she said. That's what she paid him for.

"Gimme that," she said.

He handed the broom over.

"Ernest, I specifically said to use the blower here, didn't I?"

"Jes. I *muy* sorry, señora."

"Do I pay you well?"

"Jes."

"Do I let your children use the bathroom? Did I give them lollipops for Christmas?"

"Jes."

She waited.

"*Gracias.*"

"Well? What's wrong with you, Ernest? You speak English. I won't accept any excuses."

"Jes."

"I've told you this how many times."

"*Muchas* times."

"That's right, Ernest. Do you have something else you'd like to say?"

He nodded, said, "What about the man?"

"What man?"

He lifted his dark eyebrows and looked over at the fence, the one his family had decorated earlier this morning. The gate had red, white, and blue balloons that bobbed in the soft wind. His children had blown them up, his wife had hung them up, he had pruned the apricot tree. She hadn't liked it. Something was missing. His son had said, "Piñata?" and he'd said, "Shhh." To protect his boy from a scolding, he'd guessed, "Maybe need string," and she'd said, luckily, "Yes." He'd gone and bought a box of red, white, and blue ribbons at Henderson's Fine Food up the street, and then woven them through the slats at the tip of the fence, hushing his son's critique of what appeared to be a piñata-less party.

"Who? My brother? Which one? Don't you worry about any of them! Don't give them the time of day. You're here to work, Ernest. That's what I'm paying you for, and that's what you're gonna do. All the way to sunset."

"Jes."

"You can listen to Richmond when he shows up. That's fine."

He said, "But *pienso que*—"

"He'll be dressed the nicest. Answer your question? That's how you find him. Every other man has no say here, okay?"

"Jes."

"The man," said Ernesto, nodding again toward the fence, and the house behind it, "no like the sound."

"What did I just say, Ernest?"

He shrugged, but with resignation. "Jes, okay."

"Yes, what?"

"Jes, señora."

"You stay away from excuses, Ernest. They'll kill you."

Ernesto squinted at the last statement, annoying her terribly. She'd been trying to disabuse him of the habit for years, if not for himself, then for his children. But consistent to his personal system of using excuses as explanations, he would shrug and say he couldn't help it, fingering a scar that ran from his cheek to his eyebrow. Once when he was loading up the landscaping truck with his tools, she'd taken his children aside and said, "Don't be like your father, kids. You can do better."

That was the right thing to do, she thought now. And only somebody with balls could have done it.

"Don't squint, Ernest." She reached out to straighten his brow and at once thought better of it. She had a party to attend, and couldn't afford to get dirty. That's why she paid him. To work in the dirt so that she wouldn't have to. It was called capitalism. Was called improving yourself. Money was like an adult grading system. She was a scholarly 4.0 and her landscaper, obviously, was getting straight F's. "Squinting is for losers. Squinting means you can't look life in the face."

"Jes," he said, nodding again toward the fence. "And him? What about the man?"

"I told you already! Don't worry about them! Don't let them push you around. That's what they're used to. I grew up with chauvinists. When it comes to giving orders, there's only one man around here."

"Jou?" he said, shrugging.

"No excuses, Ernest! No excuses!"

She went back inside. She walked across her spacious house at a fast, almost sliding pace, and then ducked into a bathroom, the smallest of the four, nearest the yard. She climbed onto the rim of the tub and scissored her legs open, splayed across both sides, her head edging into the space of the window.

She spied on Ernesto for a few minutes, almost certain that she'd catch him slacking off on his work. After a while, she grew bored watching him walk behind the knee-high cloud of blown leaves, whistling to himself in his contented peasantdom. She came down off the tub, mumbling, "No excuses," and then went to get dressed for the family reunion.

She had been insisting, ever since she'd bought the place, on hosting a housewarming party. She'd thrown big shindigs for her friends from the city, and with the exception of Richmond, none of her family had come.

"What?" she said now, slipping into her beige slacks. "Only the brother with the gay son can step into my world?"

She'd been there for Richie all the way to the end. It was amazing how tough she was. That she could be there for him after what Johnny had done to her in Big Victor. Most people were thrown out with the trash after a childhood like hers. Or they were selfish, thought only about themselves, never helped anyone. And yet she'd never left Richie, keeping him in good spirits by talking about her company, her goals, her lover, reminding him that she'd supported his lifestyle when no else had.

The doorbell rang. She was excited. She'd been waiting for the day when she could show off her success to the family, and this was it.

"Who goes there?" she shouted. It was the way they'd greeted visitors at Big Victor, borrowed from an old black-and-white movie, maybe Errol Flynn in *Robin Hood*. She couldn't remember those dumb films where gay men had to act straight, despite the tights, the feather in the cap, the three-haired goatee twirled into a weak point.

"Open the door!"

She sucked in her breath at a plan ruined. He was early. She'd told him to come at three, everyone else at two. Her plan foiled. She should have said four, ensure his embarrassment at being late. But she turned the knob as ordered, pulled the door, chest out, stay calm, demonstrate your betterness to this guest, and there he was, the thick waves of hair almost snow-coated with dandruff, the pockmarked cheeks spotted with psoriasis, a tinge of sin on the greasy lips, smiling his same old wolf smile, two bottom canines newly missing. Keri stood behind Johnny with a helpless look on her face that angered Mary Anna, despite her knowledge that there was nothing Keri could have done.

There was nothing she could have done.

"Hello, sister," he said, walking in, past her. "You gonna leave me out there all day?"

"Come in, Johnny," she said. "Take off your shoes."

"Hey, hey," he said, looking around her living room, eyes alight with covetousness, "what do we got here? Who'd you steal this fat-cat shack from?"

Keri walked past their guest into the house, dramatically keeping a foot of space between his body and hers, and said, "Shoes, please." She grabbed Mary Anna with one hand, the plastic grocery bag spinning clockwise in the other, and looked up at her lover.

"You don't have to tell me twice," he said.

Keri tried to pull her toward the kitchen but she stayed by the door, adamant almost aggressive in her stance, taking in his middle-class wardrobe from Mervyns, the shoddy secondhand Dockers, his best dress-ups courtesy of the Salvation Army. His utter lack of style gave her confidence, and she lifted her eyebrows up, the "butch" cut of the hair making her appear, she knew, teacherly, the house's source of authority.

"I thought I told you to look nice, Johnny."

He smiled and it made her shiver, as if the mention of dressing up was some slick insinuation about the purpose of clothes, to cover yourself and your shame, to not be naked with the truth. But this was her day, and she was finally ready for him. She looked over his outfit and saw how badly he was flunking out of the adulthood school of moneymaking, the chauvinist pig justly broke and penniless, and then she saw the considerable loss of muscle mass in the shoulders, the scarred neck thinned, the weak chest drooping, all the years of binge drinking and who knew what else eating at his insides like the South American predator she'd seen on the Discovery Channel earlier in the year. In a reenactment the wormlike fish bored a hole through the skin of a living man and thrashed itself inward to feast on the vitals, a smorgasbord of internal organs, a hundred other fish following suit, as if the little beasts were viral demons sent to feed on a lifetime of sin. The sea unleashing its most incessant agent, mercilessley, on its guest. She'd watched the episode with interest, Keri unable to stay at her side, the cadaver's legs and arms intact on the gurney, the middle of the body hollowed out of its meat, its guts, its guilt.

"What?" she'd teased Keri, patting her vacated place on the couch. "Can't stomach it?"

"Go on outside, Johnny," she said now, confident that she could kick his ass in a fistfight. *She* would overpower *him,* impose *her* life upon *his* life, use *her* power to put *him* down. Were he pinned beneath another body, he would cry out instantaneously. "The party will be in the backyard. As for me, I'll be civil to you, Johnny, for our parents' sake. No one else—not even Lazarus—wanted you to come."

"Yeah, right. As if Lazy Laz picked up his phone for *you.*"

"Johnny. Mind your tongue. If Mom and Dad were dead, you wouldn't be here. Don't push my buttons today. I'm a very good person, but I don't suffer your kind."

He smiled. "And the shoes?"

"Again, put them on outside. That's where we're having the party. Anytime you come into my house, you take off your shoes, got it?"

"Oh, yes'm," he said. "Gonna get your mother's third son a drink or what?"

"Outside. Ernest will bring you a pop."

"With fizz," he said. "Put some pop in the pop. I see I'm gonna need it today."

"Oh, no, John," she said. The thought was fast, the purpose immediate. "That was the deal. You could come to the reunion as long as you didn't drink."

He straightened himself, covered his mouth with a palm, the right corner of his upper lip lifting itself as if a puppeteer were manipulating it. "You never said anything like that."

"Johnny, you need to get sober. That's obvious. Your memory recall is clearly suffering."

"Hey, if—"

"Johnny, you're not going to ruin *my* party." She pulled Keri into her and said, "If you're not happy with your life, that's no concern of mine. This is our day and this is my house and you're going to treat it with respect."

"You're the same old bitch."

"Johnny. You're one wrong word from being asked to leave my house."

"Well, then. Can't say I haven't been in that position before. I'll take some Coke, okay?" He winked at Keri, then bent over, laughing, and reached for his shoes. "Not that kind, ladies. The bubbly beverage. American sugar water. On the rocks."

"Johnny," she said. "You better treat the help with respect."

"I always help the help." He was making his way to the back door, mumbling something under his breath that she couldn't detect, nodding at everything in her kitchen.

"Get my phone, hon," she said to Keri.

She took a kitchen stool between her legs. It was always like this. She had to clean up the riffraff of her family. Through the years, only Richmond had ever helped her. No one had ever thanked her. That's because they were men, and men were born ingrates and perverts, and what always bothered her most, she confessed in the dark intimate hours with Keri, was the way these men, despite their inherited traits, ruled the world. Soiled its sacred dirt, shit on the public street every day. That would change, already was changing, and she wouldn't hestitate one minute to expedite this change on the smallest level.

Don, her ex-boyfriend, always said, "So we get to watch *you* shit in the street now, huh?"

Keri brought Mary Anna the phone and pushed her face into her chest, leaning into Mary Anna like a wino against the wall.

"Don't worry." She dialed the digits and put the phone to her ear. "He's not going to cause you any pain. No man'll ever cause you pain again, baby. Okay? Shhh, now. Shhh. Hey, Richie! Well, where you at? . . . You are? Wait." She stood and walked to the bay window that faced the street. "Hey! I see you! Okay, we're coming!"

"It's Rich!" she shouted. They went out the door together, and then she stopped at the porch, said, "You greet them, okay?" and went back inside her house. She rushed to the same bathroom where she'd spied Ernesto earlier in the hour, and stood once again on the tub. Johnny was drinking his Coke in the shadows of the trellis, now walking toward the pool and casually processing it, almost as if it were his, as if he'd find a lavish watering hole like this in the two-story encirclement of any dive motel across the state. The unimpressed look on his face infuriated Mary Anna, and she dropped down from the tub, went back to the door, and shouted, "Hey, brother o' mine! Hey, Richie!"

"Hey." Richmond passed her a bottle of wine. "Hey, sis."

"Oh, no," she said. "Better keep this away from you know who."

"What's that?" asked Rebecca.

"Johnny demanded I make him a stiff drink."

"You're kidding."

Richmond said, "He came, huh?"

"Yeah. He promised not to drink—"

"You can't believe anything he says."

"I know, Becca, but then he said he wanted a line of coke or something, how—"

"Wait. What?"

"—oh, yeah! He said he's gonna need all the drugs he can get his hands on being around us today."

Richmond shook his head and looked at his wife. "The wrong energy already," she said.

Keri was on the brink of tears. Mary Anna grabbed her hand, and the other two moved in and hugged her.

"Sometimes you wonder," said Richmond, talking into middle of the huddle and then breaking it, "how he wakes up in the morning."

"Well, come in, come in," Mary Anna said. "To hell with him. Some people never learn how to cease and desist."

"Don't worry, girls," Rebecca said. "We won't let him ruin Mary Anna's day."

Now Mary Anna guided her guests through the posh hallway leading to the rooms, pointing out framed reprints of Renaissance art she'd bought on a week-long stroll through Cinque Terre, the black-and-white portrait of her and Keri in half-clothed repose on a bed of Asian cherry blossoms, the scrollwork on an antique Turkish vase, the arrangement of roses clipped from her garden, the framed "Call to Arms" of a feminist poet from Oakland who, Mary Anna informed everyone, would be joining the party later to recite her newest work.

"The more the merrier," said Rebecca.

"That's right!" shouted the host. She reached across her brother and hugged his wife, saying again, "You're right on, sister o' mine!"

Next she showed her guests their king-sized water bed and said, "This is where our love first set float." They laughed at her joke, and Richmond said, "Very modern." She split her legs and thrust out, from the hip, an imaginary sword, calling, "Avante-garde!" They laughed at this second joke and then she tore open the handspun curtains—"Silk! Lace!" she shouted—and tweaked the swan-necked reading lights so that the bed was lit on either side, and then jumped into the air. Her body twisted over like a gymnast's, and she landed on her back, the sheets swallowing the edges of her body on impact.

The water surged back, recentering, and pushed Mary Anna upward. She pumped her middle against the air, eyeing Keri with over-the-top lust, and grunted, "Uhhh."

Everyone laughed. She liked, when relaxed, to play the clown. To entertain the guests. When they were, that is, the right guests. She loved to dress up in bright red suits and honk horns in white face paint and press down on her plastic sunflower to squirt the unsuspecting. She loved to lift her hands skyward, her legs spread wide, an upside-down horsehoe, the prong ends of her clown boots bulbous at the toes, and shrug. She loved to shrug. She'd always dreamed of starring center stage in a traveling circus and shrugging in front of thousands.

"Wait!" she cried, and rolled off the bed. She pulled a cylinder of brand-new tennis balls from her gym bag.

"Yeaaaah!"

"And now, ladies and gentlemen, but especially ladies, let us remember that life is but a walking shadow of juggling someone's balls."

"Heeey!"

"Go, Mary Anna!"

She started into the routine in the center of the room, cupped hands blurred in the speed of her delivery, initially looking down as if willing, with her eyes, the trick into action, holding her stare to ensure the holding of the miracle, and then slowly raising her face to these people, her family, framed by the fluorescent streak of green fur in motion.

"Mary Anna!"

"Heeeeey!"

Now she began to laugh, too, and the hands seemed to mind her perfectly, and the joyousness she felt in her heart for keeping the windmill fluid brought her back to the living room of Big Victor, the memory of a summer in the early sixties, hula-hooping for her brothers. Her prepubescent body like a boy's, rail-thin child from the neck down, right through the flat chest and straight over the rib-showing abdomen, the unfeminine, uncurved, fatless hips rotating round and round in their bold weightlessness. The cheers and laughter ringing off the ceiling and walls, the energy not unlike the purely happy support at a Little League game, home base where the community came together to be the community, that storied place where all belonged, and from which she'd been denied participation based on how she peed. This despite the appeal to the National Little League Commision, a gentle plea citing her foot speed and uncommon 20/15 vision, the meat of the letter written by Richmond one late evening in August and mailed by Lazarus in the middle of his paper route through downtown Upland. So the place where almost all belonged. The XY half of all. This living room performace as close as she'd get for the time being. She picked up the pace inside the hoop, almost demonic amid the thoughtless circuitry of this game. She was laughing at how badly her brothers' mimicry failed, and worse the harder they tried, their water-heavy, baseball-prone muscles holding them down, when she saw him, mesmerized by more than her skills, breathless at the base step of the creaking staircase leading to the attic, left eyebrow suspended almost in disbelief at what he was seeing, as if he'd just discovered some secret code for buried gold in the backyard of Big Victor. The lurid bid for her body, the hoop dropping to the ground, the cry of terror misunderstood by everyone present, even Richmond.

Richmond was a fool, too, she thought now, the tennis balls ricocheting off her upturned hands, bouncing to the ground one by one, her kicking them under the bed, shaking her head at the near loss of control, but reasserting herself among the guests by laughing louder than she ever had before. The cackle made her lower neck and upper shoulders redden with blood, her fists tighten into two balls of bone and flesh and skin.

She rollicked herself calm, walking toward the window. The guests followed her, three slow steps, to take in the scene outside. Johnny was rattling along to Ernest about something sinister, gesturing with his hands like a drunken *napolitano,* his lifelong mission of locating, hustling, and finally eating the helpless taking place in their full view. Proof of a flunky's life on her property.

"Let's go have a glass of wine, shall we? There's only one person who can't take part in the drinking today, and we're not going to let him ruin this party, are we?"

"That's right!" shouted Rebecca.

"I told him a very long time ago," she said, "that excuses are like assholes, Johnny."

"Everyone has 'em!"

"Yeah," said Richmond, "and they all stink."

She took Keri by the arm and led the party into the kitchen. The wine was splendid, the talk about dot-com stocks just perfect. Before she finished her second glass, he was walking toward the house.

"Here he comes!" she blurted out, angry at herself for losing her cool.

Johnny walked in smiling, the two black holes of missing teeth on full display. He tracked dirt across the carpet and stood before them. "Well, well. I didn't know the royalty was gonna be here today. I better go back outside with the beaner."

"Shoes," Keri whispered.

"Take your shoes off, Johnny," said Mary Anna.

"Sure, no problem. What do I care if you yuppies adopt a Jap policy?"

He stood there in his shoes, not moving, looking everyone over except her, still smiling.

"Actually, Johnny," said Richmond, "there are plenty of countries in Europe where people practice the same kind of courtesy, but no one would expect you to know that."

"Nice to see you, too, big brother."

"I didn't say anything about this being nice," said Richmond. "But some things can't be helped."

"Some people, too," said Rebecca, sipping from her wine.

"We expect you to be respectful today, Johnny," said Richmond, looking over at Mary Anna and nodding. "Just because Mom insists you be at these family affairs doesn't mean anyone else wants you here."

"Blah blah blah."

"Johnny!" Mary Anna walked forward, hands on hips. "You will not treat my family disrespectfully, are we clear?" He said nothing. Richmond came to her side. "I said, are we clear?"

"Looks like you people been cleared to do anything you want."

"You will change your attitude," said Mary Anna, "or be asked to leave."

"You know," he said, walking back across the carpet in his shoes. "I suddenly realize I'd rather be outside with my beaner friend. You pricks got something stuck up your ass."

"Outside!" she shouted, index finger pointing the way.

The door slammed shut and she heard Rebecca first: "Way to go, Mary Anna."

Then her lover: "You were fantastic, baby."

"Mary Anna," Richmond said, "sometimes you make me proud to be a brother."

"I love you all," she said, and walked over to the back door, bothered by what had just happened. He was cupping water in the pool, examining it, shaking his head, instructing Ernesto, who was standing behind him, nodding. She was recovering already, her muscle memory for drama stronger than his evil. Today was a happy day. They would all wait inside her lovely kitchen, separate and safe from the bad seed of the family. The rest of the Felices were en route to visit, and she would welcome them into her life, each one, like a jester at the tent flap of the funhouse.

27

Murron Leonora Teinetoa
Nakedness on the Big Date
April 1, 2008

I'M SITTING ON AN ASIAN CUSHION in the center of a genuine American laser show, an almost naked woman spread out like a snow angel in front of me, wondering if the tacky guy who brought me to this ridiculous circus will pick up the tab. I don't necessarily expect him to, even though this was clearly not *my* idea. But then, I don't necessarily expect anything from anyone.

I'm on this date tonight following Mary's ardent advice not to think too much about Mary. But it's actually Mary's daughter who has occupied my thoughts of late. It's been a week since I left my first message with Mary Anna about taking her mother into our apartment. So far, I've gotten no response. When I hadn't heard back from her after the first few days, I decided not to share the plan with Prince, who I knew would get excited about the news. I didn't want to risk, again, putting him at the mercy of the typical Felice delinquency. I asked my mother for advice and she said to e-mail Richmond. I did. Twice. Am still waiting for an answer to either e-mail, or anything from either person.

So here we are. Here I am. Taking in something new. Before tonight, I never really entertained the possibility that you could be without clothes and yet *not* be naked. That's the big trick question of the night, our rooster laying its proverbial egg on the apex of the henhouse. My date has saved the last five cuts of sashimi for the encore. I haven't eaten one piece. He hasn't noticed. I drank down half my miso soup at the start of his feast, and that's it. I went to the bathroom just afterward and nearly puked it up right there. If he had any class, or any understanding of female silence, we'd end the show right now, and leave her there with her fish-covered flawless body.

When "the Big Date"—as he kept tagging it in his e-mails—started, she was camouflaged by rows of sushi, the cuts of fish striated between the muscles like layers of sand when a wave retreats, the sprouting spider rolls and lovely rainbow rolls running from her breasts down either side of her rib cage to meet at her belly button, which the rolls circled in a facedown tepee of temaki cones. From there, the entrée spun toward her erogenous zone in a thin line of hamachi. The visual trick for which the chef and model were apparently brought here was the ingenious fact that the fish, pale yellow in color, perfectly matched her skin. And then the theme was kept even down *there*, where the chef chose to return to five pieces of labia-pink maguro. The ginger, when squished, looks vaginal.

Now my date stands and circles the table like a beast at the kill, his hands spread out in front him like an even cheesier version—didn't think it possible—of David Copperfield.

"Wow," he says, rubbing his belly with one hand, but still at the magician act with the other. "Would you look at that? Even now, it's just a fantastic artistic arrangement!"

As we were waiting to be seated, he'd jumped, without prompt, on the "opportunity" to impress me with his "literary acumen." He talked about the battered usual suspects, Cliffs Notes criticism of *The Adventures of Huckleberry Finn* ("Because Huck, you know, he was lowbred, I'd say, but highbred in heart." He paused for effect. "Like a Cinderella for boys"), the "unverified" impossible real-life stories of Hemingway ("I heard he head-shot"—whispering it—"a

Fitzgerald look-alike on a pier in Havana") and *Why the Caged Bird Sings* ("Because"—here he shook his head—"it's caged! Duh. Come on, people!"). I almost laughed when he said Macbeth should have just told himself "to be," and forgotten all about the "or not to be."

"Yeah," I'd said instead. "Hamlet, too."

The weirdest part of the night was the constant re-arrival upon the truth about our plate: that it wasn't just a real human body but a real human body *with* a working brain. She reminded us of this anytime I almost achieved full denial, by minor miracle, of her presence.

"Great, isn't it?" she said as he practically ricocheted a California roll off his tonsils. "Can you imagine the work Sensei Dobashi put into it?"

Once in the middle of his second-to-last slice of unagi, she actually said, "If you don't get that last piece of eel, I'm gonna eat it off myself myself!"

I don't know what other words are necessary to worry my fellow Americans about the decline, or death, of our culture, but there you have it.

"Hey!" he said, after I said exactly these words to him, not worried about her comprehending the statement, not caring, really, if she did. I kept saying to myself throughout the night, Don't judge her, maybe she has kids, but even that didn't work at times. "I paid three hundred bucks for this show!"

"Must be why," I said, nodding, "you've eaten so ravenously. Gotta get your buck's worth."

"Sweetie," our plate said, "it's not my business, but I don't think you're being a very good sport."

"I have to agree with her."

"Jesus," I whispered.

"Now let's get into the spirit and feed off her body for foreplay!"

If I were twenty-two, or if I were her, I'd have slapped him right about there.

But now he's at the climax of the evening, one he orchestrated, by selection, to perfection, each nipple covered in an upside-down temaki roll, the missiles of seaweed very Madonnaesque, three pieces of sashimi covering her vagina. Her legs are pulled up so that we have full appreciation of the beauty of her role, the exact position I was in when I birthed Prince.

"Shall we?" he says, delicately lifting the temaki roll from her right boob. A sun-browned nipple pops up, pointier than the missile of seaweed that had covered it.

"Why the first person collective?"

"Huh?"

"The 'we'?"

"Yeah," she giggles, "why all that collective stuff, huh? Get moving, mister."

"If you say so," he says, reaching forward, his lips splitting open with anticipation, his tongue filling the void. "Somebody's gotta collect, lovely lady."

She's purely tickled by his flirtation with time, the suspension of revealing what he brought me here to see. Oh, but I do see. I clearly understand. He's greedy, he's a hedonist, he's a spray-tanner, he's a wannabe millionaire. He's a pusher, he's a user, he's a usurer, he's not at all what I'm looking for.

If ever I needed proof that the alluring virtual world is false, and thus dangerous, here it is. His succinct response, "I love books," seemed pure and controlled on the bed of electric impulses, and I'd ignored the void of evidence. By now, I know he meant it in the way one says, "I love the Grand Canyon."

He didn't ask me one question all night, still hasn't, and yet I can't stop thinking about myself. That I don't have a man, that I'm raising my son on my own. Tonight my stomach feels like it disintegrates on contact with oxygen, dissolving on every breath of air.

"I have to use the bathroom," I say, standing.

She doesn't care, her smile blinding. She's so proud of her nakedness that it probably extends to the nakedness inside, the metaphor
that for most of us is no metaphor. I realize that they have something
in common, these two. They are extremely happy with themselves,
quite pleased.

"Oh," he says, a little panicky. "Okay. Again?"

I nod.

"Well."

"Don't worry. It's not required that I be accompanied."

"When a lady asks to use the restroom," our plate says, "you *be* a
gentleman and *let* her go."

He rises for a moment, bowing, drops back down to his seat. "Well,
you gotta go, you gotta go. I'll be right here."

"I'm sure you will."

On our first date in the city, Lokapi and I shared plates of tako at
this hole-in-the-wall Hunters Point restaurant called Atari-ya Tai Kai.
We sat on the these tiny bamboo stools that his massive Polynesian
body completely smothered and he kept rocking back and forth anytime he leaned in to grab some fish. I said, "You're gonna wear them
down worse," and he said, smiling, "I'm used to this. I never fit into
the roller-coaster rides. I was only thirteen when they banned me and
my brothers from Great America." I kept expecting him to topple over.
He taught me how to use chopsticks in five minutes.

I saw that he was gentle. This was an odd thing since I also felt, when
he swept me up into his wide-shouldered frame, that he could crush
any of the thin-shouldered men who'd held me before. No one had
ever held me like Lokapi. I felt like a cub in his warm and meaty arms.
When I met his family, they all exhibited this same trait of gentleness.
I guess it stood out because they were so strong and sturdy—like big
circus bears—and you got the sense that they, his family—"his folk," as
he always called them—could do a lot of damage if provoked.

There were kids everywhere. I constantly lost track of names. Junior
and Malia, Tasi and Little Tama, their muscular middles wrapped

in sheet-thin *i'e* lavalavas, barefoot, always barefoot. Running every-where until told, *"Filemu!"* by an elder, which was an order to "be calm," dozens of kids I've forgotten until right now in this bathroom mirror of this unbearably lame restaurant, those beautiful kids so free and yet so sure in their belonging, so knowing in who they are.

"My Prince," I say.

When he wouldn't come back to me, when he said our son was better off with me sane, which meant us free of each other, I started to keep my belly empty in the light of day, snack on ice cream and smoothies before bed. I punished myself at night. I realized in the dead time between Leno and a rerun of *Cheers* that he meant me alone of *any* man, not just him. Not that I wasn't worth it, he was saying, but that I couldn't *do* it. That I wasn't made for it. Didn't have the circuitry of self, the requisite backstory to move into the next stage for posterity. That you can't go forward with your head thrown over your shoulder.

I read so many books my eyes stung with the speed of the passing words. I'd nod at the last good line of the novel in question, smile with an already shrinking sense of appreciation, say the requisite, "The end, folks," and then walk with acceptance to the toilet. I lived on Brazilian coffee and Big Gulps of Diet Coke, and any chance I got, I told Prince to avoid, if he could, both. "The coffee bean might be the one natural food product I don't ever want you ingesting, honey." Some days I don't think I kept in eight hundred calories. I'd walk into work and drop into my roller chair and watch the clock tick with practically human restraint into the next lagging minute. I was always worried that I'd fall off my chair if I didn't keep pounding away at the keyboard, put all my weight forward into my fingers. I'd take in twenty-eight hundred calories and discharge two thousand before the food settled. The more I thought about the mechanics of it—squat and roll my wrists onto the porcelain, finger down the throat to trigger the flood, coughing hack afterward to clear the flavor—the worse I got. Whenever I reflected on me and my story—me with Prince, me with Lokapi, me with Leticia and Gabe, me and us without Lazarus—I'd yack until I was spitting yellow bile, the kind that isn't supposed to come up, the kind that's traced with blood.

"Well," I say, closing my eyes, worried nothing at all about the "gentleman" supposedly awaiting my return, forcing me from my own mind. To get me out of the equation has been, I understand now, a kind of goal without my knowing it. Because I suspect I can breathe a little better. To take in some air and live with it when not at the center of the mind's eye. It's everything the Freudians and "Self-Reliance" Emersonians and Dr. Phils out there don't believe in, but as I can feel my stomach calm at the thought of Prince at his first prom, Prince on his way home for spring break, Prince in the nuptial aisle, what do I care about the prescribed PC formula for mastery of self?

I mean, really, who cares how I get to the goddamned show?

I just want so badly to get there.

"My Prince is waiting."

I take the road less traveled by, which in this case is an emergency exit enshrined by a manicured bridge of faux bamboo, a crown of arrow-shaped faux leaves to match. It doesn't set off one peep of an alarm out the door, and I run to my car, face to the stars in the sky, and fire it up, which is the worst kind of description for the rolling over of a Prius engine. Prince always laughs when I rev this purring kitten of a motor. I assure you that I'll be the first in the lot to purchase, whenever it happens, Ford's environmentally sound Mustang. I'll buy it for my son, actually, so he can always come home to visit his mama.

But maybe I'll just make the down payment so he doesn't turn out like my strapping date for the night, spoiled as a rotten egg. Rotten tamago. It saddens me that right now a woman out there is yearning to settle for, maybe even celebrate, the self-absorption of my would-be paramour.

The El Camino Real is emptier tonight than I've seen in some time, and I take full advantage of it, green lights for two miles running. I pass Stanford Avenue and Serra Street and the spacious, densely treed, mugger-friendly grounds of my alma mater and then, impossibly, I even make the six-lane intersection of the Embarcadero, whiz right through it without the smallest foot shift toward the brake. I may have even accelerated.

I take a right on University Avenue, the heart of downtown Palo Alto, and slow with the cars in front of me, fifteen miles an hour past the lush European fashion shops and pricey Middle Eastern restaurants, and in a matter of three short minutes, I'm already winding through the clean streets of Palo Alto's best estates, multimillion-dollar lots that stop exactly at the crosshair of Highway 101, where East Palo Alto starts, toward Pulgas—"Fleas!" Prince translated for me last spring—Avenue and MLK Park, where I take a shortcut via Myrtle Street to avoid the dark, hooded, eyeless dealers on O'Connor Street, their immediate, synchronized, furtive step back to the cover of shadows always scaring me, young men so near death, so unswayed by the beauty right under their feet. All of various tints of brown. I breathe in deep through my nostrils, the way my brother used to teach me on late-night runs through downtown Sonoma: keep the paranoid parent to herself, remember where he's at, who's with him.

"*Maternus nervosus*," some forgotten writer once put it, the use of Latin insinuating a catholic, inescapable, insect condition that all mothers have, and live by, and die by.

I start the climb upward, and can see the outline of my mother in the window of our apartment up above, her body soft and unthreatening even in silhouette. She's reading in the living room chair, probably one of the manic prayerbooks she gets prescribed each week by her priest. On her AA night, I looked the material over in her absence and thought, simultaneously, "How could you let them tell you what to do?" and "How admirable the notion of internal peace, how lovely the idea of devotion."

I finally reach the fourth and highest floor of the complex, a small hike-to-the-top price to pay for cheaper-by-a-hundred-bucks rent. Once I said something about the advantage of having windows too high to break into and Prince said, "What about to jump from, Mama?"

I didn't want to imagine what he meant.

"If there's a fire," he said, "we gotta get out."

"You're right," I said, already thinking about ladders and tying sheets together ahead of the disaster. Relieved by the elimination of the image of the last dive from my mind, a desperation he'll never, if I can help it, be aware of. "You're so right, honey."

I open the door and he's sprawled on his belly, doing push-ups on the floor. He's been watching B. J. Penn's training session at his father's house. He brought the DVD back here. Again, he's nine. He jumps to his feet and sprints to me. He's gonna knock me over if he doesn't slow down.

"Oh, Prince."

"You're early, baby."

"I know," I say. "Thanks for watching him, Ma."

"Oh, we had a blast, didn't we, Prince?"

She wants to ask me how the date went, but she fears the worst. Still worries about the fire climbing and consuming the wall. I want to relieve her of this at least, I want to share my discovery of self tonight. "I practiced how to keep from, you know"—I pull down on Prince's head, put an index finger into my mouth—"doing that when I'm upset."

"This was your date tonight? He was a doctor, baby?"

"I think he *thought* he was a doctor."

"Oh. Is he getting his MD?"

"Huh, huh. Hardly."

"I don't get it, baby."

"I'm joking, Mom. Making light of a weird date."

"Oh, I know how it is, baby. I've been on quite a few myself."

"Well, I won't be seeing him again, but if we have to reference tonight for some reason, let's just call him the Doctor of Love."

I smile at my mother's indecision. She thinks the worst of my joke, something like, A one-night stand? How reckless of you, Murron, to discard a useful man yet again! "So what happened then? Why did you go in the first place? And what was he?"

"He is—well, I never asked him. Doesn't matter. Like I said, there won't be a second date."

"I'm sorry, honey."

"No, no. It was worth the drive. We both got something out of it."

"What?"

I squeeze my son back, and we rock, together, on the sides of our feet.

She says immediately, "I see," and there's not a trace of suspicion in her voice. Sounds like hyperbole, but my mother and I have come a long way together.

"What do you want to do tonight, Prince?" I say, changing the topic so we can leave it at that. "Mama's early. Wanna get some ice cream or something?"

"Sure," he says, hopping on the balls of his feet now, hunching his shoulders. "As long as all of us go."

"Darling," my mother says, looking up at me, bending down to kiss the top of his head.

"Pow-pow-pow!" he shouts, jabbing at the air with the kind of childish abandon I miss. "I got you! I got you!"

"Prince, you calm down!"

"It's okay," I say, "huh, Mom?"

"Well, I don't want him to be so—"

"Pow! Pow!"

"—oh, I don't know."

"Violent?" I ask.

"Maybe that, yes. But not exactly. He's not *violent,* Mur."

I laugh. It's like I, Prince's mother, have just insulted her grandparenting skills. "I know he's not."

"Mom," he says. "This is a dumb conversation."

"You're right there, hon."

"Don't say 'dumb,'" my mother says.

"Boring."

"Better."

My mother's phone rings. She looks down at the number, back up at me and says, "Do we know anyone in the five-one-oh area code named Yoshida?"

"No," I say, pulling Prince in, holding on tight. He nudges his face toward my chin and tickles my neck with his nose. He's more sweet than he is tough.

"Where is that?"

"Five-one-oh is East Bay. Maybe it's one of your AA friends—"

"No."

"—relocated or something."

"I don't know anyone out there."

"Well, are you gonna pick up?"

"Hello." I hear the voice but not the articulated words. My mother's eyes widen, and after a few moments, she says, "Wait. No, no. You wait. You talk to my daughter."

She hands me the phone. I hand her Prince. "Hello?"

"Mrs. Teeny-toe?"

"Who is this?"

"My name is Denise Yoshida, and I represent the legal interests of Ms. Mary Anna Felice. I've been directed to inform you that should you proceed in attempting to move my client's mother from the Elysium Fields Hospice . . ."

I say nothing, let her get in every word she needs to finalize this immoral mess. It's not that I tune out and don't hear the two main messages: "There is absolutely no legal precedence for a grandchild to . . ." and "You will be at serious risk of facing kidnapping charges should you . . ." I process the meaning just fine, hang up after I've heard the last threat.

Neither do I say out loud to my wide-eyed mother what I'm thinking (Poor Mary, I'm so so sorry), but bead instead on the small bit of gratitude I have for never having introduced the idea in question to my wide-open son.

"She won't be moving in with us then?" he would've cried out. "Why not, Mama?"

How the hell would I have answered that?

28

Mary Anna Felice
Spring Sports Banquet at Hayward State
  University
May 16, 1993

SHE WAS ON HER MERRY WAY to Meiklejohn Hall at Hayward State University where a ceremony honoring her service to the Women's Lacrosse Club would be held. She'd invited everyone she knew, even him. He wouldn't come, of course, yet she'd sent an official invitation, anyway, so that he could see exactly how little his childhood sin had affected her in the long run. Look where she was in her life now. Look how they honored her. She was more her father's daughter than he'd ever be his father's son.

The traffic slowed and she lifted her foot slightly from the accelerator, liking very much the fluid motion of her limbs. The muscles and ligaments in her legs, from the hip flexors all the way down to the Achilles tendons, were more limber and developed than they'd ever been. This was due very simply to the newly hired yoga instructor at the graduate clinic, Ms. Keri Silverman, who'd encouraged her to press into new positions, find new places where her body could be.

The intimate tenor of Andrea Bocelli was slowly claiming the interior of her air-conditioned silver '93 Mercedes-Benz sedan, the sound system liquid smooth in this leather-bound space, the idea of other drivers seeing her operate this bullet on wheels exciting her terribly. By now the minerals of her full-immersion bath were soaked into her tanned almost brined skin, and she giddily cracked down on the Asian mint bridged between her teeth. She smiled into the rearview mirror, the sight of her meaty, overlapping gums for once not bothering her. She'd never liked the way she looked from the upper lip to the bottom of her chin. No matter her mood, no matter the tone or volume of her words, she always appeared, facially, strained. Once at Upland Elementary School, a boy had called her "monkey-mouth retard," and she'd never forgotten this, even to the present moment almost thirty years later.

Well, today she was good, unstoppable, and this meant she was happy. So much that she reached down between her legs, and right there in rush-hour five o'clock traffic, touched herself.

Here was something new, too, this discovery below the belt. She couldn't describe the sexual eureka in words to anyone, this arrival at the mountaintop of Me, not even to the very person who'd brought out the glorious celebration hidden down there in the pit of her iron-board stomach. Dusk began to open its hand upon this pollutive artery of the East Bay, and she gave no thought to any of the stories surrounding her, the thousands of lives in delicate balance, but instead saw in some secret pocket of her mind the warm candlelit shine of the tape room window, her gifted yoga teacher tickling herself with one finger on two knees, devotee at the shrine, an after-hours rendezvous to tongue-love Mary Anna into the first orgasm of her thirty-nine-year life.

"Ohhhh," she whispered, reaching deeper into herself. "Ohhh."

Now the muscles of her inner walls locked around her finger and she trembled into the happy place again, her eyelashes fluttering.

She emerged from the ecstasy, eyes widening, and slammed down on the brake with all her strength. Horns from several directions. The car came to a stop, saved by the antilock system.

The best in the world! she thought, as if she were in a demo of a thirty-second commercial for the company. Best in the world!

All at once the cars moved into their rhythm again, and she paid no attention to the angry glares around her. They couldn't be angrier than she was, after all, and unlike her, they'd been spared from damage. They resumed the race to get home, to get to dinner, to get warm.

"In my case," she said, "it's to get lauded."

She went quiet now, focusing on her driving like a teenager newly licensed, this because she was trying like hell not to let the negativity steal the moment. She knew that it was still down there, shrunken but alive, beaten but undead, beaking its cage to escape. And now her self-imposed silence soundboarded the grumble of her stomach, and she thought with bitterness of the annotated version of her life that so many people bought, the wordless poem of positivity always in the making. Only she knew what could really be written on the paper. Written out warrant for his arrest. It wasn't that she'd ever denied what he'd done. It was that she hadn't been asked. That she'd never said. Her hatred for him flouted any chance she'd ever had to speak. That, and the daily pressure of family, each member burning the fuel of the reserve, the speed and immediacy of every moment, the constant noise. Anything out of her mouth would have been pure dragon fire, a flood of flame alit in the varnished living room of Big Victor, the blaze spreading in a wild gasoline trail across the neighborhood of Third Street, the whole town of Upland, California, consumed in the heat of her life's lie.

A lie that saved the family, she thought now, angry eyes scanning the interminable line of cars on the 580. She looked to the nearest exit, dissatisfied, at once, by the number of cars using it. She wiped her dripping finger on her naked kneecaps.

The Felices happily kept together, she thought, by my miserable sacrifice.

"Get moving." Her directive came out fast and straight. "Will you jerks just get off the damned road? I got an event to be at. I actually have to *be* somewhere. I actually *have* obligations."

Not one sibling, not even Richmond, had ever thanked her, not even in his ad nauseam speeches about courage and cowardice in Vietnam, but she'd gotten through their ingratitude just like she'd gotten through everything else, and only had to look forward to that day when they would acknowledge, in whatever form, how much she'd done for them.

Only she knew, deep down, what had happened over the years. She was better than all of her brothers at one thing. She could lie. Used it every day like a credit card. All the way back to Upland and her dungeon of a room in Big Victor. Hardened, at whatever cost, against honesty. To get a better grade, to have another hour at the party, to garner favor from whatever brother, to make her father defend his only little girl, anything to get out of the house.

She knew the lie thrived down there under the thought and the sentence, spitting beast in its dark cage. The filthy breath beneath the given action. And yet one said word about the strength of her inner rodent would actually be a step away from, and not toward, understanding who she was. Because Mary Anna Felice had never considered herself a liar. Never said to herself, "She who lies is a liar." The saving of herself was what mattered, that and nothing else, the pinnacle point in Darwinian scripture: Survive.

Not preserve, she'd written in her senior quote for the '72 Upland yearbook. Actively survive.

Once a man named Don, her unemployed, live-in-boyfriend, a sculptor twenty-two years her senior, had told her precisely this: "Your lying is pathological, honey. You can keep the fear out of this thing, babe. You're always talking about the hunter and the prey. Surviving each day. You gotta take it easy. Loosen up. You don't have to protect yourself here."

She'd nearly understood what he'd said. Something legitimate, it seemed, was pushing the words into existence. But she panicked before their meaning could penetrate her system. She deemed his plea an attack levied against her person, the world constricting its hands around her throat again, men being savage men, and fell short of the message, couldn't grasp its core, didn't see the goodness in the criticism ("Criticism is neutral!" he'd kept shouting. "Neutral, you psychotic bitch!"), and, breathless, thought, Self. Self! Get. Get! Get rid of the threat.

The victim succumbed, she'd thought, the coward buckled. I am neither. I'll get what others are preventing me, unjustly, from having.

Hurried, cornered, she'd gone to a friend's house in Nob Hill and sat in, blindly, on a support group for women swingers who were trying to quit the life. The problem, her friend said aloud, was that the majority also had to quit alcohol and cocaine, which were both tougher addictions. They went around the room with their heartfelt confessions, and when it was her turn, Mary Anna said, "Men have tried to victimize me my whole life. I have four brothers, and every fucking one of them thinks the sun rises and sets at his doorstep. Well, they're right. Because *I* am the sun. *We* bring light to this planet every day. And it's not 'You're welcome' anymore. No. Now is my time. Our time."

A few of the girls clapped, and one even offered a living room couch and a business card.

Afterward, she drove across the greater Bay Area to visit half a dozen other friends, entering into each conversation with not a single sob story, no letter of regret shared aloud, no Shakespearean love sonnet that had illuminated, centuries before, the very situation in which she was suffering, none of the heavy fruit of human sadness. Instead, her friends suffered the septic venom of the cynic, no chance to answer, without input. The four-word summarizations in haltering, vicious tones, the upper-lip snarl, the gender insults in short exhalations, the eye rolling, the occasionally spat word. It was as if she'd not only never slept with Don, never housed Don, but that she didn't think Don, whoever he was, worthy of a working heart.

"I was young and dumb," she now said, twisting the rearview mirror upward.

She squeezed into the tight, amorphous, slightly budging space between cars, the tread-upon blacktop hot with the incessant track of rubber. She was almost amnesic about how close she'd been to disaster while masturbating just moments earlier. She waited at a red light, drumming her fingers on the leather-wrapped steering wheel, impatient to get to the auditorium, swiftly slapping at the Off button to silence Bocelli.

"Shut up," she said, "you blind bastard."

Finally she went through the intersection, testing the acceleration of her "Beloved Benz," as she'd taken to calling her car a minute after leaving the showroom lot, and then, half a mile down, saw it.

"Shit!"

She looked and leaned to the left, leaned right, peered fast into the rearview mirror, the car swaying with her eyes like some futuristic vehicle driven by a microchip in the brain. There was nowhere to go now. Dead-stop traffic generated by an accident up ahead, the lights and sirens like visual and auditory irritants. She exhaled so loudly she spat. She looked to her right again, not quite taking in the three dozen people perched on their toe tips, palms shading their eyes, randomly posted across the front side of the Home of the East Hayward Holy Rollers.

She read, "The ability to lie is a liability."

The weekly credo in big black letters on the church signboard.

She pushed down on the accelerator and crossed into the vacant bike lane, already preparing her plea, if stopped, to the police. She passed the accident slowly so as not to get caught and took in not the strapped prostrate body or the huddled paramedics hustling the stretcher and its sprouting contraptions into the rear of the ambulance but the positions, respectively, of the police present, and at that exact moment when she felt she could, whizzed right through the scene's very center, the flashing lights seemingly sucking the bloody gore on the road into the night air, a million red and blue particles broken from one another forever.

No one followed her delinquency, and this didn't surprise her one bit. She had to get what was hers, and they, whoever they were, had to get what was theirs. The earner's code. It was a matter of lucky timing on her part, a fortuitous accident that the civic authorities had been fully immersed in their call to duty, no concern at all to Mary Anna until she, herself, would be someday tied to the gurney, when it would mean everything.

She'd been laid out on her back earlier in the week, thirty-nine years from birth on the surgeon's table, middle-aged-halfway-to-death. The procedure perfectly safe, he'd said, the absurd 3-D welder's goggles popped down across his eyes, a flimsy crimson mirror. He looked like some cartoonish Japanese robot about to save the world from Godzilla. All this doctorly protection to get the mark of the beast removed from her flat breast, the scarred skin about to go up in the cleansing smoke of a laser hotter than the fires of hell. The scar looked like epidermal train tracks, a little boy's train, the jagged tissue of her childhood left by the sibling who'd taken her innocence, the spaces between the toothmarks like the Morse code of some feral animal. Half a mouth, four front teeth, top and bottom. He'd bitten down on her chest the first time he'd done it when she wouldn't stay quiet afterward like he'd said. He'd covered her mouth from behind, he'd covered it from above, his palms soft and oily. Only the teeth meeting beneath the skin could silence her cries. She was nine, a little girl, his only sister, and he was fifteen, no little boy, no big brother.

How did he know? she thought now. That I'd clamp down on the scream when he bit. That his locked jaw would make me lockjawed. That I wouldn't cry even louder.

That Big Victor wouldn't pick up the frequency and echo its call like it did every other sin and sound within its walls.

It was worse. She'd kept the lockjaw straight through the Bastard Johnny Period, as she'd labeled that time, her third- to seventh-grade years. She hadn't repressed. That was subconscious. When she learned what the word "succeed" meant, that it was a higher goal than mere survival, she consciously drove the live story deep into her system. She was that aware of her life, like a soldier at war. Day by day, she got better at this. By the time she was a woman, she'd allowed herself, counting the time he'd bit her, three childhood memories to keep: one to remember the goodness of her brothers, another to remind her of their tendency to talk right over the stories at their doorstep, the last as the proof of carnal evil, its aftermath. She used to throw the baseball in the street on Saturday afternoons with her brothers, the neighbors parking their cars in their driveways so the kids could play. She used to grind her teeth on the bottom step of Big Victor when the family would talk politics, the babblers never once considering the chance of a pressing issue closer to home than Washington, D.C. She used to stuff the closet with bloody sheets, deep beneath the trunk of dusty Madame Alexander dolls, clean the linen when everyone was gone, the boys at school or practice, Father at work, Mother on an errand.

Johnny beheaded every doll as a joke, she remembered now, a fifth memory that snuck in. Those damned Tonka trucks couldn't keep his lust for destruction capped.

The bloody sheets stopped when he left for Vietnam. She went to weekday Mass at the Carmelites and prayed for his death. Not once but a dozen times. She never confessed to the priest. She didn't trust the priest. She didn't trust anyone. If not a single member of the supposedly decent adult world had had the imagination to put an ear to the wall and listen for a little girl's pain, any little girl, any Mary Anna, then they didn't have the wherewithal to process the story, anyway. They didn't have the right to try and comprehend her wound. At home, she went silent to eavesdrop on the long-distance phone calls, she opened every overseas piece of correspondence in hope. She nearly ripped up those letters, which was every letter, for not bearing the news of his horrid death by flamethrower fire, death by the last clap of sharpened bamboo claws through his guts. Her heart fluttered with the anticipation of his end. She was thirteen years old.

Once she had a dream of fratricide of the truest measure, her brother Richmond finding out, by letter, what Johnny had done in Big Victor. She was above the reverie, she was omniscient. She followed her brother across the Southeast Asian peninsula, gone AWOL on her behalf, finally finding Johnny in some dark and isolated off-trail Saigon strip club, where he pistol-whipped Johnny from behind and dragged him out of the club to the empty alleyway. Her blood rushed as she watched him clutch at their brother's weak jaw, the fastest way to force a face-to-face nod of what he'd done, one little nod of admiration, and then carbon steel barrel on skin and bone, a single bullet through his head.

When Johnny came back from his tour unkilled in the war, she fought with her folks every Sunday for several months, once getting her eye blackened by a crisp short left from her mother. On Ash Wednesday, her father said, "Let's spare the rod, huh? She's confirmed, she's baptized, what the hell, huh, if the girl doesn't like hearing the homilies at church?"

They didn't understand. She still loved her savior on her knees, she hadn't yet unlearned her catechism, as they feared, like the other neighborhood kids. When Johnny walked into Big Victor with the same wolfish smile and sharp eyes, seemingly undamaged by the horror of war, handing out copies of his CIB patch as if they were political pamphlets, she knew for certain that evil was real, and that here in Big Victor was where she needed to be. Like a mission, like a calling. She stayed up past the midnight hour, she waited with a ready mind, she had a knife underneath her pillow. She would let him have her body at first and then she'd reach back and thrust the knife into his neck when he was most lost in his man lust. But he was too smart to come again. Again, she wondered how he knew. She still slept with a weapon as a grown woman of considerable success, a pistol in the drawer at her bedside, the registered and loaded .45 gifted from Richmond that she'd yet to use except at the shooting range.

She entered the grounds of Hayward State University, flashing her faculty card at the tollbooth operator with no greeting, no eye contact, zipping defiantly up the steep incline of the road to the campus above, accelerating against the gravitational forces at work against her, the world always trying to bring her down. She wouldn't let them, she'd never let them. Now she reached twice the twenty-mile-an-hour speed limit, the car popping over the speed bumps, airborne for a fast second like a bunny hop. The tires grabbed and clutched the asphalt on the landing, no traceable bounce, no American whiplash return, the European shocks intact, the tight aerodynamic tiptoe on the white-lined curves up this academic hill. She didn't dare look over the edge, she wouldn't take in the squalid crime-ridden quadrant down below, the trodden plot of land she found herself constantly high-browing. The East Bay was impacted like a beehive. Muddy as a pigsty. Not a place to live, she'd always said, not even a place to drive through. As the traffic tonight had proved. She had no friends in Milpitas, Fremont, Hayward, Oakland. God, no. Here she had clients who *needed* her. Here she had people who *paid* her.

"I reside in the city I love by working in the city I hate!" she'd joked at her coming-out party, pointing out the window of her posh gentrified SoMa suite to the lit grid across the night-blackened bay. "We flush our shit inland!"

But tonight there was nowhere she wanted to be but afloat in the municipal toilet of Hayward. She wanted to bathe in their applause, she was ready to breathe in every minute of this event. She looked at her watch, she wouldn't be late. She ground down on her bottom teeth now, as if the chipmunk motion could break apart the childhood memories just evoked. After a fast peek in the rearview mirror, she realized what she was doing, and when she opened her mouth to quit the grinding, a horrible scream sounded, unmuffled by the familiar pressure of the palm.

"That son of a bitch!" she shouted, ripping at the scar underneath her bra. She wanted to stay calm, but couldn't. "That fucked fuck!"

In the rush of a panic attack, she had decided to stop the laser procedure immediately. Right there on the surgical table. The idea of having to pay for the operation infuriated Mary Anna. Once she'd thought about the mechanics of what she was doing, once she'd envisioned the result of this act, a return to the scarless breast she'd had at age seven, she shouted at the doctor, "Stop, goddamnit!"

What else did she have as proof of her fucked childhood? She was successful, she hadn't been ruined by his perversion. She wouldn't revise history for him. He had to live with her indictment, just as she had to live with his evil. The laser would exonerate him more than liberate her, and she just wouldn't have it.

"I said, stop, you son of a bitch," she'd repeated on the table, sitting up and glaring into the red void of his goggles.

Now she could see the lights of the auditorium up ahead and she told herself at once to quit this stupid trip down memory lane, into a hell where she'd had no control, the living victim of Big Victor, and to think of tonight. She grabbed at the rearview mirror and then, anticipating unkind words to the face she couldn't stand, changed her mind, opened the door of her sedan, and said, "My night."

She walked with the confident strides commensurate with her stature. She was ecstatic with the promise of their praise. She bounded up the steps like an athlete twenty years her junior, the same long- and muscular-legged lacrosse girls whose fuzzy ankles she rapidly taped before practices and games. She could hear the friendly clamor of coaches and players mingling over cocktails, the light and simple small talk of a sport in which she'd always been remarkably apt, she could feel the honors bestowed upon her already, she could see herself leaving this place before the year was out. Better job, which meant better money, which meant a better life.

At the top step, she was stopped in her tracks, confronted with the kind of anger she liked to think she owned.

The boy's shoulders were wide and his blond hair cut tight to the skin, a Brillo pad around his head, so that, even this close, he appeared bald and masculine, a high school military recruit, front lines, in the making. Mary Anna hated him at once, looking him up and down, from the burning blue eyes to the solid kneecaps, the question "Yeah?" unnecessary.

"You better quit," he said. "Better quit what you're doing."

She immediately seized on his inability to finish the sentence in one breath. Repetition, before the whole message got out, was weakness. This kid had the passion of youth, yes, the fire of possession, but adolescence, she knew, was filled with uncertainty. Firstly, and forever, and whoever was in it. "Stop what exactly? And who are you, anyway? And how *dare* you take that tone with me?"

"I know what you're doing."

The boy was shaking, fighting back tears. He did have beautiful eyes, she noticed, his mother's eyes, the two crystals that had first mesmerized Mary Anna, straining between her splayed legs on the Hayward State University training table.

"What I'm doing is collecting my just due. What I've *earned*. That's why everyone is here. To *honor* me, okay? You're interfering with my night, young man, and I'm just not going to put up with it."

"You're interfering." He jammed a forearm over his face and dragged it across and down, the new tears already starting up, sparkling on the rim of his lashes. "You're interfering. With our life."

"Hey!" she shouted. "Don't you have any class? Any dignity? This is a university event, kid, not some locker room debate."

Just like that, Keri was at the kid's side, gripping his hand so tightly he pulled it away. She tried to nudge him into the auditorium, but he was strong, and Mary Anna could see his quadriceps lock like a drawbridge. Keri reached for his hand again and looked up into his face, as if telepathically trying to communicate the message to succumb. This only emboldened Mary Anna.

"What the *hell* are you talking about?"

The lie was enthralling. You could always win if you lied when you had to. The same with the truth. Use it when you had to. That's what people who weren't successful hadn't figured out. A truth and a lie were equal currency.

Keri looked up at Mary Anna, glowing in their shared secret, this guise to protect their intertwined afternoons. Seeing the matching crystalline eyes excited Mary Anna. Keri pulled the boy's hand to her chest, throwing him off the scent, and smiled proudly at her. Yes, this is my son, she seemed to be saying, and you are my woman.

Soon, Mary Anna knew, when the time was right, she would tell the truth about their affair, when this could be called, in selective hindsight, their courting period. Fate and romance, chance and love. When no one like this young man, whoever he was, could put the date to the act, make any party responsible for a destroyed story.

"I don't even *know* this woman!" she shrieked, as if on the raging male brink of orgasm.

29

Murron Leonora Teinetoa
First Day with Mary Capone Felice
February 9, 2010

I HAVE TO ADMIT something, okay?

There are times, even still, when the only thing it seems I know is that I have no clue about what to do with my son. Once in a while, like today, when you see one little thing so clearly—that people, truly, are fucked—I know that the best I can do for Prince is to just stay quiet, think about the miracle of discovery, the toe wiggle in the straitjacket. I'll go round and round with what's right for him, what's wrong, what I should never do with him, what lines I cannot cross. It doesn't just feel like a roller-coaster ride, raising a son in the modern world.

It feels like a war.

All he said three minutes ago was "I'm coming in, too," and I said, hesitating, "I don't think so, Prince. You wait here in the car, okay?"

"No! I wanna go in, Mom!"

He stood beside the Prius and I reached out for his wrist, spun him where he stood. His eyes widened with the kind of recognition that's heavier than a full load of laundry. I couldn't even look at him, counter him with my eyes. He's strong now. But he's always been strong. So I guess it's that he's *stronger* now. I turned and walked toward the entrance of the hospice, hoping praying believing he'd stay in the car, and wait for me, but not really knowing.

I'm very proud of Prince's strength.

And now I'm here at the bedside wondering, yet again, if what I did with my son was right, which means, I guess, that I'm mentally checking out, in part, from the only activity I've been engaged in for the last three days at Elysium Fields Hospice, trying to get Mary, whose tongue is bigger than a slab of raw meat, to suck the water out of a sponge smaller than a piece of candy. I've grown to detest these strange sponges. Silly disposable lies. We can't give her anything she'd request because the morphine she's on prevents her from forming words, we can't give her water because she can't drink it of her own volition while on the morphine, we can't put an IV into her arm because her only daughter will not sign off on it, but we can dip these little white wands into a cup, soak up half an ounce of water, if that, into the red-and-blue star on its end, force her teeth apart, and wait for her to figure out that despite the famished state she's endured for six days now, she should only press her tongue up against the roof of her mouth and not bite down on it, which will asphyxiate her if she swallows.

I can see very clearly in the movie clips of my mind the first time, more than two years ago I met this woman who, like a dream vision, was my own personal mirror of dark life-filled Sicilian eyes. I can feel, like muscle memory, the machinery of a homeless heart forcing its terrified blood through my tunnels of veins and arteries, a damaged but resilient system that somehow, as if predestined, kept pumping my body alive, how desperately I wanted to find a story here to keep for myself. And in that time, over eight hundred days, Prince has broken two bones (his right middle finger playing pickup hoops in downtown San Mateo, his left big toe skating a homemade ramp with his uncle Gabe) and made the honor roll four times, loving, at my suggestion, *The Old Man and the Sea* last spring, scored so many goals on his U12 soccer squad that they asked for a birth certificate at the end-of-the-year trophy party.

My ex-husband, Lokapi, got remarried to a blond-haired, bronze-skinned German-Samoan girl named Malia Sebald Utu in the seaside village of Amouli, a lovely ceremony to which I was kindly and weirdly invited, and which I attended with as much grace as I could summon on that beautifully backward island of honest inhabitants, shedding no tears of self-pity but crying instead out of the purity of happiness for my ex-husband and his new life and for my son and his new summertime family and against the lessons of the failure of the modern American version that I've learned, among so many other things, in this claustrophobic room. My mother and I bought an apartment on Thirty-seventh Avenue in San Mateo, the area's quality of culinary diversity unmatched, for your buck, anywhere on the peninsula, dining, as we routinely do, on compache sashimi Monday nights (fish brought in fresh to begin the week), on Spanish ceviche Tuesday nights (Mom drinks milk to combat acid reflux) and newly diced Aramaean tabouli Wednesday nights (Abe whittles rosary beads for Mary once a month). The other four nights we eat at home to save up for our dinners out.

I was laid off—"with honors," I always joke—from the *Chronicle* a year and a half ago, the budget for literary criticism no longer justified during the recession. I got beautiful letters from fans and apologies from fellow journalists I'd never known cared for books, and that meant a lot to me. Sometimes I'm amazed that we made it that far into this commoditized century. And yet the response I got made me evaluate the literary situation as not so much one with a cliff and a shove but more like the beginning descent down the steep steps of Machu Picchu, in which, of course, you can turn around and recover the ground you've lost as long as you keep your eyes off the certain death down below. Then, if you're lucky enough to make it back to the top—which means, of course, that you'll have reversed the course of modernity, a miracle hundreds of geniuses have failed to make happen on every continent in every era in every way—you'll have the problem of being alone at the top with your story. Doesn't sound too promising, I know, but still I feel good about what I'm doing with my life after they took away my column. In a way, I upped my resistance to time. I hope books don't die soon. Because I've taken up writing them, a novel in this case, my first, and maybe my last. I'm betting on the three-headed beast of diligence, sincerity, and hope over the uncontrollable behemoth of talent, though, I must admit, I still worry about my inheritance in the disconcerting hour of writer's block. But I put my head down and get through it like anything else. I've overcome my phobia about the Internet by actually earning my keep from it. So I've regressed and modernized at the same time. A compromise, I guess. During the mornings when Prince is at school, I edit online articles about every topic imaginable for an online guide called eHow. It's a safe haven for former editors and journalists from dying newspapers across the country, even the last big one back east, which was also forced to shrink to maximize efficiency. It pays the bills right now, but I don't need it existentially. If the Internet goes down, the world may choke on its own stench of burnt-out knowledge, but I assure you *I'll* be fine.

When I'm being romantic, which is often a symptom, it seems, of the writing, I try to look at the contradiction of my two activities in the same way Mishima looked at his "genre" and "literary" novels. I believe he disowned two-thirds of his books. This because he had to make money to get to his art. His personal work schedule was such that in the first half of the night he'd write the books that sold, and that he loathed, and in the second half he'd undergo a voluntary jolt of aesthetic schizophrenia and get artistic with the page, lovingly and methodically penning the books that kept his heart going until he couldn't write, or live, anymore. That kind of transformation amazes me but also seems very connected, in substance, to exactly how the world works. Which probably helps at every creative level. A constant cycle of polluting oneself and then, as it should be, cleansing oneself of the pollution. Cycle of redemption, of daily absolution.

I remove myself from idolizing Mishima beyond that because however ugly the world gets, however ugly it looks taking it on, I want to always try.

Anyway, I have to. Because two years later, I am, thank God, still a mom, and the urge to care for my son only seems, like him, to get stronger. But what's really hard about being a parent, I think, is this progressively realized notion, which is accurate in a very general way, that you have to forcibly turn off the switch to act on his behalf. You have to start letting go of the boy for the sake of his development. His growth. That you have to watch in silence, see what the wretched world has in store for him, and how he responds. That sometimes you're not allowed to even *watch* at all. That you have to trust. In a way, it's an obvious insinuation that you have to like yourself as a person, respect the parent you've been to this boy over the years. To a recovering bulimic, a recovering hater of Murron Leonora Teinetoa, and an aspiring novelist, approving of me as an idea, entity, or human being sometimes seems more foreign a notion than a little barefoot Samoan boy scaling a coconut tree in five seconds. But it can be done. He got up there all right, pumping his lithe body up the stalk on bloody knees, knocking the fruit down with a stick he'd tucked into the back of his *i'e* lavalava. Every day I like who I am enough to think clearly on these things, and so far I have the amount of self-confidence needed to keep writing this novel about a mother of five who dies alone in a run-down hospice.

So a lot happens in two years, yes, but for some people nothing happens. Nothing changes. The same bed, same room, same meals. The details that look like change—a fired nurse, dead roommate, schedule shift—are really not changes at all. This because the place remains the same. The same bickering relatives. Time doing its nasty trick of freeze-drying grudges between a bloodline, as if the three words of lasting union, "I love you," were never once uttered in a lifetime. Never whispered, or even thought. I don't mean to proselytize, I really don't, but it's hard not to be preachy on a quiet evening of near death in the Elysium Fields Hospice. The ultimate insult in nomenclature. This last story of hers, this last chapter, like a bastardized version of a game show, right between *Family Feud* and *Wheel of Fortune*, something like *Pick Your Poisonous Heir, America*. No getting around it. Someone really close to this poor woman chose to let this happen.

Mary has broken the record for longest in-house hospice patient, leaving full-blown AIDS and lung-cancer patients in the wake of her two-thousand-calorie days. The nurses, I've directly heard, despise this family. Perhaps it's a personal failing, but I lacked the loyalty to the Felices to defend them in conversation. In true reciprocity, they've ruined a few things for me, too, in minor but memorable ways. A stern but kind doctor named Yamasaki refused to talk to me about Mary's prognosis because, he said, "I'll not involve myself in the kind of rationalizations you people have been using to do this." I told him I wasn't one of "you people," but he only rolled his eyes, and by the start of the next month, he had recused himself from Mary's treatment all together. He never said hello to me in the hallways again, as if I were a plague of some sort, not even by mistake. A perfect record of his glance avoiding mine in a hundred-plus chances.

I guess it's obvious, but no one but me comes to visit any longer, not even Anthony to get away from his nagging wife for a weekend. I used to check the sign-in list, but I don't bother anymore. Johnny has been dead from a heroin overdose for a year, his corpse having been ravaged by stray dogs in a Skid Row alleyway. Richmond, I heard from my mother, bought a beachside estate on the Kona coast of the Big Island where he spends his autumns and winters, and a Victorian mansion in Portland's Alphabet District where, in perfect yin-yang balance, he spends his springs and summers. Lazarus, of course, has not once been seen here, or anywhere, for two years running, which, I guess, is just about an average absence for him. Mary Anna, I've read online, has opened a successful clown business in Walnut Creek, and last Christmas she tacked a life-sized poster of herself in a full-blown clown outfit behind Mary's bed. I've learned to look directly at it, as I'm doing now, without an active thought. Active thoughts, I've further learned, lead to dead ends with this family.

Even weirder things have happened. Mary Anna wouldn't sign off on the preparations for a Catholic burial for her mother, even though that's all the Filipino nurses and I heard from Mary every Sunday during the 2009 calendar year. Suddenly, as if an angel had whispered the news in her ear while she dreamed, Mary realized she wasn't going to get out of this place until the end. I don't know if Mary Anna's issues were theological or fiscal or if she just didn't want another hassle to deal with in her life, but when it became evident that she wasn't going to let the funeral happen, we managed to explain the particularities to a Jesuit priest at Santa Clara University and he came in without delay. Because she wasn't really "dying" of any inflicted wound or diagnosable disease, he couldn't read Mary her last rites, but he did pray for her soul. Though she'd never before met the priest, they had a plate of spaghetti and meatballs afterward (she told me how to cook it the authentic Felice way, and Leticia and I did our best) and their intimate communion so touched me that I nearly vacated my atheist post as they joyously dined to become, at minimum, an agnostic. Lest that happen, all I had to do was look around and remember where I was *at*. Still, Mary beamed with hope in that hour of her life and, honestly, that seemed to be okay with me inside. Anyway, it's what she wanted.

Which still, to this moment even, matters most.

It wasn't long afterward that I came in to visit and was given notified mail from an attorney informing Mary, and the family, of Johnny's death. I didn't want Mary to read the details of how he'd died, and I didn't dare share the lawyer's shameless attempt to recover his dead client's debt from the bedridden mother, and so I told her myself, best I could, the news of Johnny Benedetto Capone. She turned away from my hand and whimpered like my mother used to, as if clutching a ball to her stomach. She did this for half an hour, ignoring my pleas to be calm. After a while, I didn't want to be there, but I stayed in case the stress of her mourning sent her into some kind of cardiac arrest. For years now, I've had images of her rolling out of the bed in my absence and breaking her hip, mistakenly yanking a roommate's oxygen tube in the fall.

When she finally went quiet, I was caught off guard by what followed. A confession to me, of sorts. Although as I view it now, she had every right to have kept the words to herself for eternity. As it turns out, Mary knew all along that her husband had shared this room during the last weekend of his life. She'd given no hint of this knowledge the whole time he was here, but this final report about her child keyed the lockbox of this memory.

Listening to the senseless rambling on the other side of the curtain must have been worse than worrying about her sons' return from war, which at least was going on in some faraway country on another side of the world, and not in the next bed over. But true to her maternal calling, she still didn't say one bad thing about her children.

I never told her who was making these decisions about her life.

In all honesty, I never found out *exactly* how this reality came to pass. Behind the scenes, who knows which doctor signed off on what, which Felice spoke with whom, and how often? Richmond and Mary Anna, as everyone knows by now, have had power of attorney all along, but as to their private conversations, I wasn't there. Maybe, at one time or another, I might have been privy to their plans, but alas I couldn't stand the hypocrisy of either one of them. And that cookie-cutter piety of theirs. Team Anthony and Johnny, despite their directly opposed position to Richmond and Mary Anna, wouldn't go the distance with their complaint. In the end, who cares who started the fight? They, too, failed to deliver when they could have. Their stance had no substance. And Lazarus, as ever, was neutrally absent, the progenitor's bogus fruitless claim.

At my best, I wonder how some families live with themselves. At my worst, I wonder what the point of a family *is*. I remember reading in a novel somewhere that "to love another is to be the custodian of that person's decline." To this hour, I still don't understand how it's possible for this mother of five to be here in this ghetto hospice where, several months ago, a Nuestra Familia shot caller, amid late-night visits from Norteño gangbangers in 49ers jerseys and Nebraska baseball caps, died two rooms down.

One time Maggie, the head nurse, stopped me in the hallway. About a year ago, I'd guess, maybe a little longer. We'd shared a few friendly greetings since meeting each other, but really nothing more than that. I actually was just happy that we were able to have the pleasantries free of outside influence, safe from the pitiable human impulse to destroy.

"Hey, Murron," she said.

"Hi, Maggie. How are you?"

"I'm fine."

"That's great. Thank you for all the work you and your staff have—"

"Oh, no, no. We love Mary. Everyone does."

"Well, thank you—"

"She's easy to love."

"—just the same."

"You know, there *is* something, though."

"Yes?"

"I know you're not making the decisions for Mary—"

"No, I'm not."

"—but I just want you to know that I—that *we* think it's horrible what they've done."

I looked to the ground, I looked up, saying nothing.

"No, no, please. You don't have to explain. You showed up. That says more than any words would."

"Well, I—"

"No, no. I understand."

Maybe she did. "Okay."

"And you know what else?"

I smiled politely, nodded. "No."

"It's bigger than just Mary, isn't it?"

"What do you mean?"

"What do you mean?"

"Shakespearean," she said. "A cheap rhyme: the heir has failed the forebear."

"That's pretty good."

"The story of this country."

She walked off, and I thought about her words throughout the night. But if things always got worse, if everyone failed the promise of yesterday, we'd all be in the pit by now, every one of us. Life can feel like a downward slope, I know, but down has an opposite direction. Right? And Prince, I believe—I know—will improve on me, will make the world better for being himself, will go up the slope. Has to. Or maybe that's what I have to believe as a mother. In order to *be* a mother. Maybe there is no single answer to what's happened here, but I do know that each of Mary's children, like winos on a sun-drenched walk, have tripped on their own mammoth American egos. At some point, it seems, the story of how they fell doesn't matter. It's almost just filler, really. Better to say, I think, that a trail of failure, we have to believe, is just a facilitator for the real story. The better, braver story. I don't know what it takes to not be like them, but I'll keep talking to myself like a cable news host until I get it right.

I stroke the top of Mary's hand with lotion, rubbing it into her soft skin without waking her, and finally tune in to the slurping sound I've been ignoring for the last few minutes. Every three seconds her mouth slurps in air, some invisible hand pulling the lower jaw down, the tongue coming out of its hole at the same time. This grotesque sucking in of oxygen looks and sounds like the kitchen drain, at the push of a button, clearing out the debris stuck in its throat.

If they, the Felices, believe in this, it seems to me they should be here to *witness* it, as my son is doing now, his little-boy body standing in the direct center of the door, little-boy eyes unblinking, focused on me as if I have all the answers that I've never had.

"Mama," he says, taking three cautious steps into the room, stopping as if the meaning of this strange building has finally penetrated his little-boy heart, then moving toward me again. He hasn't called me Mama for years, another development that I have accepted in silence. This is the time. My moment to let my son know exactly who I am.

"Hi, baby. Come here."

"Are you okay, Mama?"

"Yes. I am now that you're with me."

He starts to cry, looking down at Mary for the first time, as I squeeze him into me. "I'm sorry, Mama."

"Oh, baby. For what? *I'm* sorry."

Now I'm crying with him, my eyes draining into the bed of bronze curls sitting atop his head, and I breathe in his smell, the strange exhilirating cross from his parents. He'll always be one half me, whether he, or anyone, likes it or not.

We're hopelessly cursed, we're fucking lucky.

"Mama?"

"Yes, baby?"

"This is real hard, isn't it?"

I take his face between my palms, and he lets me. Then, in the suddenness of a violent storm, he doesn't. Turns and reaches for the lotion, two determined pumps of cream into his own palm, the gentle steady-handed stroke across Mary's arm.

Sometimes my life is so beautiful, I want to share it all I can before I die.

30

Mary Anna Felice
Seventieth Birthday Party for Anthony
  Constantine Felice Sr.
September 6, 1983

WHAT DID HER blowhard brothers really know, anyway?

Before they had overcome their so-called crucible of Vietnam, she had known all about the terror and horror that men could retch on the world, and had she ever used it as a crest on her shoulder, did she pin it like a medal to her chest, the scarred region of disaffection that he'd clamped down on with his filthy mouth after she'd threatened to tell her real brothers, any one of them, about this secret "rendezvous"? That was, she'd bet, his first official shameless usage of euphemism, the only real skill he ever showcased other than the ability to be a demolition man with the inner lives of women. No one could deny the crime, no one could assuage the conscience, no one could alter the definition of the act with one choice word like Johnny.

He hadn't raped her in the shadows and nooks of Big Victor, he hadn't molested her in the tomb of her childhood bed, he hadn't stolen her laughter in the eternity of youth, he hadn't taught her the bodily concept of shame, he hadn't ruined her christened Catholic soul, he hadn't broken her hymen and bloodied her linen, he hadn't covered her cries with the force of his palm, he hadn't made her vomit in the hour of reflection, he hadn't taught her to lie there shivering in her sheets, he hadn't taught her that lies, like coins in your pocket, were meant to be spent on attempts at normality, he hadn't fucked her face when she pleaded soreness, he hadn't fucked her sphincter when she said she was pregnant, he hadn't given her a card to an L.A. doctor, he hadn't laughed out loud when she wept onstage at the Upland Theater downtown.

He was "just a curious kid," he'd said, "just like her."

And now they, even Johnny, were in the throes of their soldierly vanity in the kitchen she grew up in, going on and on about the mysticism of war, even, amazingly, war's *necessity*, how no story on the planet could ever match its power of narrative, how our boys these morally bankrupt days would benefit tenfold from a single minute pissing their pants in the clutches of a Southeast Asian battlefield, fraternal agreement floating around the table like a wraith ready to suffocate any intruder civilian, meaning suffocate a woman, meaning here, always, suffocate their sister. This was their private-club playground of death, the celebrated end brought on, and suffered, exclusively by men.

Perched on the hearth, back to the classical masonry that was neither supportive nor nostalgic, she watched her brothers, the wine in her glass swishing back and forth, not one drop spilling to the base of exquisite brick below. They were gripping the frosty bottles of Michelob malt liquor by the neck, as if they were about to toss a hand grenade through the living room where the women and children congregated, who somehow understood, without a said word, to let the men be men unto themselves.

They were playing bingo for prizes, and now she turned to celebrate the man of the hour as he held their mother by her plump Sicilian hips of *paesano* peasantry, the child-bearing kind that Mary Anna would never have herself. He laughed at every called-out number because life was good on this, his seventieth birthday with his family, in their house. They'd all come back to visit Big Victor for a day. Everything was good. Any way the game turned out for the Felices was fine with him. She didn't feel the same. It seemed silly, but for

some reason, she wanted to win. She hadn't won once. Every grandchild had taken a Rubik's Cube or a box of Cracker Jack or a plastic
yo-yo. Her sisters-in-law had deferred their own cheesy prizes to the
kids. She wanted to do this herself and had only remembered while
witnessing the gesture of kindness, just as she'd forget, until seeing a
pregnant woman cross the street, that she'd wanted to have children
when she'd been one eons ago. It was she who'd birthed the idea of
the bingo game in the first place, and now it seemed that without her
clown routine in the clown outfit, she'd been forgotten and left on
the wayside by her parents, her siblings, their children.

She watched her father lift his face to the ceiling at Rebecca's
bingo announcement of O-52, elated by the controlled chaos of his
brood, and what consumed her just then was how, without any stretch
of her imagination, she had given this man this very moment. And
anyone else present, too. Which meant even Johnny, the pig in the
kitchen, got this gift for however long he decided to intrude, bragging
now about a man he'd killed his first day in the field, as if he were
the long-lost heir to Audie Murphy. He'd probably read the account
in *Soldier of Fortune*. In the last twenty years of family events, she,
and no one else, had allowed each day to happen, and this eschewed
partial unshared truth became an encrypted text in her brain, became
personal gospel and personal torture both, sacrifice that made perfect
sense in her refuted inflated secret self-regard.

She walked over to the pantry counter feeling the lightheadedness
rushing through her skull like a wind tunnel of the mind, and poured
herself another glass of merlot, this gem of Richmond's from some hidden valley in central Oregon called the Willamette. Edelweiss. After
the song from the film that she'd never liked. The screen bleeding with
chirping kids and love stories that actually worked out. As she corked
the blood-red liquid in on itself, she caught one glance from the pig
that filled her lungs with fear, the infamous lascivious smirk dating back
to his childhood. She immediately understood what it meant and this
angered her. None of her brothers, neither parent, no one with their

shared lineage had followed suit. They knew he was bad, but they didn't *know* him. Which meant they didn't know how bad so-called Johnny Benedetto Capone really was. She was glad when he'd dropped the Felice, she didn't want the same last name as this man. If man he ever was. Or would be. And the folks, like two yokels, were oblivious. Didn't even know he'd earned his keep in porn. Behind their hunched backs, in front of their gleeful faces—they'd probably sauntered past his wolfish acne-cratered face a thousand times at liquor stores and drugstores and 7-Elevens, the smut bins locked away from curious kids who couldn't come up with seventy-five cents or a butter knife to pick the cheap lock.

Even now, right here in Big Victor, yet again, with everyone present, he was giving Mary Anna an unstated indication that he'd caught and admired her dexterous handling of the phallic green bottle of wine, that he'd given his nod of approval, and she knew because she knew him that his already horridly loud voice was two or three decibels louder simply to impress her, as if that were possible. The demonstrative display of heroism was devolving now into reenactment of an event, she was sure, that had never occurred, the oaken kitchen table this monster's makeshift bunker, one index finger tickling the trigger of an M16, the other cock-stroking the muzzle of the rifle, his devil's crouch behind the dinner chair no more than the soldier making himself small, as he recited from some marine manual of a bygone era, in the first blinding glare of a firefight. All to make himself big whenever his turn came to fire back. It was the flaccid cock getting hard, he said, the snake growing to full length.

"Like compression," Richmond said, smiling. "The recoiling done for the spring-loaded response."

"That only a marine is taught to properly execute," grunted Johnny. "*Semper fidelis.* Always faithful."

The brothers were drunk enough to tolerate his boasting, and even the oldest seemed respectful of his fictions—no doubt, she thought, because Anthony had never been to war himself and so how would he know what was and wasn't true about battle? She felt stuck, but not steady. Somewhat dizzy where she stood, she couldn't move toward the safety of the bingo game in the living room, not one step out of his firing range. She felt lost in this house, as she always had, betrayed by her blood, she'd been let down by a country whose so-called elite fighting unit had given scum like him a uniform in the first place, she was aghast by the lucky physics of this man, how he'd been feet or inches or centimeters from the cemetery, how that bullet built specifically to rip through his brain hadn't wanted to touch him *either*. She had shouldered his rucksack of shame long enough, her reenlistment to serve the country of his story unacknowledged by the citizens of this family, tour after tour of duty that was totally backward in concept, the victim protecting the enemy.

And now he turned his body toward her, beading on her heart, of all things, with that stupid imaginary gun, the eyes of his fraternal platoon following the path of his filthy fingers, the proverbial monkeys on the verge of covering the eyes, the ears, the mouth from the evil among them.

"Pow," he said. "I gotcha."

"Hey, Mare!" It was Anthony. "Whatcha doin' over there, kiddo?"

"Don't listen to us dumb guys." This was Richmond. "We're just as confused as anyone about this thing."

"What thing?"

Anthony's question made Richmond laugh out loud, and still standing there in the cross-hairs of Johnny's burning eyes, she was caught off guard by this freedom of expression. Richmond was the only Felice careful enough to keep his cards to himself, and now he was bowled over his elbows on the table, as if he were about to fall face-first into a dive. The others joined in now, too, each of the brothers except Johnny yukking at they knew not what, and she felt herself melting inside, as if there were a bonfire of envy in her stomach, the easy indictment of the other gender no longer a potent extinguisher of the flames. This game, she thought, is over.

"How dare you?" she muttered under her breath, repeating the words again until she stood over him, clutching at Richmond's shoulders so hard he winced looking up at her. This brother she'd always loved most, and thus the one who'd failed most. She didn't care that he was happy. All she could manage were the same words, "How dare you?," and this stupid bout of Pavlovian repetition so infuriated her that she swiveled her thin manly barren hips out of his grasp and stepped forward and slapped him across the face.

Almost in the same instant someone grabbed her from behind, and she knew it was Anthony not only because she couldn't see him in her limited range of vision but because he was shouting, "Hey!" in her ear. He twisted her away from the table and she saw Richmond stand up to tend with his weak desk clerk's hand the wound that he believed, already, to be a wound, and she reached out her arm and shouted again, "How dare you?"

"I don't know," he muttered. "I don't know what's wrong."

"Hey!"

They were spilling into the kitchen now, her oblivious parents and the gossip-starved daughters-in-law and even Richmond Jr. with his quiet probing condescending eyes, the only male heir to keep this family alive, and she broke loose from the orgy of arms and ran out of the kitchen and into the foyer, nearly crushing Anthony III, who was crawling through the hallway untended to and who, despite her inaccurate thought, was the other male heir, shouting now, "Someone watch that fucking baby!" on her way up the creaking staircase of Big Victor.

She ran into her old room and went straight to the closet. She shoved aside the dusty shoes that were piled on the floor and crawled in hurriedly, as if it were a bunker against a blitzkrieg, and closed the door behind herself and cleared a small space in the corner, dropping down like a weighted sack to her backside and pulling both feet underneath her groin. She was in the darkness again. She was alone with herself. She remembered.

She would turn herself off the instant the door creaked open and the light, like a villain, would sneak in ahead of him. Then, like a phantom, he was inside the room which, in all ways, was his room and not hers, and even as the lightless universe surrounded her yet again and seemed, weirdly, like a blanket of safety, his hand had already found her waist, and this was exactly when she became nothing and he became nothing and there was nothing at all to say about the facts of her life because the nothingness was equal all the way around, inside her, outside her, inside Big Victor, outside Big Victor, inside the grove, outside the grove, inside Upland, outside Upland, up and down every coast in the state, up and down every coast on the planet, again and again and again, all lives shoved over the edge of the cliff in the endless rape of the occupants of these cosmos.

Now she squeezed her knees into her chest and rolled down on her body like a ladybug molested by human hands, closing her eyelids to the next identically vast darkness, and cried with no regard for the world of supposed light outside the door, the promise of people out there who called themselves her own, dysfunctional lion pride who whined at the moon like hyenas.

Always the bloodcurdling noise out of the Felices, always the maxims and clichés out of the boys, always their ad nauseam recitations about the Vietnam War, as if they were the gallant mortals of some epic Grecian battle unmemorialized, as of yet, by some famous anonymous poet. She hadn't even known that Vietnam existed before they'd gone, just as they hadn't known what she'd been through in this very home, Big Victor, as they called it, cellar of incestuous shame. As far as she was concerned, that war saved her, though it didn't provide her, in the end, what she prayed for every Sunday at church, after every meal, before bed on her worn-down supplicant knees. And then when he stayed alive through the seventies, not even crippled or mangled, alive all the way to this very day, louder and brasher and unchanged in his core, she knew, and did not wonder any longer to the contrary, that there was no God no justice no childhood no redemption no family.

She couldn't talk about it, she couldn't talk about herself, she couldn't talk about her life, she couldn't talk. She'd been silent before and was silent again and this silence in no way lessened the possessive furor with which she held to her story. She could hear them coming up the staircase, and just as she leaned back and pressed against the wall to make herself smaller, the door opened and he, Richmond, was standing there against the light, pushing aside army jackets and ancient baseball jerseys with a cautious deliberateness that irritated her. He was thinking of two things at once. Save my sister but preserve these outfits.

"What?" she said. "What?"

He closed the door on them both and the darkness returned for a second and then vanished. He'd flicked on a light above her head, a single bulb. She'd heard it, but hadn't known, when the sound happened, what it was. It sounded like the hammer striking the base of an empty chambered revolver, and she knew that she'd flinched. Still afraid of noises in the dark. Any tick of Big Victor terrified her. Every time someone used the bathroom, she went still in her bed, she stopped breathing until the toilet flushed, and then shook herself to sleep.

And now this. He was sitting across from her, their knees almost touching, as if he had any right to share the floor of an old hiding place, the same closet here as thirty years ago, time as nonexistent to muscle memory as an uncaught sin between siblings. No censor on the undiscovered crime. It would happen again. And yet she knew from the look of pity on Richmond's face that he was going to talk about it. She didn't know how he knew because she'd never told a soul, not even the priest in the booth.

Had the pig actually confessed downstairs? How was that *possible*?

It should take longer, she thought. Should take the length of a childhood. They should ask for proof. And I'd show them.

"I'm sorry about all that war talk in there. War's a really disturbing thing, I know. I haven't been able to really get over it myself and we're almost halfway through the eighties. I guess it's tough being in the breach, whether you're a kid or a man. I was just a kid. Into myself, you know? So I sometimes didn't appreciate how much the families suffered, too. Still don't. It must have been hell to have us all gone and not know if we'd be back. I sometimes—"

Here she erupted into the kind of hyena cackle that was her heritage, doubled over her lap, nose pressed into her own quad, liberated, at long last, from anger and shame in the asylum-playroom of this closet.

"I'm sorry," he said now. Again.

Her laughter slowed, bubbling into hiccups irregularly spaced.

"I think I missed something."

"Who cares about your stupid war? Get over it."

"But I'm asking you now. What I missed. As your brother." This made her laugh again, one ejaculation of air laced in red wine-reddened spit. He went on, after wiping his face with a sleeve: "Please tell me what's wrong, Mary Anna. Can you? Are you physically able to?"

"He raped me, you idiot. You big-talking idiot. You idiot."

"Who?"

She said nothing.

"Who did?"

She lifted her face and looked him in the eyes. He blinked first. He blinked second. He dropped his head and said, "Was it Johnny, Mary Anna? Jesus Christ. You mean Johnny, don't you? Johnny did it."

She didn't say no and that was enough while the seconds laboriously passed and it was almost, to Mary Anna, as if the motion of him standing slowly above her was like a symbolic activation of radar that had been dormant for thirty years. He didn't look at her or, it seemed, at anything, and as his breathing picked up and bordered on hyperventilation, she began to wonder if his anger didn't come from a reshuffling of the familial past with which he was otherwise fairly comfortable, and that he'd bargained for more than he could handle by coming to this sacred hiding ground of the weak and scared.

She got the sense that suddenly he didn't like being in here with her, that it was beneath him to allow someone like Johnny to dictate the fate of a relative, that it was his job, single-handedly, to save the family, to remove himself from the insult to his personal pride, that he wouldn't accept for even another second the failure of resolution that this place, a yard-wide shelter, obviously represented, and when he walked out and returned her like a package to the pit of her own seclusion, she yelled, "A *thousand* times, you son of a bitch! Two abortions before my *fourteenth* birthday! One scar of bovine teethmarks on my chest! My *chest*! Three cowards who did shit! Who did nothing but *talk*! I heard you in your rooms! Arguing about politics and girls and what your life was going to be like! You *fucks*! Every one of you is deaf to the world! I'm deaf to it! I'm one of *you*! I *hate* who I am! I hate who you are! We're *even*, you son of a bitch! Don't do me any fucking favors! Done! Leave me alone! This family is *finished*!"

This last fit somewhat exhausted her and she decided to consign herself to gravity, crawling out of the closet and lying down in the middle of her childhood room, back and ass flat on the rug, trembling hands splayed open to the ceiling above. She put her ear to the floor and listened to the chaos below. The creaking of the floor made it sound like Big Victor was about to fall in on itself. They were all fighting, as far as they knew, over nothing. Adding noise to noise, the hollowed-out middle of her past getting bigger from the voices upon voices, sound exacerbated by sound, no shared idea, no message decoded. This was their life together. This had always been their life together.

She rolled to her side and saw Richmond walking down the hallway, the overhead fake crystal hanging in the threat of beautiful disaster, crisscrossed angles of light like daggers of ice, and she caught, almost as an afterthought, the army-issued .45 pistol in his hand, stark black against the walls of this house.

And then like a revelation finally taken in, the infamous noise of this family sputtered like a battery-drained toy, curled in on itself, and died. She heard a muffled directive: "Get out of here forever." The final response: "Well, fuck you people then." A slammed car door, the engine turning over. She got to her feet and stood there wide-eyed in the middle of the room, in virtual sexual ecstasy over the thought of a new start for the Felices, yet tremoring in the strange eerie silence that seemed, as a newfound expression, emptier than the oasis of darkness from which she'd just come.

The Felices
Prayer at the Upland Carmelite Mission
July 8, 1953

In the grave and wondrous silence of medieval penitents, they made their way under the cast-iron cross at the apex of the creaking iron gate and through the dark and crooked shadows of the olive trees, spread behind their mother in the shape of a human fan, her gloved hand pressed with a rosary to the heart in her heaving chest, her veiled head humbly bowed as if at any moment she could topple forward from the heavy burden of life perched like death upon her shoulder. She was physically moving forward through the day but mentally moving back through her life to a single day, she was in that perfect spiritual step impossible in a post-modern age, she was aligned with the machinery of Time, she breathed as if each breath were manifest evidence of her maker's existence. They heard her like that. They saw her like that. They did not think she was transforming into a saint before their eyes. They believed that she was their mother. Her position, as they saw it, started with saintliness. They were nine, seven, five, and four years of age.

Not one of them, not even Johnny, made a sound on the concrete path hidden from the sunlight by the trees. Within a year, he'd figure out that the scattered olives on the ground could be crushed, and he would crush them, each one, like a Roman centurion on the march to empire. He would be dealt with soon enough about the filth under his feet, the fire in his eyes. The priest would take his confession in the booth, already knowing the truth about who'd muddied the carpet of the sacristy, as if his chapel were no more than a country barn set to burn in the possessive appetite of a boy's heart. But that was after.

Now each boy even Johnny abided the rigid order of the hallowed world therein found at the Carmelite Mission, at whose chapel each boy had been baptized, and where Richmond, always in tears upon entering the grounds, was a dutiful and solemn altar boy. They reached the sky-blue trellis, which leaned like a child-made treehouse toward the mysterious abbey, its thin, unsturdy slats of wood held up by the wisteria branches snaking up from the ground. Their mother crossed herself at the altar to Mary, the miniature relics and fading rosaries shelved tenuously on the moist wood, the boys, each one, following in action, Richmond, the last and most affected, closing his eyes and genuflecting as though he were in another century, another country.

They went up the marble steps and into the empty foyer already at noon crystallized with the blue and red lights of the stained-glass windows. The saints that none of the boys but Richmond could name were looking down on them with the stern faces weary of a two-thousand-year mission, pushing out wooden staffs that were doubly, or firstly, wooden crosses reaching higher than their heads. The boys made their way into the church, in line behind their mother, quieter now even than they were back in the grove, so respectful they were almost tentative, pulling their hands out of their pockets to dip into the holy water and cross themselves, forehead to sternum to each of the shoulders, then back into the pockets.

There were parishioners scattered throughout the chapel in varied forms of prayer and reflection, some on their knees with their palms and fingers pressed together before them, others in the pews, heads bowed, their heads always bowed in deep sorrow and contrition. Beauty and guilt drove this place. Wonderment and pain. Healing and passion. Love and judgment. Today there were no fair-weather Catholics with crumpled *pictures of the pope in their wallets, flippantly crossing themselves as if mimicking the crazy sign one made by one's ear. Those who attended church out of the need for a social label or for the comfort of ritual and habit and mnemonic practice—they stayed away this morning. Because it was Wednesday morn, the plain and unaccomplished hour furthest from Sunday Mass in both directions, that time when only the truly devoted gathered, only the truly faithful, the truly wounded.*

And now they watched. She took a long, thin stick from a dusty glass jar at the altar of Santa Rita da Cascia and put it to the flame. The stick lit slow and true. She held it there before her face as if she were fascinated by the worldly possibility of fire, she held it there as if it warmed more than her face, her body entire, her fluttering soul, she held it as if the feeble sparkle of light could tame the savage onslaught of terrible darkness, a miracle aglow between her fingers. Then she connected the smoking tip to the single candle reserved by God for her daughter, Alessandra, her third child in this world who'd died on the blood- and placenta-soaked table at St. Jude's, suffocating on the air like a caught fish, lifeless in the nurse's shivering arms, dead before the age of five minutes. A priest was at the bedside within the early hour, rubbing the sleep from his eyes, straightening his collar, apologizing.

Alessandra, Alessandra, the defender of her own maternal heart, Santa Alessandra of Upland, California, dearest daughter, ever-dying child, an innocent named for Uncle Alexander, Il Saggio, who'd assured Mary after the families fought in the Pittsburgh town hall that out in the Wild West a fuzzy-haired siciliana and blue-eyed fiorentino conjoined against the old world lines would be no more in significance to sunny Californians than two Italian immigrants wed blasphemously in a papist ceremony, and that all that mattered in both the present and the tomorrow, as far off as it seemed, was the life of their shared story, the eternal dream, their private love in the private face of what he knew was a God of goodness. And now she had no other thought or feeling in the lighting of the candle except to be the holy automaton for a single breath of oxygen centered in the hollow of her lungs, the soft kiss, the blessed exhalation, which would give Alessandra the air she'd never had on this ephemeral earth, and lift her soul out of the mud pit of souls.

Their mother crossed herself and said a Hail Mary. She did not look back. The boys mumbled the prayer in a kind of unison that was incoherent from a distance, but that, in summation, whispered one clear word to an observer: Like "Us." Or "yes." Like "mother." She stood slowly without melodrama and went out of the church without looking at them, her boys, or at anyone, her fellow parishioners. The boys followed her, needy as once-lost sheep. They would be back the day after that, and the day after that. All the long summer with their mother at the Carmelites Mission, until school started in the early autumn breeze of September.

Still she didn't look back. She took the outside air of the olive grove deep into her lungs and she didn't look back at her boys. She walked. As if she knew with the certainty of the flame burning flesh that they would always be with her.

FEB   2013

The Felice Family Tree

Antonio Constantino Felice Sr.
b. 1913, Firenftze, Italia
d. 2008, San José, California

Maria Serafina (Capone) Felice
b. 1918 (?), Palermo, Sicilia

Anthony Constantine Felice II
b. 1944, Pittsburgh, Pennsylvania

Darlene (Havlicek) Felice
b. 1947, El Paso, Texas

Duk Soo Kim (present legal name; former birth name)
Anthony Constantine Felice III (former adopted name)
b. 1980, Seoul, South Korea

Richmond Lincoln Felice
b. 1946, Upland, California

Rebecca (Martin) Felice
b. 1947, Chino, California

Richmond Lincoln Felice II
b. 1969, San Bernardino, California
d. 1993, San José, California

John Benedetto Capone (present legal name)
John Benedetto Felice (former birth name)
b. 1948, Upland, California
d. 2009, Los Angeles, California

Cherry Ramirez
b. 1965, Cindad Juárez, Mexico

Jaime Manuel Ramirez
b. 1983, East Los Angeles, California

Lazarus Corsa Felice
b. 1949, Upland, California

Leticia McCluskey
b. 1949, Upland, California

Gabriel Lucas Felice
b. 1968, Santa Rosa, California

Murron Leonora (Felice) Teinetoa
b. 1970, Santa Rosa, California

Lokapi Teinetoa
b. 1972, Amouli, American Samoa

Prince Tamatasi Teinetoa
b. 1999, Stanford, California

Mary Anna Felice
b. 1954, Upland, California

Keri Silverman
b. 1960, Miami, Florida